To Truckee's Trail

First edition 2007, published by Booklocker.com
Revised edition 2011, published by Geron & Associates, a division of Watercress Press

To Truckee's Trail

Celia Hayes

Geron GA *& Associates*

Celia Hayes

Dedication and Acknowledgements

"This is a work of fiction, loosely based on real persons, who participated in a historic event . . . but an event which has been but sketchily recorded, and little remembered save among a few historians. The late George R. Steward was one such: an essay he wrote about the Stephens-Townsend-Murphy party for American Heritage *magazine first fired my imagination about them over thirty-five years ago. My thanks are due to him for that inspiration. Thanks also to Kathy Johnson and Craig Lockwood who encouraged me to imagine the epic journey of the party and to set it down in this form, to Oren Woody, devoted fan and reader . . . and to Mom and Dad for everything else."*

That was the dedication and thanks in the first edition of this book, which was published in 2007 and has been chugging along quietly ever since. Since then, though, I have wanted to bring out another edition which would correct some small errors, as well as to take note of some additional information provided to me since by a descendent of the Hitchcock family: in researching his ever-so-many great-grandfather as a trapper and explorer in the early 1800s – who appears as the character I called Paw-Paw – he found proof in an archived letter written by the American consul in California, that Isaac Hitchcock had indeed been to California, before arriving there with the Stephens-Townsend party in late 1844. Otherwise, this new edition contains all material in the first edition.

Celia Hayes
San Antonio, Texas
November, 2011

Members of the Stephens-Townsend Party

1 - Stephens Wagon:
(Owner) Elisha Stephens, (teamster) John Flomboy, *Dog*

2 - Townsend Wagon:
(Owner) Doctor John Townsend, Elizabeth Schallenberger Townsend, Moses Schallenberger, (teamster) Francis Deland

3 - Montgomery Wagon:
(Owner) Allen Montgomery, Sarah Armstrong Montgomery

4 - Patterson Wagon:
(Owner) Isabella Hitchcock Patterson, *Oliver, Samuel, John (Johnnie) Nancy (child), Eddie (child) and Sadie (child)*

5 - Murphy Wagon:
(Owner) Martin Murphy Sr., Daniel, Bernard, Helen and John "Johnny", Edmund Bray (Teamster)

6 - Murphy Wagon:
(Owner) Martin Murphy, Jr., Mary "Mary-Bee" Bolger Murphy, James (child), Martin (child), Patrick (child) Bernard (child), Elizabeth (infant) and Vincent Calvin (drover)

7 - Murphy Wagon:
(Owner) James "Jamie" Murphy, Ann "Annie" Martin Murphy, Mary (child) Matthew Harbin (drover)

8 - Miller Wagon:
(Owner) James Miller, Mary Murphy Miller, William "Willie" (child), Frances (child), Teresa (child), Ellen (infant)

9 - Martin Wagon:
(Owner) Patrick Martin, Sr., Patrick Martin Jr., Dennis Martin

10 - Sullivan Wagon:
(Owner) John Sullivan, Mary Sullivan (sister), Michael, Robert (child)

11 - Foster Wagon:
(Owner) Joseph Foster, Oliver Magnent (teamster)

Celia Hayes

Chapter 1 – *Preparations & Partings*

San Jose, California 1932: *"So then, Missy, is that machine of yours turned on? I s'pose it'll be best to start at the beginning, hey? My name is Edward Sidney Patterson, and I was born near Batavia, Clermont County Ohio, in September of 1837."*

* * *

Third November, 1843 . . . With a heavy heart and much trepidation, I am resov'd to leave this place, and remove to California, first for the sake of my Dearest Darling . . .

Under a pool of golden lamplight in the silent bedroom, John Townsend carefully uncorked the bottle of ink in his portable writing desk, balanced across his knees, and wrote in his tiny, careful hand:

"I fear for her health above all else. She has a delicate constitution, and cannot bear another cold winter, or disease-wracked summer such as this last without permanent impairment. Moses has been all talk this year past about the marvels of fabled California and its wonderfully mild and temperate climate. He is impatient for emigration and adventure and swears hourly to embark in company with Allen and Sarah M. I think it is the talk of impetuous youth but he is of that age to venture upon such bold enterprise. Of late though, I have begun to believe that such transportation may be my Dearest Darling's only hope of recovery to full health. In any case, she would not bear the thought of Moses' attempting such a perilous journey himself and would fret herself into an early grave . . ." John crossed out the last three words, and wrote in *"a decline . . ."*

On the bedside table, a full kettle simmered over a burning spirit lamp. Steam hissed from the spout. John set aside the writing desk. A heavy blanket was tented over the head of the bedstead and the head and shoulders of the woman sleeping fitfully underneath, a basin of water settled onto a pillow close to her head, a basin in which floated a few drops of camphor oil, their efficacy nearly spent with the cooling of the water. John emptied the basin into the slops jar, and filled it again with steaming water and a fresh installment of camphor droplets.

John regarded her face, glistening with moisture and still flushed pink with the remnants of fever, or maybe the heat of healing steam under the blanket tent that lent a spurious look of health to Elizabeth's face. Her blond hair and the neck of her high-buttoned nightgown were soaked with the sweat of a broken fever. He bent an ear towards her breathing; easy, without the gasp and wheeze that frightened him down to his soul with the threat that her weak chest and frail constitution might take his Elizabeth away from him, and leave him alone in this world.

He put back the blanket over his wife's face, and the newly-steaming bowl of water, and caught a glimpse of himself in the dressing-table mirror; a broad-shouldered man with a merry and bluntly pugnacious face. His neck-cloth was loosened, and the fine broadcloth coat that his Elizabeth insisted that he always wear – being that he was a doctor with a position to keep up – set aside. His hair also stuck up in rebellious points and curls; he had run his hands through it too often during this latest crisis. Someone tapped cautiously on the bedroom door and after a moment, opened it just wide enough to look around.

"Mose, boy, you should be in bed. It's past two in the morning," John chided his brother-in-law. Young Moses hesitated in the doorway, a gawky boy of seventeen not quite grown to his own strength, young enough to look heartbreakingly like his older sister with the same oval features and fair coloring.

"You're still awake, Doctor John," Moses said, trying so hard to sound gruff and manly. "Is she better?"

"She's sleeping easily; I think the crisis is past. I sent Mrs. Montgomery off to her own home hours since. "

John often had to speak comfortable and reassuring words to frightened relatives; sometimes they were the words that they wanted to hear and sometimes as it was now, the plain truth. John was glad of that for Moses' sake. Not only was his Elizabeth a dear sister but next thing to a mother to Moses, since their parents had died ten years ago in one of the fever epidemics that swept Stark County, Ohio.

They were but newly married then, but the best established of all the Schallenberger's children, and so Moses was left to them, a boy of six years, and all but a flesh and blood son to John. Sometimes, he reflected without grief or resentment, Moses was the best that he would have wished from any child that Elizabeth might have born to him. She had brought him a son without the agony and risk that childbirth for her would entail, and Moses was a good lad, straight and fearless and honest. John was well-content with his family; or would be if Elizabeth could only be well again, fit and rosy-cheeked, and riding a fine horse as recklessly as she once used to do.

"Until next time." Moses stepped a little into the bedroom, and looked at John, eye to eye. "This miasma, these epidemics of fever; Mr. Marsh writes about the climate in California being bountifully temperate and healthy. If we could but remove her from them . . ."

"I know, Moses. I read the same letters, and hear the same idle talk." John kept his voice low, and rubbed his forehead. His eyes felt like they were full of sand. "But it is a long, dangerous journey, and to a foreign country at that."

"For now," replied Moses. "So was Texas, once; Allen talks of nothing else than the riches to be had, should it also fall into our hands."

"It is not in our hands yet, no matter how loudly Allen Montgomery boasts of it. And it is still a wild and savage place . . ." a jaw-cracking yawn sent John's thoughts in all directions, "Sorry, Moses. I have not slept above twenty minutes these last two days. I know you are resolved on this adventure, but you are a young man with no responsibilities, no household to think on. I have both. I must consider carefully how to best meet them. Your sister must be considered, also." Another huge yawn felt as if it would split John's face in two. "We'll talk about it in the morning. Well, 'tis morning. Then after I have slept." He clapped Moses affectionately on the shoulder. "Go to your bed, lad. You must be as much in need of rest as I."

"Good night, then, Doctor John." Moses slipped away, drawing the door softly closed behind him. John yawned again. For the last three days, and two nights, he had slept, if he slept at all, nearly upright in the bedroom armchair. The armchair, cushioned with a flattened and grimy pillow and a single blanket, beckoned to him as an old friend but under the camphor-steam saturated blanket, Elizabeth stirred fitfully. In the silent house, in that sickroom, that bare movement and her thready whisper sounded as loudly as a shout.

"John?"

He lifted up the blanket; in the dim pool of lantern-light, her pupils were huge and dark. He took her hand in his own.

"I'm here, Dearest Liz."

She looked at him with a queer, fey expression, as if she were talking in her sleep and whispered, her fever-cracked lips barely moving.

"We can't let Moses go alone," And then her eyelids fluttered closed, and her hand slackened in his. She slept again as if exhausted by that slight effort. John sat back in his chair and after a moment's thought, opened the writing desk again. He uncorked the tiny inkbottle and wrote: *"I do not think of myself as a gambler, but perhaps I am so, to think of selling my house and practice, and to risk our lives and fortune on this venture, not for such earthly riches as such men do covet, but as a means that my Dearest Darling may recover her health and strength."*

* * *

Angeline Morrison Letter #1
20th January, 1844
Writ from St. Joseph
Missouri Territory,

I write imploring an answer from you with great speed, as My Dear Husband has resolved upon departing from our dwelling here, and embarking upon the trail for distant California in the spring. His friend, Allen Montgomery has long been preparing his own household for transportation hither; My Dearest tells me that he (Mr. Montgomery) has spent most of the year previous preparing necessary gear and supplies, and is most impatient for the trail season to open. Mrs. Montgomery, who lived in our household since the sad loss of her parents and was only recently engaged in marriage, is exceeding downcast by his plans.

As for myself, I have apprehensions but unlike my dear Sarah, I have the wit to keep them to myself. Indeed, my Dearest's stated reason for transportation to California is that he fears for my health, so it would be most ungracious of me – as well as casting aspersions upon his knowledge of medicine – to object. I cannot deny that I have been unwell for most of the last four years; it is most vexing for me to never be completely recovered from one ailment before falling to the next. To my Dearest, it is doubly so when none of his skills can keep the malignant vapors of summer or the bitter cold of winter from affecting me so deeply.

But Angeline, although his concern is real, I suspect it is but a pretext for indulging the restless spirit that has moved him ever on, from where he was born, to Ohio and on to Missouri Territory. When he first came to Stark County to practice medicine, it seem'd most astonishing that he had lived in so many places before. And it almost seemed natural that upon the deaths of my beloved parents and assuming the care of my brother, that we would of course uproot ourselves and move to St. Joseph. There were many doctors practicing there, and it seemed the most natural distraction from the deaths of my dear mother and father, that we should seek solace in new horizons!

I had thought we were most content in St. Joseph, but of late he has seem'd restless, and uninterested in civic matters that once were his most lively interest. The question of the peculiar institution also vexes him much, although he dislikes to speak of it, for he fears alienating friends and associates who do not share his feelings and dreads a time when he might have to voice them openly on the matter. Such a tangle . . . and I had thought my own poor condition was the cause, but now I suspect otherwise.

I shall write to you once more, before we depart onto the trail. Please write to me and tell me of the trivial doings, and little domesticities that I will soon leave behind.

Ever thy friend
Elizabeth

* * *

From Dr. Townsend's diary: *"Twenty-sixth of February, 1844: Items for the wagon, purchased from local merchants of excellent repute, represented by them to be of superior quality and sufficient for the journey: plain flour, eight hundred pounds. Salt bacon, six hundred pounds. Coffee, fifty pounds. Tea, twenty pounds. Sugar, eighty pounds. Salt, forty pounds. One barrel hard tack. Cask vinegar. Two boxes dried apples, the same of apricots. Two crocks pickles. One hundred pounds rice, the same of dried beans. Small box salt cod. Fifteen small jars of honey and preserves. Two bottles medicinal whisky . . .*

"I have had our wagon fitted out, at some small expense, to make it more commodious and comfortable. A false floor is installed, some eighteen inches above the wagon bed, below which certain stores and gear may be stowed out of the way. Three large flat-topped trunks are arranged at the rear, with a heavy mattress on top, which serves as a most comfortable bed. We have also attached a seat on metal springs to the front, which may afford a more comfortable ride, and sealed the canvas cover against rain with a generous coating of linseed oil. Mr. Montgomery has made similar arrangements in his own wagon.

"Item - purchased for the journey, one canvas tent, and a set of tin plates and such for use on the trail . . . I made the purchase of some fine china silk fabric, with an eye towards selling it in California at a profit.

"Fifth of March, 1844: Arranged the hire of a drover, one Francis Deland, who journeyed hence from French Canada and is desirous of

working his passage to California for board and bread. We intend to depart a week from today, having receiv'd notice of a large assembly at Kanesville, up-river in the Iowa Territory, intent on Oregon, our intention being to accompany them as far as Fort Hall.

"Eleventh of March, 1844 . . . we depart upon the morrow, Elizabeth and Moses and I, in company with our close friends, Allen and Sarah Montgomery. May good fortune guide us, and our Heavenly Father attend and bless our endeavors. It is so written: 'For the Lord Thy God bringeth thee into a good land, a land of brooks of water. Of fountains and depths that spring out of the valleys and hills; a land of wheat, and barley and vines and fig trees and pomegranates; a land of olive oil and honey; a land wherein thou shalt eat bread without scarceness; thou shalt not lack anything in it.'"

* * *

In the early dark, just as the pale dawn lightened the sky, the oxen stamped restlessly, and blew out their hay-scented breath, and Allen Montgomery hardly bothered to lower his voice.

"Good lord, what's keeping the woman? Fix your bonnet and come away, your ladyship. Time's a-wasting. We should be on the road to Kanesville by now." John bent his head over his saddle girth, pretending to check the adjustment of his stirrups and tactfully affected not to hear, but out of the corner of his eye could see the embarrassment on Moses' face. Moses was no doubt coloring up like a girl. He admired Allen enormously, and tried to copy his manner, a thing of which John did not wholly approve, although he wisely kept from saying so. John also liked Allen, even if he was the most hot-headed and tactless man in three counties. Francis, hunkered patiently down on his heels next to the lead ox, gave no indication of impatience, or even of having understood.

His pretty and feisty wife, little Sarah Armstrong she had been, orphaned at fifteen and come to work for John and Elizabeth until she had married the handsome gunsmith, snapped, "She's saying goodbye to the house. House . . . you know, that place which women keep, until their husbands drag them away?"

John strenuously pretended not to have heard that, either. Just as well that the two of them were well-matched in being about equally tactless. He himself had sold the house and practice, furniture and fittings, everything that could not be packed in straw, or stuffed into a trunk in the wagon. Which aside from some bits and pieces, amounted to a case of surgical implements, his books and Masonic regalia, and the set of china that Elizabeth had inherited from her great-grandmother and an assortment of trinkets, bedding, linens, and clothing.

Everything else that had adorned their home, everything dear and familiar, from the pictures on the wall and the inlaid bedroom furniture to the parlor piano that had given his Elizabeth so much joy and pride in showing off their home to her friends, all to be left behind . . . now someone else's property. Oddly enough, it gave him a feeling of curious relief, a feeling of freedom, of being able to float unbound by material possessions, like that of the early monks, with their attention focused on the divine.

A few hesitant piano notes floated out from the empty house, a stave of Mozart, clear and pure as a trickle of spring water. Allen swore under his breath and gave some vent to his exasperation by slapping his hat against his knee.

"I'll go and fetch . . ." Moses ventured, miserably embarrassed, just as Elizabeth appeared in the doorway, like a ghost in a dark merino travel dress. She tied her bonnet strings neatly under her bravely lifted chin, and pulled the door gently closed.

"I'm ready," she said simply, and took John's hand. Moses reached down from the wagon-seat, and between the two of them they boosted her up and over the great wooden wheel – one foot on a spoke, the other to the footrest, before she scrambled over the side of the wagon-box in a flurry of skirts and calico petticoats, to seat herself next to her brother with her hands folded on her lap. She nodded to John when she was settled, and he swung up into the saddle; his horse pranced sideways a little, tossing his ugly grey head until the bit jingled.

John swore under his breath. He regretted selling the trusty old gelding, Pouncer, who had faithfully carried him or drawn his trap around his medical rounds in St. Joseph and before that in Stark County for the best part of a decade. Pouncer had faultless manners, gentle enough for Liz to ride, even. But John had quietly listened to the counsel of outfitters and merchants who dealt in trade with the yearly caravans to Santa Fe, and understood immediately that Pouncer was too old, and unsuited to a rugged journey through wilderness. He would need something young, strong, and spirited, and the new grey gelding was all that, but John hadn't warmed sufficiently to give it a name or think of it as anything but "the Ugly Grey." He disciplined Ugly Grey, and waved his hat in the air.

Allen cracked his whip, and whistled shrilly to his team, and they leaned stolidly into their yokes. Francis stood up without any apparent urgency, and seemed to whisper to the lead team beasts. Then he whistled also – a low whistle, and all three yoke hitched to the Townsend wagon stepped forward almost eagerly. With a great creak and groan, the wagon lurched forward, the linseed-proofed canvas cover swaying like a bellied sail. John reined in Ugly Grey, who seemed determined to prance like a racehorse and gaily called up to his wife, who looked ahead with somber mien.

"The greatest journey starts with a single step, Dearest Liz, and I vow that we have just taken that step!"

That, as he hoped, coaxed a smile, and she called back, "'Tis a very jolting step, Dearest. Can I hope to become more accustomed to it?" She was, John noticed with approval, not looking back. Brave Liz.

"If not," he promised expansively, "I shall buy you a horse to ride before we depart from Kanesville. I had planned on purchasing another horse and two more yoke, depending on how the rules of our party with respect to a herd of spare beasts are decided."

"Why would that be?" Elizabeth reached up and straightened her bonnet, as a particularly deep rut jarred the whole wagon again. "Wouldn't we wish to take as many extra animals as we can afford?"

"Then we have the extra burden of herding them along behind, and finding fodder. It might be worth the extra effort, or it might not be. We should have another horse, regardless. Mr. Chiles ever spoke of being able to hunt, along the trail."

Ugly Grey pranced ahead, giving John the opportunity of taking a good look at his three yoke, considered so carefully before purchase for strength and docility, working together under the burden of moving a heavy-laden wagon. They moved well under Francis's direction, he thought; they merely walked, easily pulling their burden without any special effort. He rode ahead of Francis, striding next to the lead yoke, and the Frenchman caught his eye, gave a smile and a mock-salute, tipping his hat brim with the stock of the whip that he seemed to hardly use.

A good man, that; John could forgive practically anything of a man who was good with animals, who ruled them with a light hand. He had doctored animals in his time, as any medical man must when a man's livelihood might depend on the health of his horse or cow as much as on his own.

Ahead of them, Montgomery's team plodded stolidly on, around the long gentle bend in the road that paralleled the river, north and west of town, the crate of chickens lashed to the back of it bouncing to every jolt of wheels, accompanied by noisy complaints and flurries of chicken feathers. Allen's single horse and milk cow were tethered on long leads, side by side, to the back of his wagon. They would soon be out of the township, out among strangers who knew them not, floating as free as bubbles on the river, having cut the connection that bound them to a farm, a place, a town; bubbles on the river surface, joining with other bubbles, and drifting purposefully west. John reined Ugly Grey back again and fell in beside his wagon, and smiled at Liz.

"I wonder how long Mrs. Montgomery will preserve her chickens on the trail. They do not seem in a humor conducive to laying eggs."

"Chickens are adaptable," Elizabeth replied, with a ghost of her old spirit. "They will provide eggs, or a good chicken dinner, one or the other. Sarah . . . Mrs. Montgomery did not consent to this . . . expedition in the same spirit that I did, my Dear Doctor. She cannot forget how her family was dragged hither and thither, how her mother protested and her father insisted, and they moved on from one home to another, until they both perished and she was left in our care and then out of her marriage to Mr. Montgomery, had her very own little house . . . but on Mr. Montgomery's insistence, she must leave it. I fear that perhaps we did not serve her truly as friends, with her true interests at heart when we encouraged her to accept Mr. Montgomery's offer of marriage."

"He's a good man, with a good trade and a handsome devil to boot," John said. "A man like that must have a wife, and she was lucky to make such a fine match."

"Oh, certainly," Elizabeth replied, with a strained smile. "But a woman can be fortunate in her marriage, and yet not be wholly happy in it."

"Are we happy, Liz?" Impulsively, John stood in his stirrups, and reached out to take her gloved hand in his, over the turning and mud-caked wheel. "Are we truly happy, to the end of this trail and all the world encompassed in it?"

"We are," Elizabeth half rose, leaning down to briefly grasp his hand and the wagon rolled over another rut, and she sat down heavily –which knocked her bonnet askew once more. "I am happy, and you are my husband. Where you go, I go also . . . and so must Sarah Montgomery with her husband. But she is too high-spirited to submit gracefully when she must, and too young in marriage to know how to appeal to his good nature and change his mind."

"I cannot imagine anything to make Allen change his mind, once he is set on it," Moses spoke up sturdily. "Not even Sarah and I look on her as fondly as another sister. But wives are not supposed to question their husbands." Moses looked abashed and puzzled when John and Elizabeth exchanged a wry look and burst out laughing.

And the sun rose at their backs, brushing the newly green treetops with a touch of gold, and sending elongated shadows of team and wagons, horse and rider running ahead of them, stretching out towards the west.

* * *

From E.S. Patterson Interview, University of California Local History Archival Project 1932: *"My name is Edward Sidney Patterson, and I was born near Batavia, Clermont County, Ohio, in September of 1837, to Samuel Laurens Patterson, and Isabella Hitchcock Patterson. Which would make me 95 and old enough to know better, you would think. I had three older brothers and an older sister, when my father decided that we should go west to seek a better fortune for ourselves in California. He left in the spring of 1841 to go out in advance of the family.*

He sent back a letter to us, which we did not receive until mid-summer of 1843, to let us know that he had arrived safely and that my mother should sell the farm and all the fittings and prepare to follow him. In fall of the year that he had departed Ohio, my mother had given birth to my little sister, Sarabeth, whom we called Sadie, and her own father, whom we called "Paw-Paw", had come to live with us.

Paw-Paw had been in the fur trade as a young man and we were given to understand that he had traveled extensively in the west. In fact, Paw-Paw had fixed it for Pa to travel out to California through connections and friendships which he had among the Santa Fe traders. Ma was not pleased about this development: she thought he was of a light character, and was deeply unhappy about this whole prospect.

But in obedience to my father, she sold the farm, and accepted Paw-Paw's advice about a wagon and necessary supplies. She and Paw-Paw knew through friends that there was a party of emigrants assembling in the spring of the following year at Kanesville in the Iowa Territory, intending for Oregon and California, and so we made preparations to join them. She took some small things that she treasured, and fitted out a stout farm wagon that Paw-Paw approved of with a canvas cover. She had four yoke of oxen, and a milk cow from the farm. She bought sufficient supplies for the journey out of what she had for selling the home place, and took us to Iowa to take the trail to California in obedience to my father's directions. Ma was a tiny woman; she would have come hardly to your chin, missy, but there wasn't a thing she feared in this world."

* * *

Some weeks later, when the Montgomery and Townsend wagons were still a little short of Kanesville, the Ugly Grey threw a shoe and lost it in the deep mud. It had rained all morning, but now the clouds were breaking up into innocent fluffy white clumps scattered across a clear and pale sky. The two wagons had been much inconvenienced by rain, since it made the road a swampy, muddy morass, and brought the river far enough up to cover the trunks of trees on the riverbank. Francis and Allen Montgomery waded knee-deep in churned muck, and they were forced to the expedient of keeping dry firewood in the wagon so that it would burn well enough in the evenings for Elizabeth and Sarah to cook a meal over it.

John dismounted immediately, almost the minute that Ugly Grey began to favor his left rear leg, but there was no finding the missing shoe in the mud, not with the way other wagon wheels and other hoofed draft animals had turned it over and over again. Allen and Francis halted the wagons, while he did a quick search. The driver of a heavy horse-drawn dray wagon coming the other way saw them by the side of the road, and called out.

"What kind of trouble are you having, friend?"

"My horse lost a shoe. How far are we from Kanesville? Can you recommend us to a blacksmith there?" On the clear horizon ahead of them hung a hazy smear of wood smoke, too large for a single farmstead.

"Not far . . . three, four miles. That where you're bound?"

"For today. We mean to join an emigrant company there, for California. Did you just come from there? Do you know where they are camped?"

"Out west of town, in a grove of trees by the river, waiting for the river to go down," replied the drayman, slapping his reins. "And there's a good few blacksmiths there, but there's a man with a little forge set up half-a-mile back, if you ain't keen on walking all the way to Kanesville."

"Thank you for your good words." John tipped his hat as he mounted and told Allen and Francis, "Heard that? I'll stop at this roadside forge, and catch up with you at the campsite."

Just as the drayman had said, there was a wagon and tent back from the muddy road, in the middle of a little grove, with a well-established fire in a scratch enclosure of blackened bricks, sending up a straight line of smoke. Half a dozen cattle browsed in the damp meadow close by. A solitary man in a leather apron worked over an anvil; John could hear the clear regular ring of metal on metal long before they saw him.

"If I don't catch up on the road, I'll meet you in camp." John smiled at his wife, silently resolving to buy another horse, after enduring the constant lurch and jolt of the wagon for the last half-mile. He felt bruised and sore to his very bones after just this little way, whereas poor Liz had been patiently enduring it for weeks. So much for the comfort of the metal-sprung wagon seat. He unhitched Ugly Grey from the back, waved to Allen and Francis, and walked into the trees to the little campsite.

"Good morning," John called, when he was in earshot. "My horse lost a shoe a half-mile back. Might you be of assistance?"

"I can." The smith set his bit of work back into the fire and turned to look at John. He was a big, grim-looking fellow with the enormously muscled shoulders and forearms of his trade, his shirt-sleeves rolled up, and his leather apron flecked with tiny cinder burns. His face and hands were blackened with sooty grime and smoke, appearing like a gargoyle mask fringed with chin-whiskers, out of which a pair of clear, pale grey eyes the color of water sized up John and his limping horse.

Something nudged at John's thigh and the smith remarked placidly, "Don't you be moving sudden-like, she'll think you mean harm."

Quite startled, John looked down; not very far down at that, at one of the largest dogs he had ever seen, a huge fawn-colored mastiff bitch with a dark face. She sat quietly at his feet, regarding him with intelligent golden eyes.

"Dog," said the smith quietly, and made a quick gesture with his fingers. The mastiff bitch nudged John again, as if reminding him to be on his best behavior then, because she would have an eye on him, and obediently trotted away to settle herself underneath the wagon. From there she still regarded John and her master with those unsettlingly intelligent golden eyes. She had a clownish white splotch on her nose and another at the end of her tail. All of her toes on each foot were white, as if she wore dainty gloves.

"Elisha Stephens, late of the Pottawattamie Indian Agency." Her master introduced himself. "That's Dog; and you would be?"

"John Townsend . . . Doctor John Townsend, late of St. Joseph, Missouri, soon to be on the trail to fabled California." John extended his hand, but Stephens regarded him levelly and did not respond in kind.

"Beg pardon, my hands is powerful dirty. California? Heard me some talk. Tie the hoss up to this here tree, so's I can get to work."

Stephens rummaged among his tools, and a box of metal oddments, tossing a roughly shaped horse-shoe into the heart of the fire. He worked the bellows until the coals glowed cherry-red, incandescent. While the metal softened, glowing whiter than the coals, Stephens shoved his shoulder into Ugly Grey's barrel, and expertly forced the gelding to allow him to pick up his unshod foot and rasp off some of the hoof with a great metal file. John watched with interest; this was a man who knew his trade. Ugly Grey's eyes rolled nervously, showing some white, but not as much as expected.

When the shoe was softened enough, Stephens took the tongs and brought it out of the fire, laying it on his small anvil, and deftly pounding it into the right shape. He plunged it into a tub of dirty grey water, which bubbled up in great gouts of steam. When the new shoe had cooled enough, he took it up, filling his mouth with nails, and hefted a small hammer in one hand. Just as before, he shoved his powerful shoulder into Ugly Grey and took up the horse's unshod hoof. While bracing Ugly Grey's hoof in his leather-aproned lap, he spat nails into his free hand, one by one, and deftly tapped them into place, securing the new shoe.

"What do I owe you, Mr. Stephens?" John spoke with honest appreciation. It was one of the greatest pleasures in life to watch an expert do their work, especially if they were so very good that it all appeared effortless. And Stephens was truly that, as serene and self-contained as great artists are in the middle of their creations.

"Nothing," Stephens' pale, unreadable eyes gleamed in his dark face. "Pay me back with doctoring on the trail, mebbe. I'm away to California myself, in a couple of days."

"But why have you not joined the encampment with the other emigrants?" John asked, surprised out of countenance for once.

"Not one for crowds," Stephens replied simply.

"Then . . . my most sincere thanks and appreciation. Most cer-tainly we shall meet again and I am glad of that. A blacksmith is a good man to have along on the trail."

Stephens nodded inscrutably, and replied, "So's a doctor. But we won't be leaving for a good two weeks."

"Why?" John was about to put his foot in stirrup, but something of the certainty in Stephens' simple statement held him back.

"Grass is not grown tall enough yet. Three weeks."

"You've been out on the trail before?"

"Some." Stephens answered. "Some there. Some on the Santa Fe."

He didn't seem inclined to elaborate, or even feel the need to.

John swung up into his saddle, and said, "I'll look forward to seeing you again . . . by the time the grass is grown tall enough."

"I'll be there," Stephens replied.

Chapter 2 – *The Jumping-Off Place*

John caught up to his wagon and Montgomery's just outside Kanesville — a muddy and slap-together place of log cabins and flimsy tents, noisy and overwhelmingly noisome with stock pens and pigs rooting for garbage in muddy streets, as full of people as St. Joseph: Army dragoons in blue, Mexicans in black trimmed with constellations of silver buttons, nearly-naked Indians with shaved heads, sober Mormon merchants in linsey-woolsey, and emigrants like themselves with wagons full of worldly goods and children, small faces apprehensively peering out from the shelter of the wagon cover.

John took note of the stock pens, making a note as to where he should come back in the next day or so. According to Stephens they would have several weeks to rest and restock from the journey up from St. Joseph. It also amused him to overhear that the place should now be called Council Bluffs, as if that would make it any more important, or the streets less muddy.

A relief it was, to be through town, following a trampled and rutted track towards a line of low hills topped with a thin grove of trees along the river, dotted here and there with wagon tops and tents blossoming like prairie wildflowers among the thin green treetops. Rain in the morning had washed the sky clean, and the breeze smelt mostly of new grass and damp earth, only a little of wood smoke and privies, and the muddy river.

As their wagons approached the emigrant camp, children ran towards them, calling excitedly, and a tall man in a frock coat waved them down, with a beaming smile.

"Good day pilgrims," he called. "Where bound, and where from?"

"To California, from St. Joseph, Townsend and Montgomery."

"Oh, excellent, excellent! John Thorp, for Oregon." Thorp walked alongside Ugly Grey, as if some invisible force plastered him there, squinting upwards at John and chattering away.

"We have nearly forty wagons assembled, for Oregon and California both. There is a good place at the top of the hill, just under the edge of the trees, next to the Patterson wagon. You can't miss them; small wagon, with a saffron-colored cover, and many children."

Thorp seemed uncommonly presumptuous, John thought to himself. Really, was he the boss of the camp already, advising all newcomers as to just where they should camp? Just as John decided that, yes, Thorp probably did see himself as such, the man added with studied carelessness, "Oh, and we are agreed to hold elections a week from this Sunday to elect a wagon captain as far as Fort Hall. May we count on your attendance, and your vote?"

Well, that was blunt enough; presumptuous and blunt.

"Our attendance for sure," John shot back easily. "And for our vote, it depends on what we think of the nominees!"

He was amused at how early the politicking began, but annoyed at Thorp's unsubtle approach, looking to scrape acquaintance and presuming on it; the man set his teeth on edge. He could see all too plain where the camp herd had been pastured for many weeks, by the look of the ground, all chopped by hooves, grazed down to the roots and fouled by manure. It said little for Thorp's organizational capabilities. This kind of disorganization was apt to dirty water supplies and contribute much unpleasantness if they were to be camped here much longer.

Thorp waved his hat, and they moved on up the grade, as Elizabeth laughed down from the wagon-seat, "Dearest, it looks like a camp revival meeting. Will there be picnicking among the arbors, and hymn-singing, and people falling down and speaking in tongues?"

"And tediously long sermonizing? Depend on it."

"You did not like Mr. Thorp," Elizabeth said quietly with a sideways glance.

"Liked him little and trusted him rather less. He's the sort who likes to look as if he is in charge, but little favors the responsibility of it or the work itself." He answered in the same low voice, and then spurred Ugly Grey ahead a little way, looking for the wagon with a saffron-yellow cover, and a great many children.

There, right where Thorp said it would be: top of the hill, edge of the trees, the golden sun around which some smaller tents and awnings orbited, as well as a quantity of laundry and bedding flapping from lines strung between trees. John overtook a grey-beard with a limp, stumping gamely up the hill towards the Patterson camp and leading a pair of mules.

"Mr. Patterson?" John ventured, and the old man scowled.

"That's me son-in-law. I'm Hitchcock, it's me daughter Isabella you're looking for. That," he jerked his bearded chin in that direction, "is her wagon. Hers and her husband's, that is – but he's away in Californy, and I don't blame him, scrawny fussbudget that she is. I'd be there too, if I'd married a woman like her. Or China, among all them heathen. Or Hades, which 'ud be her choice."

"John Townsend. Doctor John Townsend. We're also California bound, ourselves and our neighbors the Montgomerys. Mr. Thorp directed us this way."

"Did he, now," Hitchcock scowled, muttering something uncomplimentary about Thorp under his breath.

"How many others here are California bound, besides Mrs. Patterson, and yourself?" John thought it best to change the subject off of the ambitious Mr. Thorp.

"A passel of bog-trotting Papists, mostly; Murphys, Martins, and Sullivans all mixed together. Six wagons between them and fixed on California. Good folk, though, for all a'that. I also hear tell there's an old fur-trapping man named Greenwood with his two heathen sons, looking to hire on as a wagon guide as far as the Rockies. If he's the one I know of, he married hisself a Crow woman an' went to live with the tribes years ago. All a'them Greenwoods can't be mistook, look like real Injuns, they do."

As John, and the old man approached the brow of the hill and the yellow-topped wagon, a little woman in a faded wash-dress with her sleeves rolled up and a big apron tied over all, looked up from her washtub and cried indignantly, "Pa! What are you doing with those mules? What have you gone and done?"

"Bought me a brace of 'em, Izzy, sure and a farmer's wife 'ud recognize mules? I figured to invite them into the parlor for tea," said the old man with gentle malice. "That or have them carry my traps an' goods to Californy. I ain't quite decided which, yet. Say hello to Doctor Townsend, Izzy, he's goin' with us to Californy; Doc, my daughter, Mrs. Samuel Patterson."

Isabella Patterson appeared ready to explode from embarrassment and fury at being caught at her worst in the middle of the washing and what sounded like an ongoing family quarrel, and then being introduced to a total stranger. She swiped an errant lock of dark hair off her damp forehead as John dismounted from his horse, and took her hand in his. She looked to be a tiny, quick-moving dynamo of a woman, with abundant dark hair falling out of pins and a small and oval face, whose regular features were slightly marred by a magnificently beaky nose. She had fine eyes though, and skin like a girl's.

"Very pleased, Mrs. Patterson," John ventured, at his most courtly, accustomed in his medical capacity to seeing people at their worst advantage. "I shall tell Mrs. Townsend to call on your . . . camp . . . as soon as possible, since we are soon to be travel companions."

"We shall be glad to receive her," Isabella responded with a quick, manly hand-grasp. "As you can see, our house is very open, these days. Very open indeed!" Another one like Sarah, John thought, as he touched his hat brim; not pleased about being dragged away from her own hearth, to begin a gypsy existence beside the trail. Allen Montgomery's team was toiling up the gentle slope towards where they stood, with Francis and his own following close behind.

"Until later, Ma'am . . . Sir." As John led Ugly Grey towards the open place where they could set up their own camp, he could hear the two of them starting up where they had left off. Between Isabella Patterson and her father, and Allen and Sarah, he reflected wryly, there was no necessity of waiting until the Fourth of July for fireworks.

"Here we are, for the moment, at least," he said, Ugly Grey's reins looped over his arm, as he helped Elizabeth down from the wagon seat. "Mr. Stephens at the smithy seemed to think we'll be camping here for about three weeks."

"It shall be very restful, I am sure." Elizabeth looked doubtfully towards the lively Patterson camp. It seemed there were a lot of children, romping happily and noisily amongst the clutter of tents, gear and supplies.

Then she squared her shoulders and said, "I shall have to call, I suppose, as soon as our camp is set up."

"So you should – as others will be calling on us," John answered, though he did not think that would be happening as soon as it did, a few minutes later as he was unsaddling Ugly Grey. He turned around to find two pair of eyes, watching him with intense and fearless interest; a bold urchin of about seven years, with a girl toddler dragging at his hand. The little one was sucking her thumb. They had dark hair, and something of the look of Isabella Patterson, and John said gravely, "Good morning, children. I am Doctor Townsend. Might I beg for an introduction?" The little girls' eyes rounded in astonishment over the thumb stopping her mouth, but the boy launched into full spate.

"H'lo, I'm Edward Sidney Patterson, but everyone calls me Eddie, and this is my baby sister Sadie, her real name's Sarabeth Margaret, but it don't matter 'cause she can't talk yet an' Paw-Paw Isaac says you are a real doctor an' you're going to Californy jus' like us an' Ma, an' our Pa went out there two year agone . . . is that your horse? Pa wrote an' tol' us that he was settled . . . kin I help you groom him? I like horses, we used t'have horses on our farm in Ohio, but Paw-Paw Isaac tol' Ma she should sell them an' buy mules instead, but Ma, she said mules cost too much an' . . ."

19

"Eddie," John asked, vastly amused. "Do you ever stop talking?"

"Nossir." Eddie shook his head decisively. He reached over and pulled his sister's thumb out of her mouth with an almost audible pop. "Don't suck your thumb, Sadie, Ma will give you a licking. Does your horse have a name? Ma let us name all of our teams, there's Baldy an' Socks an' Spotty. An' –"

"Here, "John handed him the curry-comb, "I'll let you name my horse, if you give him a good combing. And keep talking, that way he'll know where you are, and not step on you."

Little Eddie beamed, and set to work with energy and the greatest good will in the world, even if he barely came up to Ugly Grey's nose, while his baby sister sat in the grass and watched, thumb creeping back to her mouth again.

John walked away, hefting his saddle, remarking to Allen, who was unhitching his teams with a great rattle of chains, "On my oath, the boy's tongue must be hinged in the middle, since it flaps so, at both ends."

"Bold little squirt," Allen said, with a chuckle. "Good thing he does talk so much, I'd be coming close to stepping on him myself, otherwise."

Francis and Allen had drawn up the wagons at an angle, so they could share a campfire. Moses was setting up the tent, to complete a third side of a square around it.

"We have guests already," he murmured to Elizabeth, as she handed a box of camp cookware down to Sarah. "Master Edward and Miss Sarabeth Patterson." Elizabeth followed the direction of his look, and laughed, softly.

"Very forward, aren't they? I will take them back to their mother presently . . . it will serve as a good pretext."

* * *

From E.S. Patterson Interview, University of California Local History Archival Project 1932: *"We were camping at the Bluffs, waiting for the grass to grow for about two weeks, when Doctor Townsend's family, and Mr. and Mrs. Montgomery joined up with the emigrant camp. The Doctor was a big man, with a gentlemanly way about him. I was just a boy, but I could see he was used to being in authority. Men liked him immediately, but so did women; he could make Ma laugh. I think a lot of folk thought at first he should be elected wagon master. He and Mrs. Townsend, they brought Sadie and me back to our camp that first day . . ."*

* * *

Mrs. Patterson had finished the laundry by the time John and Elizabeth walked across to the Patterson camp. Sarah was putting the finishing touches on their open-air kitchen, and Allen, Moses, and Francis were driving their cattle down to join the main camp herd. Eddie chattered nineteen to the dozen, still dragging Sadie by the hand until Elizabeth leaned down laughing and swung her capably unto her hip.

"We're walking too fast for her, Eddie. She's too little to keep up."

"She's grown too fast for me to carry like that," Eddie retorted. "I could carry her when she was littler . . . Ma! Ma!" he called, and scampered ahead of them, "Ma, Sadie and I brung Doctor Townsend, an' Miz Townsend, too!"

"Hello the camp!" John called, as they stepped around the corner of the Patterson's tent. He looked sideways at Elizabeth and murmured, "What sort of etiquette is required, do you think, when there is no door to knock on to declare ones' self?"

"Eddie my duckling," Isabella scolded. "Where have you been and where did you take the baby off to?" She was sitting down, sorting an apron full of dandelion greens in her lap. A girl of about ten, with the same soft dark hair, helped her. "Oh, heavens above, Nancy, you finish these." She started up from the wagon bench where she sat, as John gravely presented Elizabeth to her, and Elizabeth said, "Oh, no, please don't rise. You look terribly busy, Mrs. Patterson. Would you permit me to help you with them? And if you could tell me where you found them, we have so felt the need of something green with our meals."

Elizabeth set Sadie on her feet, as Isabella smiled warmly. "Oh, that would be neighborly. We did have to walk a good distance for them, since the closer fields have been so fouled!"

John looked hastily around and drew up a three-legged camp stool for his wife to settle on, and said, "If both you ladies would pardon me, young Eddie has promised to be my guide and introduce me to some of our future companions on the trail."

"Go along then, you scamp," Isabella addressed her son, and John bowed over her hand. "Doctor, it was a pleasure. I hope you will not be strangers."

"Small chance, with young Eddie around," John answered wryly and kissed Elizabeth's cheek. "We shall return in a while, Dearest, after calling upon Eddie's particular friends, the Murphy brothers." Sadie was already leaning confidingly against Elizabeth.

To John's amusement, Eddie copied his fond gesture, kissing his little sister in the same manner, and then he said confidently to John, "My bestes' friends after Sadie are the Murphy boys . . . their Paw-Paw tells them stories, and their Uncle Jamie makes them toys. They have six wagons an' they say they are bound for Californy. I cain't think of a name for your horse, but he sure is . . . is . . . a splendid one . . . an' . . ."

Eddie's voice trailed away as he and John went down the hillside, and Isabella Patterson looked at Elizabeth and laughed.

"Warn your son that the two prettiest girls in the camp have a great many large brothers, and enough close kin to ensure that they are treated with due care and consideration. My Oliver can hardly look on Helen Murphy or Mary Sullivan without blushing as red as a girl himself, and his voice going all to squeaks."

"My son . . . oh, you mean Moses," Elizabeth said, as she took Sadie onto her lap. "He is rather my little brother. My husband and I have raised him as our son, since my parents died of the fever."

"I am so sorry, then," Isabella looked up from her lapful of greens, with a shrewd and sympathetic eye. "He looks so like you, Mrs. Townsend. Have you and the Doctor not any children between yourselves?"

Sadie curled up, a dear little weight in Elizabeth's lap, sucking her thumb contentedly again, and Elizabeth replied, "Moses would never be ungAllent to a young lady . . . my husband has had the teaching of him since he was six years old. We have no children of our own: my husband worries for my health, you see, and he is very considerate. I have not been well . . . for some time, and there has been so much sickness up and down the river of late. It is the reason we are bound for California."

"My man was after a better farm," Isabella snorted. "Any excuse will do, I think, when a man gets bored and unsettled. I should know, Pa Hitchcock never stayed in one place for a year in his life, but at least he had the decency not to drag my mother and me all over creation with him." Isabella was setting aside the tender green inner leaves into a dish at her side, "No, just you go on holding Sadie, Mrs. Townsend. Nancy and I will have these finished in two shakes. Your husband at least came up with an excuse you couldn't argue with."

"Oh, but I wouldn't argue with him," Elizabeth replied. "About going west? I would rather endure hardship at his side than suffer his prolonged absence, as you have done. You must have endured so much alone, Mrs. Patterson."

"It has been difficult, these last two years since Mr. Patterson went with the traders," Isabella said, and Elizabeth noted with alarm that her eyes were bright with unshed tears, but that she seemed to will them not to fall. She tossed a handful of tender greens into the bowl with a little more vigor than strictly necessary. "But my boys are a help, even if they are not yet men. Oliver is seventeen, Samuel two years younger. Johnny, now, he is fourteen, but as he is near tall as Samuel, everyone thinks they are of an age."

"You also have the assistance of your father," Elizabeth ventured, and Isabella snorted.

"I should, seeing that it is the fault of that old vagabond! He filled my Samuel's head with talk of California. A paradise on earth, he said it was, until nothing would content him but that he had to see it for himself. It was the very least that Pa could do, to see me and the children safely there, but he vexes me no end, always undermining my authority with the boys, and filling the children's heads with wild stories!"

"I like Paw-Paw's stories," spoke up Nancy, bravely, and Isabella fluffed up like an indignant bantam hen.

"See what I mean? Mrs. Townsend and I were speaking, Nancy . . . remember, children should be seen and not heard!"

"None the less, I do envy you, Mrs. Patterson . . . oh, for heaven's sake, just call me Elizabeth. You still have a father living, for which I envy you. Our dear parents died some ten years ago, when my husband still had a practice in Stark County and we were new-married."

"And what would your father and mother have advised you, then?" Isabella asked, still indignant. "Would they have abetted your husband in some reckless scheme, against your own wishes?"

"I don't know," Elizabeth replied, consideringly. "I cannot imagine Papa Schallenberger talking my dear husband out of anything he had set his heart on doing: he was born in Pennsylvania, and has been moving west by degrees ever since. I imagine, though, that Papa would have advised me that my place was ever at my husband's side. *'Entreat me not to leave you or to return from following after you. Wherever you go, I will go; and where you lodge, I will lodge, your people will be my people' . . .*"

"So I was also told," Isabella said, laughing shortly. "But I did not know then of the places I would be expected to go, or that I should have to find my way to them alone!"

"But you are not entirely alone! "Elizabeth took Isabella's hands, empty at the moment of dandelion greens, in her own. "We shall be in a good company, with many stout companions, and many good friends as well; of that I am sure, for my dearest darling will make it so and I trust him completely."

"Your good fortune, my dear Mrs. Townsend." Isabella laughed heartily. "I do not have the luxury of such utter dependence . . . and indeed, I think it may be one such that we may set aside, once we are on the trail."

"Whatever do you mean?" Elizabeth was baffled, and Isabella laughed again, sounding a little more kindly.

"Only that we are leaving all behind, my dear, and it might be well to be able to stand on our own feet in regards to our own preferences . . . just a fancy of mine," she added. "Think nothing of it, Mrs. Townsend – Elizabeth. Sadie has fallen asleep . . . let me take her from you, and put her to rest in the wagon."

From Dr. Townsend's diary: *"Arriving at the bluff encampment, we made haste to search out those others of a like mind to venture towards California. The largest part of these are relations, friends and connections of Martin Murphy, late of Irish Grove, in Holt County . . ."*

When Eddie had led him into Murphy's camp; six wagons loosely circled together under a large poplar tree, the elder Mr. Murphy had been sitting in a comfortable wooden chair with a child on each knee and half a dozen more, boys and girls together at his feet, telling them a story. Another man, of about the same age sat close by, whittling and listening to his yarn. Two younger men worked together in a circle of wood-chips and tools, mending a wheel, while a pretty, black-haired woman kneaded a great trough of bread dough. Another man, with hair the same jet-black, was scraping down a new ox-bow with a slip of broken glass.

But when Eddie shrilled, "Mister Murphy, Mister Murphy, I brung you another for California, he and his'n are camping at the top of the hill next to us, he's a doctor for real, an' he has a grey horse!" the older man quickly scooted the small children off his knees, saying, "'Tis enough for now, my dears, go and play . . . you too, Eddie. I need to speak with this gentleman, now." John thought, as the children romped out towards the meadow beside the camping place, *'and I thought there were children everywhere at the Pattersons.'*

"John Townsend. Eddie tells me that you are also bound for California," John said to the senior Mr. Martin; an older man, not as old as Hitchcock, with a soft Irish brogue barely abraded by long absence from his native soil, and shrewd brown eyes, very alive in his blunt-featured countenance.

"I'm Martin Murphy," he held out his hand towards John, who while attempting to seem as if he wasn't, was nonetheless sizing up their outfit and general fitness for the long journey. "And this is my old and good friend, Patrick Martin, who came away from Wexford in the same year although we did not know each other then."

Patrick Murphy, much the same age as Martin Murphy, appeared to be a lively and muscular spark, with bright blue eyes and a nose that looked as if it had been broken several times.

He shook John's hand with a strong grip. "Aye, says the lad, a doctor is it? Sure and we're honored, that we are . . . at least no plagued Englishman says I to meself, seeing you come down from the hill." He had a wicked glint in his eye, and John guessed rightly that his nose had not been broken by accident.

He returned the grip and said calmly, "My parents were English. Quakers from Norton and the family was well known locally, but they removed to Pennsylvania before I was born."

"Capital, capital!" said Patrick with a grin. "So, you've risen in the world then, is it?"

"Patrick, you'd be after teasing the wrong man," Martin chided his friend and continued, "Was it true, what young Edward was saying, you indeed are a doctor? Well, that is a blessing to have in any company. Is it true also that you are joining us? Another blessing to be sure, and are there others with you?"

"My friend and neighbor from St. Joseph, my wife, and her brother," John answered. "My friend has been ever set on California, and so has my wife's brother. I was convinced this last winter that it would be best for my wife's health if we removed also."

Old Martin looked grieved, and said, brokenly, "So, I wish we had gone sooner, and my own dear wife might have been spared. Aye, she and my boy Martin's little girl. Such an angel she was . . . no consolation that she is now in the care of like. She should have been growing up fair and happy, playing in the fields like the little lamb that she was. We could no longer stay in such a pestilential and godless place, so we came away, all of us and our neighbors – young John Sullivan and what the sickness left to him of his family, Patrick Martin, his two lads, and his daughter Annie that married my own boy James, leaving my dear Mary Ellen and the babe behind. "

Murphy's voice cracked a little, and John said, "I am so sorry. So many were lost untimely in the last year or so, to the fevers – no matter what we could do."

"Aye," Martin Murphy recovered his voice. "And they are with Him and his angels now, no doubt on that. She was a fine, goodly woman, and blessed me with nine splendid children, four having children of their own. It is in me mind, though, that I should have listened to Father Hoecken earlier than I did. But still, to have a doctor in our party is a great relief." He turned and called to the two younger men, "James . . . Martin, come and meet Doctor Townsend, who's with us for California. This is James Miller, who's married my daughter Mary and me oldest son, Martin. His wife is named Mary, also, but we call her Mary-Bee, to reduce the confusion, ye know . . ." he looked around the campsite, and remarked, "Well, they were here a minute ago."

"They walked down to the spring for water," said the younger Martin. He was a youthful version of his father, a grave and steady-looking man with the same level gaze.

Old Martin added, "Ye'll know Martin's boys when you see them, all four of them always together, and perfect imps they are, then. Dennis, come and meet the Doctor." The man who was scraping the oxbow set it all carefully down, and Old Martin continued, "Aye, you'll always know Patrick's sons by the black-Irish look of them."

"Dennis Martin." He dusted his hands hastily on his trousers, and shook hands. "Has Pa threatened to knock you down for being an Englishman yet? He'll get around to it." Dennis looked to be a little older than Moses, but with his father's black hair and startlingly blue eyes, but after Patrick's vivid self, a paler and less colorful copy. "M' brother Patrick and John Sullivan have gone into Kanesville to buy another yoke of oxen. They'll be sorry to miss you this day, but I'll guess we'll have time to make it up on the trail."

"My other boys went with them," Old Martin explained. "Jamie, that's married to Patrick's daughter Annie, Daniel, Bernard, and Johnny. We've the six wagons between us, and fifteen men; a small party, to think of going all the way alone. Do ye know of any more, who might join our company for California?"

"Just one," John answered. "A blacksmith named Stephens, camped by himself a little way down the St. Joe road."

Old Martin and his son looked at each other, and the old man said admiringly, "Och, that'll be another fine man to have on the journey with us . . . a blacksmith, is it? What sort of man might he be, if you don't mind the impertinence of me asking?

26

"A very good one, I judge," John replied, "But modest, even reticent in conversing about himself. But he says he had been out on the Santa Fe trails, and it contents me well to know that someone with experience such as that will join with us."

"'Tis good to know, then." Old Patrick looked both relieved and calculating. "Mr. Thorp, he is a foine man, for talk and all . . . but he is for Oregon, sure enough and none o' the others so bound seem inclined to go against him. Meself, I don't think he cares for us paddies . . ."

"Not that we care for him much." his son added. "But the Oregoners will have him for captain, for a' we can say about it."

"Wait and see," John said tranquilly. "Wait and see. In St. Joe, the men I know in the Santa Fe trade say that thirty to forty men in a company is best. Stephens told me he didn't think the grass would be grown tall enough for us for another three weeks. There's a little time left for others to join us, in the meantime."

Nothing so quite reassured him as the sight of the way-side blacksmith driving his team up the hill a few days later as they were finishing their noonday meal under a canvas awning stretched between handy tree branches and their wagons. Moses and Allen were exuberantly planning a grand buffalo-hunting expedition once they were out on the trail, while John listened to them and smiled quietly over his book of Chesterfield's letters, and Elizabeth mended one of Moses' shirts. Sarah was finishing the washing-up.

As she emptied out the wash pan over the side of the bluff, she straightened and said, "Doctor John, there's another wagon coming up from town. It looks like that blacksmith man."

"Why so it is." John put his book away. Stephens was quite alone, no drover and no spare stock, just the three yoke and golden-eyed Dog trailing after. At the top of the hill, John greeted him. "Stephens, you are a welcome sight. I was about to go into Kanesville and buy another horse."

"That so?" Stephens half-smiled, clean of forge-soot, but trail-dusty. The rains had finally let up, and the roads had begun to dry out. "Am I doing you another favor, Doc?"

"I appreciate your eye . . . you've vastly more trail experience than I have. Or most of the others, I have discovered, since we parted."

John introduced him to Allen and the Pattersons, and arranged to borrow Allen's saddle horse for the afternoon, Dog being bidden to stay behind and guard Stephens' wagon, while the two of them rode to Kanesville.

John pointed out the Murphy's rambling camp as they passed by it. The children were playing out in the meadow nearby; soldiers and Indians, it looked like, from the willow-branch bows and arrows, and the chicken-feathers. It also appeared that Sadie and Nancy Patterson had been unenthusiastically pressed into serving as Indians.

There was Eddie, and John recognized young Martins' sons, as alike as peas in a pod, just as their grandfather said: they had their mothers' auburn-tinged hair, and their grandfather's lively brown eyes, perfect stair-steps when they stood in a line. Their voices chimed together, and they often finished each others' sentences, presenting a united front to the world, the picture of injured innocence when accused of some small childish crime.

"I'll introduce you to them, tonight. Young Martin is the best hand with oxen that I have seen so far, very careful he is with his beasts. He doctors them himself, only asks my advice for courtesy. They're all good folk. They've six wagons among them all and at least fifteen men if you count the hired teamsters and the boys who are almost grown . . . but not a one of them ever been west of the Mississippi. It was enough of an eye-opener for Montgomery and me, just bringing our wagons from St. Joseph. I know what my own limitations are."

Stephens just looked at him, shrewdly, with those water-pale eyes. "You working on a plan, doc?"

"Yes," John replied. "They're holding an election for wagon-master, on Sunday . . . to elect a leader for all of us as far as to Fort Hall, and a secretary and god knows what. I'm going to nominate you. You'd be a better captain than that blowhard Thorp who's been angling for it since we got here. I think he's a fool and couldn't pilot a thirsty horse to water. They'd give me the captaincy, if I wanted it, just because I'm a doctor and wear a fine coat. But I don't want it." He looked honestly at Stephens. "I know my own skills. I'm good at doctoring, at least I don't kill any more of my patients than most doctors do. But I don't want to be responsible for leading all these fine folk into the desert on the strength of my fine coat and polished boots."

"But you're going anyway."

"I'd prefer to do so following you," John answered.

"Why me, in parti'clar?"

"Because I think you'd know what you're doing, out there . . . and you don't want the captaincy. And that means you're the best man to have it."

"I ain't a political man, Doc. I ain't real good with folk."

"But I am," John replied. "Leave that part of it to me."

In the mud and squalor of Kanesville's pens and corrals, John followed Stephen's lead regarding sizing up stock. "I don't think you want more'n one extra team," the blacksmith advised. "Take care of the ones you start with." They disputed pleasantly over that, and the eternal question of mule versus oxen for teams.

"Mules move faster," John argued.

"But the Injuns 'ull steal 'em, and leave oxen alone, mostly. 'Sides, you can always eat oxen, if it comes to that."

"You can eat mule." John pointed out.

"Don't taste so good. Hardly any flesh on 'em."

They leaned their elbows on the top rail of a corral full of horses; mostly browns and bays, paints and pintos, still shaggy from winter, snorting and jostling each other.

"Not much to choose from," John said, discouraged. This lot looked too wild and unbroken. There was a pretty dapple-grey, very spirited though; he quailed at the thought of his Elizabeth riding such an unschooled mount.

"That one," Stephens said, quietly. "The buckskin colored gelding, dark mane and tail – yonder far corner." It was about a hand shorter than the others, a neat-featured and spry little beast, like an Indian pony.

Someone came up to the corral rail, on John's other side, and John turned and thought in amazement at first they were Indians, silent and smelling of tobacco smoke, all three with long hair.

The oldest of them was a straight-backed and powerfully-built old man, even older than Hitchcock, for his hair had gone entirely snow white, clubbed at the back of his neck in the old-fashioned manner of the last century. He had blue eyes, clouded with cataracts. The other two, boys about Moses and Oliver's age, had high cheekbones and Indian coloring, and wore their hair in long plaits ornamented with beads and feathers in the Indian custom. All three of them were dressed in fringed leather leggings and moccasins, and tunics of hide, and trimmed alike with leather fringe and beadwork.

John said, "Mr. Greenwood?" at the same time as Stephens said, "Caleb." The old man merely nodded; seemingly he and Stephens were old acquaintances.

"'Lisha. Your friend?"

"Doc Townsend. Going t' California."

"Caleb Greenwood." The old mountain-man shook his hand with courteous firmness, "My sons, Brittan and Johnny. You are seeking a good horse?"

"For my wife," John said.

29

"Any you favor?"

"Mr. Stephens advises the little buckskin. I'd still like to see him ridden, though. They all appear quite wild."

"Britt?" said the old man softly, with a gesture. One of the Indian boys vaulted the fence, and nonchalantly threaded his way between the fractious horses. He approached the little buckskin, and grabbed him by the nose, appearing to whisper or blow into the startled animals' nostrils. For a moment, the two heads were close together, and then Britt seized a handful of mane, and leaped from the ground, straight onto the buckskin's back.

For a moment, the little horse stood stock still, and then Britt nudged his ribs with moccasined heels, and leaned close against his neck and urged him into a walk, then a trot, back to a canter and then a walk again, up to the corral fence where Britt slid down, laughing, with a flash of white teeth in his dark-tanned face.

"I b'lieve you have yourself a horse for your lady wife, " remarked the old frontiersman. "Tell her she must treat it as a pet at first and feed it apples and carrots and treats from her own hand. This one has a good heart and a sweet nature, and will carry her faithfully wherever she goes." And as if embarrassed by so many words, he nodded courteously and strode away, trailed by his two Indian sons.

"We must hire him as the trail-guide," said Stephens quietly, which John believed ever afterwards to be Stephens' very first command as captain – even though he were not yet elected to that office.

* * *

Angeline Morrison Letter #2
15th of May 1844
Writ from the emigrant camp
At Council Bluffs, Iowa Territory

My dearest Angeline:

Receiv'd your kindest answer before we departed from St. Joseph; a thousand thanks for your honest recitations of events. I will feel so distant from those happy scenes, be assured that I shall cherish your letter, and read it often, especially when we have departed these shores.

We leave in a few days, with great anticipation and enthusiasm, since the grass has now grown tall enough to feed our stock. The rains have "let up" as our trail guide Mr. Greenwood says. Such a picturesque sight as he presents, as you would think he walked out of the pages of a Leatherstocking tale! He and sons are contracted to guide us as far as Fort Hall.

My Dearest has bought me a riding horse, for my use when travel in the wagon becomes too uncomfortable and walking beside it too exhausting; he remains busy these last few days before we take to the trail, with business relating to our party, and I am relieved that he is so engaged again with these public matters. Everything promises to be so new, so different, as we leave all common cares behind, but what awaits us?

I shall write to you from Fort Laramie, my dearest friend, with an account of our adventures upon this venture. Until then adieu, from

Your loving friend

Elizabeth

Chapter 3 – *Into the Sea of Grass*

From Doctor Townsend's diary: *"Seventeenth of May, 1844: The die is cast; we depart on the morrow, in company with Thorp's Oregon-bound party. The grass is well-grown, we have made such last-minute preparations as are necessary, made final additions to our supplies and sent last letters to such kin and loved ones as we have remaining behind. We have taken every care against such contingencies as we may expect, and asked His blessings upon our journey. My good and trusty friend Elisha Stephens has been elected Captain of the party . . ."*

* * *

John sat on the wagon seat with his writing desk in his lap and the sheltering wagon cover drawn tight over the first bow. The securing flap had not yet dropped over the opening into that tiny canvas room which had been their home for a month and would be for many months yet. A few night insects fluttered around the lamp depending from the wagon bow over his head, which cast just enough light for him to write. He could look out as if through a round window, to the last of the pale color fading from the sky to the west, and the stars just winking into view. All among the trees, yellow lantern and candle light glowed within wagon tops and tents, coloring them a darker gold, like the Chinese paper lanterns that a friend of his fathers' who was a tea-clipper captain had brought from Canton and given to him when he was a boy.

Enough of looking out; he had a need to write an account of the meeting, held in the largest clearing amongst the trees, and lit by lanterns hanging from the branches overhead. They had brought chairs and benches, kegs, boxes, blankets, and ground-cloths from the wagons, and roughed out some tree trunks to serve as seats for the assembly. It was indeed like a camp meeting, as Elizabeth had foretold. John and many of the other men had put off their rough work clothes for the occasion. He himself donned his finest broadcloth coat, and Elizabeth tied his best neck cloth, and adorned her own dark travel dress with a white lace collar and linen cuffs.

Stephens did not: he came in his soot-covered work clothes, straight from the little forge. He had set that up at the edge of the camp and been kept busy ever since with mending this and that. This had resulted in Stephens becoming at least well known in the emigrant camp, if not as well-liked as he would have been if he were a more gregarious man. He had hired a single teamster to help with his wagon, a silent, wiry New Orleans Creole named John Flomboy who was as unforthcoming about himself as Stephens.

Stephens now sat next to John, Elizabeth, Moses, and the Montgomerys, his arms folded, and watched impassively.

". . . Speeches interminable, discussion endless, much as ex- pected," John wrote. *"Reviewing the required hours of travel per day, rotating the order of daily march, the observance of the Sabbath and the mechanics of managing the campsite; at which juncture I had my professional say regarding the situation of privy-pits at a good remove from any source of water we may hope to use, since the miasma arising from such may adversely affect the health of our party . . . all serving as a prelude to the serious business of selecting a leader for our enterprise, but first, another wrangle over franchise; it being manifestly clear that those who owned property, viz a wagon, should have a clear say in deciding matters affecting the party, having the most to lose.*

Much pointless discussion incited by one Mr. Hammer, a Quaker gentleman from Pennsylvania who attempted to scrape acquaintance with me by calling on connections with my father's acquaintances in the place of my birth; he insisted that heads of families should also qualify as voting on party matters on similar grounds. It eventually was determined that there existed no particular class among the entire party who were head of family, but did not own a wagon. Mr. Hammer placated into silence by inclusion of this stipulation, although I have no notion of why he took this so vociferously, save that perhaps he is of that vainglorious breed who takes an unseemly delight in the sound of their own voices.

I had been called on previously to serve as recorder, and now fell to me the task of making a complete roll of those qualified to vote."

John re-inked his pen and savored the memory of the consternation among Thorp and the other Oregon bound when Isabella Patterson stood up and calmly demanded to be included on the voter's roll, indisputably the owner of a wagon, and the head of a family.

"You can't be a voter!" cried Thorp.

An especially argumentative Oregon-bound emigrant named Shaw added, in some outrage," You're a woman!"

"That is not in dispute here," Isabella returned dryly. "However, I own a wagon, being deputized by my dear husband, who is thousands of miles away from here and cannot speak for his interests himself. In his absence, I am head of my family. And I am going to California, with my wagon, and my family. Kindly explain to me why I should not be able to exercise the responsibilities deputized to me by my husband in this assembly as regards our journey to rejoin him."

John, inwardly amused, cleared his throat, and solemnly read what had been discussed and decided upon by all present. "'Franchise is to be held by every owner of a wagon, and/or the head of a family, along with the right to call for, and to speak in any assembly of the party.' Gentlemen, I think Mrs. Patterson has us there."

"And rightfully so," Old Martin Murphy spoke up. "'Tis only right and fair, and by the rules we set for ourselves."

That surprised John, who had no idea what would move him to be such a stout or effective ally, since when Old Martin spoke, he spoke for his sons and kin, and therefore a large part of the California-bound party.

"But what about Mr. Hitchcock, your good father?" Ventured Thorp with some indignation; Old man Hitchcock took a malicious pleasure in baiting, provoking, or arguing with his daughter at every turn. He had taken his two mules and a length of canvas, and had gone off to share a campfire with his old friend Greenwood and his Indian sons on most nights, although he was usually somewhere to be found about the Patterson camp during the day.

Isabella retorted, "He is neither the owner of mine and my husband's wagon, or the head of our family, just a shiftless old vagabond with two mules to his name."

"But what of your oldest son – might he be deputized to speak for you?" bleated the luckless Mr. Thorp, and received a glare of such concentrated and withering contempt from Isabella that John thought he must surely melt into a small and steaming puddle.

"After such an unexpected diversion," John wrote," *We bent our energies to our original and long-expected agenda, that of electing a leader for this perilous passage. Mr. Thorp being nominated by those intending for Oregon, there was discussion in consideration of Young Martin Murphy; who has much to commend him, being in the prime of years, sober and the head of a family himself, but – and this was unspoken – unquestionably a Papist, unlikely to win much favor with the Oregon party. So I took it upon myself to nominate Stephens, both as a compromise, and the man I honestly think fittest for the task, tho' it is plain to me that I may have more faith in him than he does himself."*

Stephens, competent, inarticulate, and solitary, was overwhelmingly voted in as captain of the party and John himself was chosen to be recording secretary for the company – and implicitly Stephen's right-hand in the running of it. Under the lamplight in the council grove, Stephens was acclaimed as captain, and stood up on a crate, as John had whispered he must speak to all the company, now.

"What do I say now, Doc?"

"Not what they want to hear," John replied. "Thank them for their vote, and then tell them what you're going to do."

Stephens stood awkwardly on the crate for a moment, an ugly and gangly big man, ungainly in his sooty work clothes, sweating under the pale lantern light, and John realized piercingly that Stephens was in that place he hated most of all — the middle of a crowd of people, all looking expectantly at him.

Finally, Stephens cleared his throat and said, "Thank-ee for your vote, folks. I promise I'll get you to Californy, or wherever you're going. We'll cross the river a week tomorrow; the grass'll be growed proper by then. Good night t' you-all." Then he jumped down from the box and shouldered hurriedly away through the crowd.

John was detained by Allen, who said quietly, "Well, he don't seem like much, John, but I think we can work with him – better than that fool Thorp, any ways."

"I am elected recording secretary as expected, and the California party has voted to hire Greenwood and his sons as guides as far as the great Rocky Mountains, over the vociferous objects of Thorp and the Oregon faction, who object to what they term an unnecessary expense, as they insist the trail has itself been so oft-traveled and clearly marked that no guide is necessary. They steadfastly refuse to share in any of the cost for his hire."

"Dearest, why do you trust Captain Stephens so?" Elizabeth asked sleepily, after the election meeting, when they were curled up spoon-fashioned in their bed — that mattress laid over three flat-topped trunks and boxes in the wagon which took up better than half the space in it.

John considered his answer carefully; truth told, it was instinct, the instinct that served him well in the practice of medicine, but difficult to put into words. He had learned through hard experience not to ask where it came from, or worry about possible outcomes, just pay attention to that quiet little whisper of absolute conviction. He ignored it at his peril; it served him well to listen.

"He's good with the animals," he replied at last. "And he knows what he is about once we cross the river, better than any of us, except maybe Greenwood and Hitchcock. We – most of the rest of us, we have moved before. We have taken our wagons and our families from here to there, but there was always a road. We could often buy supplies, or another draft ox, and we were never at it for more than a month or so. This is . . ." he paused and thought carefully. "When I was a boy, I was taken to an acrobatic exhibition of performers who did hand-stands and tumbles, hanging by their hands from swings high above the ground. They would leap off a little stand, catch the swing by their hands, and go soaring through the air, all across the hippodrome . . . and at the right moment, let go and turn a somersault in the air and catch another swing, in mid-air . . . all with perfect timing. We are about to step off the platform, Liz. From now on, we must be able to dare, and to trust. And we must have a trail-captain who knows what it is like to be out there for months and months."

"I trust you, Dearest," Elizabeth had said sleepily. Thinking of that, John looked out of their wagon through the little round opening, at the stars and the river, and wondered if she had any idea of how immense the wilderness was, or how alone they would be, once they had swung away from their perch on the river heartland. Perhaps it was best, he decided, that she and the other women and children did not, or they would not be able to sleep so sound.

Even tonight, the night before their momentous departure, Elizabeth slept, breathing easily, her silver-gilt braid woven up for night and lying across the pillow like a bit of fine embroidery. She was happy with the buckskin pony, had petted him, and ridden him every day that they waited in camp for the grass to grow.

"I have no proper side-saddle," she lamented to Isabella, and that formidable little woman, fresh from her victory at exercising the franchise, replied, "Then ride astride. Who is there to see you being unladylike on the other side of that river? Besides, you won't fall off so easily. Wear a pair of your boy Moses' trousers under your skirt and don't pay anyone any mind about it."

John had noticed how Elizabeth and Sarah Montgomery had both looked thoughtful, as if they suddenly comprehended the kind of freedoms that lay across the river, besides the much-advertised perils.

Children's voices from the Patterson camp, sleepy and querulous; John smiled to hear them. Sadie had almost stopped sucking her thumb, and learned to say a few emphatic words now that her mouth was not corked up by it; "Don't! Horsie! Mine!" Eddie alternately charmed and appalled, with his total and complete fearlessness in every situation. John felt that children being frightened was a good thing; they were kept from danger by their fears, but Isabella averred that Little Eddie feared nothing in the world, and moreover usually walked serenely straight in the direction of any available danger – which of course frightened the very daylights out of her.

"We are to assemble tomorrow, before dawn, and move to the riverbank to begin crossing," John wrote carefully, *"where there is a rough landing, and a single flat-bottomed scow to ferry the wagons over, thereby saving considerable time. Capt. Stephens plans to swim the stock, against the advice of Thorp and the Oregon party. I spend much time in vexatious dispute with these gentlemen . . ."*

The sky had entirely darkened now, pricked by a brilliant spangle of stars. John sighed and corked his ink-bottle; enough of this for tonight. He closed the lantern and let the canvas apron fall over the round opening, but even when he was in bed he lay awake for a long, long time, looking up at the curving canvas roof and remembering the acrobats soaring confidently through the air.

It did not go well in the morning, for dawn came under lowering clouds, and they packed the last of the cooking things in a fine drizzle of rain, and left the cook-fire to go out of itself.

"You're needed down at the river, Doc . . . you an' the boy, too, if your man can manage your wagon hisself." Stephens appeared out of the grey rain, his hat-brim dripping like a roof-edge. "We're going to start swimming the stock."

"I shall stay in the Montgomery wagon and keep Sarah company." Elizabeth pulled her shawl around herself. She had meant to ride on this first day, but she gave the reins over to Moses with a certain amount of relief. They had been ready for several hours, waiting in a huddled mass of wagons and teams for their turn to cross the river. It looked to be a tedious business, unhitching two wagons at a time on the river bank, man-handling the wagons onto the waiting ferry, and diverting the loose stock into a steadily growing herd, milling about on the riverbank.

The ferry lurched ungainly in the river, poled away from the landing by two of the Indian crew. They were entirely naked save for a brief loincloth, even to their heads, shaved of all but a long top-knot like a horses' tail. They seemed stoically indifferent to the rain that streamed down their bodies.

"Dollar a wagon," said Stephens, laconically. "Extra for stock. Good business, while it lasts. "

Out on the river, the current caught the flatboat, and pulled it swiftly along the heavy line strung between banks. They could just see the opposite bank, where more of the shaven-headed Indians hauled away at a long rope attached to the flatboat. A similar rope paid out from the near bank as the scow moved away, close to where Stephens and John watched.

"Dropped the rope," Stephens remarked, as there was a flurry of shouts and gesticulating from the Indians on their side of the river. "Current's got it."

"What'll they do?"

"Watch."

A small dug-out canoe shot out from the riverbank, two Indians digging short paddles into the muddy water, achieving a nice burst of speed, aimed for where the tow rope had dropped down into the water. One of the paddlers slipped into the river as smooth and confident as an otter and vanished under the surface.

"They can swim?"

"Handy thing to know, living on the river,"

The swimmer surfaced a few seconds later, bearing a loop of rope, and handed it to his confederate in the canoe. They paddled back to the river bank and beached it on the bank.

"Fine show for us," Stephens remarked. "A little fun for them. Start moving the cattle towards the river. Force them as far out as you can, until they begin swimming for the far shore. You mind getting wet?"

"I can't swim." John pointed out gamely.

"That horse of yours can, Doc. When he gets deep in, take your feet out of the stirrups and hold on to your saddle horn."

But even with the assistance of men and boys on foot, shouting and waving their hats, the cattle would not go far enough into the swirling river. They turned back and clambered over each other, bellowing frantically, or were swept down to the mud flats below the landing, and mired to their shoulders. Finally, nothing could induce them to venture in farther than the shallows, even as their numbers were added to, as wagons were unhitched and slowly rolled onto the ferry landing. John wearily concluded that in a brute physical contest between a two-hundred-pound man and a two-thousand-pound ox, the ox was eventually going to win out on that one. He found Stephens helping Old Man Hitchcock and a resentful Mr. Shaw, trying to dig one of the stuck oxen out of the muck.

"Captain, I think we're going to have to try something else."

"Agreed, Doc." Stephens looked around, very thoughtfully. "You know, they ain't real bright sparks, oxen. Not like dogs."

"Or pig; real clever, pigs. I saw an elocutin' pig once, in a traveling menagerie," mused Old Man Hitchcock. "But an ox ain't any great shakes, no more'n sheep, an' they have to put a bell on the lead sheep, 'cause all the rest are too dumb to figure out how to get out of their own pen."

Stephens suddenly lifted his head. "Doc," he asked casually, "Who has the most biddable, tamest ox in this party?"

"That 'ud be Izzy," Old Hitchcock answered right away, and John nodded agreement. "I seen her and the other children yoking them together of a morning, and Eddie driving them, an' that li'l squirt ain't but knee-high to a grasshopper."

"Doc, get one of Miz Patterson's boys, ask him to bring one of theirs on a long halter down to the landing. Hitchcock, see if you call to mind any of that Injun sign-talking, and get those two with the canoe to row a little ways out in the river."

Hitchcock began chuckling, wheezily. "Cap'n, that's a notion in a million . . . how to lead an ox to water, an' get him in the drink."

John spotted the saffron-yellow wagon top easily enough; just a little ahead of his own, already unhitched by the landing. He waved to Sarah and Elizabeth, and leaned down to speak with Isabella, and the boys.

"Captain Stephens requires the loan of the most biddable of your oxen, and Oliver, with a very long halter. He has an idea to get them into the deep water."

"Socks," replied Isabella decisively. "He's as tame as a kitten. He would follow any of us into a house and curl up in our laps if he could. Oliver, find Socks and take him to Cap'n Stephens."

Oliver took up a long halter from their wagon, and John gave him a boost up to ride behind him, into the milling herd of muddy and unhappy cattle penned by the river bank. They located Socks easily enough, and Oliver snubbed the long halter around his horns. He clumped readily after them, waded hock deep, knee-deep, chest-deep in the water as Oliver tumbled into the canoe and the two Indians slowly paddled out into deeper and deeper water.

Socks followed trustfully, swimming strongly, and Stephens commanded, "Now! Get 'em going!"

Slowly and ponderously, other oxen moved into the water, deeper and deeper, in Socks' wake; a few, a scattering, then as if reassured, more and more of them, a broad and threshing arrow of nostrils, horns, and backs cutting across the river. The trampled river bank emptied and as other teams were unhitched, they trotted obediently into the river, hardly needing encouragement from the horsemen and boys waving their hats and shouting.

Two and two the wagons made the slow trip across. In the late afternoon, with only a portion of the wagons and most of the cattle on the other side Stephens sent Old Greenwood and his sons across to scout for a good camping place. They swam the last of the loose cattle and sent a party of young men to stand guard over the cattle and horses, since they could not move the remaining wagons and families over until morning.

* * *

From E.S. Patterson Interview, University of California Local History Archival Project 1932: *"We'd only gotten some of the wagons over, by the end of the day, so there we were, half and half. Ours was over, and Mr. Martin Murphy, and John Sullivan's and one or two others. Doctor Townsend sent his foster son and some other of the young men to mount guard, fearing that the local Indians would try and steal cattle, for they had that sort of reputation then. Amongst the guards that night was my brother Oliver, Moses Schallenberger the doctor's boy, and Johnny Murphy – all bright and daring young sparks. They had pastured the cattle, and let them feed, then rounded them up into the corral made from chaining the wagon tongue of each wagon to the rear wheel of the wagon before, or chained them to the wagons. Around midnight they became bored with watching the cattle and the wagons whilst all slept.*

They had a mind to play a trick on John Sullivan, who was something of a sober-sides, for all that he was not that much older. He was continually nervous about the Indians, and about his oxen being stolen, and he was plagued particularly as he had a very pretty sister and always had to act the part of a severe papa. She married a Mr. Sherbeck in San Francisco, eventually, but not after leading all the other single men of the party in a merry dance.

It was Oliver's idea, and he put it to Moses who thought it very funny, but he worried that the Doctor and Captain Stephens might be angered, so they went to Martin Murphy, who was more or less in charge, and put it to him. They might not have worried; Martin thought it a fine jest, too. They had pastured the cattle, put some of them into the corral for the night, and chained others of them outside to the wagons.

In the wee hours, Oliver quietly unfastened John Sullivan's cattle and drove them into the woods, and after some minutes Moses and Bernard gave the alarm. John Sullivan sprang up and gave chase after his property, and after some brisk exercise and listening for the jingle of their chains, recaptured them and brought them back to his wagon, where he chained them to the wheels again and returned to his bedroll. In a little while Oliver loosed them and drove them farther into the woods, and Moses giving the alarm. John Sullivan sprang up with some uncomplimentary words about the pesky Indians and gave chase again.

This time Oliver had driven them much farther away, and when John Sullivan stood himself up on a fallen tree to listen for the jingling of chains, Johnny Murphy was hiding close by and fired off a shotgun, both barrels full of birdshot into the air. John Sullivan went running back to camp shouting that the Indians had shot at him, and talked ever afterwards of the narrow escape he had. Meanwhile, Oliver and Moses brought back his cattle, circling around from another direction.

Over the next days, Captain Stephens made mention of their determination and skill at retrieving John Sullivan's animals twice . . . and then remarked at how odd it was, that no one else's stock had been disturbed. But my brother Oliver spoke up, saying it was that John Sullivan's cattle were white, and thus were better seen in the dark, and Captain Stephens, he smiled a little. I think he knew, or guessed something of what had really happened, but he said naught else on the matter, even when John Sullivan told the tale again of how the Indians had tried to steal his oxen and shot at him.

The Doctor did give a great lecture several days after to the corporals of the guard, and all the young men, about the seriousness of their duties, and not to give way to the temptation of larks and practical jokes . . ."

* * *

From the Diary of Dr. Townsend: *"We are at last over the first obstacle on our journey, at some cost, having lost some cattle to the river, being swept away, or stuck in deep mud and drown'd . . . this also being the cause of some lack of amity between'st ourselves and the Oregon party. I was called to attend to Mrs. Thorp, she being ill, and Mr. Thorp himself blaming Capt.*

Stephens for his insistence upon haste. Much contention from Mr. Hammer who insists on being solely guided by divine revelation revealed through his dreams, and Mr. Shaw, guided by a penchant for trouble-making, who seems to have quarreled with one and all.

We must now make preparations for crossing the Elkhorn River by constructing a boat from two wagon-boxes waterproofed with hides sewn closely over all. Capt. Stephens revealed peculiar foresight by having provided his wagon with a number of stout metal pulleys, such as are used on ships of the line, and a great quantity of good rope . . . The contents of each of our wagons and the wagons themselves must be thus laboriously transported. My Dearest Darling and the other women went aside from the scene of our toils to perform their own toils, viz. laundry, it for once being a fine, fair day with abundant sunshine . . ."

* * *

Elizabeth carried a large bundle of bedding packed into her washtub, leading her pony along the river bank towards where the women of the party had set up an open-air laundry under the poplar trees. She recognized Mrs. Thorp and some of the other Oregon-bound, a little further along at the water's edge, where the water ran clear over a clean gravel bottom, as if they were holding themselves a little apart from the Murphy women and the outspoken Isabella. She had two more bundles of clothes and bedding tied to her horse's saddle. Laundry day, such as it was, and perhaps a chance to properly dry out some things that had been damp and musty, seemingly for weeks; A day not to spend in the saddle, or in the wagon, not to be incessantly moving.

A warm breeze rustled the ever-trembling poplar leaves, and cloud-shadows chased each other over gentle-rolling hillsides of grass. Sheets and blankets were already spread out to dry on the sweet clean grass, that prairie grass they had waited for to grow and feed their cattle. There was the sound of laughter, as merry as schoolgirls, under the trees, and Elizabeth unaccountably felt old. Dear Isabella was the only woman older than she, and Sarah – just lately wed, the only one without children – and sometimes Elizabeth felt quite alone; alone and isolated by her husbands' profession and stature. It had not mattered so much back in St. Joseph where there were many other women, where she had affectionate and longtime friends. Neither Sarah nor Isabella would have been counted amongst them then, except in the most cursory fashion.

But today she had put on a faded old wash-dress with the hem turned up, and she had brought a bucket of soap and gone to seek the company of other women and Isabella looked up from her scouring to smile, and exclaimed, "My dear Elizabeth, you are an angel, I had wondered how we were to carry all this back with us. And you have brought more soap, and another tub! We are boiling water to scrub everything as clean as can be, and the girls are rinsing it all in the shallows. We may not have such another chance for weeks, so Mr. Greenwood has told us."

She gave another vigorous scrub at her washboard, and tossed the results to her daughter Nancy, who stood in the water with her skirts kirtled up above her knees, along with Helen Murphy and Mary Sullivan. The girls were rinsing the laundry clean in the shallow current, splashing back and forth with joyous energy. Eddie and Willie Miller, and Willie's stair-step cousins, Martin Murphy's little boys, were spreading the clean-rinsed laundry over the prairie grass to dry.

They had kindled a fire, over which a number of steaming kettles were set. Sarah, and Mary Miller, and the Murphy brothers' wives, Annie and Mary-Bee, had placed their washtubs close together. Elizabeth placed her own next to Sarah, regarding it with faint loathing. She did not much care for doing laundry, but it was a woman's lot, and might as well do it with a fair face, and in good company. Eddie magically appeared with a bucket of water dipped from the river, and ran back and forth alternately with kettles from the fire and buckets from the river until her tub was full enough to begin.

"I think it very well, that I was advised to make all our trail bedding from dark calico," remarked Isabella. "This will all smell quite fresh, and at least I can think it clean for a while yet without the evidence otherwise that white bed linen would present."

"God tempers his winds to the shorn lamb," remarked Annie Murphy. Her black hair gleamed in the speckled sunshine with a bluish luster like a blackbird's wing. "I can only hope that He," and she crossed herself hurriedly, "is doing the same with regards to our bedding, and taking away something of our sense of . . ."

"Smell?" said Mary-Bee Murphy. She was young Martin's wife. Their four little boys were distinct among the children, as they had her own dark-auburn hair and unfortunate freckles. "I dearly hope so, since the smell of salt-junk makes me so ill in the morning of late."

"You are not . . . truly . . ." said Mary Miller, laying a hand on her belly, which while generous, barely showed under her loose wash-dress and full apron.

43

"I think so," Mary-Bee Murphy sighed "I have not had my courses since we left home, and I thought it was worrying . . . and no little grief at leaving the little one."

Annie reached over and patted her hand, comfortingly. Elizabeth already knew from John, how Old Martin's wife, and Young Martin's and Mary-Bee's baby daughter had all perished together in the worst of the epidemics, some two years ago; and now this new grief of leaving their graves behind.

"Perhaps the blessed Virgin will grant this one be a girl," Annie said softly and Mary-Bee smiled a little tearfully, and answered, "I do hope so, those imps of mine need a sister to tease and torment them."

Isabella had the absorbed face of a woman rapidly doing up sums, "My dear, do you realize your child shall be born when we are just arrived in California; such good fortune for you both that we will have a doctor among our company."

Mary-Bee looked a little cheered, and Isabella whispered to Elizabeth, "You should tell your husband, my dear Elizabeth, I have served as a midwife on many occasions, and will be more than happy to be of assistance . . . Mary will be brought to child-bed in the next two months, I judge. On the trail, but a blessed event, none the less. You are not hoping for such for yourself, then?"

"I might yet," Elizabeth said tranquilly. "My husband has been very tender of my poor health until now, and would not permit me such a risk, but they say the air in California is marvelously healthy – so healthy, I vow the very thought of breathing it has made some improvement. I have not had one of my sick headaches for some weeks now."

"You are out in the fresh air every day. Indeed, we can scarce avoid fresh air," Isabella said, robustly, and the other women laughed. "And I think if you did not lace your corsets so very tightly, you might find you can take in more of that good air."

"I should then have no shape at all," Elizabeth protested, "And what of the support that tight lacing lends to a woman's weak bones?"

"It hardly matters to your weak bones, if custom demands that women be laced so tightly that a woman of fashion cannot walk across a room without fainting," Isabella replied.

"Why, Mrs. Patterson, I believe you are an advocate of rational dress!" Elizabeth exclaimed, and Isabella giggled like a school-girl and lifted the hem of her stout dark-colored wash-dress to reveal a pair of voluminous, baggy pantaloons of the same material, gathered at the ankles.

Elizabeth clapped her hands. "How very, very clever and completely modest! But you must be very brave to wear such a daring garment. Mrs. Bloomer insisted that such things would be very, very comfortable and healthy. But I would fear the laughter of all. What does Mr. Patterson think of this?"

"He has more sense than to care for such matters," Isabella replied, "but Oliver liked to die of embarrassment, and Samuel and John made much sport of my Turkish trousers, until I challenged them all to a footrace and won." Elizabeth had a sudden mental vision of the tiny woman, limbs pumping madly and her hair falling out of her pins, hurtling across a meadow in a blur of rational costume just ahead of her teenage sons. "And at the end of it, I leaped over the fence with perfect modesty," Isabella added smugly. "Not a word from any of them after that but I made my skirts just long enough to cover them. I have not Mrs. Bloomer's capacity for absorbing ridicule . . . but out here, they can ridicule away!"

"I believe they have no time for anything but the teams and wagons," remarked Mary. "Mr. Miller has barely spoken to me in days. He attends to Willie and the girls for a little while in the evening and falls asleep where he sits, with his plate in his hand. Were it not for him snoring in bed and his dirty shirts I would scarce know I had a husband at all."

"And for that, also." Annie roguishly glanced at Mary's bulging apron-front, and they all dissolved in shrieks of laughter, which only stilled when the old trail-guide, Mr. Greenwood, appeared silently in the grove, almost within their circle.

"Good morning, ladies." He looked around, nodded to them all and spoke softly. "Just to let you know, my boys are standing watch on us all, yonder, from the top of that hill. The country round here is safe enough commonly, but it's best to practice keeping watch now, for the odd ruffian."

"Oh, we are safe enough," Isabella said firmly, and from a basket of clean laundry at her side she produced an ancient dragoon pistol. The corners of Greenwoods' mouth quirked, and Isabella added, "It's loaded, and I keep it near me always. Mr. Patterson had me practice with it before he went to California. For all I must use both hands, I am quite a fair shot."

"Doubtless," Old Greenwood answered with dry amusement. "It relieves my mind, ma'am, knowing you had thought on certain precautions for this journey." He nodded at them all again and departed as quietly as he had appeared.

"Does he not frighten you a little?" asked Mary with a shiver. "He dresses so like a savage himself, I am sure he is gone over to them entirely and the boys are hardly any better."

"He does not frighten me," Elizabeth answered thoughtfully. "He speaks well, like an educated man now and again. He may dress like a savage, but I don't think he is one at heart. He is rather more like a hero in a Leatherstocking tale."

"Stuff and nonsense," Isabella snapped. "He is just one of those silly men who wanted to go wandering around in the wilderness, instead of settling down and working at a good trade to support his family.

The other women were a little taken back by her vehemence, and it was a few moments before Mary-Bee ventured, "Still . . . have you noticed? He is quite a handsome man, for all of his considerable years."

"He is, that," agreed Annie. "Curious, isn't it, that most men are handsome in youth and decline from that as they age, but there are some who are plain youths, but make handsome and vigorous old men."

"Quite vigorous," agreed Mary, coloring a little. "He claims to be fourscore, at least, but his sons are just barely out of boyhood." She blushed even more deeply as her sisters and Sarah giggled, and drew a shocked rebuke from Isabella.

"Mrs. Miller! Consider the girls! Little pitchers have big ears!"

Elizabeth bent over her own scrub board, to hide her own smile, as Sarah said, "Whatever tonic Mr. Greenwood has taken all these years, I hope then that my own husband never partakes of it!"

"Mrs. Montgomery, for shame!" said Isabella, scandalized, and Elizabeth hid another smile and wrung out one of John's shirts, thinking as she did so that in such company, this journey might just not be as terrible as she had feared.

* * *

From E.S. Patterson Interview, University of California Local History Archival Project 1932: *"There was always much to do with crossing rivers, and it seemed like we were forever having to stop and cross one. Sometimes the men could double-team a wagon through a shallow river, since enough of the oxen would have their feet on the river bed to keep it steady and moving. Captain Stephens turned out to be good at organizing river crossings; he was a fair hand at judging if we could just go straight over, one at a time, or if we might have to set up a ferry as we did on the Elkhorn. There had been a lot of rain that spring, and the rivers all remained higher than most years for many, many weeks.*

"For a lot of us this established him as a good leader almost at once, but Mr. Thorp and the others in the Oregon party were galled by his leadership and contested his every decision. It was often up to Dr. Townsend to intervene and smooth things over."

Chapter 4 – *Pilgrims' Progress*

From Dr. Townsend's diary: *"Twenty-second of May, 1844 With much labor we have crossed the Elkhorn River and reassembled our wagons and teams on the far side, and ventured out into the Desert."*

From E.S. Patterson Interview, University of California Local History Archival Project 1932: *"Oh, it was glorious to see! I can close my eyes and see it still, mile after mile of that beautiful green grass, full of wildflowers it was, rippling in that sweet clean wind, as if thousands of little animals were running through it. The wagons coming over the top of the hill, those canvas covers shining in the sun, and the feel of it when we children ran through it in our bare feet, with the sun on our faces, and butterflies and dragon-flies all going every which way in the sunshine . . . Ma said I had to look after my baby sister, Sadie, but I didn't mind, she was the closest thing to a real pet that I had, way back then.*

And we had chores to do, too. My brothers and I had to get up in the dark when Ma waked us, and round up our oxen, find them where they had strayed to in the night. O' course, they never went far, ours were as biddable as dogs, they came when we called their names. We had four yoke to start with, and they all had names: Socks and Spot, Baldy and Blackie, Fergus and Red, Corny and Star, and the milk cow, Goldenrod. My sister Nancy had to milk Goldenrod in the morning, while Ma fixed breakfast, and my brothers and I hitched up the teams. We'd have eaten breakfast, and packed up everything by sun-up, and then Cap'n Stephens would have someone blow a horn. It was one of the Oregoners had the fancy notion to bring a horn.

Later on, we didn't have anything like that, just the Cap'n come along, and saying to Ma, "All ready and hitched-up, Miz Patterson?" and Ma would say "Surely, Cap'n Stephens," and then she would drive the team herself, but that was later on, after we left the Oregoners at Fort Hall and it was just our eleven wagons."

From Dr. Townsends' diary: *"Our days begin very early at 4 AM, for we must be ready for the days' march by 5:30; wagons packed, the teams all hitched, everyone fed and ready to roll out."*

* * *

The day began with a knock of a fist against the wagon box, close by John's head in the dark, and the voice of whoever had the overnight watch on the cattle-herd, making the wake-up rounds. "Doc Townsend . . . you awake?"

"Aye, I'm awake." John pulled on his trousers and boots in the dark, and then shook Liz's shoulder. "Dearest, time to rise."

He clambered out of the wagon through the front, loosing the canvas apron against the morning air and taking the lantern with him, before he climbed down to the ground. He stumbled to the fire that his family shared with Allen and Sarah, kicked the coals apart, and tossed some small kindling and some buffalo chips on them. The fresh stuff lit readily and he took a small twig from the fire and lit the lantern from it. He hung the lantern in its accustomed place on the first wagon-bow, and yawning hugely, set off on the short journey to the men's privy pit. Returning from it to his wagon, he passed Mrs. Patterson, wrapped in a shawl and jacket over her night-dress, returning from the women's privy pit. They pretended not to see each other.

On returning, John went directly to the tent where Moses and Francis slept, pitched just outside the wagon-circle that protected the horses and mules, and opened the tent-flap. He could see Elizabeth's shadow moving in their wagon.

"Mose . . . Francis: Time to rouse, gentlemen, time to rouse." Moses groaned theatrically, and pulled his pillow over his head, but Francis grunted and threw off his blankets. He pulled on his trousers and shirt, and padded off towards the men's privy pit. John gave Moses another shake, took up Ugly Grey's bridle and climbed over the wagon tongue, secured for the night by chains to the Montgomery wagon, in search of his horse. Ugly Grey often chose to be skittish in the mornings, prancing and dodging his master as if playing a game for some minutes, before allowing John to slip the metal bit between his teeth, and pull the leather bridle over his ears; a game, a part of the morning ritual.

When they set up camp every evening, they parked their wagons in a rough oval; just far enough apart to angle the wagon tongue and chain it to the wagon ahead, securing a corral inside for the horses and Old Hitchcocks' mules. They set their campfires and tents on the outside of the circle, with the privy pits dug close enough to be safe, but distant enough to spare sensibilities, and loosed the oxen and milk cows to graze under the guardianship of two men chosen by rote to keep guard throughout the night.

Stephens adamantly insisted on a night guard and the inclusion of every man and boy old enough to participate in it, a pair of them watching from sundown to midnight, and another pair from midnight until morning reveille. There were no exceptions, not even for Stephens himself, although he was often to be found patrolling at odd hours through the night. John wondered if the man ever slept entirely through the night; he thought not. At least the fact that Stephens claimed no privilege of exemption for himself reduced the level of complaint regarding his leadership to mere background grumbling.

Moses had roused himself by the time John returned leading Ugly Grey, and busied himself with taking down the tent. His and Francis' bedrolls were already bundled up, ready to be put back into the wagon. The fire had caught nicely, a kettle already sending up steam. Elizabeth, with her hair in an areole around her face, was grinding coffee. Sarah was mixing up a batch of dough for fry-bread, balancing the bowl on her knees. By the Patterson wagon, Isabella already had bacon on the fire, and the smell of it mixed appealingly in the cool morning air.

The camp slowly roused into waking life, evidenced by the voices of men and women, and the cries of "Catch up! Catch up!" mixed with the jingling of tack and chains, and the clatter of breakfast preparations. Women bustled in and out of the shadows around their campfires, about their morning chores, while the men pulled on their outer garments and shouldered the task of hitching up the ox-teams for the day's travel.

John hastily kissed Elizabeth and bade a hurried "Good Morning, Dearest Liz", and she smiled and replied, "Good Morning, dear Doctor," and no time for anything more, as he had to saddle Ugly Grey. It might be that cattle had strayed far during the night, or chosen to hide in the cottonwoods and other brush along the winding creek-bottom and the river adjacent, where they had camped the night before. As oxen were found and yoked and hitched to wagons, it would become clear if any had strayed.

Francis led up the first yoke, and John hastily unchained the wagon tongue and pulled it around. Now to capture Elizabeth's buckskin pony, who tended to be even more coy in the morning. Elizabeth had finally named the pony Beau, after Beau Brummell, laughingly saying that he was a dandy, and in truth so vain that he would stand and admire his reflection in a pool of still water before dipping his muzzle into it to drink. But Beau had another vanity, a taste for sweets, and when he tired of evading the halter he would step trustingly up and nuzzle hands and pockets.

By the time John had Beau captured and saddled, Moses had brought up the second yoke, and Francis had them hitched. Allen Montgomery was securing his lead yoke to his own wagon. Elizabeth poured John a mug of coffee, scalding hot and sweetened with molasses, and he sat with her on the wagon bench while she combed out her long hair and pinned it up for the day's travel.

"I long for the day when our oxen are as tame as the Patterson's teams," John remarked, idly. "They all come to the boys without having to be chased all over creation. Their wagon is ready to roll out whilst everyone else is still rounding up their beasts . . . that rowan-colored beast of Millers' is a particular plague. He runs and hides in the brush, or over the brow of a hill, every morning without fail, and then puts on an air of innocence when he is caught."

"For shame, Doctor," Elizabeth chided him, laughing. "How can a mere animal express a human feeling?"

"I don't know he manages," John insisted, "but he does. We find him a half-mile from the herd, strolling back and forth, nibbling a little at the grass, and I swear he is laughing at us for the trouble he has caused."

"I don't believe a word of it," Elizabeth said, "Oxen laughing at you, and being sly!"

"Your Beau Brummell is clever enough to have you bringing him sweetmeats," John countered. "And you say yourself he is as vain as a peacock. Why should an ox have any less of a personality?"

Sarah, busy about the fire, and the plank laid across a pair of kegs that served as kitchen, remarked, "That pony minds me of Mr. Montgomery sometimes, always so certain that everyone is looking at him."

"Sarah, dearest, your husband is truly among the handsomest of the younger men, no wonder that everyone should look upon him and marvel . . . although there is a handsomer among the older gentleman."

Elizabeth and Sarah exchanged such a look, and simultaneously began to laugh. John thought '*Best not to know why women are laughing about men, it's mysterious, and best left unexamined*'; similar to all those occasions when he had to pretend not to hear Thorp's friends in full complaint against Stephens' rule as captain.

Still laughing, Sarah handed John a plate of hot bread and fried bacon, and he accepted it with gratitude. "A culinary marvel as always, Mrs. Montgomery; we have butter this morning, I see."

"We shall, for as long as the cow gives milk," Sarah replied briskly.

Elizabeth added, "We have made a marvelous discovery. A covered bucket of fresh milk hung under the wagon by the grease-bucket in the morning will have churned itself into butter by early afternoon."

Allen accepted his plate with a surly grunt, and John frowned. It worried him more than he liked to say that Allen preferred cutting a dashing figure in front of women, and favored the company of the young and unmarried men over that of his own wife. Allen and Sarah were but newly married, but still; above all in the world John prized Elizabeth's company and companionship, and was as eager as a lovesick boy to spend time with her. Responsible men like young Martin, and James Miller held their wives in much the same generous affection. Just the other day, he and Allen and James, and young Bernard Murphy had ridden out at nooning, scouting for buffalo.

James was teasing Bernard about making calf-eyes at one of the girls in the Oregon contingent, saying, "How will you ever have the courage to ask her father for her hand if you can only look at her with a moon-face and never be bold enough to speak to her outright?"

Allen laughed bitterly and said, "Pay no mind, Bernard. While women are all for marriage, it's not clear to me that all men need be!"

It was an odd, mocking thing to say, and John wondered still, although the others had passed it off as a joke. But it remained that Allen and Sarah often times behaved like strangers to each other, and it did not escaped John's notice that Allen spread his bedroll under the wagon at night, and at meals Sarah barely spoke to him at all.

Stephens appeared silently in the campfire-lit circle, leading a paint-pony he had bought from a party of passing Pawnee Indians, and shadowed as always by Dog.

John groaned, "How many not found, this morning?" while Elizabeth exclaimed with pleasure. "Good morning, Captain Stephens. Will you have some coffee?"

He looked as if to say no, but Sarah handed him a full cup of it, and he said instead, "Six, including Miller's rowan."

John wolfed the last of his breakfast, handed his plate and cup to his wife, and tossed Beau's reins to Moses; this was becoming a predictable part of the morning, riding out to find animals which had strayed from the herd, beyond the easy reach of drovers and men on foot. Oxen might have been dumb, as Old Man Hitchcock pointed out, but they were creatures of habit, and some of them liked to wander far. So far, they had always been able to locate the wanderers after a brief horseback search along the river bank, or where the grass grew with particular richness.

"Miller, that ox of yours is going to make some Sioux tribe a feast they won't ever forget," John said when they returned the prodigal to his impatient master, and less venturesome yoke-mate. "And I swear, I won't mind a bit . . . I might just ride up and ask them for a taste."

"When it happens, get a taste for me, too, Doc." James Miller snapped the yoke on his errant and peripatetic property. The sky had begun to pale in the east, attended by rosy clouds whose color deepened, while the stars faded, all but the brightest and largest.

"I do believe it may rain today." Old Greenwood sniffed the air like an ancient hunting hound. He too was mounted on a spotted pony, like those ridden by his sons.

"Keep that in mind as you scout," Stephens said only, and Greenwood and his two boys rode off, in the direction of travel they would take today.

John recollected how the Oregon-bound Mr. Hammer had said so scornfully, "Wouldn't it be better to hire a man who could see the trail?"

Only later did John think of retorting, "But this is a man who can smell it!"

He and Stephens nodded to each other, and then wheeled Ugly Grey and the paint pony, and rode in opposite directions around the camp, where each wagon stood hitched and ready, drivers at the alert beside their lead teams, women and children scrambling up to their places in the wagon. All the portable detritus of their camp gathered up and packed, all the disposable left behind; the campfires burning out, the privy pits with the last shovel-full of dug-up earth thrown upon their contents, the places where the horses and the oxen had pastured, trampled and grazed over. All the water casks filled, everyone fed, the last of the loose herd gathered up, the last child, dog, and horse accounted for and in their place.

Stephens and John met at Stephen's wagon, where his three yoke stood patiently in harness, waiting for his drover's command. It was a marvel to John, how Stephens with just his one silent teamster worked so efficiently by himself in breaking camp. Like the Pattersons, he was always ready to roll out twenty minutes before everyone else; all those years of experience on the trail to Santa Fe.

Now Stephens stood in the stirrups and waved his hat towards Thorp's wagon; the clear silver notes of a bugle winged up into the morning sky. Who was first today? Oh, the quarrelsome Shaw, last in line yesterday, and let none forget it. Shaw's heavy-laden wagon angled out of the camp-circle, bullwhip cracking like a pistol-shot, followed by the Clemmons family, then Prather, Thorp, Jacob Hammer – who preferred to depend on his visions and prayers in the conduct of the daily journey – and the other Oregoners, then Stephens, the Murphy and Miller wagons, Sullivan's and Martin's, Fosters', and his own, and the Pattersons, with Allen bringing up the rear, trailed by the loose herd. Stephens would ride ahead for the morning march, in advance of the first wagon.

John wheeled back to his own wagon where Francis stood ready and Elizabeth impatiently waiting in Beau's saddle, ready to be riding along in the cool of the morning with the outriders, free of the constant jolting and dust attendant upon travel in the wagon. John himself would be riding close to the lead wagon for the day's march, while other mounted men flanked or circled the line of wagons, which moved at a slow pace of oxen plodding, and tended to spread out as the day wore on, since the travelers were desirous of avoiding the dust kicked up by the hooves and wheels ahead.

The sun rose up from the hillside at their backs, into a blue sky flecked with milkweed puffs of cloud in which the wagons were the only evidence of a man-made world. The only things moving in it besides themselves were birds and insects springing out of the grass, the cloud-shadows rolling over, that and the river always on their left, wide, shallow, and muddy brown. John had heard the same witticism about it being "too thick to drink, and too thin to plow" too often in the last couple of weeks to be amused any more. He took it in mind to ride up to the top of the tallest rise, just ahead of the route of march, and see if he could see much of the way forward from there, as well as the entire line of wagons. Ugly Grey cantered ahead, eager to move faster after being held to a gentle stroll. He tackled the hill as if he wanted to tear great chunks of it off with his hooves, plunging up and up until John reined him in at the crest and turned him around. Grey pranced restlessly, even so. John dismounted and stretched. It was quiet, up here on the hill, nothing but the wind rustling in the endless grass, and a hawk on motionless, widespread wings floating in circles overhead. He seemed to be an immeasurable distance from the wagons, crawling below, the clamor of their passage – shouts of teamsters, and the sharp crack of whips, the voices of children – barely disturbing the cathedral quiet. They would pass through this vast deserted grassland, make their camp and move on, leaving it to the silence of the blowing wind, and the harsh cry of a hawk; nothing which would know or care that they had once passed through.

He counted the wagons as they passed below, took note of the outriders, the trailing loose herd, the gaggle of women and children walking alongside, like goslings after their mothers. He shaded his eyes; could that be little Eddie driving the Patterson team? It must be; John recognized Eddie at a distance, from the sling on his arm. Three days before, Eddie fell from the moving wagon and broke two bones in his left arm. John helped Isabella set the bones and bind them up, and himself dosed Eddie with syrup of opium. This way, it looked as if his mother was keeping a close eye on her adventurous child. John didn't think it would last: Isabella would take her eye off him for a moment, and Eddie would be off on another appalling adventure.

He looked ahead to the west where a fast-moving horseman, a mere dot at that distance, kicked up a puff of dust on the farthest ridge-line – one of the scouts, returning. John remounted; he wanted to do a quick pen and ink drawing of the wagons as they looked to him just now, moving against the background of the river and the rolling country on the far side, with the green islands set like emeralds in the river, which the angle of the morning sunlight turned to a sheet of silver. Perhaps he might do it this afternoon, if Old Greenwood's son was not bringing back word of some particularly laborious obstacle in their way. The horseman came over the next ridgeline. Britt Greenwood; no one else rode so like he and the horse were actually one creature.

Ugly Grey, of course, was not interested in going down the hill as fast as he came up it. John could feel him grinding the metal bit in his teeth, and placing his feet just so. A human would be grumbling crossly under his breath. He urged him across the slope, and intercepted Britt at Stephens' wagon.

"It's a creekbed, with a steep drop-off, both sides," Britt reported. "We went upstream and down, nearly as far as the river, and it's the same all the way."

"Take a party ahead and dig out a ramp, as much as you can," Stephens ordered. "Make a start. We'll finish it when we get there."

On his way to pass the word and take the pick and shovel from his wagon, he passed Elizabeth and Isabella, walking together, leading Beau with little Sadie perched in the saddle and squealing with excitement and enjoyable apprehension.

"I'm taking up road-building at this time of my life, and I'm afraid I have need of your Beau again," John told his wife. "Mrs. Patterson, would you be able to send Samuel and Oliver ahead on Beau with whatever tools you can muster?"

"Of course," Elizabeth lifted down Sadie. "Time to walk, sweeting, poor Beau has work to do!"

Road-building – or at least that part of it relative to creek banks, was getting to be something they were well-experienced in. John's pioneer party, composed of all the boys and men who were not actually driving wagons or with the herd, picked a place where a side gully had broken down some of the steep wall of the creek bed.

Patrick Martin was at it already, as John had come to expect. The elder Patrick might have been hasty and hot-tempered but also generous to a fault. He had the energy of two men and near the strength. No matter if it was digging out a ramp for the wagons or felling a tree to use for a wagon-brake, Patrick was first there and fastest, wielding shovel or ax in a furious storm of dirt or wood chips.

Sweating mightily, John and the other men broke it down even more, prying rocks out of the creek bank and rolling them to the bottom to make the foundation of a ramp. They used buckets and wash pans to carry more soil dug from the top of the ramp to fill in at the bottom, packing it down with buckets of creek water. They had rough-finished the down-ramp, and begun tearing down the bank on the opposite side for the up-ramp, when Shaw's lead wagon caught up to them.

"It's just wide enough." Stephens surveyed the work accomp- lished. "Lock wheels going down, and double-team going up."

"You'd have to do it again, Cap'n, in another two miles," Old Greenwood sat slouching in the saddle of his horse, looking down at the makeshift ramps. "But that I found the place where I came this way, 'bout ten years ago it was, with two wagons and a pack-train . . . it's rocky, but passable. I blazed the trees either side, and left a trail back even a farmer can find. The water is deep in the middle, but the stream-bed slopes nice and gentle."

"We're gonna move on after this? I don't know why you're in such an all-fired hurry," grumbled Shaw.

"We only made six miles since hitch-up," Stephens said abruptly, and walked away.

The old mountain-man looked at Shaw with an expression of peaceful serenity and drawled, "Whoever's going to camp in the snow and eat rocks in six months – ain't gonna be me an' my boys, suh."

They chained a sturdy tree-branch, thrust through the spokes of each wagons' rear wheels, locking them into place and throwing up huge gouts of dust, as each one skidded down the ramp. Then they had only to laboriously draw the wagons one by one out of the creek bed by double-hitching their teams. It was dusty, exhausting work, and the sun stood close to overhead by the time they were done with it.

"We'll noon at the next creek, and rest before we cross," Stephens directed, his face masked in dust. John thought there would have been the usual rumble of discontent from Shaw and Thorp and their adherents but that they had already crossed over. He turned to remount Ugly Grey, and there was Elizabeth, bearing a canteen and a tin cup, and a towel soaked in cool water from the creek.

"We took the children a little way upstream," she explained, as John gratefully wiped his face and drank his fill. "Eddie collected some pretty pebbles, and we saw the dearest little frogs about the size of my thumb hopping all around, and dragonflies with eyes like jewels. And Sarah and I picked a basket of wild cherries . . . which are not entirely ripe, but will taste extremely fine in a pie tonight. We have found a patch of wild onions, also," she added.

"We will feast like lords tonight, then," John said. "I must make a note of it in my diary!"

"You had better," Elizabeth twinkled at him. "Mr. Montgomery ventured off the trail a little way while waiting to cross the creek and managed to shoot an antelope for our supper."

"In that case, a kingly repast indeed, and well worth a long entry." John kissed his wife and swung himself up into the saddle again, wincing slightly as he took up the reins. He had some blisters on his palms, and an ache in his shoulders from laboring at the earth ramps; not as trail-hardened as he would like to be, obviously. Back to ranging the length of the train, keeping watch on the flanks. They were crossing Pawnee territory, Old Greenwood had told them a few nights ago.

"Not what they used to be." Old Greenwood sounded slightly mournful, "They got cleaned out by the smallpox an' then the Lakota ripped them up good. They won't be looking for trouble any time soon. Good for us, I'd be guess'n."

"Better safe 'n sorry." Stephens said, and John agreed most heartily with that sentiment.

They got to the second creek as the sun reached the highest overhead, and heartily glad to see it, to unyoke the oxen and let them drink. A pretty place, with the poplar leaves shimmering in constant movement overhead. They dined on the cold bacon and bread left over from breakfast, but Elizabeth spread out a blanket on a patch of grass in the shade, and brought out cool water and a shrub made with vinegar and a little of the sour wild cherries mashed with sugar.

"A picnic in the farthest wilderness," John said gratefully, and dozed for a while in that murmuring shade, while the oxen slapped flies off their flanks with their tails, and children played along the creek banks.

After a while, he roused himself and walked up stream, slapping at an occasional mosquito. He smelled smoke; around the gravelly bend he came upon Patrick Martin, Joseph Foster, Old Martin's hired man Ed Bray, and his own man, Francis. Patrick and Joseph had lines dangling into the water at midstream; Ed Bray had set his to one side, as he deftly gutted a fat silver trout. Francis was tending the fire, where three or four more fish threaded onto a frame of green willow twigs were grilling gently over it.

"Speak you now softly, sor," Patrick rumbled, in his soft Irish brogue. "For the fish are still hungry . . . how they would be biting in the morning, with the mist on the river and all . . . oh, that would be a foine sight."

"We had a longing for the taste of a bit of trout, so we did," Ed Bray was also Irish, wiry and weathered.

Patrick said, "Faith, and me old friend does not set as good a table as any in the land?"

Bray sighed and replied, "Well, as my wages are paid those meals . . . still, I had a longing to taste something else, now and again, and the rivers are so full, they fair leap out and array themselves on a griddle . . . speaking of which, how are they doing, Frankie?"

"Ver' fine," replied Francis. "Anodder few minutes, I 'tink."

"Don't forget the salt, Frankie," Joseph Foster told him. He settled himself against the weather-polished trunk of a fallen tree and sighed, "Doc, this is the life, I swear to you."

Joseph Foster was a small, spry man, cheery as a cricket, still quite young although he had already lost much of his hair. In all the weeks of travel, John had never heard a cross word from Joseph, or anything other than the greatest good cheer in the world, even when his wagon tipped over on a steep creek down-drop a few days before. Joseph's wheel yoke were so badly tangled in their harness that one of the oxen broke its leg and had to be dispatched.

Foster butchered the fallen ox on the spot, and borrowed another from the Murphy's spares until he could purchase a replacement at Fort Laramie, saying, "It's an ill wind that blows no one any good. Roast beef for all tonight, and won't it taste good after salt junk and pemmican?"

Fair-skinned and freckled, he had been much plagued by sunburn.

He was blistered and reddened on his exposed face and hands, and John said, "Joe, you'd best cover yourself better from the sun, there'll be nothing left to you but a little crisp like a bacon rind."

"Fortunes of the trail," Joseph replied cheerfully. "D'you fancy a taste of fish, Doc? We only brought four plates, though."

"The doc's a gentleman," said Patrick, ever genial. "Can't ask a fine gentleman to eat with his fingers."

"I've already eaten," John protested, but Francis handed him a plate with a bit of broken, grilled trout on it, and it smelled so tempting that his resolve broke down. And it was good, slipping of the tiny white bones of it and meltingly tender.

"Good, m'sieu, no?" Francis smiled shyly.

"Marvelous – my compliments to the chef," John replied, and Francis said, "M'sieu jests, I am not a chef, merely a hired driver."

"You might be able to pass yourself off as one in California," John answered, "for sure, I almost wish I had hired you as such," and Francis protested, "No, m'sieu, Madam Montgomeree does the cooking very well. It is just that one longs for something . . . a touch of the different."

"Aye, we're only along for the fishing." Ed Bray was laughing. "A little of that for me, Frankie . . . thanks. No, Doctor sor – we are just as keen to reach California as you, just that we have not the wherewithal for a wagon and stock and supplies and all. So we contract to work our way, in exchange for board, and that's the way of it for poor men such as Frankie and meself."

"Speak for yourself, Bray!" Joseph had pulled forth another sleek silver-gleaming trout. "I heard the fishing was grand. And so I packed my traps and set out, and if this is anything to go with, California is a land such as true anglers dream of."

And Patrick Martin caught John's eye, and laughed, and John thought it was well that some were having the time of their lives, fishing in a wilderness river in the middle of the great desert.

Now on the move again, he squinted at the sky, off towards the south where the pretty and creamy white clouds of the morning were piling up and up and up, into a great tower, brilliantly white at the top, but flat and dark across the bottom, pressing down on the plains south of the river like a great grey flat-iron. A grey veil hung from the bottom of that cloud, and a gusty south wind brought a teasing breath of moisture and the smell of rain. John rode towards the head of the train where old Hitchcock stumped along leading his mules and Greenwoods' pack pony.

"Looks like we're gonna get wet again," Stephens said laconically, as a bolt of blue-white lightning shot from cloud to land, too distant for any sound but a faint rumble. "Close up as much as possible, and keep a close eye on the loose stock."

"And me with my rheumatiz," complained Old Man Hitchcock as the thunder grumbled again.

"It looks as if it would just pass to the east of us if we keep going," John ventured. Although it seemed as if the cloud spread, pressing closer and closer against the earth, and there was a queer greenish cast to the air as the sunlight winked out.

No, they could not outpace this storm entirely, but perhaps they might avoid the brunt of it. Ugly Grey seemed to tremble with unease, and John could hear oxen bellowing as a mighty crack seemed verily to split the sky right over their heads. The clouds darkened to the color of lead, and pressed even closer as if twilight was falling in the very middle of the day. A mighty gust of wind sent the wagon covers swaying and the women's skirts to flaring out. Down in the river bottom, the wind lashed the trees in a tumult of green leaves, tossing like waves in a storm at sea. Up ahead, he glimpsed Elizabeth pulling at Beau's reins; she must have been leading him, walking with Sarah and Isabella and the children, and now Beau pulled away from her, in a head-tossing, snorting panic, as thunder crashed again overhead. Sarah screamed, barely heard, and John raked Ugly Grey's flanks with his heels.

"Sarah!" he shouted, when he reached the struggling women and the panicky horse. "Give me your shawl!"

She looked barely older than Sadie at that moment, her eyes huge and dark with panic. John snatched the shawl off her shoulders and threw it over Beau's head.

Unable to see, he stood, head drooping, and John took the reins out of Elizabeths' hands and shouted, "Get in the wagon, both of you! I'll see to Beau!"

The storm was upon them, now impossible to count the seconds between the flash and the noise, while gusts of wind flattened the grass. The rain announced itself first as a growing rustle on the grass, pattering in random wet splotches. Elizabeth and Sarah picked up their skirts and ran. The first few fat drops resounded like pebbles on the wagon top, and then the full force of it swept in, and the light pattering became a full-throated roar. Sarah and his wife were safely in the wagon. Through veil of rain, he could barely make out the dim shapes of other wagons and their teams. They had all slowed or stopped as the rain swept in. A fringe of silvery drops fringed his hat, even, and suddenly something smacked his shoulder, and Ugly Grey seemed to start. The sound of the rain on the canvas next to where he stood between Beau and Ugly Grey took on a deeper note. The grass was suddenly full of bouncing white pebbles the size of marbles, and the rain flailing his shoulders and the horses' backs was ice cold. Yet he seemed to be sheltered from the worst of it, and almost as suddenly as it had begun, the sky lightened, and the hail stopped.

Sarah and Elizabeth peeped out from the wagon cover, still quite shaken from the sudden violence of it all. "Dearest, are you quite all right?" Elizabeth's voice trembled. "You are soaked."

"I am quite unharmed," John replied. "I apologize for shouting, Dearest. The storm looked to be quite violent and I feared for you both. I must go and see if anyone has been injured."

"Then I will take back Beau," Elizabeth said, with a stronger voice. "And Sarah will want her shawl returned to her."

* * *

From Dr. Townsend's diary: *"Caught on the trail this afternoon in a storm of some violence, with hail of some one to one-and-a-half-inch diameter and much heavy rain, fortunately of no lasting duration. No very great injury to our party taken, but a great fright to us all. Mrs. Thorp o'ertaken with a fit of hysterics, Mr. Magnent the cattle-driver sustained a great many bruises about the shoulders from the hail, and Mrs. Patterson sustained a blow on her head from a piece of hail whilst attempting to shelter her oldest son from the worst violence of the storm . . . "*

From E.S. Patterson Interview, University of California Local History Archival Project 1932: *"There was a storm we were caught in, along the Platte I think it was, oh, an incredible sight to see it come in, across the river bottom, and worse to be caught on the trail without any shelter, lightning everywhere, and hail the size of slingshot. Ma shouted at us all to get into the wagon and button up the flaps tight, but she caught up an iron pot-lid to cover her head and went to see to the team, as my brother Oliver was driving it and the oxen were snorting and getting to be fractious because of the hail and lightning. Ma held the pot-lid over Oliver, and she was hit on the head by a hailstone, raised a great welt the size of a goose-egg, it did. Doctor Townsend chided her afterwards, why didn't she get into the wagon like the other women, and Ma said right back to him, because she couldn't think of anything except for what she could do to protect her children . . ."*

* * *

The afternoon march dragged, seemingly endlessly; John realized that he had been struck by hailstones also when his shoulders began to ache. The weary day's march told on them all, in the voices of women raised, chiding fractious children, drovers impatiently snapping their great bull-whips over the backs of the teams they drove, teams which were tired and thirsty. Only Old Greenwood did not seem wearied, of all the men, slouching easily on his painted Indian pony, as he and John rode by Stephen's wagon.

"Two more miles, if that," Greenwood said. He and his boys had found a good place to camp the night, a sheltered meadow, tucked into the curve of a low rise above the river, with a freshet of water coming down from the higher ground, plenty of deep green grass for the animals, and stands of trees on the low islands in the river for firewood.

"Why are the largest trees on the river islands?" John asked, curiously. "And not on the banks, as elsewhere?"

"Fire," Greenwood answered, "In the fall when the grass is dried, these plains are plagued with fires. Sometimes they are started by lightning, sometimes by the tribes . . . they say it makes the grass grow more richly, but it burns everyhing before it, save what is protected by the river channel."

"Then we are fortunate to be venturing here in the spring, when everything is still green," John said, and the old man sighed.

"You are that, Doctor . . . it is a horrible sight to see, a line of fire across the horizon, moving through the grass as fast as a man may run, and everything . . . everything, rabbits and antelope, prairie hens and all, leaping and running from it all, as fast as they can."

"You must have seen many strange sights in your journeys to these desolate parts," John ventured, and the old man sighed, reminiscently.

"I have that, Doctor, I have seen many marvelous things, things that put the accounts in Old Strabo's Geography to shame. There is a place where fountains of hot water spring up out of the ground, and natural cauldrons of mud bubble as if overflowing from the infernal regions. There are places, I have heard, where rivers run into the desert and sink without a trace into the sands. I have seen brave Indian warriors test themselves and worship their gods by thrusting sharpened bones through their own flesh and dangling from the roof of the council house by leather thongs attached to those bones, chanting for hours until their flesh tears loose and they drop down to the ground. I myself knew a man, a white man, who was captured, and made to run naked to amuse the warriors of the Blackfoot tribe, and he ran barefoot for a day, outdistanced them all but three, and killed them with his bare hands. I have seen lakes in the high mountains, as blue as sapphires and so clear you can see twenty, thirty feet down, and valleys of trees all turned wondrously to gold in the fall . . . I have seen sights so beautiful and terrible as to turn your heart forever away from those places our kind call civilization."

"And yet you speak like an educated man," John said, wonderingly. "You know Strabo, and the classics."

"No 'counting for taste, Doc." The old mountain man smiled. "A wise man goes where his heart tells him to go, not where other folk think he should go. Tell you truth, though, sometimes I miss such things. Not commonly, though."

"I have a small library," John ventured, on impulse, "in my wagon. I could not countenance leaving them behind, since I had collected them with no little trouble. I have a volume of Byron's poetry, Lord Chesterfields' letters, and others such as Heroditus' histories and *Pilgrim's Progress*."

"Bunyan?" Greenwood chuckled. "Seems fitting – considering. I'll think on your kind offer, but my eyes are so bad, I would need one of the boys to read it to me, and they don't care so much for the exercise of it. But thank-ee, anway, Doc."

As the sun slanted towards the western horizon, turning a reach of the Platte to molten gold, the first wagons reached the appointed camping place for the night. Old Greenwood's boys had already marked the quadrants of the wagon circle, driving four sticks into the ground with a bit of cloth flagging the end, and fluttering in the light breeze. Tired men and boys unharnessed weary oxen, turning them loose for the moment to drink at the riverbank.

A party of older boys set off to cut wood, while women and older children gathered small dry kindling from where it had fallen from trees, or from skeleton branches left scorched and bone dry by last year's fires, flashing over the prairie and leaving nothing green above ground. The smoke from cookfires and the ringing sound of someone pounding in tent-pegs filled the grassy bowl of their encampment, along with the voices of women, and children laughing.

John circled the wagons one last time, and slid down from Ugly Grey so tired that his legs fairly buckled underneath him. He barely felt strong enough to unsaddle Grey, sending him with a slap on the rump into the central corral.

The chore of chaining up the wagon tongue drained him utterly, and he thought he might be trembling from the reaction of all the long days' labors and alarms. He poured a dipper-full of water over his head, and it ran down, soaking his hair and shirt again as he took a long drink, and felt somewhat better.

Sarah and Elizabeth had busied themselves around the campfire, from which came the most extraordinarily savory smells, and Moses appeared from the river-bottom with an armload of wood. A roast sizzled on a spit arranged over it — Allen Montgomery's antelope, and John's mouth filled. Elizabeth hastily set aside the pie she was constructing, and brought him a tin cup, a cup most marvelously cold to the hand, and refreshing to drink of.

"Mrs. Patterson and I gathered a quantity of hail in a milk-bucket, before it melted," she explained. "And buried it in a flour-barrel. We thought it would be a treat, to have something so cold. Isabella thought upon making ice-cream, but there was only just enough to make some more cherry shrub for everyone."

"A most blessed thought," John said, and drained it with sincere appreciation. "Ahhh that was most welcome, my Dearest Liz . . . I might just be able to stay awake long enough to dine without falling asleep into my plate."

"You had best," Elizabeth ordered. "Sarah and I will not have our bravest efforts go unappreciated. Not only are we dining on roast antelope, but we found wild peas along that creek were we nooned . . . they do not taste so well as from the garden, but they are green."

"It smells so wonderful; might I not have a little taste?" John pleaded, and reached for the cooking fork.

"No!" Elizabeth mockingly slapped his hand away, and so he must content himself with resting a while, sitting on a box and leaning against the wagon-wheel while the women cooked and Allen cleaned his hunting rifle, but it was all the better for having waited for it, and they ate their fill around the campfire, as the sunset colors – gold and purple and orange – faded out of the western sky and stars bloomed so large in the sky over their heads, it looked almost as if he could reach up and pluck it from the sky, as one would pluck a wildflower from the grass at ones feet.

From the direction of the Murphy campfires floated a thread of music, a penny-whistle and the complicated patter of an Irish drum. Old Murphy and one of his sons, playing to amuse his grandchildren, joined presently by a fiddle, and the merry laughter of children dancing with each other by the campfire, as the stars bloomed overhead. John leaned back against the wheel, and smiled. Perhaps he would take Elizabeth by the hand, and they might walk down to the Murphy's and dance to a penny-whistle and fiddle under the stars. Or he might fall asleep first, content to know they were another fifteen miles closer to California.

Chapter 5 – *Trade Goods*

From E.S. Patterson Interview, University of California Local History Archival Project 1932: *"Oh my, Missy, you have no notion of what it looked like when the buffalo herds covered the earth, all along the Platte Valley they were sometimes, covering the ground like a great woolly brown blanket, and the sound of their hoofs like thunder, shaking the ground and your heart in your very chest! We was near caught in a stampede, and oh my, the sound of it! And another time a great herd of them crossed our route of march as we was all strung out. There they were, crossing between the wagons as casual as you please, and all the men could do was put the women and children into the wagons, and keep meandering along, as quiet and as slow as we could, moving through the herd as they grazed. They were huge, hairy beasts – as like to an African lion as a cow.*

"Some of the brave young sparks tried to hunt them as they would any other animal, but it was a waste of ammunition to shoot at their great heads, for their skulls were inordinately thick, to say nothing of the layers of mud and hair matted like armor on their foreheads . . . Finally Paw-Paw told Mr. Montgomery and the other young sparks the trick of it; to aim for a spot on the buffalo's side, just behind the forelegs and about a third of the way up.

"Anything else was a pure waste of lead. Mr. Montgomery, he put eighteen shots into an old bull, oncet and still that old bull wouldn't go down. Mr. Montgomery, he was that mad. Paw-Paw and old Greenwood, they was looking down their noses about buffalo hunting, themselves. It was for greenhorns, and about as easy as shooting fish in a barrel. Them two old men, they had trapped beaver in their time, which called for much more skill, the way they looked at it . . . but the buffalo made prime eating, I tell you what. We did not lack for meat, all along the Platte."

From Dr. Townsend's diary: *Fifteenth of June, 1844 . . . This day having crossed to the Loup River, we have commenced to travel along the south bank thereof, the terrain very gravelly, but open. Our passage is swift, unimpeded by the quicksand along the Platte, which we must eventually rejoin. Much good hunting, particularly of antelope . . . the women are able to gather abundant wild plums and cherries from thickets . . . there are few trees save for cottonwoods, which grow wherever there is any water at all.*

"John Murphy afflicted with a fever, and there are other illnesses amongst the party which keep me oft from my bed at night and other business during the day. Young Master Patterson suffered a slight concussion in falling

down a steep bank and striking his head on a large stone . . . This day passed an enormous village of "prairie dogs," which look not so much like dogs as very large squirrels, which live in burrows below ground, and spend much of their day standing sentry on top of small conical mounds built up from the spoil of excavating said burrow. At the slightest hint of trespass or danger, they chatter loudly, and dive down into their safe burrow, and seeing that, every other nearby does alike.

"At night we hear the howling of the prairie wolves all around our camp; not true wolves as Mr. Greenwood tells me, but smaller tawny-colored beasts, very cunning thieves. We think it is they who have taken the last of Mrs. Montgomery's chickens, which have not laid for some weeks, so we were intending a fine dinner of them, but alas! We must make do with prairie fowl!"

* * *

At the end of another day spent toiling along the gravelly banks, and dampening down a fight between the contentious Shaw and an equally contentious old fellow named Darby, John would have thought he was owed a bare few moments peace in which to eat his supper; but no, that was Jamie Murphy hesitating at the edge of the firelight.

"Good evening, all," he said, a little awkwardly. Elizabeth and Sarah had just put out the plates. Allen was pouring a trickle of boiling water down the barrel of his long rifle, followed carefully by a twist of clean flannel.

"Jamie, what say we look for buffalo, tomorrow," Allen said heartily, "Say man, are you up for it or not?"

"Oliver and I are going to go hunting," Moses chimed in, but Jamie said, "I really . . . I wanted to have a word with the Doctor. It's just that . . . my wife says that I am worrying too much, but with my brother being so sick."

"Whatever is the matter then," said Allen in puzzlement, and Elizabeth caught John's eye and murmured, "I'll save your supper, Dearest," as John concealed a very small sig, and reached up for his medical bag. He had of late been keeping it handy, just under the wagon seat. "Johnny's not taken a turn for the worse, has he?" Old Martin's youngest boy was a year and a half older than Moses, and had been recovering slowly from a fever that left him weakened and barely able to move.

"No," stammered Jamie. "It's m'daughter . . . it seemed like she was burning up with the fever tonight, and couldn't take a bite of supper. Annie says it's nothing but a childhood sickness, but . . . if you wouldn't mind taking a little look at her, Doctor."

"Not at all," John said reassuringly. "Better safe that sorry, Jamie."

He followed Jamie towards the cluster of Murphy family wagons, thinking that Annie Murphy, a sensible and hardheaded woman, was probably right. But Jamie adored his only child, and took her little injuries and illnesses much to heart. He played the fiddle sometimes of an evening, but more often spent his little leisure with whittling small wooden figures and dolls; toys for Mary and the Miller children and young Martins' boys, things that he made and gave away freely without a second thought. Jamie, like his father Old Martin, was adored by his small nephews and nieces.

Now, Annie looked up from mending one of her husband's shirts, under a lantern on the wagon-box and the last of the dying daylight, and exclaimed in exasperation, "Oh, Jamie, you did not need to bother the Doctor. She is sleeping fine now. It was only a little too much sun!"

"I am not bothered, Mrs. Murphy," John answered. "I wished to make certain myself, since so many others have been made ill from bad water and such, and thought it at first to be nothing more than some minor ague."

"Well, as long as you are here, and it's no trouble at all." Annie put aside her sewing, and John thought that she might herself have more been than a little concerned. Despite her words, there was a look of relief on her face. Parents did after all bury children, and the memory of how Martin and Mary-Bee had left their baby daughter to a lonely grave back in Holt County must have been in both their minds.

Annie followed him into the wagon with the lantern, to where Mary lay already restlessly asleep under a couple of blankets. She was about Eddie's age with Annie's crow-wing black hair, and the blue eyes that came from Patrick Martin. She had tossed a little in her sleep, the bedcovers were disarranged, and the black eyelashes on her closed eyes were half-circles of silky fringe on her cheeks.

She clutched a little wooden horse in one hand, and Annie whispered, "Jamie made that today and so it would be her favorite. He has it in mind to make a whole Noah's ark for her. Mary sweetheart, the doctor has come to take a look at you."

"No need to wake her," John cautioned. He felt her forehead, and swiftly ran his fingers under her jaw, feeling for any swellings there. "There is no fever now, she has perspired a little, and her forehead is cool. The glands in her neck are not swollen. She was not complaining of a sore throat, was she?"

"No," Annie answered.

"What about her appetite? Did she eat supper?"

"No, she seemed not to hunger . . . but she was thirsty. Mrs. Patterson said she should drink some of her herbal tea that she made for her, and so I did let her, unless you thought she should not . . ."

"No, I cannot think that Mrs. Patterson's herbal brews can do much harm to a healthy child . . . and perhaps it did some good after all, for she is sleeping without a fever now."

John resettled the blankets around Annie's daughter, and Annie said remorsefully, "I'm sorry for Jamie dragging you from supper for nothing . . ."

"No," John answered. "It's never nothing until I have taken a look for myself. For all I know, you both would fret your own selves into an illness over worrying about Mary here and then I would have two patients, and frankly at this time I have all the patients I can manage."

* * *

Eighteenth of June, 1844: "This day one Vance, a hired man with the Oregon party, died after being ill and delirious for several days. All remedies applied had no effect upon his illness, which was much exacerbated by the necessity of travel. Mr. Vance was buried with dignity and the full rites of his beliefs, and our fervent prayers that he may be the only such loss that our company sustains.

"Sadly, we must leave his resting-place unmarked, although not unrecorded. Our Mr. Greenwood warned us that the natives, being curious or avaricious, would unearth and desecrate the body unless extreme measures to hide his resting place were taken. Alas, this necessitated interring Mr. Vance close to our trail, as we could then run the loose herd over the grave. We have recorded the approximate location, but in this wild and featureless country, I do not suppose anyone will ever be able to find where he was laid to rest, until the day of the Resurrection, when we all shall stand before our Maker!

"This day of travel brought us within sight of a great ruinous castle, off in the near distance seemingly with the river at its foot in the manner of a moat, with a wreath of mist all around upon which it appears to float. This marvel was in view of our train for many days and held the attention of all, as we discussed much on what it most resembled: a vast domed courthouse, a pagan temple of old, or an ancient walled fortress with many towers and

bastions and the stump of a central tower crowning all. The view of it at around sunset, when gilded by rays of dying sunlight against a darkening sky was most sublime.

"Much disputation between ourselves and the Oregon party, Captain Stephens quite out of sorts and bad-humor'd in this respect, saying that, 'those lazy so-and-sos would rather play cards, and dance and fiddle around the fire of an evening, and rise with the sun of a morning, and dawdle all along the trail the next day', and I own that I too am grown impatient. The Oregon party are even racked with dissention among themselves; William Case came to me this morning, full of impatience and vowed that he would soonest travel with us to California than abide one more day with them. I fear to some of our fellow pilgrims this journey is a long holiday, whereas to our Captain, it is a business, out of which we must earn a profit, and essential that we move as expeditiously as possible.

"We have passed near the foot of a great sky-ward pointing finger of rock, like a shot-tower or a giant's chimney, which we have had in view for some days, it being a particular feature of the landscape, even though it is some miles distant on the other side of the river. The air is so clear that judging distances is a matter of great difficulty: objects which appear to be only a few miles distant are often a considerable distance removed!

"Mr. Greenwood insists to me that when he first traveled this way, many years ago, this monument was yet a quarter again as tall as it is at present. I suspect him of jesting in this particular, but Mr. Hitchcock said the same, and both gentlemen with much laughter told me that the natives name for this landmark translates very roughly as 'Elk Brick.' Both he and Captain Stephens say we are making excellent time on the trail . . . the days being quite warm, but the nights are quite chill, I deduce that imperceptibly we have climbed to some higher altitude than formerly.

"The country to the south of the river presents a most wondrous aspect, a series of high and cliff-like bluffs presenting the appearance of a vast walled city of towers and spires, entirely inhabited by giants, and ornamented with every order and style of architecture known to mankind. These ruinous bastions appear to rise directly from the banks of the river opposite, and at sunset this evening presented a picture of overpowering grandeur: the shadows and canyons between appeared a deep azure color, while those portions illuminated by the dying sunlight took from it a brilliant golden hue . . ."

* * *

"They call it Scott's Bluffs," Old Hitchcock spat into the dust, and his mule snorted and bridled sideways a little. "Goes on for miles. Rougher country than this."

"I can see that," John said. "It looks like the castle of the gods." He and Stephens had ridden a little ahead with the two old men to pick and mark the night's campsite. Moses and William Case had tagged along, hoping for a shot at an antelope or one of the amazingly long-eared and speedy rabbits who had confounded not a few of the parties' dogs.

"Who was Scott?" Moses asked curiously. "Did he live here-abouts?"

"Naw, Sonny – he died hereabouts, round about fifteen year ago."

"Twenty," Old Greenwood said, and Hitchcock shook his head.

"I ran into him at Ashley's rendezvous in '26. He was lively enough then. Heard tell he was hurt in a flight with the Blackfeet during the Bear Lake rendezvous, two year later."

"Hiram Scott, he was one of Ashley's brigade leaders back in the earlies . . . strapping young hoss, round and about from St. Louis," Greenwood interjected. "He and his partner would bring out supplies to here and there, and take back the furs. Got cut up bad at that fight in '28, couldn't leave out with his partner . . . man named Bruff, Bruffy, something like that. But Bruffy was agonna wait for him at these here bluffs for him to catch up. Scott had two friends stayed behind with him until he was well enough to travel . . . trouble was, he never got much better. They built them a bullboat after he got so's he couldn't sit a saddle no more, and brought him down the Sweetwater a piece. But they got caught in the rapids and lost all their guns and food but what they had on them. Still managed to carry Scott all that way, although he was in a real bad way and got worse."

"They got to where Bruffy promised to wait for them, and he'd lit out . . . gone on down the river." Greenwood took up the story, sitting easy in his pony's light saddle with his rifle crossways on his lap. "They'd had a chance to catch up, if they could only move fast."

"Sick as he was, Scott had sand." Old Hitchcock shook his head, sorrowfully. "He told his two friends to leave him – he was dying, he said he didn't have no chance a'tall, but they might have a chance, and he didn't want them to throw it away."

"But that was horrible," Moses burst out. "To think of leaving him all alone! Didn't they have any loyalty . . . no pity for him?"

"They did, sonny." Old Hitchcock spat again. "But pity don't come into it, in that there situation. They were good men, they knew the score, and so did he. Catching up to Bruffy's party was their only hope. So they propped him up, with a gourd of water by his side an' a couple of blankets and promised they would come back if they could, and that was that."

The two old men were silent for a moment, looking at the great stone pile and thinking, John was sure, of their days in the mountains.

"Did they come back for their friend, at least?" Moses asked. The sun slipped a little lower, intensifying the colors even more. They could hear the first of the wagons coming up the rising ground below them, harness jingling and the teamster's irritable voices.

"No, sonny, they weren't able to catch up to Bruffy for weeks, and they felt sure Scott wouldn't have lasted long, all by himself. Will Sublette found his bones the next year, buried them proper and decent."

"Funny thing, though," Greenwood commented, "Sublette found him a good few miles east of where his friends said they'd left him – as if he had managed to crawl a ways by himself. Full sand and grit, that hoss – he was a ways from giving up, I reckon."

"But he wished for his friends to save themselves," Moses looked solemn.

"A brave and noble gesture," John said. "And a mournful fate, but a magnificent monument. Perhaps not so mournful, though, to have this view as your last sight on this earth."

"I'd sooner have a sight of Californy in front of me," Old Hitchcock said, and spat again.

Out of sudden curiosity, John asked, "So, have you seen it yourself . . . truly?" and the old man shook his head regretfully.

"Don't tell m'daughter – I truly have, but Izzy'd never let me see the end of it, she's so caught up in thinking of me as a foolish old man with my yarns. I was trapping this side of the Great Basin, round about twenty year gone, and Joe Walker had gone, two, three times for Cap'n Bonneville. He told me all of it that he seen, so green and mild . . . the hillsides all gold in spring with wild mustard, or gold with tall grass in the fall . . . blue mountains off in the distance, and little streams tumblin' out of the mountains, with bright shiny gravel at the bottom. I had to plumb go see it myself. Ol' Joe, he made it sound like a paradise, and the other boys of his'n that I yarned with, they said the same. I wintered over and came back through Santa Fe in the spring."

"Mr. Hitchcock, you have the soul of a writer of romances," John remarked, and the old man chortled richly and dropped a lewd wink.

"Allus wondered what they called it," he said.

Old Greenwood shook his head, remarking as he did so, "Hoss, if your yarns weren't so entertaining, they'd call you a bald-face liar."

"That be what they usually say," Old Hitchcock retorted.

* * *

From Dr. Townsend's diary: *"We are no more than a few days away from Fort Laramie. My Dearest wife, as well as others, are composing letters to be posted back to our loved ones, as this will be the first outpost we have reached since departing from Iowa from which such missives may be dispatched . . . At last, crossed over the Platte River and now travel along the southern shore of it, much plagued by mosquitoes, nothing more dangerous than that, although Mr. Murphy's wagon was overturned in the crossing. No damage, although all their wagon's contents somewhat wetted . . .*

"Consulted with the indomitable Mrs. Patterson this evening, who tells me that in her judgment, Mrs. Miller is within a week or two of her time of confinement . . . we are advis'd this day against approaching the Fort, by an emissary from the commandant, Mr. Bissionette, to wait a day, that he may take council with a great assemblage of the Sioux, some four or five thousand of which are camped with their families adjacent to the fort.

* * *

"Not sure what ought to be done in this case, Doc," Stephens remarked immediately upon reception of Mr. Bissionette's dismaying message. The hoofbeats of his messenger's horse still echoed, and the dust of his passing had not even settled, but the stranger from the Fort had been noticed and was being remarked upon, for heads were turning toward Stephens and John from all up and down the line of march.

"See what Greenwood will say," John answered. Word of four thousand Sioux camped around Fort Laramie was not particularly reassuring intelligence, even if Commandant Bissionette was correct in saying the Sioux had brought their wives and families with them. So had the wagon party, and any fool could see the emigrant party was well outnumbered, and as Old Man Hitchcock freely reiterated, the Sioux were anything but fools. John added, "Consult Old Man Hitchcock, too. He claims to speak the Lakotah language, and he was out this way frequently, to hear him tell it."

"Waste of a day," Stephens grumbled. "Tell the boys best not hunt too far from the train tomorrow. And douse the fires after dark. We don't need to tell everyone we're here."

"You think that they won't know it already?" John asked, and Stephens grunted.

"Mebbe. But we don't need to announce ourselves with a brass band, neither. We'll talk it over with Greenwood and Old Man Hitchcock as soon as we make camp tonight."

Hitchcock stumped over to Stephen's council-fire that afternoon in gleeful good humor, trailed by young Eddie, chattering away like a magpie.

"Lots of Injuns, Paw-Paw? Will we have to fight them? Ma said . . ."

"Don't talk nonsense, young-un," they heard Hitchcock saying indulgently. "Clever men work out a way not to have to fight. Commonly, they look big and mean and ready to fight – so much so that they hardly ever need to."

"I just now realized where young Eddie inherited his gift for loquacity from," John jested quietly to Stephens, whose rare smile came quick and was gone again almost at once.

"Took you until now?" he said. Dog sat up alertly as Old Hitchcock sat down with a barely stifled groan. Greenwood was already hunkered on his heels at the fire, and Stephens gentled Dog's ears until she lay down again at his feet.

"Hell to get old," Hitchcock remarked, rubbing his rheumatic knee. "But on the whole, it beats the alternate."

He and Greenwood chuckled sourly, and John recollected Greenwood remarking, *'Suh, there may be old mountain-men and there may be bold men among them, too, but there are damn few who are old and bold.'*

Now, Hitchcock continued, "Well, Cap'n, I take it we ain't going to fight the Sioux tribes? Good. They'd give us an almighty pasting, an' hardly break into a sweat."

"We're going to be excruciatingly polite to them, I expect," John said. "But it would help to know how we should approach them. They are camped around the Fort, and we can hardly go around them."

"No." Old Hitchcock scratched his stubbly jaw, with a raspy sound. "No, can't do that. Would be bad manners, and look like we're afeerd. They ain't anything like the Kaw, back at the river. The Sioux, they're the lords of all these here parts."

"But what are they like?" John persisted.

Old Hitchcock scratched his jaw again. "Proud as Lucifer," he answered at last, "Every man jack of them. Touchy for their honor, like the knights in old times. Fearless warriors. Hold their word, once they have given it mostly and generous when they feel like it. Good company, in the main. And handsome, straight-limbed folk. They dress well and like personal adornments, as they count such things, and their lodges are clean."

"Our advice is, to treat with the Sioux as if they were our equals," Greenwood said, quietly. "Honorable and well-armed equals. We make no offense, or offer any unwelcome familiarity, or braggadocio, but show ourselves to be confident and courteous . . . and moving on, as soon as possible."

"Cap'n Stephens, did I hear right?" Hitchcock asked curiously. "That there messenger, he did say the Sioux were all around there with their women and children, to trade and all, not lookin' for a fight?"

"That's what he said, several times."

"Ah," The old man sat back. "Then I make a suggestion, Cap'n. To show our own good will, and straight intentions when we get to the Fort, we send word through the Commandant, that we are happy to trade . . . and I'll take some of our women and children to the Sioux camp to trade with them."

"We couldn't possibly send our wives and children out to treat with them in their own camps!" John burst out indignantly, but he saw Greenwood nodding in sober agreement.

"They'll come to our camp in any case," he said. "I think there would be little risk, or no more than there is in bringing your families out here anyway – and much to be gained. No better way to demonstrate fair intentions, for a start, and to reciprocate their courtesy. Or even demand a little of it."

"What do we have which they would desire, assuming it's not our scalps?" John asked mordantly.

"All sorts of little trifles you would hardly miss," Old Hitchcock answered, readily. "Needles, pins, and buttons. Lengths of calico, and any sort of metal. Pots and pans. I myself have a pack full of needles, and beads and other pretties that I brought this far with the intent of trading on the way as needed."

"And what would we be trading our bits and trifles for?" John was diverted.

"Dried meat," Stephens answered this one. "If they would sell it to us out of what they need, come winter, and horses."

"Moccasins and leather garments," Hitchcock added practically. "Cured leather and buffalo hides, and any other curios and ornaments as they choose to offer."

"Well, I can see the advantages of trade," John sighed. "But I do not like the thought of Mrs. Townsend and the other women walking into such a lions' den."

"Boldness may carry the day," Greenwood said. "Tell her . . . tell any of the women who wish to trade not to show their apprehension."

"Put fear aside," Stephens said, looking down at his strong, blacksmith's hands, resting on Dog's fawn-colored head. "And look confident, always."

"We should call a general meeting and let everyone know what is expected," John suggested, and Stephens shrugged.

"Your show, Doc. One thing. Greenwood, do the Crows war with the Sioux, this season?"

"Not so far," Greenwood answered cautiously.

"Good . . . remind your boys. I'll be sending them with Hitchcock and the women."

* * *

Angeline Morrison Letter #3
24th of June 1844
Writ from the Trail near Fort Laramie

My Dearest Angeline:

We have been bidden to wait for a day before approaching the Fort, and so we take a day of rest such as we have usually not had, since departing from the Bluffs. Our journey was much impeded by heavy rains at first, which had made the water in numerous rivers which we had need to cross much deeper than what our Guide, Mr. Greenwood, tells us was more usual. I should tell you now that my health, always of such concern to my Dearest and to friends such as yourself is presently much recovered. My Dearest says it is because we are removed from the bad air along the river bottoms, that the air is very dry and clear, suited to someone with a constitutional weakness of the lungs. Others have been ill, as we journeyed, but not myself. (Dearest says that was caused by the drinking of bad water, from the river itself.)

We are to trade with the Indians, camped around the Fort; they value such trifles as we may spare, and so in great anticipation of this expedition,

Sarah and myself, and Mrs. Isabella have searched our wagons for such little things as we may offer in trade. I shall offer some blankets, a box of odd buttons, an ivory needle-case with five stout steel needles in it, and a metal kitchen-fork with a broken tine. The other ladies have all made similar collections, but I fear that only Mrs. Isabella and myself, and perhaps Miss Murphy and Mrs. Case express any anticipatory pleasure in the outing we have planned. Mrs. Isabella's father was long engaged in trade, and has engaged to escort a party of us into the Indian camp, assuring us over and over again of our perfect safety there. My Dearest and Captain Stephens join in such assurances . . . Mrs. Thorp, of the Oregon party succumbed most promptly to an attack of the vapors when it was suggested that she join us.

I know not how often the mail travels from Fort Laramie, dearest Angeline, but it is in my hope that you should have received this missive by winter, when we are safely arrived in the pleasant paradise of California, and I may pen a fuller account of our adventures upon the trail.

Until then, adieu from Thy dear Friend

Elizabeth

From Dr. Townsend's diary: *"This day around noon approached the Fort, which presented a most curious sight. The country around has become quite sere and brown, being at the height of summer, but the meadows around Fort Laramie remain lush and green as they are watered by many streams of sweet water, and encamped around are the conical skin lodges of the Sioux, in such numbers as to make our hearts grow faint, a veritable city of lodges and brush bowers. The fort is a rectangular compound built of packed mud bricks and a timber palisade above, with a pair of taller towers at opposite corners, and a great overhanging gatehouse guarding a commodious entrance . . . the gates stood open in a welcoming manner, as if there were no need to ever contemplate closing them, while the multitudes came and went.*

"We rolled a little beyond the fort, and chose for ourselves a pleasant open space to make our camp, being much aware that we were the cynosure of all eyes. Captain Stephens and myself accompanied Mr. Greenwood and certain others of the party to present our compliments to Mr. Bissonette . . . I at least took care to dress in the best that I possessed, and we were received most graciously by that gentleman, whom we thanked for his assistance. He in turn welcomed us to the settlement, and promised to send on our invitation to trade with such individuals of the Tribes as were interested . . . after our reception, we wandered at will about the establishment, and marveled at how freely intermingled were people of diverse races."

* * *

John shrugged his shoulders, under his best broadcloth coat which unaccountably felt tighter. He had not worn it since the elections under the trees east of the great river. Stephens had dressed as he always did, and so did Greenwood, in his leather Indian jerkin and leggings.

John was painfully aware that Greenwood looked more at home here then he himself did. Stephens had preferred to return to camp, leaving John at the fort to cope with the hospitality offered by Mr. Bissionette and to see what supplies and services the fort offered. Not much and that expensive, John decided, after a short survey of the trading post shelves. He found the two old men sitting outside, silently watching the passing parade of humanity.

"You are correct, sir, they are absolutely splendid physical specimens," John ventured.

Hitchcock rubbed his knee and replied, "Aye."

"They'd make the finest fighting cavalry in all the world, could they fight under discipline," Greenwood said regretfully.

"Aye," said Old Hitchcock again. After a short time, he asked, "Caleb, remember the very first time you came out here to the mountains?"

"Seems an age," Greenwood replied, "And yet again, just the blink of an eye. There were places I went, where I was the first white man any of them had ever seen. Fat times and the streams all full of beaver, then."

"Just a handful of men," Old Hitchcock mused. "Count them on the fingers of your own hands, a couple times over, but all of this once was our'n . . . all the pelts you could trap, all the trails you could follow to the end, every green valley a garden of Eden, all the pretty squaws you could woo, and blood-brothers you could fight back to back with against their enemies and yours. Come back to civilization every three years with a pack of pelts, send money to your family, and then go back an' do it again."

"Rare times," Greenwood said sadly. "Rare times."

"Aye. We all thought we were made of iron, ten-foot tall and bullet-proof."

"Were? Speak for yourself," Greenwood said with a glint of a smile. "But it doesn't turn back the clock for my wife's people, nor for the Lakotah. When I first passed this way, there was no fort, and now there is. And it's been rebuilt twice . . . thrice? There were just tracks then, tracks of our own pack-trains, and now there are iron-shod wheels cutting ruts into the ground, more and deeper every year. In our day, it was easy enough for men like you and me to step into their world," he jerked his chin towards the Sioux camp, "and then step back to our own blood, but there were few of us, and we could take up their ways, and no one thought the worse of us, because the Tribes were all that there was out here."

"Aye," Hitchcock sighed morosely. "And there'll be more, next year, and the year after that. If I were a Sioux, I wouldn't be a'feared of our wagons, Doc. Our wagons are here and gone the next day. They can trade with us, steal a horse or an ox for amusement, but they'd have no reason to war against us until the day that our wagons come here and stay. And then there will be no going back and forth between our peoples."

"Stay here? In this desert?" John laughed. "I cannot imagine anyone wanting to stay here but the wild Indians and they are welcome to it, in my opinion."

"It's not yours to decide, Doctor," Greenwood said. "In any case we will be in California or singing in the choir eternal before things may ever come to that pass. Take no heed of us, just the memories and regrets of old men, lamenting a lost paradise."

* * *

From E.S. Patterson Interview, University of California Local History Archival Project 1932: *"Ma and Paw-Paw said we were going to trade with the Indians at Fort Laramie, that some of the women from the party were going to trade for dried meat and supplies, and that Sadie and I might come but we must not show that we were afraid. Paw-Paw told us that we should act as if we were going to call on folk in another town, but that we should be polite and treat them just as we would our equals.*

"It was Ma and Mrs. Townsend and Mrs. Montgomery and Ellen Murphy and Mrs. Case, that I remember, Ma and Mrs. Townsend dressed in their best and put up their hair, and Paw-Paw and the Greenwood boys, who looked so like Indians themselves, coming with us, and one of Paw-Paw's mules to carry everything we had to trade.

"I remember Paw-Paw taking me by the hand and walking with me straight into their camp, close by the fort it was ... he could speak their lingo, and none of us had ever known that! It seemed like we were expected, all their folk looking at us so curious, and Paw-Paw talking to them as calm and level as you please, and showing them what we had to trade ... they came around us, so curious.

"One woman, she was so took with Sadie, she set her on her lap, and was stroking Sadie's hair, and chattering to her friends, and she asked Paw-Paw a question. Paw-Paw, he shook his head, held out his hand to Sadie, an' called to her, he said, "Sadie, come here, child," an' Sadie wriggled off her lap an' came right back to Ma an' Mrs. Townsend, an' hid herself between their skirts. Paw-Paw, he said to Sadie, "Sadie, stay with your Ma and Miz Townsend, you hear, child?" Then he struck a bargain for Miz Townsend, traded a fine buffalo robe for two blankets, but I noticed that he never took his eye off Sadie, not for one moment after that.

"I got into a fight with an Indian lad, 'bout my age, just then. He came up and hit me on the shoulder, and I hit him back, and we took to tussling like a pair of puppies in the dust, and first I was on top and then he was, and then me again, 'til one of the Indian men pulled us apart. He was a big, splendid man. He and Paw-Paw looked like they was no end amused, and Paw-Paw said, "Go an' play, boy," so we did, while Ma and Mrs. Townsend and them sat on blankets and dickered for dried meat and moccasins an' such. At the end of the day I gave the Indian boy my spinning top that I had in my pocket, and the big Indian gave me a sheath-knife with a wooden handle that I have still."

* * *

John would never admit to anyone how relieved he was to see the little trading procession return to camp, for that would mean acknowledging how apprehensive he had been for their safety . . . apprehensions that the women obviously did not share, for they seemed at first to be quite exhilarated by their adventure in the Indian camp and most pleased with the results.

Old Man Hitchcock was positively smug. "A fine profit, this, a fine profit, and would have been even finer if we had traded little Sadie to the woman with little bells sewn all over her dress."

"Pa! How could you even think to trade our flesh and blood!" Isabella went up in incoherent flames while Old Hitchcock rubbed his bristles and tried to keep a smile off his face, and Elizabeth cried, "Oh, surely he is joking, my dear Isabella! Dr. Townsend, tell her that he is being a terrible tease!"

"She offered two ponies for the little one, an' I think I could have talked her up to four," Hitchcock said, and Isabella burst into tears.

"Mr. Hitchcock! Now see what you have done!" Elizabeth stormed, and John realized that perhaps it had been rather nerve-wracking for the women after all.

Hitchcock put his arm around his daughter's shoulders and embraced her, saying shamefacedly, "Izzy, Izzy, girl. Stop crying. I was jesting with you, girl. You was always too serious." Isabella hiccupped, and scrubbed her face with the handkerchief that Elizabeth gave her. "Dry your eyes – that's a good girl. Izzy, you should know about my tall tales by now."

Isabelle hiccupped again. "You're a wicked old man, Pa, I do know that."

"Aye, I am that," he admitted.

Elizabeth took her hand, and said, "I do wish I could have traded for her dress though. It was magnificent, and sewn all over with little sliver bells, that chimed so enchantingly whenever she moved."

"She's the wife of a rich chief," Old Hitchcock said. "Makes it easier for him to find her in the dark."

John choked on his own laughter, and both women chorused, "Mr. Hitchcock!"

"Pa! For shame!"

"I regret that you did not trade for it, since it seems to have pleased you well," John recovered his voice. "What other barbaric wealth did you come away with? We had some little trading here, but all they offered were ponies. Captain Stephens traded a box of metal scraps for two such."

"A very splendid buffalo robe," Elizabeth replied. "And some pairs of moccasins adorned with very pretty beadwork. Mr. Hitchcock most particularly advised us to trade for dried meats and fruit, to add to our stores. And Isabella bought some more moccasins and a pretty necklace of shells for a birthday present for Sadie – which I think must be sea-shells, but as we are thousands of miles from the nearest ocean, I cannot think how they came to be here."

"In trade, my Dearest; the same way you came to be here to purchase them. You've all done very well today, although I so very much regret that you felt the slightest apprehension regarding your safety."

"Oh, it was not so bad after the first moments." Elizabeth laughed "I do own, though – they kept looking at my hair, and at Miss Murphy's, and I could not really tell if they were admiring our coloring, so unusual relative to theirs, or of they were speculating on how well it might adorn their lodges!"

John laughed, a great relieved laugh, "Brave Liz! The former, I am sure. And we shall be good guests and move on as soon as it is courteous to do so."

Later, though, he spoke quietly to Old Man Hitchcock. "I know you passed it as a joke to your daughter, but did you think that Indian woman was in earnest regarding trading for little Sadie?"

"I'd say so," the old man replied thoughtfully. "She's younger than they usually like when they take them into the tribe from outsiders – usually they take 'em Eddie's age, or a little older. Old enough to not be trouble taking care of 'em, but young enough to be biddable."

"If they wanted little Sadie or any of the other children," John ventured, "would they just take them, do you think? Would they dare?"

"Not from here, not at the Fort. They ain't fools and it 'ud cause too much trouble. Naw, I think the chief's wife just liked the looks of little Sadie, and thought she might venture an offer. She didn't seem at all put out at being refused . . . but still an' all, we'd ought to keep a close eye on all the childer until we leave."

* * *

From Dr. Townsend's diary: *"Thirtieth of June, 1844: Departed this day from Fort Laramie, much refreshed by the rest, but with some apprehensions regarding our continued attachment to our scalps. We were treated with every courtesy by the Sioux during our short stay, but I could not shake a conviction that our slight intercourse was like to that of sharing a large enclosure with some wild and beautiful jungle cat; a cat with beautiful markings, a supple body and very sharp claws, which deigned for the moment to purr and rub its ears 'gainst our hand, whilst we being always uncomfortably aware that it is, should it choose or the mood take it, capable of rending us in a trice to the very bone.*

"We have jointly resolved, however, to travel separately from the Oregon party, our differences being simply too great to encompass in one single company. We are in the advance by about a day's journey; we have arranged, however, to remain close enough to come to each other's aid. I own it is a great deal more restful, not having to constantly intermediate between Mr. Thorp and Captain Stephens or the quarrelsome Shaw, and whomever has recently attracted his animus.

"We have traveled some 600 miles since departing from the jumping-off place, in a little more than a month and a half . . . excellent hunting along the Sweetwater Valley: Moses, Allen Montgomery, Johnny Murphy and Joseph Foster went to hunt buffalo at our nooning this day, since we had seen a handsome herd close by. They intended to catch up to our caravan by

nightfall, but by sundown they had not returned. Captain Stephens gave permission to burn campfires all night; Mr. Murphy and my Dearest are in no little distress because of this ..."

* * *

"I do not see why Captain Stephens does not send out a party to search for them!" Elizabeth spoke in a distraught whisper. She and Old Martin had been stoic all day and into the evening, even as they looked towards the eastern horizon every few minutes. Now she lay next to John in their bed in the wagon, but she was sleepless in spite of the day's toil.

"Because it would be a pointless effort, Dearest," John repeated patiently. "They are able men, and well equipped to look after themselves. Allen and Joseph are, anyway. They are undoubtedly camped for the night, and intend to catch up in the morning. Moses and Johnny are as safe with them as they would be with the wagons." To no effect; he could almost feel the tension vibrating in her. "Try to sleep, Dearest . . . you cannot help Moses by staying awake all the night."

"He might be near to a man grown, but he is still my little brother," Elizabeth answered miserably. "Mama gave him to me almost as soon as he was born. 'Here is your baby brother' she told me. 'You must look out for him.' She had not the strength to look after him properly, so she gave him to me, although I was only a little older than Isabella's Nancy. And he was such a very dear baby, so much better than any doll. He said his first words to me, and took his first steps for me, and I taught him his first letters . . . and when Mama and Papa Schallenberger both died and he was left to us, it was as if he were really our child."

"Liz, he is not a child to be coddled. You cannot go around keeping him from bumping his head or skinning his knees . . ." John started to say, but Elizabeth turned away from him, exclaiming, "You are heartless, Doctor Townsend, quite heartless!" and John knew that she wept, and why, and knew also that there was nothing to be done until morning. Presently she slept, and so did he, but in the middle of the night he woke alone, no Liz breathing quietly next to him.

She was at the front of the wagon, a ghostly figure wrapped in her largest shawl. She had drawn back the flap that covered the round opening and stood looking out, with the moonlight streaming in. Outside the cattle moved restlessly. The night herd guard walked by, his footsteps crunching quietly on the ground. He spoke quietly to Elizabeth; Bernard Murphy, by the

83

sound of his voice, although too quietly to hear what he had said, and Elizabeth replied. Far away in the hills above the Sweetwater the little prairie wolves wailed and yelped.

"Dearest . . . they would not have traveled through the night and risk being shot by accident in coming to our camp at night," he said, and she started and turned towards him. "In the morning, Liz. We'll look to see them in the morning, not before. Come back to bed, then."

"I know," she answered softly, and let the flap fall. He could not see her, except as a vague shadow against the canvas, but heard the rustle of her shawl, and then a gentle movement of blankets as she slipped between them again, to lay close-curled against him. "Please don't be cross."

"Never . . . well, never for long, Dearest."

* * *

"They returned to us at midday, leading their horses packed generously with the results of their hunt, although having to leave much of the meat to wolves which pursued them most tenaciously. They made light of their adventure, and were astonished at our worries on their behalf, saying there was no cause for it in the least . . . My Dearest made only a mild complaint to the lad, and denied being over-much concerned . . . We have much to do with drying the buffalo meat. Cut in strips and hung from the wagon covers, it looks as if they were adorned with a red-brown fringe.

"Ninth of July, 1844 . . . three days travel brought us to Independence Rock, a great grey monolith recumbent upon a low sloping bank of scree, above a wide and shallow valley where we intend to rest for a day to celebrate the 4th of July. There are the faint traces of those parties who have passed this way in seasons previous; ruts worn through hard-baked soil, bare circles where campfires were set, places where branches were broken for firewood . . . in many places along a canyon which forced us away from the river, the water was so heavily charged with alkali salts as to be distasteful and even injurious to drink.

"Moses and I, in company with the young Murphy brothers and their friends the Sullivan boys, intended to climb up to the top of the rock tomorrow morning, and paint our names and the names of our party, as Mr. Greenwood avers has been the custom for many years; we are encamped only a little way from the bottom, and I would like to sketch a small scenic view of our wagons in camp. Alas, I am thwarted once again . . ."

* * *

At a leisurely breakfast, unencumbered by the burden of catching the horses and rounding up the teams, John set down his coffee and asked, "Where is Mrs. Patterson this morning?" With the party reduced roughly by half, the wagons and campfires described a tighter circle, the spaces between campfires being much reduced. Young Nancy presided alone over the Pattersons' campfire, with quite touching gravitas, serving up the morning meal to her brothers and Sadie and Old Hitchcock.

Sarah and Elizabeth looked at each other, and John was aware of a spark of unease.

Elizabeth said nervously, "Mrs. Miller's time came, very early this morning. Isabella went to her at once. She told us it would be hours before you were needed, and that I should not wake you just yet, she would send as soon as it was necessary."

"Liz! I am the doctor; I should have been called at once! I might very well not be needed at once, but I would prefer to be the judge of that myself, and not leave it to some back-country herb-wife!"

Elizabeth quailed; he so very rarely raised his voice as other husbands did, or spoke harshly to her. It felt like slapping a child, and he regretted saying so with such bluntness. But his wife and Isabella had conspired with the best of intentions to spare him from duties he was oath-bound to carry out, and it angered him.

But even though tears stood in her eyes, she lifted her chin and said, "I know that very well. But you are also Captain Stephens' second, and the co-leader of this party, with very great responsibilities, which leave you very nearly wearied to death. You fall asleep with your supper half-eaten, and the fork halfway to your mouth – you are wakened by some emergency half the nights, and are on guard over the cattle the other half, and are at everyone's beck and call in between, and if you aren't allowed some sleep now and then, you will fall sick yourself, and who would look after us, then?" she finished illogically. "And where would I be then, out in this wild country, all alone?" She gulped, and added in a steadier voice. "Besides, Isabella is a very good midwife, and she has born six of her own, to boot. She says it takes simply hours and hours. She was only called a little while ago, so why you should feel like a laggard for another half hour of sleep and a good breakfast, I don't know. You could at least finish your coffee."

Having his gentle wife suddenly round on him like that felt as if little Sadie had suddenly grown fangs and sprung at his throat, but in the middle of his shock and surprise, John illogically felt a kind of pride; that she could be so fierce on his behalf, and unyielding in her defense of his welfare? Greenwood had said once of his Crow wife, *'A good wife will re-load for you, a great one will take up a knife and slit your enemies' throats.'* Not quite what he wanted of his Liz, exactly.

Now she said, in a very small voice, "Don't be angry at me, Dearest. You were sleeping so very sound. And I was going to tell you before you and Moses went up to the rock."

"Have some more griddle-cakes." Sarah put two more on his plate, and John realized that she and Moses had been watching this all with the liveliest interest, and all his hasty anger drained away.

"Ah, Darling Liz," he sighed, and took her in his arms. "You are right, and I have been very inconsiderate of my own welfare. The next time this happens, will you promise to tell me so privately?"

"If she won't, I will," Moses neatly scooped another griddle-cake from Sarah's platter, and Sarah slapped his fingers.

"Children!" Elizabeth said in an attempt to mimic Isabella's tones, but it didn't quite come off, and they all laughed, just as Eddie came around the corner of their wagon and said, "Ma says it's time, Doctor Townsend."

Chapter 6 - *Ellen, Independence*

"10th of July, 1844, encamped upon the Sweetwater River; appended is a sketch of our camp as it appears from the top of the Rock. I climbed up myself this morning; it is actually much farther from the Rock; distances are deceptive in the pure and clean air. Mrs. James Miller gave birth to a daughter yesterday around mid-morning, attended by myself and Mrs. Patterson. This is her forth child, having already one young son and two daughters . . ."

* * *

They had pitched a tent, the Murphy's had, and all the Murphy women were hanging close about with Mary Sullivan, boiling water and setting out clean towels and sheets. Sarah and Elizabeth came trailing after John, once little Eddie had delivered his message and gone happily off to play with Willie Miller, and Michael and Robert Sullivan and the little Murphy boys. James Miller and Old Martin sat a little way off, saying little, as John ducked head and let the tent-flap fall closed behind him.

Outside the tent, it was cool, the cool of an alpine morning, but it seemed warm inside, too warm. After the sweet clean air outside, it smelled inside of human sweat, and blood and other fluids. Mary Miller lay in the middle, on a straw-tick and propped to nearly sitting up in the lap of her sister-in-law Annie. She was wearing a shift, rucked up to her thighs and soaked to the point where it clung to her breasts and belly; a pretty woman as all the Murphy woman were, even in the extreme of child bearing.

"Good morning, Doctor," she gasped. "It's nearly time, I think. Mine always went fast."

"Good morning, Mary . . . about how long have you been feeling the pains?"

He picked up her hand to feel the pulse in her wrists, but she gripped his with strength that left white and bloodless marks on his fingers, as the pain passed over her like a tidal surge.

"Since last night . . . but only small pains, and irregular . . . James sent for Isabella when I couldn't sleep."

"The waters burst about two hours ago." Isabella held Mary's other hand. "And since then, the pains are much stronger, down to about three minutes apart."

"A drink of water . . ." Mary gasped, and Isabella briefly held a cup to her lips.

"Only a sip, Mary dear, no more." Isabella set the cup aside and gently patted Mary's face with a damp cloth.

"Thank you" Mary sank back into Annie's arms. Her eyelids drooped closed for a bare few moments of what looked like sleep, until her belly went rigid again, and Isabella chanted softly, "Breathe dear, breathe. One and two, and breathe . . . one and two."

When it passed, John said, "Mary, I am going touch your belly, and see if I can tell how far the baby has dropped . . . oh, yes. Good . . . well down . . . good heavens, yes, there's the wee little feet there, I can feel them quite well . . . very good, Mary, the babe is the right way around."

Mary smiled faintly, the flesh under her eyes already dark with exhaustion. "All my babies are good . . ." she whispered. "They all have come easily . . . as easily as is possible, I suppose . . ."

"That is good to know . . . although I have brought my patent pair of German forceps; but if it is as you and Mrs. Isabella say, I shall not need to use them."

The minutes and hours of time, ticked away, measuring the pains, marked out by Isabella's gentle chant. Mary-Bee replaced Annie at Mary's shoulders. When the tent-flap was lifted, the bright light outside stabbed at their eyes and John realized that he was stiff, from kneeling on the ground.

Isabella saw him wincing as he changed position, and said, "Take some air, Doctor, and stretch yourself a little. We can spare you a few moments."

He blinked in the sunshine outside; it was well past mid-morning. How long had he been in the birth tent? Hours? It seemed like all the ordinary activities of camp had paused, waiting patiently . . . or no, not all of it. The children were nowhere to be seen. James Miller and Old Martin Murphy started up from the fireside, seemingly from the same place they had been before, as soon as John appeared.

"No, no, nothing yet," John said hastily. "And she is doing splendidly well. It won't be much longer, James, truly it won't."

"Leave the doctor take a little refreshment," Old Martin rumbled comfortingly, and handed John a rough sandwich of camp-bread and cold bacon. "Here, Doctor, eat up. Mary is in the best of hands." How long had it been since breakfast?

John realized he was ravenously hungry and wolfed it down entire before asking, "Where is everyone?" The camp seemed nearly silent without the sounds of children at play or the voices of women. It was good to sit for a while, outside in the fresh air, and revel in the quiet of it all.

"Moses and Mr. Greenwood have taken them all on an expedition," Elizabeth said calmly. She and Sarah sat side by side on a bench taken from Murphy's wagon. Annie Murphy was pegging out newly-washed laundry on a line strung between two wagons. "They have gone to the top of the Rock to paint their names."

"We thought it best to give them some amusement," added Martin Murphy.

"And the drovers have taken the cattle a little away for fresher pasturage. Is it not so delightfully quiet? We can hear the birds singing at last," Elizabeth remarked.

And also the half-stifled cries from the birthing tent, John thought. He wished that Elizabeth and Sarah had gone also with the children. He did not mean to linger, but the moments without responsibility weighing down his shoulders were so very, very rare these days. There was an odd, choked-off moan just then, and Isabella called from inside the tent. Sarah gripped Elizabeth's hands; both of them looking very white. Of the married women in the party, they were the only two who had not yet born children of their own. John shouldered his way into the tent again, followed by Annie, hardly noticing that Old Martin had clapped him on the back, saying, "Praise God, only a little while longer!"

"It's coming, now." Isabella had slipped around to join Mary-Bee Murphy in propping up Mary, lifting her to almost sitting upright.

"Grasp your knees now, dear . . . on the next pain, bear down as hard as you can . . . push, push, push!" Mary cried out, the loudest that she had so far, and Isabella said, "Can you see the head, yet?"

"Just the top . . . she must push again, harder."

"There now, Mary, dear . . ." Isabella stroked her forehead, as she lay gasping against hers' and Mary-Bee's shoulders, "Catch your breath, the babe is nearly here . . . one more big push, you can do this, be our brave Mary, when it starts again, breathe deep and bear down, as hard as you can . . . you can do this for us, you can do this for the baby . . . here it comes again, one big breath . . ."

She and Mary-Bee hoisted Mary upright again, and Mary closed her eyes and cried out.

"The head is out," said John calmly.

"Bear down, Mary, bear down!" commanded Isabella, and the rest of the babe slithered out of Mary's body and into John's hands, as Isabella cried, "Oh, Mary, 'tis done, and it's a girl, a beautiful little girl!"

The baby breathed at once, a pale little thing with dark purple-pansy eyes and a pursed rosebud mouth, flecked all over with little clots of bright red matter. Annie handed John a clean towel to swaddle the child, and she held it while he tied off the cord and slashed it clean through. Mary fell back gasping and crying triumphantly, "Lord be praised, give her to me! Is she all right, all her dear little fingers and toes?"

"A moment, Mary . . . let me look at her." John peeled back the towel and did a swift assessment, while the baby looked up at him, in short-sighted astonishment; yes, all her toes and fingers, that soft little boneless starfish grip, closing around his thumb, her nostrils and mouth clear. John pinched her, and the bonny purple-pansy eyes screwed up half in astonished betrayal and half from the pain of it. She wailed in lusty outrage, and John said, "She's perfect, Mary, not a mark on her anywhere."

Mary lay back, gasping, as the afterbirth came away; an enormous clot of spongy, blood-sodden tissue. It seemed to be all there, all of a piece, and John nodded reassuringly to Isabella, both of them knowing well how a portion of it retained in the body could fester and poison the mother. She did not seem to be bleeding any more than was usual, and John could not see any tearing of tissues attendant on delivery.

"She's crying! Give her to me!" Mary demanded, and John wrapped the baby and placed her in her mother's greedy arms. Isabella passed him a basin and towel for his hands.

Footsteps outside the tent, and voices; James demanding, Annie saying, "It's a girl, James, for the love of Jesus; can't you have a bit of patience?"

Outside the tent, Old Martin's urgent voice, "How are they, Mary and the little one . . . what does the doctor say?"

John sighed at the look of Mary's arms tenderly curled around the baby's tiny, swaddled form. "Mary? Let me show the little one to her father and grandfather. I'll take her away for just a moment, and let Isabella and Mary-Bee help you wash, and comb your hair, so James can come in and see for himself that you are fit and fair."

Mary nodded wearily, and surrendered the little bundle to John, giving up herself to the ministrations of Isabella and her sisters. She looked to be near exhaustion, and who would not be? John cradled the baby — so very solid feeling in his arms for such a little mite — and carried her out into daylight to meet her father and grandfather.

James Miller took her from John, touching her face with his finger. "She has the look of Mary, do you think?" he asked Martin, who gripped Johns' hand in both of his, and could hardly speak at first for emotion.

"Bless you, Doctor; bless you for bringing them both safely through this trial,"

"In fairness, Martin, Mrs. Patterson had the greater part of it." John said honestly.

"Aye, so she did," tears stood in old Martin's eyes, "she is a rare woman, Mrs. Patterson . . . we are fortunate to have you both in our company."

"Have you thought of a name for the little one?" John asked. James could hardly tear himself from contemplating his daughter: her tiny fingers were already wrapped around one of his and no doubt around his heart as well. Elizabeth and Sarah cooed admiringly. Stephens had appeared silently, trailed by Dog.

"Ellen, for her grandmother, God rest her soul, and Independence for a middle name."

"Suitable for the day and the place," John murmured, and old Martin took out a small corked flask from his vest pocket.

"I brought this from Missouri," he explained. "'Tis a bit of holy water, blessed by Father Hoecken. We'd best to baptize her here and now, I am thinking, for the safety of her immortal soul." James nodded, agreeing, and old Martin looked around at the small group: John and Elizabeth, Stephens, Sarah, and James with the baby. "Aye . . . loose the covering over her head, then."

Old Martin rested his strong, work-worn hand on the baby's forehead, and his lips moved in a silent prayer before he opened the flask and intoned, "Ellen Independence Miller, I baptize thee in the Name of the Father, and of the Son, and of the Holy Ghost." He dribbled a little water on her forehead and traced a cross in it, three times, at each name of the Trinity. Little Ellen squirmed a bit, and her rosebud mouth pursed up, as if she wished to nurse. "Aye, back in the old country, they say that would be the devil himself departing," old Martin said, comfortably. "So she is saved from sin, at least . . . all but gluttony. I think she is hungry now, James. Best take her to Mary."

Annie and Mary-Bee had emerged from the tent, carrying a bundle of soiled towels and linen between them, and then Isabella with her own little case of midwife's implements and aids.

"We shall celebrate tonight," Old Martin said, and took her hand in his. "I have already blessed and thanked the Doctor, and now I should thank and bless you doubly, Mrs. Patterson."

"Children are a great gift to us, Mr. Murphy," Isabella returned. "I am obliged to help whenever I can, but it is always my pleasure and I consider myself already blessed when I have helped another safely into this world."

"None the less, add our blessings to those that God already showers upon you." Old Martin embraced her as if she were one of his own children, and it seemed to John that Isabella returned his affection with the grace of a kinswoman. Releasing her, Old Martin shook Johns' hand once more, while Elizabeth also embraced her, saying softly, "Dear Isabella, you look quite exhausted . . . come back with us, and rest yourself at our fire, Sarah and I will fix you something light and refreshing to eat."

"Mrs. Miller should rest for a day, before we move on," John said, and Isabella nodded in agreement. "The constant jolting of the wagon might prove injurious." He turned to Stephens, "Can we spare another day here, Captain? It is a restful place, with plenty of water and grass."

"I don't know if we can spare it," Stephens replied, "but if you judge it best for Mrs. Miller's health and recovery, then we must risk it. Perhaps we can devise a way to make it up later on."

"See what Greenwood or your father suggest." Old Martin nodded towards Isabella. "He has often talked of his journeys out here."

"He often talks," Isabella said wryly. She spoke without the irritation in her voice which formerly accompanied mention of her father. "Then, gentlemen . . . we leave you to your considerations." She nodded courteously and took her leave.

"A rare woman," Old Martin said. "A rare women indeed . . . my own wife was just one such."

"I had often wondered," John mused thoughtfully, "why you had taken her part when we were setting up the offices for the party . . . at that meeting, do you recollect, before we crossed the river to begin this journey? We all barely had met, and knew nothing of each other, and yet you spoke out so strongly."

"Aye, I remember very well," Old Martin said. "And every day of this journey, and this one most of all, has given me reason to think I did well to speak so." He paused, seemingly to order his thoughts, or even to put them into words. "When I said that Mrs. Patterson was a rare woman, and like to my own wife, I did not mean to say anything more than they are of the same spirited and fearless nature. She looked rather like Helen, with red-golden hair. And somewhat like Mrs. Townsend, as to her features, otherwise." He sighed, a little. "Mary Ellen Foley feared nothing in this world, or even the next, being a devout and honest woman. Not departing with me from Wexford and everyone and everything we had ever known, and taking ship with me across the wide ocean and leaving Martin and his sister Margaret behind already with families of their own . . . not setting up in a little cabin we built ourselves, or moving on as the spirit took us, and building a cabin a little bigger than the first . . . she was at my shoulder always. We were given more children, fine upstanding boys and girls – and no little credit due to my Mary Ellen for that. So when I saw Mrs. Patterson with her children, just as mine looked so, such good lads they are, and pretty little misses too, and herself so resolved on taking them to California . . . well, it minded me of Mrs. Murphy. Supposing I had fallen ill and died when our children were still young, and left her a widow, instead of her being taken from me as it happened? What if she had been a widow, all alone in the word with our children, and trying to look after them as best she could? And, I thought to meself – aye, I would have wanted to see someone step up for her, and see that she could look after her own interests. She's a fine woman, so Mrs. Patterson is, she should be able to look to her own rights, as I would have wanted Mrs. Murphy to look after her own."

"I did not mean to pry," John said. "It was just something I wondered about."

* * *

From Dr. Townsend's diary: *"The air is most marvelously clear, and it is a most easy climb to the top of this great granite mound . . . there are a great many names chipped or painted onto the rock. I brought a chisel and a small hammer with me and took a great pleasure in adding my own name and that of my Dearest to this great registry of travelers . . . out in the distance to the west, one can descry the tops of distant peaks . . . we are joined by William Case and a number of wagons from Thorp's party, whom we thought to be a day or two days behind. Mr. Case has grown exasperated with the pace set; as expected they have taken their ease along the trail, and consequently are nearly a week behind us . . .*

"Captain Stephens has given orders that we are to douse our campfires after sunset, lest they attract hostile notice from Sioux war-parties. This is an order that is not terribly popular in all quarters, although most of us admit the necessity of it."

* * *

"No, I shall not put it out!"   Mr. Derby glared across the burning campfire at John, and his whole family murmured indignantly and rebelliously in the twilight behind him. John sighed; why had not Derby and his ilk remained with Thorp, instead of returning like a bad smell to plague him? Stephens had given plain orders that no fires were to be burning after dark. Young Johnny Murphy and Patrick Martin were on guard-watch this evening, and John himself as corporal of the guard. The boys had fetched him, as Derby had not put out his fire. John had gone, armed with a shovel, in addition to the rifle slung over his shoulder.

"Mr. Derby, I must ask you one more time to douse that fire. We are passing through a place where the Sioux are known to be a danger and Captain Stephens . . ."

"Captain Stephens is an old granny!" Derby snapped. "There is no danger here, and I'll not put out the fire for him or any other."

"Perhaps you'll not, but I will." John's shovel bit into the mound of dry soil ringing Derby's fire-pit, scraping it back into the hole from which it had been dug, and in short order the fire was smothered. "Good night to you, Derby." He turned on his heel and walked away, silently damning Derby for a pig-headed, arrogant fool. It was that long hour after twilight, after supper and the going down of the sun behind the western mountains. Some folk were still wakeful, but most tired enough after the exertions of the day to look to their beds and a night of sleep with relief and a certain amount of anticipation. Children had been put to bed, and there was but a faint candle or lantern glow from most of the wagons or tents as he paced the long circuit around the outside of the camp.

As he walked quietly by the Montgomery's wagon, he heard angry, barely stifled voices from within; Allen and Sarah. As he passed by, Allen let the front-flap fall behind him, saying over his shoulder as he leaped down from the box, ". . . haggle and peck at me as you do, why should I endure it, I was only being as polite as you tell me . . ."

"Not in that way to Miss Mary Sullivan!" Sarah raged at his departing back, and then they both caught sight of him. Sarah drew the wagon-flap closed with an angry gesture of her arm, and Allen strode off towards the darkness outside the camp-circle.

As he passed by his own wagon, where everything seemed quiet and closed down for the night, Elizabeth remarked quietly from the darkness,

"They are not happy, Dearest. They have been quarrelling most spitefully all of this evening." She was sitting, wrapped most snugly in her most voluminous shawl, on the long wagon bench, leaning up against the wagon wheel where John was himself wont to sit. With a sigh, John sat down beside her, and she leaned her head contentedly on his shoulder as he set the rifle within reach. "It is most cheerless, not being able to burn a fire after sundown . . . and even less so with Sarah and Mr. Montgomery forever snapping at each other. Then she rejects all sympathy and climbs into their wagon, and he goes off to play cards or spend the evening spinning wild yarns with the hired men or the Murphy boys, and if and when he finally returns, they fight again."

"Darling Liz, there is not much I can do about a man not wishing to spend a quiet evening with his wife," John replied.

"I know you cannot," she said, and they sat contentedly for a moment, and she continued thoughtfully, "I do not think he cares much for the companionship of women . . . oh, he likes women well enough, but have you never noticed, that there are men who enjoy friendships with women, who think much of their wives and daughters' intellects, and then there are men who do not? They may marry and love their wives, but they keep their true friendships with other men . . . and for choice would rather be away from their home hearth." She sighed again and continued, "Well, I can hardly blame some of them, for some women are very silly and have feeble intellects and very boring conversation . . . but still, one cannot help but notice."

John was diverted. "So whom among our party are of the first sort, Dearest, and whom do you see as of the second party?"

Elizabeth giggled, "Yourself, of course, but I fear Mr. Montgomery is of the second and Mr. Hitchcock, also. Captain Stephens cares not for any human company at all. And . . ." She broke off, as John rose from his seat with a muttered curse, for a campfire had bloomed again. Derby, damn him.

"Sorry, Dearest . . . duty calls," he said over his shoulder, catching up his rifle as he went.

Derby's fire burned bravely, like a lighthouse in the darkness of camp, and the greater darkness of the wilderness around them. It may have drawn eyes outside the camp circle, but he knew for sure it had the attention of those nearby. There would be a greater audience for this defiance of Stephens' orders, and John's temper rose high to match it.

"Put it out."

"No." Derby stuck out his chin defiantly. "I will not and I don't think it would be healthy for anyone to try it."

John turned and kicked the fire apart.

"It would not be well for you to light that fire again, tonight, Derby."
He trampled the coals into the ground, scuffled dirt over the remains, and
when it was quite extinguished, he stepped closer to Derby, as close as
dancing partners, and lowered his voice to a menacing growl which only
Derby could hear. "Hold this in mind, Derby – we are passing through
country that the Sioux war-parties roam, attacking who they will. If your
actions attract a raid on this train . . . a raid which results in harm to any of our
families . . . my wife, one of the children, any of the boys guarding the cattle
at night . . . you will have more than Sioux arrows to worry about." Derby's
eyes dropped to the rifle that John held, across his body. "You wish a fire at
night, Derby? Then be so kind as to camp hereafter where your fire will only
call down the Sioux upon your own stiff neck. Good night to you!"

As he left, he made sure to jostle Derby so that the smaller man
staggered; an ungentlemanly gesture that he was immediately ashamed of.
Stephens stepped out of the shadows between two wagons before he had gone
very far, with Dog at his heels.

"Problem?" Stephens asked in his mild, laconic way.

"I hope not," John answered grimly. "On my oath, I'd not mind if Old
Derby did loose his scalp to the Sioux through his own idiotic stubbornness."

"You'd mind," Stephens answered, and John knew that he was smiling.
"It's no credit on a wagon master to lose a man from the train, even if it is his
own doing."

* * *

From Dr. Townsend's diary: *"Mr. Derby complain'd directly to
Captain Stephens the next morning, not knowing that Cap't Stephens had
witnessed the transaction of last night. The captain took my part, and Mr.
Derby swore a mighty oath and declared that he would not travel with such a
crowd. He has camped about half a mile from our camp every night for some
nights, but lit no fires after dark. However, as we nooned this day, Britt
Greenwood and some of the boys who went to hunt buffalo said they had seen
the tracks of a large body of Indians. This party had no mares or colts among
them, which suggests a war party. That night Derby's wagon camped with us;
he has submitted most agreeably to the rules.*

*"Twelfth July, 1844: We have departed the vale of the Sweetwater, and
approached South Pass summit. From here, Old Hitchcock tells us, all
streams flow towards the west. Some of us rejoice, thinking that this means
the end of our journey is in sight . . . but no, alas. We have only come about*

half the way, and according to Greenwood and Hitchcock, the easiest half. To the north of here we discern tall mountain peaks, wrapped in eternal snow, even in mid-summer . . . mysteriously, the buffalo have vanished from the landscape around, as if spirited away . . . encamped on the Big Sandy, where the trail runs south and west, to the Green River, and then back north and west again. Old Man Hitchcock has proposed departing from the established trail and going directly towards the Green from this point."

* * *

"Captain Bonneville took wagons that way in '32," Old Man Hitchcock insisted. "Clear all the way from here, not more than 25 miles. It's more'n eighty miles that way around. Going straight across to the Green would save us a week, at least."

"But do you know that for sure, from having been there," Old Martin asked sharply. "Or is it just from talk you have heard?"

"Talk," Hitchcock admitted grudgingly. "But it was informed talk, from several and at different times, and I saw the tracks, coming north along the Green the next year."

"What do you think of this notion, Captain?" Old Martin looked at Stephens, across the campfire, where he sat with Dog's great head resting on his foot.

"A gamble," Stephens said simply. "This whole venture is a gamble."

"We need to make up time," John said, thinking of the two days waiting for Mary Miller, and the birth of a child at Independence Rock, and before that, four days at Fort Laramie, resting and trading with the Indians. "The straight way across is surely shorter than going south and then north again. At best, it couldn't possibly be longer."

"Oh, yes it could," Greenwood put in. "If the country is rough enough, it surely could. But I had heard tell of Bonneville's expedition, and no one said ought of the country being impossible for wagons."

"We know it was done, twelve year ago," Old Hitchcock insisted. "We know of it being done, and there were no tales about it being especially difficult. And Caleb or I would have heard them for sure; trappers and such gossip worse than old women."

"So, do we trust your word on it?" Patrick Martin demanded. "Look, I know nothing of this country; I'm a thick Irish farmer with itchy feet. I couldn't tell a Sioux from a Pottawatomie without a label and you'd best make the lettering in big square letters at that. Are your secondhand tales and old mountain gossip good enough to lead us through? Tell us true, Old Man, because you're asking us to bet our kinfolk's lives on it!"

"Yes," replied Hitchcock firmly.

Greenwood looked meditatively into the fire, "Myself, I'd go it alone, based on tales and gossip. When it's all said and done, it's from men I'd trust my own life to. And that I have done, over and over."

"I'd gamble," Stephens said simply. "It's a good hand."

"Shall we vote on it, then?" John suggested quietly. "A show of hands, majority to carry?" A murmur of assent went around the meeting. "All right; all for departing from the established trail, and going directly towards the Green River from here?"

Eight, ten, eleven hands, twelve and thirteen hands went up around the fire, none very hastily. "All opposed, who favor remaining on the established trail." Four, five hands. "The motion is carried,"

John sat down, and Stephens said quietly, "Anyone who does not wish to join us should camp here, and wait for Thorps' contingent."

"Or whoever is in charge of them by now." John added under his breath, and Stephens continued, "I'll not force anyone along who is that fiercely opposed."

"No, we'll go as a party," Patrick Martin had been one of the holdouts. "I'll not break with you on this. I just wish we were doing so with more information, that's all."

"When we reach Fort Hall," Stephens said, "we'll know even less about the trail ahead from there than we do now, and a longer way to go than twenty-five miles. Think on that, gentlemen." Isabella cleared her throat, and Stephens nodded. "Lady, too. We'll not always know the way, or what we find at the end of it; best consider on how we'll manage it."

"Well, it's only twenty-five miles," Patrick sounded as if he were still trying to convince himself it was so.

* * *

From Dr. Townsend's diary: *"We ventured off the established trail, thinking ourselves a day and a half from the Green River, and took no further preparations than a little more water, and planning to travel a full day and as much more as would see our company entirely across as desolate a piece of wilderness as I would never hope to see again. But we did not reach the river by sundown, or moonrise either. Our advance scouts found no good camping place, so we were obliged to make a dry camp. We spent a worrying and sleepless night, much affected by the pitiful bawling of the cattle, tormented by thirst and hunger, and in the morning awoke to find forty head of them run off."*

* * *

"Ye unmitigated 'ald liar!" Patrick Martin roared. "We followed ye into this hell on your word, and now we have lost a fair portion of our herd? I demand satisfaction, 'an the right to thrash ye within' an inch of yer worthless pagan life . . ." The Irish came surging up to the surface in Patrick in such moments of sentiment, or anger, as he undoubtedly was at this moment. His son Dennis clung valiantly to one of his arms, and Old Martin Murphy to the other.

Isabella Patterson and John similarly penned in old Hitchcock, Isabella shouting fearlessly, "For pity's sake, have some sense! He's an old man, how dare you threaten so!"

Old Martin deftly held Patrick fast, his own Irish coming out at full strength. "Ach, Patrick, me old friend, ye know ye canna' do that, you'd break your knuckles on the auld bones of him, and then where would we be?"

"Liar!" screeched Old Man Hitchcock. "Liar, you call me a liar? Izzy, let go of me, I'll thrash this priest-ridden, bog-trotting Papist to here and Californy and back again, old man or no! I told ye fair I had never been along this path, but I was told it was no more than twenty-five mile! You know how hard it is to judge distance, out here! Yes, you've been misreading every distance since Fort Laramie. It's a plain wonder to me you can find your way out of your own outhouse, let alone your own way from the Mississippi to here!"

"Mr. Martin, Mr. Hitchcock, enough of this!" John roared. Rather to his chagrin no one appeared to pay the least bit of notice.

The other women and a scattering of children watched from the wagons or the campfires. There was a circle of angry men around Patrick Martin and Old Hitchcock. They had spent an unhappy night in a dry camp, rationing the water, and had awakened late to apparent disaster. Forty head of cattle represented most of the spare beasts, and unfortunately, two yoke of Patrick Martin's were among them.

With some effort, Patrick broke free of his son's grasp on his right arm and swung a great haymaker at Old Man Hitchcock, which would have very nearly broken the old mountain man's jaw had it connected true, but for

Hitchcock cannily bracing himself against John and Isabella and efficiently kicking Patrick Martin in the crotch.

Patrick doubled over on the ground, while Dennis cried out, "That was a dirty blow!"

Hitchcock snarled, "Sonny, there's no fair fightin'. Where I learned it, them as fights' fair is dead before the first winter. You'd best see to him, Doc, and leave go of my arm!"

"You all had enough?" Stephen's quiet voice cut across Patrick's half-stifled moans, Isabella's remonstrance with her father, and Dennis's loud indignation. John helped Patrick to a sitting position; he looked quite pale, as if he were about to heave up his breakfast. In back of Stephens, Greenwood slouched easily in the saddle of his paint pony, looking down on it all with amused exasperation.

"He gonna be all right, Doc?"

"Only his pride is hurt," John said, and Old Martin Murphy, forgetting Isabella's presence, added a ribald diagnosis of what also must be hurt as well and then lamented, "Och, I was forgetting your presence, Mrs. Patterson! Beggin' your pardon, I had no intention of offending your good self!"

"Men," retorted Isabella. "Sometimes I am driven to think you keep most of your brains there. No, I am not that much offended, Mr. Murphy."

"The boys and I went hunting for tracks," Old Greenwood drawled. "Them oxen of yours, they went all over the place . . . we found their tracks all right going in all directions back and ahead, but I saw something elst just as it started to get light."

"I want you all to see sompthin'," Stephens said, in his most laconic way. "All of you. Martin . . . can you walk?"

Patrick grunted, and John helped him to stand and walk after Stephens and Greenwood, a little away from the wagon circle to the top of a low rise of land. Down to the west of them, a steep walled dry gully cut across the land, the far side of it illuminated by the rising sun at their backs.

"Look yonder," Greenwood gestured towards the gully, and they did so, but there was nothing to be seen but the same thin scrub and hard-packed ground they had been traveling over for more than a day and a swath of pale dry gravel across the length of the gully, where water had once flowed. There was nothing different ahead of them than there was behind, save for the line of desert scrub broken by their wheels and wagon-beds, and trampled to the ground by the feet of their teams and the spare herd cattle. "D' y'see there?" Greenwood said, impatiently after a moment. "The bank of that gully, just there. Look familiar?"

"Ah," John said, as enlightenment dawned. There was a gap in the gully bank – obvious, now that it had been pointed out to him. The vertical bank of the gully had been dug away, and a sloping ramp cut into it, an opening precisely as wide as a wagon. It looked, too, as if there was another ramp on the near side, just opposite, where the desert brush grew low and sparse.

Old Martin Murphy gave a great shout of laughter, and slapped his knee with his hat. "Jesus, Mary and Joseph, Paddy, you owe the man an apology, look you there, plain as day! Indeed and there was a wagon brought this way, and more than one, looking at the trouble taken for it to cross . . . and how many creeks did we cross in just the same way?"

"It almost looks as if there is a track," Isabella offered, diffidently. "Where the plants were trampled and broken . . . they have grown back, but not to the same height and vigor as those nearby."

"Ten year, twelve year ago," Greenwood nodded. "Good eye, Mrs. Patterson. "There's your proof that Bonneville did come this way. Those would be the traces left of his wagons – things grow slow in the desert, and the marks stay for a while."

"We'll not need to break out the shovels and dig our own road over, at any rate," John said. "And that's proof to me that we are on the right trail."

"Aye," Patrick Martin assented handsomely, although he winced when he stood straight upright, and offered his hand to Hitchcock. "I spoke too hastily, and in anger. It does not get us back our cattle, though. What are we supposed to do about that, hey?"

"Get them back," Stephens answered. "Caleb says we're only half a day from the Green. We'll send a mounted party back from there."

"Just one thing," Patrick Martin said. "The next time we do this? Go taking unknown cut-offs into the desert? Cannot we send a long scouting party ahead, y'know, a quick look around, find where the water is, and how long we'll need to go for it?"

"Aye, that's a capital idea," Old Martin said, and around him there was a buzz of agreement.

Stephens shrugged and replied, "Cross that when we get to it."

* * *

From Dr. Townsend's diary: *"Arrived at the Green River about mid-day, to our very great relief. Captain Stephens immediately sent out six men led by Young Martin Murphy, who feared that the strays had gone back to the Sandy. Young Murphy sent three of the six to search the banks of the Green, and himself backtracked with Moses and Dennis Martin to search the vicinity of our previous camp on the Sandy. Whilst on this errand, they were forced to conceal themselves in a small defile from a war party of Sioux, which rode so close by their hiding place they could hear them talking to each other. . . .*

"Finding the missing cattle taking refuge in the meadows by the Sandy, they rounded them up without further adventure and retraced our path without any untoward incident. We plan today to move on towards Bear River, as soon as it is light . . ."

* * *

John re-inked his pen. He had been negligent with his diary in the last few days, what with the alarms attendant on venturing along an untested trail, the near-fisticuffs between Old Hitchcock and the hot-tempered Patrick Martin, Elizabeth's fears for her little brother, and trying to smooth the rough edges off Stephens' terse and abrupt manner. Really though, Stephens had been quite masterful when he showed them the place where Bonneville's wagons had gone, defusing a lot of doubt and anger at being led out into the desert on the thin say-so of two old men with their aging memories.

But now there was some kind of ruckus on the far side of camp; the Murphy women were suddenly snatching up smaller children and clambering into the wagons, and little Jimmy Murphy, the oldest of Young Martin's boys, came running from their campfire.

"Injuns!" he gasped, pale underneath his freckles. "Lots of them, coming up from the river! I saw 'em, they're all painted up, only men! Capn' Stephens and Old Greenwood say it's a war party!"

Elizabeth dropped the pan of dishes she held with a gasp and an almighty clatter of tin ware, and Sarah caught her hands. The two women clung to each other.

Allen cursed a mighty oath and roared at them, "Get in the wagon!" as he caught up his shotgun.

John hurriedly corked his precious bottle of ink as Moses tossed him his own rifle and took up the other. Yes, there were Indians coming up from the river bank, a lot of them and well-mounted, the sun brave on their feathers and painted skins, and the restless movements of their ponies. Well short of the wagons the main body of them stopped, and three men on foot came out from among them, walking slowly in advance of the main group. When the three on foot reached a point midway between the war party and the wagons, they hunkered down on their heels, and looked towards the camp, obviously waiting for some kind of response.

At the Patterson campfire, Isabella had conjured up the old dragoon pistol from wherever she kept it, and Eddie, Nancy and Sadie clustered behind her like bantam chicks taking shelter behind their tiny but fiercely protective mother. Oliver and Samuel had rifles too, and Old Hitchcock knelt just behind them, an oddly calm and steadying presence, with a hand on each of their shoulders.

John looked around the camp, all the normal bustle of eating breakfast and breaking camp for the days' journey entirely ceased, and a bristle of rifle barrels sprouting from behind every solid bit of cover. John spared a glance at young Moses, and thought with a sense of shock how resolute the boy looked. No, he was not a boy, John realized ruefully; Mose had been doing a man's work all these months on the trail.

Here came Stephens, pacing along, elaborately unhurried and empty-handed with Dog loping at his heels, pausing to say something to Isabella and Old Hitchcock, something reassuring, to judge from the way they seemed to relax in some indefinable way. Old Hitchcock said something to the boys and Isabella and followed after Stephens.

"They've sent three unarmed men out to parlay," Stephens said quietly when he came up to John, Moses, and Allen. "I judge we are in no danger. Caleb thinks they are Snakes, or Shoshone, maybe. He guesses they are hunting the Sioux party that Young Murphy and your lad spotted yesterday. I am taking Caleb and Hitchcock to smoke tobaccy and see what's going on."

"You are risking too much for us," John said.

Stephens grinned, a flash of teeth in his sunburnt face, "I'm as fond of my scalp as you."

"And we have more guns," Old Hitchcock pointed out, equably. "A lot o' firepower pointed in the right direction does tend to make negotiations fairly honorable, Doc."

John drew in a deep breath, for the first time realizing that he had been all but holding it, and Moses said sturdily, "We'll cover you, Cap'n Stephens."

"'Preciate it," Stephens said, his tone as dry as dust.

All around the circle of wagons, little knots of men and boys, and a few women also, knelt or crouched behind sparse cover of wagon wheels or piles of harness. A tiny movement in the lee of a clump of desert brush flanking the wagon circle caught John's eye. His heart sank momentarily, before he recognized the Greenwood boys, nearly invisible in their dust-colored buckskin. Britt looked back at him, and made a brief gesture of acknowledgement. There was a rustle of skirts at his back, and Elizabeth was there, pale but resolute, with another rifle in her hand, and a bullet-pouch and powder-flask over her shoulder.

"I'll reload for you both if it need be," she said firmly. "Isabella showed me how."

"Brave Liz," John said. The bullet-pouch rattled a little in her shaking hands. "I don't think it will come to that, they have sent three men out to parley with Captain Stephens."

Now Stephens and the two old mountain men were walking out from the camp, empty hands held clearly at their sides. Dog shadowed her master, until he made a quick gesture and she sat down, just outside the wagon circle, watching alertly. When they reached the three Indians, Stephens, Greenwood, and Hitchcock also hunkered down on their heels; they seemed to be conversing, partly in words, and partly in sweeping gestures and hand movements.

Now Greenwood gestured in response. Slow minutes ticked by, nearly every eye focused on the little parlay party, but when Stephens stood up, and the Indians did likewise, John was aware that the tension had suddenly seeped away. Stephens walked back to the wagon circle in the same unhurried way he had walked away from it, but he walked loose-limbed and relaxed. The two old men also walked casually.

As soon as they were within earshot, Stephens called, "Rest easy; we were right. They're after the Sioux war party. They want no fight with us, just curious is all."

"They're going to be right neighborly, too," Greenwood said. "And help us swim the stock over the river."

"Do you trust them?" John asked warily, as Stephens strode on towards the Murphy's wagons.

"Well, today I do," Greenwood answered. "Might be a different story tomorrow though. I guess for today they hate the Sioux more than they like the look of our plunder. I also think they'd like to see us moving along and out of their range." He moved on after Stephens, passing the good word to the others.

"Then we should finishing packing." said Elizabeth firmly, and she took the rifle out of John's hands and stepped up onto the wagon wheel to slot them both into their places under the seat. "Don't stand there like a goose, Moses, go help Francis finish harnessing the teams."

"I think you'd best keep it for the time being," John said, as Moses made to hand his rifle up to his sister. "We don't want to look warlike . . . but we don't want to look like fools, either. Brave Liz – that was well done, volunteering to load for us."

"I have come a long way, Dearest," Elizabeth said.

John answered, "So have we all."

Elizabeth hopped down from the wheel, as spry as a girl, and went on tiptoes to kiss his cheek. "But I have come farther," she said simply, and John caught her hands and looked at her, seeing her with new eyes; the color in her face, a little darkened by sun, and her hair jammed up any old way under a man's hat secured with a scarf tied under her chin. Her fingers were callused and coarsened by work and by Beau's reins, and she was wearing the same faded travel dress and a shapeless coat over it that she had worn for the last week, and John's memory went piercingly back to the invalid she had been eight months ago, gasping for breath under the camphor blanket on the morning that he had decided on this venture.

"That you have, Dearest, that you have."

Chapter 7 – *Continental Divide*

From Dr. Townsend's diary: *"Sixteenth of August, 1844: Fort Hall, upon the Oregon Trail. We depart upon the morrow from here and within a few days turn southwards and aside from the established road. The Oregon company has caught up to us whilst we were encamped here. Mr. Case and the others who had accompanied us since Fort Laramie upon the Sweetwater remain wholly resolved upon Oregon, and part with many expressions of sorrow and the most sincere good wishes for our successful translation to California.*

"Captain Grant, the factor of the establishment of Fort Hall has given us information concerning a party and the trail that we are resolved to embark upon; to whit – A small company guided by an old comrade of Mr. Hitchcock's named Jos. Walker and captained by a Mr. Chiles departed intent on California at about this time last year. Capt. Grant has no intelligence upon the happy conclusion of their journey, save only that their wagons had planned to depart from the trail at the Raft River crossing and strike out into the desert, following the route of Mary's River into the desert sink, and to essay a crossing of the mountain barrier beyond. Aside from that, we know as little as we did three months ago.

"Some of our party, fearing their supplies may run short, were desirous of replenishing them here, but were utterly dismayed at the cost of doing so; flour at one dollar a pound, et cetera. We were able to trade for a little stock of dried meat, and consider that our spare oxen constitute a food reserve sufficient for our needs. Captain Stephens has required of me to compile a complete listing of our party, with their condition and property, a copy of which being left with Captain Grant against some kind of dreadful misfortune falling upon us. The greater portion being of the Murphy family or connections thereof, I begin with them:

"Martin Murphy, senior; widower and farmer by trade, accompanied by those of his family yet unmarried: Daniel, Bernard, Helen, and Johnny. and a hired man, Edmund Bray."

John had come to like the Murphy paterfamilias; prosperity and material success had not dulled the sharp ambitious edge that the old man must have had in him, since migrating from his poor, green island so many years ago. And Old Martin was shrewd enough about his own limits, unlike many a self-made man. He placed much the same degree of confidence in Stephens that John himself did. John had treated him for a touch of bursitis – aside from some rheumatism in his hands, which did not prevent him from playing the penny-whistle for the amusement of his grandchildren – he was as fit as any of his sons. Johnny, the youngest of them, had been ill for many days as they had traveled along the Loup River, from the same fever that killed Vance, but he had since recovered his youthful energy and vigor.

"Martin Murphy, Junior, a farmer by trade; with him his wife Mary and four sons, aged from twelve to three years: James, Martin, Patrick, and Bernard, and a hired man, Vincent Calvin. Mrs. Murphy is in a delicate condition, expecting to be delivered of another child approximate to our arrival in California."

"I am praying to the Blessed Virgin that this one is a girl!" Mary-Bee Murphy had told him, laughing ruefully, as she rested her hands on her pregnant belly. "Another boy like the rest would have me tearing out my hair. I'd never survive running after five of them all the day, truly I wouldn't."

"James Murphy, likewise a farmer by trade, wife Annie, daughter Mary, hired man, Matthew Harbin."

John had made a physic for Matthew Harbin's piles, and had treated him for a long graze across his arm which had gone septic with mustard poultices, and been called to attend little Mary, usually by Jamie who doted on his only child.

"James Miller, a carpenter by trade, wife Mary (daughter to Martin Murphy, Senior), son William, daughters Frances, Teresa, and Ellen; the youngest being an infant of ten weeks and delivered whilst on this journey."

John smiled to think of tiny Ellen Independence, and Mary Miller's exhausted but triumphant face. Like her father, like the other Murphys, they had some small prosperity on this earth, but counted a larger part of their riches in their children. Besides attending that birth, John had also doctored James' left hand; back on the Elkhorn crossing, as they were disassembling wagons for their makeshift ferry, James had broken two fingers, caught between a wheel and the axle.

"Patrick Martin, farmer, a widower with two grown sons, Dennis and Patrick." That very day, Patrick had gotten into a long-anticipated fight with one of the factor's men; leave it to him to find the only Englishmen within a thousand square miles and get into a fight with one of them straightaway. He had come to John to be treated for split knuckles on his right hand.

"Broke it on the jaw of an arrogant Englishman, so I did!" he had announced triumphantly. John reckoned they would be fortunate to leave Fort Hall without Patrick getting into any more fights with the Englishmen there.

"John Sullivan, farmer, with his grown sister Mary, and two younger brothers, Michael and Robert, aged about eleven and fourteen."

The Sullivans were a distant family connection to the Murphys: In his early twenties, John Sullivan seemed oddly older, a sober and responsible youth, having the charge of his orphaned younger brothers, and vexed by the flirtatious ways of his sister, who along with Helen Murphy were the only two marriageable girls in the party, and consequently much admired by the younger unmarried men. Mary Sullivan had gone to Isabella for some unspecified female ailment: it probably wasn't serious, for Isabella would have consulted with John if it was, instead of just mentioning it to him, but the poor girl blushed as red as a beet when John asked after her health offhandedly.

Robert had fallen, climbing down from their moving wagon, early on, and broken his collar-bone and his younger brother had gouged his hand on a sharp branch, while gathering firewood. Their stores of supplies were the lowest of all in the party, a matter of guarded concern for Martin Murphy, who had taken his worries to John when there was nothing at Fort Hall in the way of supplies.

"Allen Montgomery, a gunsmith by trade, wife Sarah."

Funny, that John Sullivan could appear to be grave, sober, and reliable while barely twenty, and Allen — his senior in years — conducted himself generally as a careless and irresponsible youth. As for the Montgomerys' health, Sarah had burned her hands several times on hot kettles over the cook fire, and once had asked after a physic that would make her courses more regular, and then hastily said, no, there was nothing the matter, when he had asked with concern if she had been very much delayed in them. "No, only a few days."

"Mrs. Samuel Patterson, with children Oliver, Samuel, Johnnie, Nancy, Edward, and Sarah, aged from seventeen to three years of age."

Aside from young Eddie's continuing adventures, to which he had added being roundly sick from drinking too much water from Soda Spring, the Pattersons otherwise had little need of John's doctoring, Isabella being a fair hand at that herself, with her box of medicinal salts and herbs. In the early days on the trail, Oliver's shoes had raised great blisters on his heels, which had become infected, and Sadie had been bitten on the wrist by some kind of insect that raised a great red welt.

Otherwise, Isabella and the older boys managed the days of travel very well. John did fear that the Pattersons, like the Sullivans, might run low on supplies if the journey lasted much longer than another three or four months. Watching Oliver, Samuel, and John wolf down their evening meals, John wondered nightly if Isabella underestimated the ravenous appetites of three boys who were doing men's work.

"Elisha Stephens, blacksmith and elected captain. Hired man, John Flomboy."

Flomboy drove Stephen's team, while Stephens himself ranged on horseback with the advance party. John had not been called to treat either of them for illness or injury, although Dog once had torn the pads of her right forepaw on a sharp rock, and left a long trail of bloody footprints in the dust behind Stephens' wagon, until Oliver Patterson, driving just behind, took notice and called for John. John inked his pen, and wrote carefully; *"I am proud to call him my friend, and can think of no one better fitted to lead us unto the wilderness, even with his distinct oddities of character."*

"Joseph Foster, farmer and wheelwright by trade, hired man, Oliver Magnent."

Joseph Foster, still chipper and cheery, trying his luck with his fishing pole, every river they came to. His hired man, Oliver Magnent, was another French-Canadian like John's driver, Francis Deland.

"John Townsend, doctor of medicine, wife Elizabeth and brother-in-law, Moses Schallenberger, with hired man, Francis Deland."

John considered his list again; he must finish it soon and the copy for the factor as well. The sound of a fiddle came from across the campsite; so many wagons drawn up here it seemed like a town. It would be the last of any sort of settlement they would see until they got over the mountains into California. Lanterns and campfires burned yellow, gold, primrose in the twilight, and voices, the clatter of supper clean-up, the noises that cattle and horses made as they bedded down for the night, all of this floated on the evening air.

Women's voices, the laughter of children, and Old Martin's penny-whistle and Elizabeth, all verve and drama, reading *Pilgrim's Progress* to

Eddie and Sadie, over at the Patterson's campfire, all of them floated on the night as well, the complicated symphony of the trail, and John set his pen to paper again.

Elizabeth continued to be well, riding Beau, or leading him and walking with the women and children, as if all the summer agues, all the nights of struggling for breath, the days when she was prostrated with headaches, had been but a series of vile dreams. It pleased him also that Moses spent rather more time with Young Martin, John Sullivan, and with Dennis Martin, better models for Moses and the Patterson boys of what a man ought to be than Allen Montgomery.

"The above listed all are wagon owners: we are accompanied also by Isaac Hitchcock, trader and trapper, and Caleb Greenwood, trail guide by profession, with sons John and Brittain."

Old Hitchcock's two mules with their packs held all of what the old trader needed, although John rather thought that some of his heavier possessions and stores must be in the Patterson wagon. As for Hitchcock's health, he complained of rheumatism, only to be expected in a man of his years, but little else. Caleb Greenwood did not even complain of that, but it was clear to John that the cataracts in Greenwood's left eye would cost him vision there within a few more years. He and his sons also lived out of their small pack train and from hunting; John often wondered how fast they would have been able to travel were it not for the wagons.

"So this being an accounting of the company in which we now travel, much reduced in numbers after three months of experience, but each of us now having a fair sense of each other's qualities and capabilities. We are risking much in this journey, but I cannot think of better company in which to venture forward."

"Nineteenth of August, 1844, at the crossing of the Raft River . . . Cannot imagine anyone having to use a raft to cross a bare trickle such as this! Captain Stephens has ridden ahead a little, with the Greenwood boys. He thinks to have espied the trail of last year's party, as it stands out best at a distance, going over the next rise of land; with little rain falling throughout the year, the wheel ruts remain clear in sand as in dried mud, as well their passage is marked in broken sage, and the clear places where campfires burned. This morning, we have finally turned aside from the trail, following a little stream into a broad and well-grassed valley. Old Hitchcock tells me this is called Kassia, or Cassia Creek. Grass is plentiful along the streams, which

*are small but providential, but the uplands all around are burnt and dry,
supporting only sparse sage and a species of cacti . . . passing a great bowl-
like valley studded with rock outcroppings like candied fruit . . . the heat is
unrelenting, and the dust boils up from our passage describing a pillar like
that which led the Hebrews out of Egypt and into the Promised Land."*

* * *

Day followed weary day, plagued by dust, a fine powdery grit and
baked by the sun, with never a pitying cloud in the sky. When the wind blew,
the dust was everywhere and in everything, caking on sweaty faces and limbs
like some itchy and dun-colored mask. The women despaired of keeping it out
of their hair, or from penetrating the bedding: the dust was everywhere, and
inescapable. Allen Montgomery swore he even felt it gritting in his teeth in
every mouthful of bread that he ate.

They seemed to crawl, like ants over an endless and featureless platter.
There were no landmarks to catch the eye once they had left the spires of rock
at the tangled tributaries of the Raft River, nothing to see and mark their
progress by, only an endless succession of low ridges and dales, like an ocean
in a flat calm, sparsely covered with sun-burnt grass and the endless and
eternal sagebrush. Only along the creek banks was there anything green to
refresh the eye, or taller than a man to cast a comforting shade.

"I don't know which is more of a plague," John remarked one day
during the noontime rest. "The dust or those poor damned Digger Indians."

He and Stephens, with Greenwood and Old Murphy, were resting in the
shade under a length of canvas rigged between the side of John's wagon and a
pair of cottonwood poles, and keeping a watchful eye on a pair of nearly
naked Indians going around to the other wagons begging. Most of the other
families had set up something of the sort for a bit of shade by their wagons.
They had taken to nooning in the hottest part of the day, while the sun was
directly overhead. While they watched, one of the Diggers suddenly ducked
and scooped up something from the ground, and ate it, with apparent relish.

"Lizard, mebbe . . . or a cricket. It's a delicacy, round these parts,"
Greenwood explained, and Old Martin said, "Jay-sus, Mary and Joseph, that's
something pathetic."

"They ain't Sioux," Stephens remarked.

"And that's the plain truth," Old Martin said. "The Sioux are gentry;
these are tinkers, picking over the rags. 'Twould be an honor to be killed by

the Sioux, I'm thinking, but a right embarrassment to be killed by one of this poor lot. At least the Sioux are clean."

"We're not exactly fragrant ourselves of late," John pointed out, and Stephens cracked a brief smile. "How dangerous are Diggers?"

"Not very," Greenwood admitted. "More given to thieving, here and there."

"Naught too hot, or too heavy, eh?" Old Martin said humorously. "Still and all, I wouldn't want them as enemies, not if there's a grudge in their black little hearts and a sharp blade in their hand. Our cattle . . . saints preserve, what is he doing?"

John Greenwood suddenly appeared purposely around the corner of Sullivan's wagon with a quirt in his hand, where the ragged pair of Indians importuned Mary Sullivan and the boys for something more to eat. They could not hear what John Greenwood was saying to them, but his voice sounded angry, and when he struck out with the quirt, the smack it made on the Indian's bare shoulders sounded harsh in the desert silence.

"There's no call for that," exclaimed Old Murphy in shocked disapproval. Old Greenwood was already up and halfway to the Sullivan's. "They're only begging, the poor tinkers. Caleb had best rein in that boy of his before he brings down trouble on the lot of us."

"He's a hothead," Stephens agreed, watching Old Greenwood and his son alertly. "Half-Crow hisself. The only reason the Crows ain't at war with the Diggers is they ain't gotten to it yet."

"Give them time," John said. "And let us be out of the way first."

"We'll have to keep an eye on him." Old Martin sighed." I'll tell my boys, quiet-like."

"Anyone else liable to borrow trouble?" Stephens asked thoughtfully. "Montgomery? Any of the young bucks?"

John shook his head. "None of them seems to hate Diggers the way the Greenwood boys do."

"I'd tell Greenwood to keep his lads on a short lead." Old Martin advised, and he did, but when trouble came of the young men of the party and the Indians, it was not provoked by the Greenwoods.

Were it not for the necessity of keeping track of it for his diary John might have lost all count of days, as they followed Mary's River farther and farther into the desert. They had no need of the faint traces left by Chiles' wagons the year before; the river itself, shallow, sluggish, and a slash of green across the desert was their road and guide.

At night the stars hung low and brilliant, as thick in the velvet dark sky as dust motes in a sunbeam, until the moon floated free of the horizon, waxing and waning and waxing again. But among the constellations of early morning, the hunter Orion swung farther and farther up into the sky, a harbinger of autumn and winter to follow. One morning, as they were saddling their horses for the day's march, John saw that Stephens was looking at the stars too, standing there holding his horse's bridle, with patient Dog at his feet.

"What date are we at, Doc?"

"The last week of September," John answered. Stephens didn't say anything else, but John wondered if he also thought of the snow-topped mountains off in the distance as they had crossed the great divide at the height of summer.

That very day for the first time, John thought he could see a faint dark blue outline on the edge of the sky ahead, just where it met the farthest dun-colored fold of desert, but the dust of the day came up and masked it all and he thought he had been misled by a mirage, shimmering and elusive like a pool of mercury, until the sun set. Clear against the orange-gold sun was a distant jagged outline.

"The mountains," said Old Man Hitchcock that evening, with immense satisfaction. He lit his pipe from a twig thrust into the embers of their shared campfire. They had taken to building them from sage, hacked out of the low desert bushes and piled up in a shallow pit. It burned down to an aromatic steady fire, much more satisfactory than the buffalo chips they had to burn back on the Platte. John and his family and Sarah and Allen Montgomery had lately begun to share a campfire with the Pattersons, as it tripled the quantity of sagebrush cut for the one fire. Supper was over, and the few dishes scoured with handfuls of sand, and washed at the water's edge. The day's heat fled with the sun.

John stretched out his hands to the fire gratefully and asked, "How far away are they?"

"No idea. I've heard a hunnert miles from the Sink, an' I've heard fifty – and there's still a mite 'o current to the river, so we ain't at the Sink yet."

"What is the sink?" Elizabeth asked curiously.

"Ma'am, it's a great flat place in the middle of the desert, where this here river spreads out into a marsh and just flat-out sinks into the sand and vanishes."

"How peculiar," Elizabeth remarked. "To think of it ending, just like that, when we have been following it for such a long time. Were not we always taught that a river should empty into an ocean? Water flowed naturally from the highlands down to the sea. This all seems quite odd. So, you and Mr. Greenwood are convinced there is a river coming down from these mountains, into this . . . sink, as you call it?"

"That's it in a nutshell, ma'am." Hitchcock puffed away, while Isabella, mending a tear in a pair of Eddie's trousers, rolled her eyes and muttered under her breath, "Old fool. You've never seen it, but you know it must be there."

"Ahh, Izzy, Izzy, Izzy – blessed are those who do not see and yet believe. 'Tis one of those great truths, which I have yet to see disproved. It rains in mountains; in the winter it snows, and when all that snow melts, the water runs down out of those mountains. Wherever there are mountains in this great western desert, there are rivers of water coming out of them – where the water comes down, that's where men can climb up into the mountains and mebbe cross over them."

"But you do not know exactly where this river might be?" Elizabeth ventured, and Old Hitchcock puffed on his pipe and replied, "We can make us an eddicated guess, ma'am."

Isabella snorted in derision. "Educated fiddlesticks!"

"But what are we going to do when we get to this sink where the river ends?" Elizabeth asked.

"We'll camp for a couple days, rest the cattle," Hitchcock said. "I reckon Cap'n Stephens will send out a couple scouts, see if we can track them wagons from last year. Mebbe they found the way over the mountains, mebbe not. Make a couple of casts north and south to look for that river . . . we have time."

But not terribly much of it, John thought, remembering Orion swinging up in the star-field every morning.

In another couple of days the river ceased to resemble a river at all and became more of a marsh, with great swales of green rushes, the haunt of water-fowl, fringed with mud and alkali ponds, alive with deer and antelope. Stephens and the two old men consulted and led the wagons around to a fair stretch of meadow on slightly higher ground.

"We'll stay here a while, rest the teams and do some hunting," Stephens said to the scouting party — John, Coung Martin Murphy, and the Greenwoods. They could see the mountains clearly now, a haunting blue shadow, clearest at dawn and again at sunset.

"I swear the teams are in prime condition," Young Martin said. "They're fitter now than when we left Missouri." Just then, Dog suddenly barked, a sound more like a deep and startling baying, and launched herself fruitlessly after a flock of ducks at the water's edge. They rose from the water in a storm of agitated wings as Dog plunged after them. Stephens whistled, and she returned instantly, wet and baffled.

"Not unless you grown wings, girl."

Behind them on the meadow, the wagons deployed for the night camp, so practiced were the drivers by now that it all seemed like some vast clockwork. The smaller children and the women had already been gathering firewood, collecting promising sticks of dried wood as they walked.

"I wish't we hadn't lost those three to the alkali," Stephens said.

Two of the Murphy's stock and Isabella's lead ox, Socks, had drunk from a pool of tainted water and died of it. The children wept for Socks, so tame that he had followed Oliver trustingly into the river on that first day when they had swum the oxen over the river and commenced this journey. Isabella might have wept a little too, but then she had put her cherished milk-cow in harness to replace Socks.

"Or the pony that John Greenwood said the Indians stole," Young Martin added.

"John Greenwood is always ready to blame the Indians for any loss . . . real or imagined." John said. Left to him, and if he did not respect Old Greenwood so much, he'd have gagged and bound the younger man and carried him all this way in one of the wagons. Of late, the Indians had been a different sort, rather less wretched and rather more dressed than before. Paiute, said Old Greenwood, with a little more of a fight in them than the Diggers formerly. And Hitchcock had dryly commented that with the fight they had to get any sort of living out of the desert, no wonder they had no energy left for anything more.

And John looked at the distant mountains, in all their sunset glory and visibility, and thought of how close they were to that goal. Just the mountains, just the mountains and over them before the winter snow; just that little bit farther. He would have a grand house for Elizabeth; she would be healthy and fit for the rest of her life, and play the piano again. He would school Moses with his fine library, instead of living this vagabond life in a wagon, camping in the wilderness, like a bunch of old Martin's tinker gypsies.

Stephens held council in the morning, as girls and women carried baskets of laundry to the water's edge, and cattle stood near to their shoulders in grass. "Two long scouts. We cast north and south of here for Chiles's tracks," he said. "Three to four in each. Greenwood takes the north; I'll take the south, but not more than a day."

"Fat hunting country," Hitchcock remarked. "Keep the young bucks busy."

"So that's the plan, then?" Old Martin ventured. "We rest and restock, and mend the wagons here for the last push?" Stephens nodded. "Ah, then 'tis a fair place . . . a little short on good timber though. And if you do not find their trail, or that grand river of yours, then what do we do then, hey?"

"Cross that bridge when we get to it." Stephens abruptly stood up. "Who's with me, and who's with Greenwood?"

John volunteered to ride south with Stephens, and Allen Montgomery, and Patrick Martin and Dennis went for the north with the Greenwoods; a hard days ride in the saddle either way of it, casting west and south into the dry desert which lay between the sink and the mountains. They found the traces almost at once, but Chiles' party looked to have gone south. They followed it as far as they dared until early afternoon, when Stephens reined in his horse at the top of a rise, from which they could see the faint tracks scribbled over the next rise, and the one beyond that.

"I don't think those boys knew any more'n we do," he said. "We'll head on back, see what Greenwood found."

When they returned to camp Greenwood had not returned; fortunate in a way because it meant that his sons were not there to make a bad situation worse.

Old Martin met them with a grave face. "Doctor, there's been some trouble with your lad, you'd best come quick."

"What kind of trouble? How badly is Mose hurt? Is Liz with him?" John's heart sank within him clear down to his dusty boots, and Old Martin said quickly, "No, not that kind of trouble . . . he caught one of those pesky tinkers stealing away his halter."

Old Martin led him rapidly toward a knot of men, Murphy's sons and the Sullivan boys, and a handful of Indians gathered around Old Man Hitchcock. Hitchcock was in full hand-talking spiel, gesturing and making signs with his fingers; it looked as if he needed no help. John didn't see Moses at first, off to one side with Young Martin.

Moses looked angry and aggrieved. John thought instantly of a guilty boy caught in some mischief; Young Martin just looked angry, pale with it and lecturing Moses in a furious undertone. Old Martin continued, "You know that fine one of his, braided out of colored rope . . . he missed it, and looking around, spotted one of those Indians, wearing a fine blanket trimmed all over with bird feathers it was, but the halter hanging down beneath it as fine as you please, and with all his friends around. And your boy grabbed it back, and the Indian was angry then, he drew up his bow and nocked an arrow, and all his friend did the same, and your fine lad took up his rifle and pointed it at him."

"Oh, god, no!" Johns' blood ran cold at the thought of what shooting one of the Indians might bring down on Moses and the rest of them.

Old Martin patted his shoulder. "No, Martin struck up his rifle and took your lad aside, and Hitchcock came and began to talk sense before everyone got offended . . . well, offended very much more, as I judge. Isaac had to talk very fast, and for a good while, but I think he has got them all properly soothed . . . but you'd best talk to the lad."

"Doctor John!" Moses cried as soon as John came up to them. "Tell them that thieving wretch tried to steal away my own property, and I caught him fair and square! Are we to continue submitting meekly to these insults?"

"Yes," Young Martin replied bluntly, before John could even begin to formulate a reply.

Old Martin stepped in front of Moses and regarded him compassionately. "Yes, my lad, you should. That's the short answer, and this is the longer one, and why 'tis necessary. Better men than you have taken worse insult . . . better men than you have been turned out in the road by the landlords, and seen their sisters and wives treated like common whores, and had to learn their letters in the hedges and leave the land that their ancestors bled for, generation after generation. And they endured it, because to strike back would have cost their lives, and all of those lives they held dearest. So, you had a small thing taken from you, and yes, it was stolen, we are clear on that, and you've a right to be angry – but lad, ye canna let the anger lead you to act rashly! There are many of them, and poor ragged savages they might be, but they are here, the Lord Himself only knows how many, w'their bows and arrows, and knives, and we are just a bare handful passing through!"

Old Martin had the gift, John thought, of weaving spells with his voice, as if he had only to talk and talk in that gruff but musical Irish voice to compel agreement and obedience, and Moses already looked a little less angry. Old Martin continued, "If you and John Greenwood want to start a war with them over trifles, I'd say 'Be my guest', have it. Have as many as you like if it just fell on your own heads, but this is my sons and daughters and the children in the way of it, an' that is where I say, we canna risk provoking them!"

"They are stealing from us, night and day, and anything that isn't nailed down," Moses protested. "I'm sick of it, and sick of having them take advantage . . ."

"Moses, that's enough," John kept his voice low, although he wanted to shout. "Be silent. You could have set off a massacre of all of us, with your temper and thoughtlessness!"

Old Martin shook his head, pityingly. "Lad, lad, be listening to me. Don't be thinking of it as stealing, if you like. Think of it as us paying a toll, to pass through their lands, only instead of coming to us fair and open with their hand out, asking for the price of it, they amuse themselves by collecting it piecemeal. What have we lost, now, really? Some few clothes, and a couple of blankets, and some bits of bread and meat, and maybe that pony, but myself I think the wretched beast just strayed. We can afford to hand them those trifles. After all, they might have come to us and asked for an ox an' that we couldn't do."

"They could help themselves to the oxen any time they wished," John pointed out. "We guard them as best we can, but if they wished, I am sure the Indians could bleed us dry. You may like to think we are kept safe by our own efforts, but we are also secure because to this point I do not think they feel any great urge to harm us."

"We must not give them any reason to wish us ill," Old Martin added. "D'ye understand now, lad?"

Moses nodded grudgingly, but with a stormy face. "I understand, but I do not like it at all, Mr. Murphy!"

"Aye well, lad – we're not asking you to like it," Old Martin said, clapping him on the shoulder. "Just to keep your temper and put up with it for a little longer." He stumped away, and Moses looked at the ground, and then at John.

"You're angry, Doctor John, like Martin was. I am sorry; I did not think it through."

"At least Young Martin did," John said gravely. "And you must remember our situation also, and think carefully before you act. What you do may affect more than just yourself, for as long as we are part of this company."

"I will remember next time," Moses promised.

"You must, Moses lad, you must. We have get to get out of this desert, and over those mountains."

"I'll do better, Doctor John, I promise I will do my part."

"We shall all have to do that," John said with a sigh, and his eyes sought the thin blue lines of the mountains once more.

Chapter 8 – *Humboldt Sink*

From Dr. Townsend's diary: *"Third of October, 1844, encamped in the desert sinks by Mary's River, in considerable perturbation about the direction of our continued journey. We are resting ourselves and our animals, repairing the wagons and re-provisioning ourselves, whilst some of us explore nearby. This morning came to our camp by chance, an old Indian . . ."*

Towards dawn, a mist rose up from the marshes, burning off as the sun rose iridescent and pearly, among the voices of waterfowl and frogs, and now the rattle of iron skillets and spoons over the fires, fires that in the pallid early morning light, burned with a pale primrose flame. John leaned back in his accustomed seat, resting his back against a wagon wheel, and reflected on how the hardships of this journey made one so appreciative of small innocent pleasures like a cup of good coffee and hot bread baked over a fire.

"The Lord save us all – just like clockworks," Sarah remarked, in resigned exasperation. "Here's another one of them. We might as well set another plate every day!"

"What? Oh, an Indian." Elizabeth straightened from bending over the Dutch oven, and John glanced down, reassuring himself that he had set his rifle within close reach, leaning against the wheel and easy to hand. "Sarah, my dear, I do not think he is a beggar . . . look, he just walked by Murphy's campfire."

"No, you are right, he doesn't look as if he wants a handout," John agreed.

The Indian appeared to be immensely aged, although that might have been due to the hardships of life, without a spare ounce of flesh on him. He was all but naked, seamed and scarred and burnt brown, but bore himself with enormous dignity and assurance; he was, John felt instantly, a person of consequence.

The old Indian strolled with leisurely purpose through the camp, observing it all with mild interest, as if he were paying a formal call on new neighbors. He also carried no weapons other than a short knife and a small bundle slung over his shoulder. John blinked in sudden astonishment, as the Indian passed by their campfire and their eyes met; did the old man nod his head to him, as a white man would in passing by a slight acquaintance on the street? No, the old man was not a supplicant. They watched him walk by the Patterson's wagon. By this time every eye in camp was on him, and it was clear where he was going.

Greenwood and his sons had built a small campfire just beyond; Old Hitchcock commonly joined them in the mornings. It seemed like some kind of signal passed among the three old men; Greenwood, Hitchcock, and the mysteriously confident old Indian. As John watched, Old Hitchcock creakily stood up and unrolled a blanket, spreading it flat upon the ground with the hospitable gesture of a grand host inviting an esteemed visitor into the parlor. The old Indian settled onto it unhurriedly, cross-legged on the ground. Old Hitchcock sat and Greenwood too, after gesturing to Britt.

Britt left off saddling his pony, and came to the Townsend's fire. "Pa, he says for you to come. Bring some bread. Enough for five. The Old One is a chief, he thinks. I am fetching the Captain, Pa says for him to be there as well."

John wiped his mouth – any man alive could have told the old Indian was a leader of no small consequence, just from his very bearing and assurance. Elizabeth handed him the bread, five slices wrapped in a clean towel on a tin plate, and he joined the three old men, sitting on the blanket, in the pearly light of a desert sunrise. Stephens also arrived, carrying a couple of tin camp mugs into which Greenwood poured coffee, and passed a mug to their visitor. He tasted it, and could not entirely hide a dislike of it. John, in obedience to Old Greenwood's nod, handed out a piece of Sarah's good camp-bread to all of them, and the old Indian ate more than just a courtesy bite. He ate with evident good enjoyment, and they ate of their own, while John and Stephens followed Hitchcock and Greenwood's cue and waited with as much tranquility as they could pretend to.

Hitchcock and Greenwood were much better at this than the younger men. It seemed as if there was all the time in the world to get to the purpose of this, the purpose for which all their lives hung in a balance. And to John, watching intently, it seemed that he could see and understand the gestures and expressions as plainly as if they were written in one of the books in his small library.

The old Indian finished his morsel of bread, seeming to relish it, and made a sweeping gesture, encompassing the whole camp, the wagons and the penned horses, the campfires with the women and children gathered around them.

Who are you, what are you doing here? What is it that you want?

Old Hitchcock made a walking gesture with his fingers, and pointed at the distant mountains; in a way, John realized, he was as good with his hands as Old Martin was with his voice, a master musician, conveying acres of meaning with a minimum of voice and motion.

We are here, and just traveling through, we want to go over there, but –

He watched as if mesmerized, and the old Indian did also, eyes opaque with mild puzzlement as Old Hitchcock gathered up a double handful of sand, and then another, pouring it out onto the middle of the blanket between them. He flattened the mound of sand, and in part of it, traced the outline of the river and the marsh. He stood a few blades of green grass in it, to indicate the marsh itself.

"Your canteen, Caleb," he asked. When Greenwood silently handed it to him, he uncorked it and poured a little dribble of water to indicate the river, and a pool of it for the marsh. Looking at the Indian's face, Hitchcock pointed at his little model, and made another of those sweeping gestures; the camp, the marsh, and the river to the east.

Here . . . this is the place were we are.

The old Indian nodded gravely.

I understand.

Then Hitchcock took another double handful of sand, but instead of pouring it out all at once in a heap, he dribbled it in a long narrow line to one side of the sand model of the sink marshes. He modeled it into a series of mounds, a mountain range in miniature, took up another handful and did the same again. He passed his hand over the little peaks of sand, and pointed at the far distant blue range to the west, then made that walking-fingers gesture, along the near side of his modeled range.

These are the mountains. We want to cross over them, but there is no path.

Comprehension bloomed, and John thought the old Indian might have come close to smiling. He looked at the sand ranges, thoughtfully, then reached out with one hand, and flattened the middle. He carefully re-molded the sand peaks, with a gap between them, and took Greenwood's canteen, just as Hitchcock had done, and traced a little dribble of water running through it.

Then he poured a few drops in the middle of the space between the sand range and the marsh, re-corked the bottle and levelly met their gaze.

There is a river in the mountains. There. And a spring in the desert, half-way there.

Hitchcock pointed at the sun, and traced its path across the sky, and then moved his hand from the damp patch of sand indicating the marsh, to the little sand range.

How many days?

The old Indian held up two fingers.

Two days journey.

Hitchcock pointed first at Stephens, then at John himself, finally at the old Indian, and gestured at the mountains.

Will you show them?

A brief, almost imperceptible nod of assent, and Stephens said,
"Have your boys get him a horse. Doc, you and I ride."
"We'd best take one more . . . just for safety."
"Who's up next on the rota for out-riding?"
"Foster."
"Good. He's one of the better shots."
It took a moment to fathom that remark, and John looked at Stephens, horrified. "He's not a hostage . . . surely you are not thinking of shooting him, after he shows us this river, or if his people try to attack ours!"
"No, the Chief here is mebbe what passes for an honest man in these parts and I'd as soon he was safe with us." Stephens scratched his jaw thoughtfully. "Jus' wish I knew why he was being so helpful to strangers, that's all."
"Easy enough," Greenwood answered. "Either he is a Good Samaritan, or his folk wish we would just move on down the road a little way and out of their lands. Stop spoiling their hunting, and distracting their young bucks."
"Whichever it is, it's to our advantage," Hitchcock said. "I'd not go looking a gift horse in the mouth."

"If we ain't back in five days, don't send any lookin' for us." Stephens got to his feet and gave John a hand up. "You two and Murphy take everyone south, follow Chiles' tracks, and do the best you can. Doc, you and I best saddle up now, and take us plenty of water."

* * *

From E.S. Patterson Interview, University of California Local History Archival Project 1932: *"So, Cap'n Stephens and Doctor Townsend and Mr. Foster all rode out into the desert, following that old Indian. Cap'n Stephens had him a big old dog, big as a pony she was, and she liked to follow him ever'where, but as they left camp, he snapped his fingers at her, told her to "stay", and she sat down right on that spot, watching after them 'til they was no more'n little dots out in that desert. And she sat there, looking after the direction they went, didn't move from that spot, didn't eat, didn't hardly sleep none, just looking after the direction they went, making a little whine, deep in her throat.*

"Ma, she got to worrying, sent my sister Nancy with a basin of water and some scraps from dinner for Cap'n Stephens' dog. Nancy said the dog drank a little, but didn't eat none. Nancy said she took her by the collar, tried to bring her into camp from that spot, but the dog pulled away, an' showed her teeth, even growled a little, which she never done to any of us, and finally Ma said, just leave her alone. Three days Cap'n Stephens dog sat there, waiting for them to come back."

* * *

John went to his wagon, gathered up extra canteens and took the bundle of food and supplies that Sarah, ever competent and foresighted, had assembled for him, and Elizabeth said, "Dearest, do you want to take your journal with you?"

"No." John had leaned down and kissed her from horseback. "I shall make a long entry upon our return."

Her voice quavered, "Do you trust this man . . . this wild Indian who has promised to guide you to the river?"

"Aye, yes, I do." John's instinct in judging men – and women, too, come to think on it – had almost never played him wrong. He had long learned to trust that small, cool judgement, that judgement that told him to trust Stephens, Murphy, and Old Hitchcock and the others, the same judgement that warned him off Thorp, all those long months ago at the emigrant campground outside Kanesville. The same judgement that told him that he should press his suit to marry Elizabeth, on that long-ago morning in Stark County when he went to call on a well-to-do merchant's family and first laid eyes on her, playing the parlor piano.

"Don't fret, Liz, Stephens is the most sensible man I know, we aren't in any danger," or, as he silently added to himself, *any more than we are already.*

"I dislike being left alone." Elizabeth handed up another filled canteen.

"You aren't alone." John looped the strap of it around his saddle horn where it hung with three more against Ugly Grey's withers. "You have Moses to look after, and Sarah Montgomery and Mrs. Patterson to keep you company."

"You know what I mean."

"Dearest Liz, I'll be back in four days, I promise from my heart."

"I know." But she couldn't keep the fear and bewilderment out of her eyes, any more than Dog could when Stephens snapped his fingers and bade her sit and stay, as they rode away into the desert, and camp and dog grew small in the distance behind them.

The sun burned down, pitilessly from a harsh blue sky, baking the ground underneath. Their horses' hoofs scuffed up quantities of fine, bitter-tasting alkali dust. John tied a large calico handkerchief over his nose, and the lower part of his face, to try and keep from breathing it. Foster had already done so, more to shield his sunburned and peeling face from any more exposure than to prevent breathing dust. They looked, John decided, like the veriest desperados. The old Indian led at a cracking pace, seeming to be impervious to the temperature and the dust. Once or twice, when their horses seemed to flag, he looked over his shoulder, and seemed to be encouraging them,

"*Truck-hee, truck-hee!*" he kept saying. "*Truck-hee.*"

"What does that mean, do you think?" Foster asked when they halted at midmorning to pour out a little water for the horses and pass around a canteen for themselves.

"Could it be his name, mebbe?" Stephens ventured.

"Hell of a thing to have a guide you can't talk to." John dampened his handkerchief and tied it over his face again.

"Me, I'd learn that hand-talking language from Old Man Hitchcock," Foster remarked. "Or, I would if I were going to do this trip ever again. Oncet

I get to Californy and get me a nice little farm, with a trout stream nearby, I ain't gonna set foot off it. Or sleep on the ground ever again, either. Ma Foster's little boy Joseph has done about all the traveling he is ever gonna do."

"But not today, he hasn't," Stephens replied. "Let's ride, gentlemen, our guide wants us to move on."

The old Indian watched them, seemingly with a mix of concern and impatience. Foster waved reassuringly and said, "Truck-hee, truck-hee."

The old man looked mollified, even a little pleased, and Foster made an aside to John, "Well, at least now we know it ain't something rude in his lingo."

On and on, across the baking and featureless ground, the sun blazing a slow arc over their heads, their path chosen by their tireless guide towards the mountains, and pitiless heat drying the moisture from their mouths and clothing. Mirages like quicksilver pools danced and shimmered on the horizon. They spoke little and drove their horses at as fast a pace as they dared. Very late in the afternoon they came upon the springs, heralded by a stench of sulfur. In the middle of a barren desert valley, a number of pools of water steamed and bubbled away like a pot on the boil. The biggest of them spurted like a great stinking fountain a good few feet into the dry air. Another was elevated in a pyramid shaped wall of reddish clay to the height of a man, and vented steam with an ominous rumbling sound. Yet another overflowed a shallow basin, a lively trickle as white as milk.

They sat on their horses for some moments, marveling at the sight, until John remarked, "In my medical opinion, Foster, it would do marvels for your health, if you would take the waters. The ancient Romans thought very highly of the medicinal properties of natural hot springs such as this, and built bathing pools and temples around them. Many such places remain popular today amongst the quality and nobility of Europe."

"No foolin', Doc?" Foster pulled his kerchief off his face. "Certainly stinks enough to be good for what ails you."

"Alas, this spring is a little short of the amenities," John admitted. "No assembly rooms, no gardens, no medicinal bathing pools . . . nothing which makes a visit to such a spa so enticing a prospect."

"I reckon we'll survive." Stephens swung down from the saddle and unshipped his small hatchet. "We'll have to dig a channel, run off some of this and let it stand until it's cool enough for the horses."

"*Truck-hee, truck-hee!*" said the old Indian. He slid down off Greenwood's pony like an otter slipping from creek bank to water. Stephens was already hacking out a small channel in the bank of the biggest pool.

"I guess this is where we camp tonight," John unsaddled Ugly Grey and piled the empty canteens in a heap. He still had one half full of water. Even lukewarm and straight from the river-sink, it no doubt tasted better than the stuff from the hot springs.

"We'll have to cut fodder for the teams," Stephens remarked thoughtfully. "There's nothing here but mud."

"And load up water in everything that don't leak," Foster added. "How long is it? Two days, didn't Chief Truck-hee tell us?"

"Two days, maybe less." John answered. "Depends, too, on how fast you are moving. I think we made about fifteen miles today, moving faster than a man on foot, or following a team and wagon."

"Ain't no wood either." Foster unstrapped his bedroll. "Say, that patch of sand here, or that patch of sand over there . . . so many nice patches of sand to choose between."

"Long as you ain't settled on the patch with an ant nest in it." Stephens cracked a smile.

"I like a lively time in bed as well as the next man, but that don't include a passel of vermin." Foster shook his head.

"My good man, cast no such vile aspersions on St. Joseph's finer lodging houses," John said. "I have it on good authority that the vermin in the beds there provide quite the liveliest of nights, and at no additional expense."

"Speaking of lively nights," Foster lowered his voice slightly, "shall we draw straws on keeping a watch during the night? On the horses and Chief Truck-hee?"

"I'll take the first watch, after we eat. Just as well there ain't no wood, I wouldn't want to build a fire anyways."

"What about when we come back with the wagons," John asked. "We can bring along wood . . ."

"No," Stephens shook his head. "We'll not set up a camp. I'll talk it over with Greenwood, but it might be best to just haul straight on through. Start at sundown and just carry on."

"I'd agree on that."

John brought out his own supplies. Sarah and Elizabeth had supplied him with dried meat, some tack and dried fruit, and the rest of the mornings' bread baking. Chief Truck-hee's little bundle seemed to be a little dried meat wrapped in a tattered blanket. John offered him some bread, and he took a little of it, and then wrapped himself in the blanket and hollowed a place for himself in the sand. The old man dropped off to sleep as simply and rapidly as a cat curled up in a familiar place, and John envied him that ability profoundly. He, like Foster, did not look forward to sleeping on the ground. By then the pool of water run off from the hot spring was cool enough for the horses to drink, although they did not seem to relish it in the least. He lowered the empty canteens by their straps into the least-muddy of the springs and let the water run gurgling into them until they were filled, heavy and dripping, and radiating heat.

"Might keep us as warm as a fire would," Foster ventured. "Still and all, I wish we had brought along fodder for the horses today."

"We'll get an early start after we've had some sleep," Stephens said. "Doc, I'll wake you in three hours, then you wake Foster in three. Foster, when your three hours is up, wake us all, and we'll head out."

Perhaps he was getting used to the hardships of the trail, for it seemed that he only lay for a few minutes, looking up at the stars; huge they were, hanging so close above him that it seemed as if he could reach up and pluck one from the sky as easily as he could pick a rose from an arbor just over his head. And the next moment, Stephens gently shook his shoulder, and he was reaching for his rifle before he was entirely awake.

"You awake, Doc?"

"I am now. Wish I had some coffee, Captain."

Stephens' teeth gleamed in the faint starlight, as he handed John one of his canteens. "It ain't real hot, Doc, but it is coffee. I emptied a whole pot into this here canteen this morning, and it's been soaking in that there hot spring since sundown. I thought we might have need to stay awake."

John drank gratefully – yes, coffee, hot and strong, banishing sleep and one of the few comforts on this long scout. "Thank you, Captain. This reminds me of the main reason I backed you for the captaincy back in Kanesville. You think of everything, days before the rest of us even get around to considering the possibilities."

"I try, Doc," Stephens shrugged; John thought he might be embarrassed by such off-hand praise.

"Other men try, Captain . . . you *do*, without any fuss about it. When I want to give myself nightmares, I think of what might have happened to us if Thorp had been elected captain at the first."

"No need. We'd have made our own way before very long."

"Perhaps." John pulled his blanket around him against the chill of a desert night. "Still . . . we gained some days on the trail when the traveling was easy when we might have thought to take our ease. That was your doing, gaining us a little more time before the snow sets in."

"We'll need those days now, I think," Stephens replied, and looked to where Orion would be striding up over the horizon. "Good night, Doc."

"Good night, Captain Stephens." John said, and Stephens pulled his own blanket around himself, and as swiftly as Chief Truck-hee had dropped into sleep, was himself gone in slumber.

The horses fidgeted at the end of their pickets, and the stars overhead blazed in midnight glory. Foster was a faintly snoring bundle, but Truck-hee stirred and rolled over, under his ragged bit of blanket. His eyes gleamed in the faint starlight for a moment, and John thought he seemed a bit surprised to see anyone still wakeful.

"Truck-hee, Chief, truck-hee," John said soothingly, and it seemed that the old man smiled a little in the starlight.

"Truck-hee," he replied, and the gleam winked out, and he was another blanket-covered bundle, snoring faintly under the glorious, ever-wheeling stars. Three hours later, John shook Foster's shoulder, and handed him the canteen of coffee, newly heated in the hot spring.

"Doctor, you are a gentleman and a scholar." Foster uncorked the canteen and gratefully swigged down sufficient of the contents to render him awake and alert, re-corking it with a gasp. "And a damn-fine judge of horse-flesh. I am in your debt, always."

"It was Stephens who brought the coffee," John pointed out, and Foster took another swig,

"A gentleman too, and a very considerate one, and I am in his debt as well. How is Chief Truck-hee?"

"Sleeping the sleep of the blameless," replied John, and he lay down and pulled his blanket around himself, but it was in fact Chief Truck-hee who waked him by shaking his foot, and Foster was holding the canteen of coffee – nearly drained by the weight and gurgling sound of it when he tipped back for a deep swig of the contents — and saying,

"Morning, Doc. I think Chief Truck-hee wants us to saddle up and ride."

"Better to travel in the cool of the day." Stephens had already rolled up his blankets and saddled his pony. It was still dark, but the sky in the east was lightening somewhat, and the stars there looked pallid. A few minutes to water the horses from slightly cooler water, drawn off the spring during the night, and they were mounted and away with no temptation to linger at the springs. The sooner they found Chief Truck-hee's river, the sooner they could bring the wagons over this last stretch of desert and be done with it. They urged the horses to a trot, and made good time in the coolness before the sun rose at their backs, and the temperature soared until it seemed the ground shimmered like the top of a stove.

"I thought yesterday was bad," Foster said, when they paused to rest and water the horses around mid-day. "But this beats all." He poured a little water into his handkerchief, wrung it out over his head so the water dripped down over his face. He passed the canteen to Chief Truck-hee, who drank sparingly from it.

"*Truck-hee, truck-hee,*" he said, as usual, and waved an arm towards the west.

"The oxen will have a hell of time in this." Stephens' pony stood with head drooping, hoof-deep in fine, shifting sand. They seemed to be going up the flank of a long, gradually sloping ridge. They had been so for hours, never quite seeming to reach the crest of it.

"I don't know what Greenwood will advise." John took the canteen from Chief Truck-hee. The water in it was as warm as blood and tasted vile, only temporarily soothing his heat-cracked lips. "But I agree with you, Stephens. We'll be better off attempting passage of this desert at night – anything to alleviate the strain on the teams."

"Will we be able to find our own tracks in the dark?" Foster asked. "I'd not want to become lost in this hell on earth and go in circles all the night."

"We'll steer by the stars, Foster, as sailors do," John said. "Stephens and I have been keeping note of the North Star, relative to us — just to make sure we were not being led in circles ourselves this morning."

"By gum," Foster exclaimed in admiration. "I'd have never thought to do that! I was just trusting the Chief here and thinking we would just follow our tracks back to camp."

"Always best to think on other plans." Stephens took the canteen from John and drank deeply of the distasteful stuff.

"Reckon that's why you're the captain, then." Foster said, and took back his canteen. "Any idee on how much farther?"

Stephens squinted at the sun, far overhead. "'Bout noon now, I'd say. Chief did say it was two days from the marsh. We made good time; I'd guess another three-four hours; sundown, at the latest."

"*Truck-hee, truck-hee,*" said the Chief, making a waving motion towards the west."

"Wish't I knew what that means," Foster mused.

"In this case, probably something like 'gentlemen, let's meander a little farther along this invitingly scenic trail,'" John answered wryly.

"His lingo sure packs a lot 'o words into a little, don't it, Doc?"

"You've never studied Latin, Foster."

"Can't ever say I had the pleasure."

John laughed, and pressed his heels into Ugly Grey's sides. "Then I shall while away the next part of this journey conjugating Latin verbs for you, Foster."

"Hey, that ain't something illegal, is it?"

"No, but there are many schoolboys who would disagree in the strongest possible terms."

"Hell, listen to the Doc talk long enough, Foster, you'll be as eddicated as he is." Stephens looked over his shoulder, as John filled his lungs and began declaiming to the desert, "*Amo . . . I love; amare
. . . to love; amavi . . . I have loved; amatus;* loved . . . oh, damnation, I have forgotten what comes next."

"Don't worry about it Doc, I figure I'm already as eddicated as I need to be." Foster sounded cheery as always, probably smiling broadly under the sodden neckerchief tied around his face.

In mid-afternoon, the sun slanting about halfway down the sky in front of them, they finally topped the long, shallow ridge, and were able to look down the other side — a vast and featureless sweep of sand, as far as the eye could see . . . but just on the very edge, right on the horizon, a thin scribble of green lay across the desert, with dun-colored hills beginning to mound up towards the blue mountains beyond.

"*Truck-hee!*" The chief waved an arm towards it, and John murmured, "Truck-hee indeed. Gentlemen, I believe there is our river, and the key to getting over the mountains."

"What are we waiting for, then?" Foster made as if to spur his horse, and Stephens said, "Easy does it, it's a good few miles off."

But they could see that thin random line of green and it heartened them to have their destination so clearly in view, incrementally becoming larger and more distinct, a line of green trees, the poplar trees which meant water and plenty of it. Their horses became restive and energetic, almost dancing with impatience; they could smell water, sense the moisture in the air, and the scent of lush green pastures.

Soon John could smell it also, and he and the others allowed the horses to trot, and then canter. The sand and dust rose in a great plume behind them, and then their hooves drummed on firmer ground, they shot across a thin strip of pasturage, and reined them in on the gravelly bank, half-crazed with thirst and the glory and richness of it all. Water, sweet water with green rushes growing all around, and yellow and green poplar leaves rustling and whispering overhead. He leaped down and let Ugly Grey plunge into the river, up to his knees in it, while he lowered his head and drank in great gulps of water. Stephens' pony and the others waded in, and John knelt on the bank and dipped his hat into it, pouring a great scoop of fresh water over himself. Foster kicked out of his boots and waded in with the horses, stretching out his arms and whooping like a madman before falling flat into it with a mighty splash.

John poured another hatful of water on himself and thought how beautiful this place looked, after that desert. The afternoon sun lay golden in this grove, sifting through the leaves, and a little breeze rustled the tall clumps of rushes. Great dragonflies and other insects hovered above the water, and the murmur of water melded with the sounds of leaves and insects into one tranquil symphony.

Chief Truck-hee stood quietly on the bank, holding the reins of Greenwood's pony, watching them for a moment with what John read on his face as great satisfaction, and even a bit of gentle amusement.

"*Truck-hee*," he remarked one last time, and then handed the reins to John, settled his blanket bundle on his shoulder, and padded away along the river bank, vanishing like a wilderness sprite among the rushes and dusty golden bars of sunlight slipping down through the trees.

"Let him go." Stephens halted John with a hand on his shoulder, even though John had no intention of stopping the old man, "He kept his end of the bargain."

"I'd still like to know," Foster sat up in the water and retrieved his hat, "if this river has a name."

"It does now," John said. "I'd name it after the old man, and call it Truck-hee's River."

"Truckee?" Stephens shrugged. "Have to call it something, I guess. We'll camp here, and head back in the morning."

"It purely is a beautiful place." Foster looked around appreciatively, "You sure was right about taking the waters, Doc . . . I feel better already."

Chapter 9 – *Forty-Mile Desert*

From E.S. Patterson Interview, University of California Local History Archival Project 1932: *"Three days Captain Stephens and Doctor Townsend and Mister Foster was gone in the desert with the old Indian . . . funny thing, they thought his name was Truck-hee, because that's what he kept saying, over and over. We were so grateful for his help, guiding them to that river, they named it after what they thought his name was, but it wasn't his name at all! Truck-hee really meant 'all well' or 'everything satisfactory!' But he was a chief, right enough, the chief of the Paiute tribe thereabouts, and a very well-thought-of man among them. Rightly, too, I have to say . . . he took the compliment so well, that he took "Truckee" as his name after that.*

"A good man, right enough. Died of a tarantula bite, years later; he was given a splendid funeral by all the folk thereabouts, Indian and white. Buried him with a Bible that John Fremont gave him, so the story goes. Anyway, I'm wandering. Privilege of old age, so they tell me; 96 years old next April, I'll be. I've outlived all my brothers and sisters, even my little sister Sadie. Outlived my wife and three of my children . . . can't get more privileged than that, hey?

"I think Captain Stephen's dog saw them first. She commenced to whine, and then to bark. She warn't no dog that barked much, commonly, so that had everyone's attention – especially since she had been sitting on that very spot since they went, and Captain Stephens bade her stay. They came riding out of the desert, leading the extry pony, that dog barking fit to beat the band. Ma, and Doctor Townsend's wife, and the other women came running out . . . most of the young men were out hunting. We had been busy all those three days, patching up the wagons, and the women were washing things, and smoking meat over the fires and all. Such a sight they was, all dirty and sun burnt, but grinning all over. Chief Truckee had led them right to that river, all right. Captain Stephens snapped his fingers at his dog, and she went to capering and leaping about, and running back and forth. Miz Townsend, she reached up and hugged the Doctor . . . ah, such a lovely woman she was. I had a bit of calf-love for her, you see. Just a boy of seven or eight, I was then, but she was the most beautiful woman I'd ever set eyes on, and brave she was, too. About broke my heart when she went, but she and the Doctor went together. Within days, I was told. Some comfort in that, I suppose; she never had eyes for anyone but him, big jolly roughneck that he was. Capable man, he could deliver a baby or doctor an ox and build a road; can't say that about doctors these days."

* * *

"We found it!" John shouted, waving his hat over his head, as they rode into camp. "We found it, right where the Chief said it was!" He slid down from his saddle and swung Elizabeth off her feet; she was laughing and crying at the same time into his shirt-front. Old Hitchcock hobbled up from Greenwood's campfire, Eddie at his heels. "And a beautiful, beautiful river it is, too. Liz, don't cry – why are you crying?"

"I was worried about you!" Elizabeth brushed her cheeks with the edge of her hand.

"Nothing to worry about, Dearest, it was only the desert . . ."

At his side, Foster clapped Old Hitchcock on the shoulders, saying, "Ice cold, straight from the mountains! Two days travel, a little less on horse, as you can see. We're close to Californy at last, Old Man, close enough to taste it!"

"We ain't there yet," Stephens said quietly. "Down, Dog." Dog sat obediently at his feet, but her tail kept wagging, and she pressed up against her master as if to reassure herself that he was really there. More men gathered around the three scouts and their horses, drawn from their chores; Old Murphy, beaming joyfully, James Miller with a hammer still in his hands, a happy babble of voices repeating the good news to the lately arrived.

Stephens finally held up his hand. "Folks, we're tired, hungry, and saddle-sore . . . we found the river, but it's been three days in the desert to get to it, there and back. Give us a mite to clean up. Doc and I'll call a meeting for tonight, after supper."

"We'll not be leaving from here right away," John added fairly. "It'll be worse than that cut-off between the Big Sandy and the Green. We'll have to carry all the water we can and cut two days worth of fodder for the animals." A dismayed murmur rose from all; the memory of that leg of travel and the temporary loss of 40 head of cattle was clear. This desert would be even more desolate and comfortless? "We'll go over it all tonight after supper," John said again, and Moses appeared and took Ugly Grey's reins out of John's hand.

"I'll take care of him, Doctor John." Moses looked at him critically. "You might want to . . . um, wash up, a little."

"You should." Elizabeth recovered herself. "You're as bristly as a bear." She went on tiptoe and kissed him again. The crowd had melted away, reluctantly, and John went to the waters' edge below camp with a bucket and a rag, stripped off his filthy shirt, and poured water over himself until he began to feel somewhat cleaner.

"It works better with soap," said Elizabeth from behind him. "I've brought your shaving things and a clean shirt."

"Bless you, Liz," John said gratefully. She also carried a clean towel and a basin of warm water. "It was a hell of a scout on horse with a small party, Dearest. It will be even worse with the wagons."

"We'll manage," Elizabeth replied tranquilly. She perched herself on a rock at the water's edge. "With Captain Stephens and you, and everyone . . . we'll help each other, and we'll manage."

John upended the bucket and sat upon it, with the basin and soap at his feet, and commenced scraping beard-stubble off his jaw and from under his chin. "We'll need to." He rinsed off the razor. "We can't stay much longer here, in any case."

"What does Captain Stephens plan?" Elizabeth lifted her skirts a little; she had moccasins on her feet, rather than shoes. She slipped out of them, and dabbled her feet in the water as playfully as a child.

"He is going to suggest that we travel at night. The heat during the day is hellish, Liz. It's forty miles at least, so Stephens estimates it. The last stretch is in deep sand; we'll be lucky not to loose at least a couple of oxen there unless we take good care. There's not a scrap of grass from here to old Truck-hee's river, and only one spring of water, and it's boiling hot and tastes utterly vile to boot." He scraped at his face again with the razor. "There . . . did I miss anything?"

"No, I don't think so . . . oh, little bit, just so." She stepped out of the water and took the razor out of his hand. With a look of great absorption, she ran the edge of it over the last bit of bristle. "There," she remarked with satisfaction. "You look quite respectable again, my dear doctor, not like some shiftless ruffian of the trail . . . or you will, once you have put on a shirt again. I missed you terribly, these last four days. Since we wed, I think it has been the longest we have ever gone without seeing each other."

"Once over the mountains," John ventured, taking up her hands in his, "we will be in California, and I doubt I'll have to go on such a long scout ahead of the train. Therefore, I think I may safely promise that we will not ever be parted for so long again."

He kissed her fingers, and she laughed a little and replied, "No, promise rather that wherever one of us goes, the other will follow after in a little while."

"Always, Liz, always," and he kissed her fingers again, and she laughed again and pulled away to gather up his dirty shirt and the towel and basin and all.

"I think I may soon need to cut your hair as well, Dearest," and she slipped her feet into the moccasins and carried her burdens back to camp.

* * *

From E.S. Patterson Interview, University of California Local History Archival Project 1932: *"We were another couple of days, camped at the sink and making preparations. Captain Stephens brought out his sharpening stone, to sharpen knives and sickles, as we needed to cut all the grass and rushes that we could carry with us. We spread out tent canvas, and piled up cut fodder on it, and rolled them up into great bolsters and tied them onto the backs and sides of the wagons. Mr. Miller mended as many empty barrels as there were, with wood scraps and tar and bits of unraveled rope, and we soaked them in the marsh so the wood might swell again and seal up any leaks. Ma and Mrs. Townsend and Mrs. Armstrong cooked up enough bread and beans and meat and such to last us for two or three days, for as Captain Stephens said and Mr. Greenwood said too, that we would travel straight through without stopping save to rest the cattle for a few hours. We rested a little in the afternoon of the second day, and ate a good meal, and as the sun went down, my brothers and the other men hitched up the teams, and Captain Stephens led us out into the desert."*

* * *

One after another as the sun set in a red-gold smear against the lavender-colored mountains, the wagons lumbered away from their camping place, to the gentle accompaniment of the frogs and night birds singing in the marsh, and the querulous voices of smaller children, put to bed in the wagons but unable to sleep for the motion of it. Greenwood and Stephens carried lanterns with them, and lit them as darkness gathered; not as if they needed the light to retrace the scouting party's tracks, but rather as a guide to the wagon drivers urging their teams on. Those were plain under the starlight, across the pale desert sands, and clear as daylight when the moon soared over the horizon.

"It reminds me," Elizabeth remarked, "of those winter nights when there was a fresh fall of snow on the ground and a full moon behind the clouds . . . it was night, but everything brilliantly lit, as bright as day."

John circled the slow-moving procession of wagons and returned to walk with her and a knot of women and older children walking close by the Patterson wagon. The light evening breeze bore the dust away from them. She led Beau, and he walked beside her leading Ugly Grey.

"It's almost like walking in snow, too," Isabella spoke up. She and Oliver were taking turns driving; now she walked with one arm around Nancy's waist, leading Eddie by the other hand. "Don't drag your feet, children, it just makes the dust worse."

"Ma, I'm thirsty," Nancy said, and Elizabeth unhooked a canteen from Beau's saddle horn, and handed it to the girl.

"Don't drink any more than you need," John said. "Often, but not too much. We'll need to save as much as possible for the horses and the teams and to walk as much as possible ourselves to spare them."

"How long must we walk, then?" Nancy did her best to sound brave.

"As long as you can, sweeting," Elizabeth replied cheerfully. "And when you are a little tired, I'll let you ride Beau for a little, and when you and your brother are really, really tired, you can sleep in the wagon for a while."

"I'm not tired," Eddie spoke up sturdily. "I can walk for miles and miles and miles yet."

"That's our brave Eddie," Elizabeth said affectionately, and Eddie fairly glowed.

John kissed his wife, and swung into the saddle again for another patrol, the length of the train. Not near the long chore it was, in the days when they traveled with the Oregoners; now just the eleven wagons, and a scant handful of spare oxen, and Old Hitchcock stumping along with his two mules. Old Martin walked with his younger sons, his daughters, daughters-in-law, and his grandchildren, although it touched John enormously to see that he was carrying the smallest grandson on his shoulders, and young Helen carried tiny Ellen Independence for Mary Miller. Old Martin was declaiming one of the epics of old Erin as they marched along through the night.

"So it came to Queen Maeve, that it seemed as if she didn't own anything at all, if she had not a bull of such splendor among her herd, so she called the herald McRoth into her court to find out if there were any such in the whole kingdoms of Ireland, and the herald McRoth said to Queen Maeve 'I know indeed where there is a bull even better and more excellent than he, in the province of Ulster in the cantred of Cooley, in the house of Dare

MacFinna . . .' and Queen Maeve ordered him to go, saying to McRoth the herald, 'Ask of Dare for me, a year's loan of that bull . . .'"

Even Mary-Bee Murphy walked, carrying a basket of small things, and leading her sons linked by their hands.

"You should not overexert yourself unduly, Mrs. Murphy," John said with some concern as he overtook them on horseback.

Mary-Bee flashed a smile at him. "Oh, I am not the least bit tired, Doctor Townsend . . . I have promised Isabella and my husband that I shall ride in the wagon and rest when I feel the need of it, truly I shall."

James Murphy walked by his team, driving them with his voice, while tenderly carrying little Mary in his arms. She was asleep, her head on his shoulder. And so they walked on, children stumbling with weariness until they were put to bed in the wagons or into the saddles of horses, and led by their elders.

At midnight, John finished another circuit of the wagons; he found Elizabeth leading Beau, with Nancy and Eddie dozing in the saddle. "Captain Stephens is sending me ahead with Foster and Greenwood's boys," he said to her, "so we can run off water from the springs and let it cool off enough for the cattle . . . three hours should be enough."

Elizabeth pulled her shawl closer around her shoulders. "It does seem so much colder at night out here," she replied. "Take care, Dearest."

"We'll be resting at the springs for a couple of hours before moving on; you should ride for a while. This is the easiest stretch."

Elizabeth shook her head, "I am fine. I'll rest when you do."

Using shovels this time, it didn't take long to break several new channels, laboring like well-diggers in the moonlight, in clouds of sulfur-stinking vapor. When they were finished, John tied Ugly Grey's reins around his wrist and simply cast himself down on the ground to snatch a little sleep, while Britt Greenwood watched for the wagons. Britt shook him awake when he spotted the lanterns bobbing in the distance like a pair of distant yellow glowworms.

They dared not unharness the teams entirely, lest they repeat the experience of having them run off in search of water, but led them in yoke to the pools of cooling spring water to drink. The oxen relished it as little as the horses had, but drank. Once re-hitched, the men scattered mounds of fodder in front of them where they stood in harness, and allowed them to rest and eat of it as they wished. John found Elizabeth lying on top of their bed in the wagon, fully dressed even to shoes, and fast asleep, the deep sleep of utter exhaustion.

She had managed to unsaddle Beau and leave him picketed next to a bucket of water and an armload of green stuff. Moses and Francis had spread blankets underneath the wagon and slept also, but it was no more than a brief respite of an hour or so. They ate of the cold food prepared for the journey and moved on, stumbling with weariness through a night that seemed endless until the stars paled and dawn came up at their backs.

John thought he had moved to somewhere beyond weariness, aware only of a slightly giddy feeling if he moved too fast, as he patrolled the length of the caravan, pausing at each wagon or family. The sun arced higher in the sky, and the heat of it poured down relentlessly. The night-time coolness fled as if it had never been. The Sullivans and the Martins were at the tail on this day. Mary Sullivan led her younger brothers by the hand, while her brother drove their wagon.

Patrick Martin waved cheerily. "Holy Mother and all the saints," he exclaimed. "When I am judged before the Lord, I will be able to say that I should go to heaven straight away, as I have already served in Purgatory."

"I hope you have the right of it, Patrick," John replied. The Patterson children walked uncomplainingly with Isabella, although Sadie cried in silent misery, her tears drying on her cheeks nearly as fast as they fell.

"Here," said Old Man Hitchcock to his grandchildren. "This is an old Indian trick; put a little pebble in your mouth to suck on. You won't feel so thirsty, then. Sadie-girl, you want to ride on one of Paw-paw's mules? Ups-a-daisy, there you go. Now, boys, I was once chased by a war party of Comanche through a desert just as bad as this."

Elizabeth had wakened in the wagon around sunrise, and was walking again, leading Beau. She smiled at John, "Nothing seems to bother him, does it?"

"He's a tough old bird," John replied. "I used to think most of his stories weren't true, and now I am beginning to wonder if most of them aren't the Gods' own truth."

"Well, the one about being scalped by the Blackfeet – that's not true," Elizabeth mused. "But, now that I have seen the hot spring back there, I think the tale of the great fountain of water spurting out of the ground might be true."

"A little exaggerated, maybe," John admitted.

Old Martin strode like a patriarch of old among his sons and grandsons, still in full spate. *"Now Cormac had three companies of warriors, who came to Cruachan; the first company was arrayed in mantles of green, with many-colored cloaks wound about them, and fastened with great silver brooches.*

They wore tunics woven of golden thread reaching down to their knees, trimmed with red gold thread. Bright-handled swords they carried, aye, splendid swords with hand-guards of silver, and long shields. Long shields they bore on their left arms, and each man carried a broad, grey spearhead on a slender shaft in the other hand. 'Is that Cormac, yonder?' everyone asked, and Queen Maeve made answer 'Indeed, it is not . . .'"

Each one of the adults carried a child.

"Anything to lighten the wagons and ease the burden for the teams," Young Martin Murphy said gravely to John. "This sand is wicked cruel on their feet, and they must pull twice as hard." He patted the neck of his lead ox as it plodded stoically forward. "I think we will not know just how much we depend on them, until we must carry a like burden ourselves. A good thing they ask so little of us – they certainly get very little in exchange for their great labors."

No, thought John, only a kindly bullet at the end of things, after drinking bad water, or miring in quicksand, or breaking a leg when a wagon tipped over on a steep hillside. Allen and Sarah were quarrelling bitterly; John did not know what about, for they stopped when they saw him riding closer. Allen was red with sunburn and fury, Sarah's voice sharp with irritation.

"Then see if I care when we get to California!" she snapped. "You may please yourself then, and so shall I!"

John sighed: one of those things it would be best to pretend he did not hear. He said instead, "Captain Stephens says we will rest for three or four hours at noon, wherever we are when the sun is overhead and it is hottest. Allen, can your team manage for another couple of hours?

"Think so," Allen grunted, and swabbed his forehead with his shirt-sleeve. Sarah said something under her breath and walked a little slower, letting their wagon run ahead while she dropped back to walk with Elizabeth and Isabella.

Foster pulled the handkerchief off his face and grinned hugely at John from where he trudged, sinking into the sand at every step beside his laboring team. "I am telling them all about Truck-hee's lovely river, and all that beautiful cool water and the green leaves overhead," he said, cheerily as ever. "So help me, I think they are listening to every blessed word. It cheers me up no end to think on it, myself."

"We'll be there in another day, with luck," John said, although to even hope of it in this soul-scorching heat, with the wheels biting deep into the hot sand with every step the oxen took, seemed like the veriest illusion. Old Greenwood and his boys walked with Stephens, leading their ponies and pack string in the van a little way ahead of Stephens' own wagon where the scout party's own trail ran clear, a churning of the sand marked with shod hoofs where they had gone and returned.

"How're they doing back there, Doc?" Greenwood strode along, as strongly as any of the youngest men. "This is a rough road, no mistake."

"Quite well, considering," John answered. "Everyone's teams are pulling strongly still, no one lagging behind. The oxen are terribly thirsty though. Everyone is walking who can. Allen Montgomery and his wife are quarrelling. Old Hitchcock and Mrs. Patterson are not. The smallest children are tired and cross. Mary-Bee Murphy is riding her brother's pony, at the insistence of her husband, father-in-law, and myself, strongly backed by a committee formed of all the other Murphys. Old Martin is well launched on an epic tale of war and slaughter in Old Ireland, and I think that I am slightly touched by the sun, or as Hitchcock would say it, 'tetched.' This concludes the morning report, Captain Stephens."

"You're thirsty," Stephens said. "Take a good long drink of water, Doc."

"No, actually, I am not," John insisted. "I am a doctor, I am fully competent to make my own diagnosis!" but Greenwood passed him a full canteen and commanded, "Drink half."

"We're supposed to save as much for the teams as we can," John protested, and Stephens replied, "Won't do us any good, if you have sunstroke, Doc. Drink."

"No one authorized you to practice medicine." John grumbled, and Greenwood said, "They wouldn't have the nerve. Drink." John obeyed, but didn't admit that he felt only slightly better for it afterwards.

"We'll rest in two hours," Stephens said, squinting at the sun nearly at zenith. "And start again at sundown. We can loose the oxen then. They'll not dare leave the water and fodder we'll put out for them."

"At least that will lighten the wagons somewhat," John remarked, "of the extra water barrels, at least."

"We might consider lightening them even more," Stephens said thoughtfully.

"You've used a fair portion of your supplies," Greenwood pointed out, "which has lightened the burden gradually as we traveled farther."

"But we have brought extra traps with us," Stephens answered. "Things for which we have little use or need. Good thing to consider, dumping what we can spare and moving on."

"It may come to that," John allowed, and after a moment confessed, "I have a case of books in my wagon, and of little use in this instance. It might spare my team the effort of hauling another sixty or a hundred pounds if I dumped them out of the wagon this instant."

"So are the smaller children of little use." Greenwood replied crisply, "yet their parents carry them, willingly. Your books are a promise of future fulfillment, just as the children are, Doctor. Do not consider for a moment leaving them. They are as much a part of what we are and what we stand for as the children, and being such are irreplaceable. No, cherish your books, Doctor Townsend. If you are that concerned about the burden I will carry some of them myself."

They crawled along, the constancy of creaky wagon wheels and jingling harness occasionally broken by an ox bawling in misery, and the snap of a whip. The children suffered in silence, all but tiny Ellen Independence, who wailed a thin, constant complaint and could not be comforted.

At last, Stephens said, "Here. We'll rest here until sundown."

There was nothing in particular to distinguish that spot, only that the sun stood directly overhead; simply that it was as good as, or as bad as any other, and the bawling from thirsty team animals had become nearly constant. Like automatons, everyone worked to spread out the fodder and carry wash-pans filled with water, around which the animals clustered so thick, shoving each other and packing so tightly one to another that it was impossible to refill them for some little time once the desperate stock had drunk them dry. The women spread out blankets on the stand, in the shade underneath the wagons, or under canvas stretched from the sides, for the heat in the little spaces inside was unbearably stifling. No one had much of an appetite for lukewarm meats and stale camp bread and crackers, and almost everyone just lay themselves down to sleep.

"I am sorry, Dearest." John set aside his plate. "I am only thirsty. I will force myself to eat, but I cannot confess to any enthusiasm for it."

Moses had wolfed down his own portion, and now he said, "You should eat, Doctor John. But I'll take that, if you aren't hungry."

"I do not see that anyone has much of an appetite but you." Elizabeth took John's untouched plate, and tipped its contents onto Moses'. "Well, perhaps when you have rested a while . . ."

"Only for a short while," John replied. "Stephens has asked that we set a watch on our cattle; he fears some of them might be crazed with thirst."

"He is asking too much of you, Dearest," Elizabeth said indignantly, "You must have a care for everyone else but yourself, and I won't have any more of it this day. You both have had no more than two hours sleep, but I slept long in the wagon this morning. I will sit and watch the silly cattle . . .

and you will rest." She flung his plate back into the box with the other camp tin-ware and took up John's rifle with a fierce and determined look. She sat down in a flurry of faded calico skirts by where John lay, and lifted his head onto her lap. "I can see the animals from here, and I will know if you exert yourself in the slightest."

Moses chewed his last mouthful of camp bread and remarked, "Really, Doctor John, I wouldn't argue with her, when she's this way."

"I have no intention of arguing . . ." John answered, and then he dropped like a stone into deep, deep sleep, and remained there until the sun went down and the camp roused and prepared for the final desperate push.

Before harnessing the teams, they put out the last of the cut fodder and all but a barrel or two of water, thinking to save that last to dole out little by little. The oxen sounded querulous and miserable, even Foster's team obeying with reluctance. The coolness in the air that came with sundown and the short rest had somewhat revived animals and humans alike. They marched on through the moonlit night with renewed energy. They were almost at the end of the desert torment, surely? Stout souls like Elizabeth and Old Hitchcock, Old Martin and Joseph Foster rallied the faltering and exhausted.

"It's a marvelous river. "Elizabeth's voice lilted. "Doctor Townsend told me it looks like a river that flows through the Garden of Eden . . ."

"How does he know about the Garden of Eden," Eddie asked, and Nancy answered scornfully, "He just does, silly."

"And in the middle of battle, the great king Conchobar heard that the fight had gone against him three times from the north." Old Martin was in fine form, under the golden moonlight, reciting for his grandchildren. *"Then Conchobar cried out to his guardsmen, the men of the Red Branch: 'Hold ye here a while, ye men!' cried he; 'even in the line of battle, that I may learn who has attacked us three times from the north! Then vowed the men of his household: 'We will hold, for the sky is above, and the earth underneath and the sea all round, and unless the heavens fall with showers of stars on the face of the world, or the blue-bordered ocean break over it, or the ground yawns open, we shall not move a thumb's breadth backward from here, until the very day of doom and of life everlasting until you return to us!'"*

"Green trees and water, boys, green trees and sweet cold water," Foster snapped his whip over the laboring team.

"We crossed a wicked desert like this once before." Old Hitchcock stumped along. "Four days at it, we were . . ."

They rested a little at midnight, with the oxen standing in harness. They were fractious and unhappy by then, since the water was nearly gone, and with having to pull hard against the deep sand.

"I think we are close to the top of the sand." John consulted with Stephens and Greenwood after a short scout ahead. His head ached abominably. "But with the moon gone down, I can't say for sure. The teams are moving faster, though."

"Aye, so they are. I think we must be on the far side of it, now."

"Were it daylight, we could see the river from here," John explained to Greenwood.

"Pass the word," Stephens said.

"It'll give everyone heart," Greenwood said. "And tell them too, that when the oxen begin to smell the water, they might get a little jumpy. Remind all to be on their guard."

"It takes a lot to set an ox to stampede," John said cautiously, and Greenwood answered, "But when they do, they stampede real bad."

"Especially bad if they're still hitched." Stephens added grimly.

Knowing that they were close to the river though revived everyone's flagging energies, and at first everyone was glad of the oxen walking faster, pulling with more energy than the plodding lethargy of earlier. But the crackle of whips and irritated shouts from the drivers filled the night. Ugly Grey began fretting at the bit as John did a circuit of the march; yes, the animals were fractious, barely obedient to their drivers, maddened beyond all endurance by the smell of water. One of Foster's oxen began to bellow, and toss its horns, and the frantic contagion leaped like a wildfire, a crash from within a wagon, and a woman screaming, oxen bellowing and a storm of dust rising up.

"We're losing them, Captain!" John shouted.

Stephens stood in his stirrups and cupped his hands. "Circle the wagons, circle them now, and let the oxen go! Un-harness them and let them go!"

The half-dozen loose cattle pounded by, throwing up great gouts of sand, swiftly followed by two boys on horseback. John thought one of them might be Moses on Beau. The column split and circled in a storm of sand, cursing, and the bellowing of unhappy oxen.

"Let them go, let them go!" he circled the camp, waving his hat, "Unharness and let them run before they do any damage!"

In the maelstrom, he caught a brief sight of John Flomboy clinging to the neck of one of Stephen's frantic animals, shouting and beating it about the head with his whip-handle, and Bernard and Johnny Murphy struggling to free the yoke from another. One of old Hitchcock's mules flashed by with its pack nearly under its belly. Two, three, four loose animals charged through the camp, maddened beyond any control and somewhere a child screaming piteously. That was Mary Murphy in her father's perilously rocking wagon, and James shouting to her to stay still, stay where she was.

Dog was barking somewhere in the middle of it, a deep ringing bay like a very hellhound. The terrible cracking sound of rending wood, oh, god, was one of the wagons going down? More loose animals plunged away, two of them still yoked together. Old Martin's wagon stood free, all the animals away, Young Martin and Mary-Bee huddled underneath it with the boys; at his own wagon Elizabeth and Francis struggled valiantly to free the last yoke. More loose oxen, one with a broken leg dangling free and horrible, chasing after its fellows, and a riderless horse, reins and stirrups dangling loose. Ugly Grey snorted and reared, jibbing sideways as a handful of loosened oxen bore down like phantoms out of the dust, but they were there and then gone, and left silence settling with the dust after them. His head pounded, he felt sick, sawing at Ugly Grey's bit, battling for control of his frantic horse. He caught sight of Elizabeth sheltering under his wagon, cast up like some kind of bizarre shipwreck askew in a tumbled sea of sand, but hoof-beats pounded out of the dark at his side, and Stephens shouted, "We need to ride hard, Doc!"

"Liz!" he shouted to her, "we'll be back when we can!"

She came out from the wagon calling, "Just get them back!"

"Well, we sure as hell ain't going anywhere less'n we do!" Stephens grunted, and they were away in the dark, following the stampede trail, even in starlight as broad and unmistakable as a city road. They passed some of the teamsters on foot, Old Martin with John Sullivan and the Martin brothers. "Go on w'you!" Old Martin shouted. "We'll catch up!"

* * *

From E.S. Patterson Interview, University of California Local History Archival Project 1932: *"Oh, that was something frightening . . . not that they nearly stampeded, that all happened so fast, Sadie and Nancy and Ma and me barely had time to be frightened. Rather, it was sitting under the wagons in the desert all alone, waiting for the men and Captain Stephens to come back. All the men had run after the cattle, or taken their horses and left us. Oliver and Samuel and Johnny had gone after the cattle, too, and there we were, all the women and little children, sitting under the wagons in the dark with just a little water. Ma had her old dragoon pistol, and she spread out a blanket for us and told us to sleep. Mrs. Miller with her baby, and Mrs. Murphy who was going to have a baby, they sat under the next wagon with all their children, and the baby crying all that while. We were all so thirsty . . . and then the sun came up and we could see a cloud of dust, and it was the men coming back, driving the herd ahead of them. Such a welcome sight as I'll never forget! The oxen had all drunk as deep as they wished and eaten all they wanted . . . but five or six ran off, and we never found them again, and one of Miller's had panicked in harness and manage to break it's leg.*

"They brought us canteens of fresh, cold water, and it tasted so fine! We hitched up, and carried on towards the river, which was as welcome to us and seemed every bit as beautiful as Mrs. Townsend had promised: a river out of the Garden of Eden, with lush green grass everywhere, and beautiful trees, golden trees on the hills all around, and good hunting. Best of all, the river came out of the west, down out of the mountains, like Chief Truckee said, and we followed it until we came to a beautiful meadow . . . but the canyon walls closed in, and one morning we woke up and there was snow all over the ground . . ."

Chapter 10 – *Truckee's River*

From Dr. Townsend's diary: *"Eleventh of October, 1844 . . . encamped for several days upon Truckee's River, to recover ourselves and our teams from passage across the desert . . ."*

Birds: he could hear birdsong, and water gurgling softly close by where he lay. A cool breeze fanned his face and arms – very peculiar, for the very last thing John could bring to memory was a dark maelstrom of sand and stampeding cattle, and himself and Stephens riding hell for leather after them with the other men. He'd been fighting a cracking headache all that night and the day before, that and fear and thirst, which were all minor things next to the task of keeping the wagons moving, because to stop would be to die of thirst in the desert.

He felt limp, and exhausted, as if a fever had burned through him. Where was he? Was this some paradisiacal garden? No, that was canvas overhead, with leaf-shadows dancing across it. He was in a tent, with the sides rolled up, lying on a tick mattress spread out in the shade provided. If he turned his head he could see wagon wheels, and beyond them a stand of water reeds and a willow thicket, swaying gently in the breeze.

Not paradise, but nearly as good as that; Chief Truckee's beautiful river, midday by the look of the sun. What had happened to him, then? John decided that he must have been taken ill. His hair felt damp . . . and when he reached down, lifting the blanket over himself he realized that he had been entirely divested of clothing and boots.

So much for getting out of bed.

"Liz!" he shouted, crossly, and immediately regretted it, because his head still hurt. "Liz! Where are you! Where are my clothes?"

"We took them away," Elizabeth answered softly, and he felt a fool, for she had been sitting here all the time, underneath the tent, right by the pillow that supported his head. He heard her dress rustle, as she turned and called, "Isabella, he's awake!"

"Oh, good!" he heard Isabella reply from nearby. In a moment, she appeared herself, brisk and bossy, fluffing up like a banty hen. "In his right mind?"

"I think so," Elizabeth replied. "He wants his clothes."

"Well, he can't have them," Isabella replied. "Not yet, anyways."

She brushed her fingers across his forehead, and John batted them aside and snapped, "Why are you two talking about me as if I weren't here? What happened?"

"No temperature," Isabella said matter-of-factly. "Elizabeth, my dear, I think you may have the worst patient on the face of the earth."

"Petticoat government!" John complained. Isabella relented.

"Sunstroke, that's what it was. Doctor, you were rushing about in the heat, all during our crossing of the desert. Captain Stephens says you felt ill, and drank water only sparingly . . ."

"Well, of course, we had to save it for the oxen." John did feel the perfect fool, not having seen the symptoms in himself.

"You collapsed at the river," Elizabeth said softly. "As all of you were rounding up the cattle. Captain Stephens had Moses and Francis stay and attend you. They carried you to the river and put you in the shallows. You seemed to be burning up with fever, so . . ."

"Yes, that was the best thing to have done . . . stay, then . . . who hitched up our team and drove the wagon here, if Moses and Francis were tending to me?"

"I did," Elizabeth replied serenely. "Isabella and her boys and Captain Stephens helped, of course, and I have been watching Isabella drive for months on the trail. It didn't seem that hard at all. Oxen are not terribly clever, are they? You had revived a little by the time we arrived here. The boys set up the tent, and we have been taking turns sitting by you ever since. That was yesterday morning . . . Isabella said we must make you begin drinking water with a little salt in it, and that we should be sponging you with cool water, and keep you lying still."

"The worst of it was over by last night," Isabella added, "You were merely sleeping very deep. Which was good; before that you were muttering and complaining about pains everywhere, and worrying about the oxen, and sometimes again we couldn't make you drink . . ."

"You didn't recognize us, at first," Elizabeth said, and John heard the clink of a cup against a water jug. "Which frightened us all, terribly. Here – if you like, we'll assist you to sit up. Isabella will fetch Captain Stephens. He wanted to know when you woke up. Now, drink this."

She held the cup to his lips, and he drank greedily. When he lay back, it was to recline against some more pillows. The leaf-shadows overhead danced in the breeze . . . no, the desert crossing seemed now like a nightmare, fading in the light of morning.

"This is such a beautiful place," Elizabeth continued. "Or perhaps we only think it so after all the trouble and hardship endured to get here. Shall I bring your writing desk? I don't think you run any risk of over-exertion, writing in your diary."

Footsteps, outside; Stephens' voice mingling with Isabella's and Dog's padding footfalls. "Doc? You up to receiving visitors?" Stephens ducked under the tent. The look of relief on his craggy features was unmistakable.

"That might be, but I'm hardly dressed for it. They won't bring me my clothes," John answered, and Stephens looked amused.

"Don't be silly, Dearest. You'll have them when you have rested a little more." Elizabeth sounded indignant.

"Frankly, Doc, I'd be more apt to hog-tie you to a tree if that would keep you flat-back for a while longer. You gave us a hell of a scare, Doc, a hell of a scare." Stephens shook his head. "And there I told you, back in the desert, to drink more water. We weren't gonna run that short."

"So . . . did we get all the cattle back? I just cannot recall anything after that," John asked, and Elizabeth started to protest. "Liz, Dearest, I promise I'll rest. I'll rest and write my diary entry, but I must know what happened, first."

"I'll bring your writing desk, then." She brushed his cheek with her fingertips, saying as she left the tent. "Please don't agitate him, overmuch, Captain Stephens."

"I won't," Stephens promised solemnly. As soon as she was out of earshot, he added, "A good wife, and above the price of rubies. You are a lucky man, Doc. I had worries about Mrs. Townsend at the start of this. I'm glad to say they were misplaced."

"Worried about Elizabeth?" John was puzzled. "Did you think she was not equal to this journey?"

"Well, you know her better than I . . . or so I would hope. Being her husband and all." Stephens sat Indian fashion, as Dog curled herself into a compact, fawn-colored shape in the sun, just outside the tent. "She did not seem like a woman suited for all this at first look. Mrs. Patterson, she looked to be more the usual woman, one fit for life out here. Hardships strike but make stronger, like steel. Your wife looked like something delicate carved in ivory, would shatter at the first blow but she turned out to be good steel underneath."

"I've always known that."

"You did? Better than I knew, Doc. Strikes me that a man needs to have a good idea of who he really married, that way life don't deal him out any more bad surprises than are strictly necessary. Anyway, back to trail business." Stephens sighed. "No, it ain't all that bad. We lost six through the stampede, and one we had to shoot, through being leg-broke. Couple more didn't come through the desert real well. Might be able to nurse them, might have to shoot them for meat. Might be able to find some of them, too, looking up and down the river, but I wouldn't hold my breath about it. Greenwood and his boys been scouting west and upstream; It looks good, Doc, looks real good. But we'll have every animal yoked to a wagon, once we hitch up again. There ain't a spare herd."

"But we've only to get over the mountains now," John answered after a moment.

"That we do," Stephens looked as if he might have said more, but for Elizabeth returning. "We'll move on when Greenwood and the boys return and the teams are rested. Miz Patterson said you're on the mend, and fit to ride in a day or two, so that works well."

"And we are through the worst of this journey, are we not?" Elizabeth averred cheerily, but John noted how Stephens seemed to hesitate before he replied, "Should be, Miz Townsend, should be." And tipping his hat to her, he slipped out of the tent.

Elizabeth set his desk beside him, and sat on the edge of the tick mattress. "It does seem such a pleasant place, Dearest Doctor. It almost seems as if we were picnicking in the country for the pleasure of it. I might almost be tempted to lie down on the grass and rest my head on your shoulder, as if I were a silly girl with nothing on my mind but the next pretty dress to wear."

"Why, Mrs. Townsend, I do believe you are flirting with me," John remarked as he opened his writing desk, and she giggled.

"La, Doctor Townsend, you might very well be right! No, I shall just keep you company, as you write, and if I should rest my eyes for a little bit . . . we are chaperoned by the entire party, so I doubt that anything the least untoward shall happen." She fell comfortably silent them, as he began to write, and he saw after a few moments that she had indeed fallen asleep.

* * *

From Dr. Townsends' diary: *"I was myself afflicted with a case of sunstroke, and many of our party are much exhausted by the exertions necessary to cross the desert. For the moment, we are counting our blessings in having safely reached such a fortunate place as this, and have named it after our benefactor who guided us hence . . .*

"Thirteenth of October, 1844: We have followed Truckee's River in a westerly direction. We experienced some little trouble in coming through some hills, where the river descended through a steep canyon . . . we continue to be abundantly supplied with grass, firewood, water, and game et cetera . . . this day entered a fine open upland, a grassy meadow surrounded by low and rolling hills."

From E.S. Patterson Interview, University of California Local History Archival Project 1932: *"Ma and us and everyone else, we were all right happy, once we had got to that river and out of the desert. We thought, well, we were nearly there. We came up river to an open valley, place where the city of Reno is now. It was all an open meadow then, with the river running through it and willow thickets and cottonwoods and poplars all around, and more mountains ahead. Now and again we saw patches of trees, up higher, with their leaves all turned to bright gold. Paw-Paw said they was aspens. Now and again there was frost on the ground of a morning, and a little bit of ice in the water buckets, but we paid it no mind at first, until one morning, there was snow on the mountains and all around of our camp, a dusting of it, like fine white sugar."*

* * *

"Oh, Dearest," Elizabeth groaned one morning, as she slid out from under the warm nest of blankets and the buffalo robe, shivering as she pulled on her dress and stockings and shoes. "I think now of how hot it was in the desert, and how much I longed for coolness, and now that we have it, I could wish for a little more warmth. Why is it we are never very long in a perfectly comfortable place, but must move on to some new extreme?"

"Because it is in our nature to never be entirely content." John hastily pulled on his own outer garments. "Silly of us, I know, but Adam and Eve were not entirely satisfied with Paradise, were they?" He undid the canvas apron at the front of the wagon, and stopped, dead still. "Dearest Liz, no wonder it is cold this morning . . . it has snowed during the night."

Elizabeth peeped around him, looking out at the clean white fall unmarked by anything save the restless cattle. "It is not so very deep. Surely it will melt during the day." Happy shouts of delight came from the Patterson's wagon, and from the Murphy camp where the children had already begun throwing snowballs at each other and at James Murphy.

"Perhaps," John answered, but the chill he felt was not entirely due to the snowfall. He pulled on his own coat and went to look for Stephens. He found him with Greenwood and Hitchcock, all three of them grave and sober, around Stephens' new-kindled campfire.

"It's a light fall," Hitchcock was saying. "It prolly won't stick, but the point is, it's mid-October now and we can't count on more than another three, four weeks of clear weather."

"What do you say, Caleb? Morning, Doc." Stephens nodded at John. "We was just considering the snow. Any idee how much it piles up of a winter in these here parts?"

"You know what I've said before; skedaddle now," Greenwood said bluntly. "I never trapped in these parts, so I don't know for sure, but I seen it plenty deep otherwise. I'd guess eight, ten feet, but I don't want to be around to make sure."

"Pack everything on your back and walk out," Old Hitchcock enlarged on Greenwood's answer, but John shook his head.

"We couldn't possibly carry enough to feed all, not if we'd have to carry the children also."

"I'd agree with you on that, Doc," Stephens rested his hands on Dog's fawn-colored head, "since we don't know how much farther to the summit. But we might have to consider it, sometime."

"Later than sooner, I hope." John asked, and Stephens answered cryptically, "I ain't a one for waiting 'til we have no choice at all."

To the relief of John and others, including Old Martin Murphy, that snow melted rapidly in the warmth of the day, leaving little trace of it by afternoon, although the children were deeply disappointed.

"I fear that we are on borrowed time, Liz," John spoke quietly in the wagon that night. Elizabeth curled spoon-fashioned against him, her back tucked into the curve of his body, and her head just under his chin. He held her close, under a sufficiency of quilts and the buffalo robe spread over all.

She held his hand in hers, against her cheek, and murmured sleepily, "How so, Dearest?"

"The snow . . . winter is coming on. The trees in the higher elevations have turned all colors, weeks since. How many mornings has it been that we found ice in the water buckets? It's been freezing at night, and I think it will be colder the farther we advance into the mountains. We've always known we must be over the mountains before winter has been well established."

"Mmmm . . . perhaps the winter will be no more than like what we have always known . . . two or three big storms, and snow just up to the bottom fence rail, and all else frozen still and solid. That might not be so very dreadful."

"Ah, Liz, we could only hope that it would be a winter such as we are accustomed, then we would not have so much concern. But Greenwood and Old Hitchcock have much experience in the western mountains — although not in these — and they both aver that the snow becomes impassibly deep in that season – that any kind of movement is next to impossible, and how can the cattle dig down for fodder, as they are used to do? We must feed the cattle so they may continue to pull the wagons, which are full of our stores and serve to shelter ourselves. Greenwood and Hitchcock, they have always favored pack-beasts, moving fast with little, living off the country."

"But they are hard men, accustomed to that sort of life and method." Sleepily, Elizabeth had put her finger on the crux of it. "We do not have enough pack animals to move us all along, all the children, and Mary-Bee Murphy in security and plenty. Is it possible to use oxen as pack-beasts, Dearest? I think not, for I assume we would have seen such being done already."

"No, they are accustomed to pulling, not directly bearing a burden upon their backs," John replied.

Elizabeth kissed his hand, that lay under her cheek, and said drowsily, "I think I would sleep now, my Dear doctor; sufficient unto the day are the evils thereof."

In the morning there was no new snow, only frost coating the ice and crackling like broken shards of glass under foot. Sarah already had the fire going, and Elizabeth brought the coffee mill closer to it, and began grinding coffee beans for the first pot of the day. The winter dark pressed close upon them, and Elizabeth pulled her heaviest shawl closer. John had gone off in the direction of the men's privy pit, yawning hugely. But he dropped a light kiss on Elizabeth's face, and after he had gone, Elizabeth noticed that Sarah looked wistful.

"I wish that Mr. Montgomery did that," she said, after a moment.

"Does he not?" Elizabeth said in some surprise. "Perhaps it is because he is newly come to the married state and has not developed certain habits of affection. Was Mr. Montgomery not gAllent in his addresses to you before you wed?"

"No more than any other," Sarah shrugged. "And seeming for a while afterwards. . . . But of late, it seems we can barely exchange two words without snarling at each other like a pair of wild cats."

She sat down suddenly on the wagon bench next to Elizabeth and dropped her head into her hands. "I don't know what I expected of being married . . . but not this."

"It is only the difficulties of this journey," Elizabeth said in compassion, for Sarah seemed truly unhappy. "They try us all, very deeply."

"Not you and Doctor John," Sarah answered vehemently, and now she had tears rolling down her face. "Nor does it try Mr. Murphy and Mary-Bee, or Annie and Mr. Jamie . . . they seem content in each other's company in spite of it all. But Mr. Montgomery seems better to like spending his time among the other young men, as if he had no wife at all. I know not why we married; only that custom commands that a man have a wife, and a woman a husband!"

"But even if there is only mutual respect, and obedience to custom at the outset, one may come to truly love one's helpmate after marriage." Elizabeth took one of Sarah's hands in hers. "Love can grow, after a fashion; you and Mr. Montgomery seemed well-matched, of a good age to marry, and of similar temper. Sarah, dear, I beg you to nurture the liking you had for each other when you first were wed – surely you had good reasons in your heart for accepting his suit?"

"I did, then," Sarah smeared the tears on her face with the back of her hand. "He was handsome and spoke well. He had a good trade, and was a fine match for a poor orphan without any family and also he had Doctor John's approval."

"No more than that?" Elizabeth was a little taken back. "But surely, there must have been something else, something that drew your particular regard?"

Sarah shook her head. "No. Not much more than that. Did you not marry Doctor John for much the same consideration?"

"I was not then an orphan," Elizabeth considered thoughtfully. "And though I would never say so to anyone but you, Sarah dear – my Dearest has never been considered handsome. But he had an excellent profession, and was very well spoken. He talked to me of books, and matters that he was interested in, and so attracted my regard above other suitors."

"And after you were wed, did he still seem so very fine to you?" Sarah asked, and it seemed with some bitterness. "Were there as many good qualities to him after marriage as there seemed before?"

"Oh, yes – even some of which I was not aware at first, although I think I sensed it from the start."

"And what was that?"

Elizabeth smiled with great fondness. "He is utterly reliable in his care for me and for those he loves, for his patients and those who rely upon him. He is like a rock for security upon which we all depend, like the parable."

"Mr. Montgomery is like sand," Sarah answered wonderingly, as if she had just thought of that. "He is like sand, borne away by the current. It is not my fault, then, it is just the way he is." She squeezed Elizabeth's comforting hand, and it seemed that she suddenly looked more cheerful. "I would not have thought of it in that way! You are a true friend, not just because you have words of wise comfort, but that they make me see things in a way that relieves my own mind. Do not worry for me, Mrs. Elizabeth. I will pine no longer over what cannot be repaired though my own efforts."

"I will be glad for you." Elizabeth resumed grinding coffee beans. "Although I am not entirely sure what I said which gave you comfort."

"Don't worry, then," Sarah lifted her chin, "for I will not. We will be in California soon, and Mr. Montgomery and I will make some accommodation to each other."

Unfortunately it seemed that every day brought an evil in the weeks as they followed Truckee's river into the upper canyon above the meadows. Steep hills drew tight on either side, as if the canyon walls closed in like the jaws of a trap.

"It ain't any better around the bend." Stephens slumped wearily in the saddle, his pony standing knee deep in frigid water. John and Patrick Martin, and Old Martin's younger sons labored in deeper water with a long pole, attempting to lever a tall standing boulder out of the way. The wagons and their teams waited; some of them in the river, waiting for the way to be cleared; the only passage here was in the river itself.

"Push down!" John gasped. "Put your back into it, man, it's moving!"

"One . . . two . . . three!" Patrick shouted, and on the last count, they bore down on the lever with greater effort, and the boulder heeled over with a crash and splash, now lying flat enough in the current that the wagons could pass over without too much difficulty. All five of them squelched out of the river and sank gasping on the narrow bank.

"Cheerful words!" John said. "Exactly . . . what . . . I . . . need to hear."

"Faith and I'm getting too old for this," Patrick answered. "We've crossed the river how many times is it, just to make a mile, this day alone?"

"Eight times, and one more around the farther bend," Stephens replied. In mid-stream Old Martin's wagon negotiated the rocks, rocking violently as the iron-shod wheels rolled over and among rocks hidden in the streambed.

The three of them held their breaths, as it tilted one way, nearly tipping over, then righted with a crash and a jolt.

"And I thought it was rough going, back on a road in Missouri," John observed. He was well soaked and his boots sodden. He could barely feel his feet, numbed from immersion in the river's icy water. All of the men were numbed, cold, and exhausted by the end of a day struggling to move the wagons, but the oxen were in worse case.

"Did you ever hear about the poor Irishman?" Patrick stood, wearily, balancing the pole over his shoulder. "Who was in a bad way, and the landlord said, 'Now, Paddy, cheer up, things could be worse'" And Poor Paddy cheered up and sure enough . . ." Patrick spun out the point of his joke. "Sure enough, things got worse!"

"Must be your way of telling us, there are two great rocks around the next bend," John said wryly and Stephens answered, "And a fallen tree wedged between."

"Jay-sus," Patrick sighed. "Ah well – who's got an ax now?"

Day after day, they struggled on, chilled, wet, and aching, fighting the rocks and an icy wind that whistled down the canyons. The oxen's feet softened from constant immersion on water, bruised from rocks until every step was a torment for them. Finally they would not move unless it were in water, which both relieved their pain but worsened their condition, and urged by a drover who must walk at their side, hip-deep in water himself.

Most days it seemed like they did not pick a campsite, merely stopped when they were tired enough to drop. And even then, John found little rest for himself; being called to doctor the hurts and bruises of the day, stitching up gashes in hands too tired to swing an ax well, feet and ankles bruised on rocks.

"Why then, did you not move out of the way?" John inquired of Joseph Foster. "You could see it was going to roll in your direction, couldn't you?" He was gingerly feeling along Joseph's right foot, purple and bruised nearly all over, searching for broken bones.

"I don't know, Doc, I just don't know. I think I was either too tired to move, or just too tired to care."

"I don't think you've broken anything, since you can bear weight on it . . . but for the love of God, Joseph, move yourself from the path of the next boulder that the Martin boys are shifting out of the way."

Day after day, Greenwood and his boys rode ahead, sometimes with Stephens, always coming back to report more of the same; the river and the rocks, steep canyon walls on one side or the other, grey granite walls hemming them in, until one afternoon the clouds loomed up, sparkling at the edges where the sun caught them. The first fat white flakes began drifting down like feathers as they made camp for the day, despair in their hearts. Snow that fell this thick and fast, this was nothing that would melt in the warmth of the next day's sunshine.

Winter was here, and they were fairly caught in it as in a trap, still on the far side of the mountains. By morning, there was more than a foot of it on the ground, and the oxen lowing in despair for now the grass was buried deep. Martin Murphy cut some green pine branches, hoping that they might be at least tempted to eat of something green, to no avail. Nothing to do the next morning but move on, sick with apprehension, sick with cold that went straight to the bone, driving on the tormented oxen in a veil of fast-falling snow.

"There's a wider place, three or four miles on," Greenwood reported. "Shallow and open, with a great stand of rushes . . . they ate rushes in the desert, they'll eat them here when there's naught else above the snow."

And so they did, but with such eagerness that two of them died of a surfeit, but as Young Martin said, optimistically, "As long as we camp where they can find rushes . . . they'll have some fodder at least."

Until the snow buries the rushes, John thought, and wondered how many more days that would be.

"There's not an end to it," he said that night to Elizabeth. "The desert crossing . . . that was bad, but we know there would be an end to it if we just kept moving. This . . . there's no end to it. It's been . . . what, three weeks since we came up from the meadows, since that first snow?"

"We have come far up into the mountains," Elizabeth answered. "Did you not notice how the trees changed?"

"I was too busy chopping them down," John grumbled.

"There were cottonwoods and willows around the river in the great meadow, lower down. And then there were aspen trees, and then pines and sage mixed and aspen trees still, but I think we have moved quite far up. I have only seen pines in the last day or so. We may be near to the very roof of the mountains, Dearest. If I recollect, the only thing higher on a mountain than pine trees, are no trees at all."

"We can hope, Liz, we can hope. That may be what we have most left of . . . hope."

* * *

From Dr. Townsend's diary: *"Thirteenth of November, 1844. This day with much the usual toil came to a confluence of the river which has been our guide. The river itself bends to the southwest, ascending a narrow but lightly wooded canyon. The tributary tends directly in a westerly line, a broader and more open vista, which terminates in a mass of great grey mountains, veiled in snow. We must make some kind of decision; but as we have twice before been guided by fortune to strike directly west, I am in no doubt of what our choice on this occasion will be . . ."*

Chapter 11 – *The Choosing*

From Dr. Townsend's diary: *"Fourteenth of November, 1844 In the wilderness at the fork of Truckee's River. This day, I can scarce put pen to paper, being distract'd with grief and worry. Our party is split yet again, this again being of our own decision. My own Dearest is gone ahead with five others, judged fit and sound, and without the care of little ones to attend. Yesterday, our labors brought us to where a tributary came down from the mountains, athwart our path and leading to the south. We made camp in late afternoon, and Captain Stephens called a meeting."*

* * *

"We can't take the wagons much farther," said Young Martin flatly, as if daring anyone to argue with him. "Unless we follow the west tributary." He dropped down onto an upturned cask that he was using as a stool, and wincingly pulled off his waterlogged boots. He peeled off his socks, which were also soaked.

"Out of our way," murmured Old Hitchcock, looking into the fire, past his eternal whittling, and his knife-blade. "The long way around."

"The long way around may prove the shortest," answered Stephens gently. "We done well before, heading straight west; at the Green, and again from the Sink. I'll wait to hear what Isaac says."

He sat a little way back from the fire on a half-rotted fallen log, Dog at his feet. Her great fawn and black head lay on her forepaws, golden eyes going back and forth as if she was paying intelligent attention to the conversation. The fire was the smallest of the three outside the circle of wagons and tents, set up on the lee side a barrier against the icy breeze roaring down from the high mountains and the cold that came at sundown, the cold that was most particularly felt when the exertions of the day were over.

Allen Montgomery, and the Murphy brothers, Jamie, Daniel, Bernard, and Johnny, hunkered around the fire. It had the air of an informal meeting of the men, while the women cooked a sparse but much anticipated meal. The horses and Hitchcock's precious two mules were close-picketed for the night just on the other side of the wagons, inside the circle jostling each other for mouthfuls of tall dry grass bristling up from the day's accumulation of snow and armfuls of green rushes cut from the riverbank by the women and older children.

Around that fragile shelter of canvas, brush, and fires, the snow was trampled to a muddy slush. At other fires, Isabella, Sarah, and the Murphy women moved in an intricate ballet, skirts, shawls, and sleeves carefully held back from the fire, as they cooked the evening meal: stew and cornbread that tasted like sawdust with no butter to spread richly on it, dried apples stewed with a little spice. Even Isabella's milk cow had gone dry, months since.

Mary-Bee Murphy sat with Mary Miller on a wagon bench, dandling the baby Ellen, while her sons and Willie Miller and their cousin Mary leaned on Old Martin's knees, or sat bundled in shawls at his feet as he told them another endless story about miracles, and goblins and old heroes of Erin. It was hard to judge by a casual looking, John thought, of how far along Mary-Bee was, all bundled in shawls as she was, but she still walked lightly. She was not far enough gone in pregnancy to be awkward, but she tired easily.

His glance was drawn finally, as it always would be, to his own Liz, her hair silver-gilt in the firelight, wrapped in two shawls and the buffalo robe that Old Man Hitchcock had traded for her from the tribes at Fort Laramie. Sitting on another wagon bench, she had Sadie in her lap, Nancy and Eddie leaning confidingly against her under the shelter of that buffalo robe.

Poor Liz, she had never been any shakes as a cook, had never even had to be, let alone over a campfire. But to do her fair, she tried her best, at a cost of burnt fingers, scorching her own apron, and upsetting a pot of beans and near to putting the fire out. Isabella spoke out in tones of mixed exasperation and affection, somewhere back along the trail when the three families had begun to share a campfire. *Elizabeth would do them all favors if she could but stay away from the fire and the hot kettles; chop the vegetables, if she would be so kind, and read to the children, give them lessons and keep them out from underfoot.*

In that mysterious way she had of seeming to know when he was gazing at her, her eyes lifted from the book and met his for a smiling moment, quiet communion among the crowd around the campfire. He was here, she was there, and yet they were alone together. And then she went on reading to the children, and he was supposed to be also paying attention to the needs of others in the party.

They had all become a tribe, John realized, a tribe of nomads as like to any of the Indians, bound together, sharing hardship alike with those moments in the evening, those rare moments of rest. Across the trampled circle, Moses and Dennis Martin stepped out of the darkness between two wagons, each with an armload of firewood. They piled their burden roughly beside the largest of the fires, and a storm bright burst of sparks flew up like fireflies meeting the stars overhead.

" Tonight, after we've supped."

"A meeting?" John was startled back from his nearly simultaneous contemplation of his dear wife and of Young Martin's left foot, dead white, nearly bloodless, propped up on his knee. "Pardon – I was lost, considering this interesting combination of foot-rot and frostbite. Dry socks, Martin, dry socks and liniment. Contemplate sealing your boots with tallow and paraffin. Other than that, consider staying out of the water as much as you can . . ." There was a dry laugh, shared around the circle around fire. In the last three weeks, they had been forced into the riverbed time and time again, as it provided the easiest, and on occasion, the only passage for the wagons.

"We must consider what we should do now," Stephens said. "We might send a party ahead, along the south branch."

He fell silent, as Mary-Bee Murphy came with a basin and a steaming kettle, and Isabella bearing a dry cloth and her box of medicinal salts. "Doctor, tell him to soak in this for a bit and dry them carefully. We'll bring a set of dry stockings presently, and dry his boots beside the fire."

"Mrs. Patterson, you are a tonic." Extravagantly, John caught her hand and took it to his lips. "And an excellent nurse; I shall see that the patient follows your advice to the letter."

Isabella gave him a very severe look, as Mary-Bee awkwardly set down the basin and filled it with steaming water. Isabella added salts and gathered up the socks and the sodden boots. Mary-Bee looked as if she would say something more, but she merely patted her husband's shoulder and followed in Isabella's wake. "See that he does then, Doctor Townsend, see that he does," Isabella shot, over her shoulder.

When she was gone back to the cook-fire and out of hearing, Stephens remarked, "A good woman is above the price of rubies."

"I long to meet the man who would play Petruchio to her Kate," John said, just as Greenwood appeared as silently as a ghost in the circle of firelight, shadowed by Britt and heralded only by the scent of tobacco smoke.

Stephens grinned, a flash of teeth in his whiskered face. "Nearly as much as I'd like to be warm again, and over those pestilential mountains; he must be a formidable man. I imagine a very Ajax."

"Not so," said Hitchcock seriously. "M'son-in-law's a very mild-tempered man. Never has much to say for hisself."

"Married to her, who'd wonder?" ungallantly ventured Bernard Murphy *sotto voice*, as Greenwood sank onto his heels and held his hands to the fire, looking every day of his fourscore. Britt took up a seat next to Stephens on the log and casually gentled Dog's alertly-raised head. She lay down again with an inaudible "woof." Stephens merely lifted his brows, and Greenwood sighed.

"Not so good for wagons, Cap'n. Not 'less you had a month of good weather and a hundred strong men and them with an ax in either hand. Horses? Yeah, easy enough. We blazed it, two, three miles, far as we could, 'fore sunset. Horses and pack-mules. It looks right promising otherwise, but I've always said if you want to be over these mountains by winter, you'll have to leave all your traps and ride hard."

"No." It was Isabella's voice. She had returned unobtrusively to the fire-circle, joining the men, as was her right as a wagon-owner and the head of a family. "We cannot just leave our traps, as you say. We have chosen out all the most valuable and useful of goods, and brought them all this way; we cannot just drop them by the wayside as things of no consequence."

Greenwood shrugged. "They're only things. You can get back things, or something like them."

"Things? Things, as you say, but our things! We considered them very carefully; these are things that are not only valuable to us, but things that we need! They are not frivolous possessions, but necessary tools to earning our livelihoods! Without those 'things' we should be beggars, dependant upon charity." Her keen hawk-glance went round the circle of faces, and John thought of his books; the case of surgical instruments, Liz' precious china tea set that came from her grandmother whose family had brought it from Germany and cherished through generations. "And what of the children? Can they ride hard? Can Mary Miller ride, with a baby at breast, or Mary-Bee Murphy, so close to term? The wagon is our shelter, our home! I'll not be a beggar, I'll not be destitute. What if any of us fall sick, through lack of shelter? What do you say, Doctor? How many of us would be fit to leave all behind and ride hard?" Her hard, inimical glare pinned him, challenged him to speak, to venture his opinion.

"The very youngest or those of a weak constitution could not endure very long in such conditions as this without shelter," John stammered. As many times as he had talked this over with Elizabeth in the privacy of their bed, he was still stuck on the two-horned dilemma, having never come to any conclusion in his own mind. "Nor the very old, either –" Old Hitchcock snorted derisively at this, and would have said more but for his daughter's fierce gaze swinging around towards him. "The wagons . . . they are at least of some shelter. I would not choose to leave them. I do not think we could carry enough food and blankets and tents on our backs for the weeks of traveling we still must endure . . . not if we had to carry the weakest of us."

Stephens sighed, lines of weariness and responsibility harshly grooving his features in the firelight. "Our supplies diminish every day that we spend this side of the mountains. I know that my own do, so I assume the same of you all. Old Man, how far do you think we might be from Sutter's Fort?"

"I do not know for sure, "Greenwood answered bluntly. "A week's journey on a good horse to the summit, maybe longer; his place is down in the flatland, on the river, a good piece from the mountains on the other side."

"What sort of man is he? If we sent a messenger asking for aid, would he send it?"

"Aye, he would. I know nothing of him at first hand, though. But he is accounted to be generous, and he has ambitions."

"As do most men, but I've a hankering to know what he has ambitions for." Stephens stood wearily and stretched. "Doctor, I'd like to call a meeting – not now, after we've all supped. Not just the wagon-owners. Everybody. Tell them it's to consider sending out a small party ahead. He saluted Isabella with a touch to his hat brim, "Pardon, all. I shall check on the stock. No," he added as Greenwood looked to get to his feet. "You've earned some rest, Old Man." Dog's eyes had snapped open as soon as Stephens moved, and now she lurched to her feet and padded after him into the darkness outside the firelight.

John sighed; he was wearied to his very bones, how Greenwood must feel after his long scout today he could only imagine. The old man must be made of iron and buffalo sinews to have endured this kind of odyssey for years.

"Supper's ready," said Isabella abruptly. "The table is set . . . that is, if we had a table."

John stood and bowed elaborately, offering her his arm. "My dear Mrs. Patterson, then may I then escort you to . . . our lack of table and our evening repast?"

Isabella nodded regally, her lips twitching with her effort not to laugh. "How very kind of you, my dear Doctor." She took his arm with a flourish, and they moved with elaborate gentility across the trampled mud to their own fire, where Elizabeth watched them, laughing, while the children stared in baffled astonishment.

"La, Mrs. Patterson, I fear you are flirting with my own husband!" she said, while Isabella dissolved into hearty and infectious giggles.

"My dearest, I am wounded at the heart!" John slapped his chest theatrically. "How could I consider being unfaithful to you, even in thought!" He sank onto the bench next to her, as the children had sprung up to help Isabella pass out tin plates.

He added in a low voice, "Although I confess I now can see how Mr. Patterson's affections might have been drawn towards our own Kate."

"Because she is altogether splendid," Elizabeth replied. "But too many men are fools. A pretty face and a kind regard is all that is necessary for their attentions. A strong mind and a stout heart are not obviously apparent."

"I am properly rebuked," John said, and they sat together in perfect companionship under the buffalo robe, while Sadie brought around the tin plates and her brother a pan of cornbread. Isabella carried an iron Dutch oven, from which the most savory scents emanated. She carefully doled out a ladle and a half to each. Across the fire John saw that Allen and Sarah sat next to each other, but separate.

Elizabeth followed his gaze, and intuited his thoughts, perfectly. "They are not happy. I doubt they will ever be. They married in haste, thinking they would come to love each other, but I cannot see how that will happen under the trials of such a journey as this."

"Perhaps when we get to California," John ventured. "It may yet work out." He took a mouthful of the stew. "Oh, this is truly succulent fare . . . or am I just amazingly hungry?"

Elizabeth twinkled merrily. "It is a Luccellian feast, is it not?"

"This cannot be a potato, surely? I thought we had eaten the last of the potatoes months ago. Murphy made such an event of it; I made a note in the trail diary."

"No," Elizabeth replied. "Those things that taste somewhat potato-like are roots of water-reeds. The Indians eat them, even dry, and grind a sort of flour out of them or so Mr. Hitchcock says. And we found stands of wild onions when we first came up into the mountains. Truly, this wilderness is a garden if you know where to look."

"Ah, well." John looked with new interest into the contents of his tin plate. "We are well served and well fed, Darling Dearest. I could not ask for better companions in all the world."

"So." Elizabeth ate with renewed interest. "What does Captain Stephens think we should do next?"

"He wants to hold a meeting." John replied. "I think he wants to send an advance party, following the creek towards the south, whilst we move the wagons west along the main body. We cannot spare too many men, or horses, though. But at least, they could bring fresh supplies and teams from Sutter's."

"Who will he send?" Elizabeth looked around the camp. "Who can be spared? Who can be asked to leave their families behind?"

John followed her gaze. Across the fire, Moses and Allen laughed together. Sarah's back was to her husband; she talked quietly with Isabella, who seemed to be listening with half an ear while she supervised the children. A tiny worry-line appeared between Elizabeth's level brows.

"He'll ask for volunteers first."

"Moses will ask to be sent, I am sure of it."

"Liz, dearest, he is not a child any more. He is a man, or close enough to it. And we will talk it all over tonight after we have supped."

Elizabeth's merry mood seemed to have fled though, and they ate in companionable silence until they could see that other men were drifting to Stephens's campfire, carrying benches and stools; Old Martin Murphy and his sons and James Miller, Patrick Martin and his boys, young Sullivan, and the various drovers. Sarah and Elizabeth hastily scoured the plates clean and followed Isabella. John clambered up into the wagon for his little writing-case; he had a sense that he ought to be taking the minutes.

The wagon-owners settled themselves in the first circle around the fire: Stephens and Greenwood, Isabella and her father, Allen, Martin Murphy and his sons, and James Miller, John Sullivan, and Patrick Martin. Wives, older children, brothers, and hired men filled in the spaces and spilled over to a second circle, and stood in the gaps behind benches and chairs brought out from the wagons. Coming to the confluence of waters meant a very real decision about what route to take now, a decision with nearly unbearable consequences, now that snow had been falling for weeks. No wonder Old Martin looked particularly worn, and cosseted his grandchildren. Fully half the party was his blood kin, and he the person most responsible for bringing them here, too.

"Aye, we must send for assistance, while we can, "Old Martin agreed. Like Isabella, he would not countenance abandoning the wagons; consensus regarding taking the slightly more open but possibly longer route along the creek was complete.

"And how many shall we send? And who can we spare, when we'll need every strong man to move the wagons, hey?"

"No more than six, "Greenwood replied. "Strong riders, with little gear and just enough food. Eight of the horses are in fair condition, still; six to ride, two for spares and packs." He cleared his throat and spat thoughtfully into the fire. He seemed almost to hesitate before saying more. "Whoever they be, 'twill be six less on the foodstuff left to the main party. And they need not all be men, either." That was a notion to cause an intake of breath around the fire, and a sudden, thoughtful silence.

Old Martin was the first to break it. "I'd not countenance asking a mother or a father yet, to leave children behind in a place such as this No, no, never, 'tis an unnatural thing y'd be asking. Not even the heathen savages would ask such."

"No," Greenwood agreed. "But among the tribes, women without children commonly ride with the hunting parties. They do the butchering and dressing out, and cooking and all."

"What a wonderful time they must have, doing all the work of it!" Sarah said, in a voice that carried just far enough, and there was a rustle of wry laughter from the women on the edge of the campfire.

"So how do we choose the six; should we draw lots from among those of age, young, fit, and without children?"

"Aye," agreed Old Martin readily. "But it is in my mind we should first pledge to assist the families of those chosen, whatever they may require. Our needs might leave them short of a provider and ready hands."

"So – are we agreed on that, then? To draw lots for a place and to see to the needs of any family left short?" Stephens' ugly, lined face appeared more than usually like a grim, fire-gilded gargoyle, looking around the circle. "We are agreed then? Are there any exceptions?"

"None but you, Captain – and the Doctor. You are more needed here with us."

"I had no intent of leaving this company, until we are all safe," replied Stephens dourly. "Nor does Doctor Townsend; so, how many will draw?" He leant down and began pulling stems of dried grass from the brown tufts which were still untrampled around his log seat."

The quiet murmurs ran around the campfire, quickly tallying names; Alan and Sarah, Greenwood's two sons, Stephens' young drover Tom Flomboy, Oliver Patterson, old Martin's youngest children, Daniel, Bernard, Johnny, and their sister Helen. The four drovers, Edmund Bray, Vincent Calvin, Matthew Harbin, Oliver Magnent, and Francis, John's own hired man. Joseph Foster, and Moses' close friends, Dennis and Patrick Martin. Not the Sullivans; after some discussion. John and Mary had the care of their younger brothers. But that left Moses himself . . . and his Elizabeth. John's heart seemed to turn over in his chest; all of them, fit and strong, young and childless, twenty of them, nearly a half of the party.

Stephens cut twenty straws, and then cut six of them in half. He set them in his palm so they were all level and then closed his fist. He held out that fist towards Allen Montgomery first, then Britt and John Greenwood. Allen and John Greenwood drew long straws, and so did Britt. Moses also drew a long straw. His disappointment was obvious, but John hoped that his own relief was not. The hired men drew in a body: the Irish drover boys and Stephens's drover lad, the dark Louisiana French boy whose name was such a tongue-twister; all drew long, but Oliver Magnent and Francis Deland both drew short. Joseph Foster stepped forward to draw: another long.

"Tarnation take it, another two months of this!" he said, in good-humored disappointment. "And all on short rations, too!"

"Daniel, Johnny, ye and Bernard step forrard. Where's Helen?" Old Martin chided his four youngest into the circle and looked on with a deathly countenance, when Helen, Johnny, and Daniel all drew short straws. Oliver Patterson stepped forward into the firelight to draw.

Stephens looked at him with a particularly severe and interrogatory frown. "Boy, are you of age for this venture?"

Oliver blushed deep red as Isabella said, white-lipped, "He will be eighteen in three months."

Oliver drew a long straw though, leaving a pair of wispy straws in Stephens' fist; Sarah and Elizabeth stepped forward, and John's heart felt as if it turned over entirely within his chest. Sarah drew a long straw, and could not hide the disappointment on her face.

Elizabeth then took forth the last of the straws from Stephens's hand: a short straw for the horse party. Elizabeth, not Moses; John was shaken down to the soul. Old Martin looked hardly better.

Stephens let the murmurings of excitement and sympathy die down and quietly said, "Doctor, take down their names into the trail journal. I'll want to talk to them, all together. They must leave in the morning, as soon as we are ready." He spoke a little louder, to the gathering at large. "Thank-ee all, sitting out in the cold for this. It's only trail business we had to settle tonight."

Taking their cue, the women began chivvying away the children who already had not been settled to bed. The younger men and the families of those who had not been chosen drifted away from Stephens' campfire in their wake; after such a day of travel, a warm bedroll had a powerful and irresistible allure.

As the evening meeting broke apart, Greenwood thoughtfully sized up the six chosen. "You were well-guided, Cap'n . . . they are well-suited. Among the women, Mrs. Townsend has the best seat, and little Helen is young and strong. It is good that her brothers are among them, they are both good hands with the beasts and fearless about venturing into wilderness. Magnent and Deland are good shots, and as trailwise as they come, besides being used to the cold and the snow."

"For me, I am glad Mrs. Townsend is amongst them." John said. His voice sounded hollow to his own ears. "The cold and the hardships are so extreme I fear for her under these circumstances, and welcome any means for her to escape farther exposure to the winter chill."

"It may be best at that." Old Greenwood looked grim. "Would that I could urge all to travel so light, and escape these mountains. At least they will be six less appetites upon the supplies we have left."

Old Martin and his children, Elizabeth and the two French lads, all of the chosen lingered by the fire as they were bidden. In the firelight, Elizabeth looked as young as they; all of them so eager, fired by the prospect of adventure, just as they all had been six months ago at Council Bluffs, when the grass was lush and deep, escaping the drudgery of a mundane existence. Now they looked fair to escape another one, of everlasting cold, and the brutal labor of moving the wagons another mile or so farther up the river, the river whose jaws were closing in on them like a trap.

Stephens looked at them and smiled wryly. "No great words . . . wish I did. Ride hard. Look after each other and the horses. Get to Sutters' place and bring back help."

"We shall!" Elizabeth's chin lifted, and her eyes were fired with determination. "We are leaving our kin and dearest ones, and our friends, knowing that their very salvation depends on us. Depend on us, Captain Stephens, we will not fail."

And even if Old Greenwood seemed to hide a half-cynical smile, the others – Helen and her brothers, the two Frenchmen, all shared the same look of bright dedication. They could not fail; they would throw themselves at the high mountains, the rocks and rivers and the ice, they would win through it all, they would come through, rescue their families, and John's heart felt as if it would burst with a combination of pride and dread.

"And we will not fail, "Elizabeth whispered, when they lay tucked together in their bedroll of blankets and quilts and the trusty buffalo robe, all spread out on top of the platform of boxes and flat-topped trunks in their wagon. The drawstrings and flaps were drawn tight against the cold. A kettle of coals taken from the fire lent an illusion of warmth to the tiny, canvas-walled room. A pair of flat stones heated in the fire, wrapped in a blanket and tucked in the bottom of their bed produced a slightly more convincing degree of warmth, together with the warmth of each other, curled spoon-fashioned.

Around and outside this fragile shelter came the quiet, near-to sleep voices of Isabella's children, Allen Montgomery's irritated voice raised and quickly hushed, a quiet crunch of regular footsteps in new snow, the horses pawing the frozen ground, searching for more of the thin dried grass. Under it all, a nearly-imperceptible yet menacing rustle, the constant sound of more snow falling, brushing the canvas and pine branches; fat flakes like feathers, like falling leaves.

"I wish . . ." said John, into her hair, hugging her dear and familiar self into the shelter of his own body, "I wish that we . . ."

"Had not taken this journey?" Elizabeth picked up the thread of his thoughts as expertly as she had always done. "Oh, my dear, never wish that. No, never. For I am glad that we have, even if this would be the last night we spend in each others' arms . . . and it will not be," she added firmly, and took his hand in hers, and held it first to her lips, and then her cheek. After a moment she continued thoughtfully. "I almost feel as if my life before we started this journey was lived in shadows, a sort of half-life, and then I came out into bright sunshine. Did not we decide upon this great adventure partly because of my own health? And now I am in good heath, and have shared your life in a way that I never could before. In our present emergency, I am accounted strong enough to be given a great task, a responsibility? There should be no greater reward, I do not ask for any such. Dearest, there is nothing to regret. I love you all the more for having made this possible. Have no fear for me . . . I will be safe, and we will not fail."

"I pray that shall be so." John tightened his arms around her, at once wishing for this night with Elizabeth never to end, full knowing it would be the last they would spend together for weeks if not months, and yet wishing that it were tomorrow already, and the agony of parting already over. He was torn between pride in her courage and worry for her that shook him down to his bones.

"We should go to sleep, Liz, you'll need as much rest tonight as possible."

"Mmmm. Don't stay awake yourself, watching over me," Elizabeth said teasingly, but John did try to fight off slumber for a while, until sleep claimed them both.

And then too soon it was dark morning, and snow still falling, and he was standing, wretchedly tongue-tied in front of people, for once. He had promised Elizabeth back in the desert that he should not have to go on a long scout again and be separated from her. And now, ironically, she was riding on a long scout, leaving him to plod behind.

"Promise me rather, that wherever one of us will go, the other will follow after in a little while," she had said, and so he would be following after, but it was bitter, bitter. Moses and he had saddled Beau, rolled up the buffalo robe and two or three blankets around a pitiful bag of dried meats and hard-tack, and a little ground coffee and strapped them behind her saddle. Isabella and Sarah had fussed over what to send with her, just as the Murphy women had fussed over Helen, Johnny, and Daniel.

Old Martin had tears rolling down his cheeks as he gave his youngest daughter a boost into the saddle. Daniel's paint pony danced impatiently, crunching the fresh-fallen snow underfoot; the lads were eager to be away.

"Dearest, I must go now." She leaned down from the saddle, and brushed his cheek with her lips, and then she was gone, following the rest of the mounted party. They were veiled in falling slow before they reached the first bend and were lost to sight, but he was almost sure she turned in the saddle and lifted her hand in one last farewell.

Chapter 12 – *The Very Roof of the Mountains*

From E.S. Patterson Interview, University of California Local History Archival Project 1932: *"There was snow falling every day that we moved the wagons along the river. I don't think we knew how bad things was, until Ma told Mister Stephens to kill the milk cow. We were only children, you see, but my little sister Sadie, she cried and cried. We all cried, even Ma, I think. That was the one milk cow we took from the old farm in Iowa, and Ma, she still scolded us for crying. The men and Ma had consulted and decided to leave six wagons at the lake, and continue on with the teams that were still fit."*

From Dr. Townsend's diary: *"Twentieth of November, 1844 . . . still encamped at a lake in the mountains, endeavoring to find a way over the rampart of the mountains. There are three notches in the mountain wall to the west, the lower of the three appears to offer the clearest path. Captain Stephens has called another meeting."*

* * *

It seemed to John almost a twin of the meeting a week before, when Elizabeth and the others had drawn straws for the fast-moving party to go down the south fork, instead of carrying on west with the wagons: the fire burning on a bed of cherry-red coals, throwing up a shower of sparks, as another armload of wood we tossed into it, Stephens looking like a grim, bearded gargoyle.

"Folks," he said, quietly, "Thanks for coming round. It's too cold for a long palaver, so I'll bite the bullet first. It's been brought up before; we ought to leave the wagons –" He held up his hand, at the murmur of disagreement around the fire, and Isabella cried out, "We can't! How can we manage with the children!"

"Miz Patterson, we already been all over that ground. I already know how some of you would be in a passel of trouble, trying to pack out enough to keep everyone fed an' sheltered. So here's my thought. Leave five or six wagons here, pack the rest with just what we'd need. Pool the fit oxen to double-team those wagons. And," he looked serenely around the group of faces gilded by firelight, half in flickering shadow, "I'll be the first to say I'll leave my wagon here and put my team in the pool and come back in the spring to bring it out. Anyone else?"

"Yes." John said. "Mine also." He felt half-defensive about it, especially looking at Moses' face. "While I value the property in it, I valued the wagon more as it sheltered Mrs. Townsend. Since she is gone with the horseback party, my team might better serve those of us who still need shelter."

"I'll add in my team," Joseph Foster spoke up. "I've only got but two yoke left, and there's not much left in the wagon anyways. But she's a stout little bit of carpentry and just about the only thing I own. I'll sweeten Captain Stephens offer; I'll stay here to watch over the property and wagons that any of you care to leave here. I'd build a little cabin and hunt for my supper."

"I'll stay, as well," Allen Montgomery spoke up abruptly. "I'd just as soon bring my wagon out in the spring – if my wife may travel on under yours and your fathers' protection, Mrs. Patterson."

"She has it," Isabella protested warmly, at once, and put her arm around Sarah, whose expression transparently warred between anger and relief. "Sarah, you are dear and welcome. You should move whatever small things you need to our wagon, and stay with us as long as necessary."

"I'll stay, also." Moses spoke up, suddenly.

Stung, John cried, "No, lad . . . what shall I tell your sister?"

"That I stayed to guard our family's property," Moses pointed out with perfect assurance.

Meanwhile, Old Martin had been consulting in whispers with Young Martin and James, Patrick Martin, and James Miller.

Now he said heavily, "Patrick and I have agreed to leave our wagons also. Martin and James have little childer, and Mary has the baby. I think it a good plan, Stephens — the only thing we can do now."

"Some of the oxen are not fit enough, even double-teamed," Young Martin said. He looked troubled, and Stephens replied, "That's the other part of it. We'll have to cull the ones that are failing. It's cold now enough to keep the flesh wholesome for weeks . . . we can even leave some for the boys to live on until they can hunt proper." He sat back, his big hands dangling over his knees. "Well, those are my thoughts . . . shall we go ahead and vote proper on it?"

"No," Old Murphy replied. "I think we're pretty much agreed."

"We'll need to work on it pretty brisk now," Stephens said, "before another storm comes in on us. Sort out the supplies tonight. Tomorrow we cull the oxen and repack."

"No other thoughts then, gentlemen . . . and lady?" John asked.

No one had, and he lingered behind with Stephens as the others scattered to their various bedrolls. "Captain . . . it's about the only way we had out of this mess, a compromise like that."

"Aye, well, I hope I didn't leave it too late," Stephens sighed. "We might be in a real pickle yet, Doc. If anyone sets up wrangling about staying or leaving, or fighting over this or that – I leave it to you to settle. I ain't real good at soothing over folk, and tomorrow's not a day I am looking forward to."

Nor am I, either, thought John, n*or am I either. Now I have to think on what little I can take with me, since I must beg for space in someone else's wagon for it.*

After the meeting, he sat in his wagon, turning over one of Elizabeth's shawls in his hand; perhaps if he folded it small, and tucked it into a bedroll. There was so little he could take now — a change of clothes for himself, and his rifle, and ammunition for it. The writing desk and diary, of course. Those were small, and so was the box of surgical tools and medicinal supplies. He drew out another box, the one with Elizabeth's grandmother's tea set. It was not something he wanted to leave behind; they had left so many things behind in taking part in this great adventure; this was the only frivolous, unnecessary thing they had left that he valued at all, and only because Liz loved it so. He sat with her shawl in his hands, looking at the boxes that he must find a place for.

A quiet footfall on the wagon step, and Moses' anxious voice; "Dr. John, are you within?"

"I am here, lad, what's the matter?"

Moses pushed aside the canvas flap and climbed into the wagon.

"Nothing, Doctor John . . . I was just. Oh." Moses let the flap fall behind him. "You miss her."

"Terribly," John replied. The wagon bed jostled slightly, as Moses stepped across the small space of it, and sat down next to John on the edge of the platform of boxes and trunks where their bedroll had been, where he and Elizabeth had slept curled into the shelter of each other all these months since departing St. Joseph.

Moses rubbed a fold of Elizabeth's shawl between his fingers. "I miss her also, Doctor John. I cannot recollect my mother; only Liz."

"You cannot? Truly? But you were . . ." John thought back to that awful summer of epidemics in Stark County, the summer after the spring when he and Liz had married. "You were well-grown when you came to live with us, a boy of six or seven, if memory serves. Surely that is old enough to remember your mother?"

"But there were a good many of us, Doctor John; Liz the oldest, and me the youngest. Haven't you noticed that with the Pattersons? Mrs. Isabella is so taken up with the management of the team, the business of the trail, and preparing meals, that the care of the youngest goes to the older children and so little Sadie is cared for day to day by Nancy and Eddie. They are the ones who take her by the hand, and comfort her when she is frightened. So Liz was to me. She took care of me until your marriage, then she was gone for a little while, and then she was there again, and I thought nothing of my mother and father at all because it seemed that you were both all but my parents. Truly, I can not remember my mother, and Father Schallenberger only a little; it has always seemed to me that you and Liz were all the family I needed or desired."

"So have I often felt," John replied, "that you were as much a son as we would ever have wanted."

"So, then," Moses answered, "I must do this; I must stay behind with Joseph and Allen, and look after my families' property and interest." He looked down at his hands, rubbing the folds of the shawl together. "I am nearly grown, Doctor John. I owe something, after my bad temper at the camp on the other side of the desert when I nearly brought down a massacre on you all. I owe it to you all to stay behind. You said yourself I had to consider others."

"So I did, so I did." John set his arm around Moses, as if he was still the little lad of six or so. "Back on the desert, I promised your sister that wherever one of us should go, the other would follow after in a few days as soon as we could. Whatever am I to tell her, that you are left behind in the mountains?"

"Tell her that it was my choice and my duty, Doctor John," Moses replied.

"I shall have to do that," John sighed. "Well, I will leave my library behind, so the winter will not be wasted as far as your education is concerned. Read of them as you can; those books will not serve you wrong."

"That I will," and at those brave words, John felt as he had when he watched Elizabeth riding towards the turn of the south-bound river branch, and turning back to look at him one last time. All of his family was gone, or about to go from him, leaving him alone. All he would have after that would be his obligations to the party and his duty as a doctor.

In the morning, he took the box with the tea set to Isabella, fixing breakfast, and bluntly asked if she had room for it.

"Of course," she said, heartily. "Mind you, there's some things I'd like to store in your wagon, in return. Nothing like this little box, several times that size, but we've room enough for all your supplies and things. We've been friends all along this long trail, you've only to ask." And then suddenly he thought there were tears in her yes, but she seemed to force them back by sheer will, saying then, "There's only one favor I would ask. And that's to come with me when they shoot the milk cow."

It was a doleful, melancholy scene, under the grey granite mountains and the sweet-scented green pines, culling the herd; the drovers and the wagon-owners standing about, as John, and Stephens, and Young Martin went one by one among them; poor, pathetic creatures, wincing as they stood on their tender feet, slab-sided and the hollows of near-starvation under their gentle and bewildered brown eyes.

These were the oxen bought with care and consideration in the markets of St. Joe, or Kanesville, or brought from the home farm in Ohio or Missouri, patient and trusty, obedient and gentle enough that little boys like Eddie and Willie Miller could drive them, bring them to harness even. They were bought and used well, and sometimes used hard, doctored with turpentine and tar, most of them with affection of a sort . . . and now some of them were at an end and the rest to be used even harder, but they all had names, and their character and history well known.

Isabella held the halter close and petted the nose of Goldenrod the milk cow, "There, there, my sweetie, there, there," she crooned, just as she must have done all those mornings on the trail, and those morning before in Ohio, before poor Goldenrod became a pathetic wreck of a cow with her ribs standing out and all the plump flesh rendered off of her. Isabella gave her a handful of withered green grass, gathered from the meadow where the main herd was pastured, where they stamped the snow aside and had thrown down armfuls of cut rushes, where John and Young Martin were examining them, one by one.

Isabella led her gently aside from the meadow, trailed by the puzzled children, away from the other oxen and towards the ice-water lake with John, where Stephens waited with some of the other men and commanded in a harsh voice, "Now, do it."

Stephens took aim with Isabella's dragoon pistol, and shot the gentle animal through the forehead. The cow folded up in a tangle of limbs and bones, while the children cried out, bewildered and Isabella turned towards them and shouted, "Don't you dare cry, any of you. It had to be done, and there's an end to it! Go back to the wagon, now! Do you hear me! Go back to the wagon!"

The children fled; Eddie, his sisters and Johnnie holding each others' hands and sobbing, and Isabella stern and furious, like one of the ancient goddesses demanding a blood sacrifice. John went on, his heart heavy within him, working with Young Martin, examining this ox or another, pronouncing this one fit, or fit for a little while longer, or this other one to be led gently around to the lakeside, and dispatched.

One of his own, a couple of the Sullivan's, one of Isabella's, another of the Murphy's . . . it went on, and on, only it was not all that many, truth be told. It just seemed like it. The slaughter-field presently became sodden with blood splattered against the trampled snow, the bloody hides thrown in one heap, the reeking viscera raked into another, scraped bloody bones in a third; grim work, not with much honor in it, John felt. Perhaps there was some kind of atonement one could make for a sacrifice of this kind. He had heard that the Indians had some sort of ritual, maybe there was something in Old Martin's beloved church rites. He almost hoped that merciful nature would cover it all in snow, make it vanish as if it had never happened, even if such a happening would be to their disadvantage.

And suddenly he wanted to go back to the wagon, that tranquil little place where he and Elizabeth had lived, near to where Moses and Joseph and Allen were marking out where their little cabin should be, cutting logs and using the best of the culled oxen to drag the logs. It would be a tight, trig little place, calked with brush and mud, and roofed with cattle hides . . . the hides from the cull, and thick-piled brush over top of it. They would be warm, sure enough, with all the bedding left behind in the wagons, and well-fed, with their rifles and ammunition left to them. Moses might very well be safe, snowed in for the winter in this valley just below the mountain pass, safe in the care of two trusty men like Allen and Joseph.

Walking past a thicket on the way to his wagon, he thought he heard a sound, a half-stifled moan, as if someone were hurt and trying to keep silent. Thinking it was one of the children, John paused and looked closer into the cluster of barren branches growing at the base of a large tree. Seeing nothing, he was about to move on when he heard it again. The snow at his feet was printed with many footsteps, but a pair of them seemed to go straight within the thicket's clustered bare branches. He shouldered through them, and there was Isabella, leaning against the tree trunk with her balled-up fist at her mouth, stifling her own agony of grief by biting so hard on her own fingers that she had drawn blood. There was more blood dabbled on the hem of her dress, from the slaughtering field.

"Mrs. Patterson, are you taken ill?" he ventured, uncertainly, and Isabella shook her head, her eyes overflowing. She took her hand from her mouth, but nothing came but terrible, gasping sobs, and John put his arms around her, and held her close, while she stifled them in his coat front. No, not ill, just grief, which he had seen and coped with it before, although it always made him feel particularly helpless.

They stood so, Isabella leaning against him, as if she were relieved to have someone to lean against for a moment, and John realized that she was really a very tiny woman. Her shoulders felt as narrow as a child's. It was just that Isabella was so masterful she appeared larger, a force of nature. Now she leaned against him, wracked with grief and guilt and fear besides, and all the worse because she must not let any of it show. There was no privacy in the camp, and she had no one else in the train to carry a burden like this with, no one at all except her old reprobate of a father. Silently, John held her, until the storm of it passed: Liz's good friend, messmate and wagon owner, voting member of the company and for him even a kind of a professional colleague; for all of that, they would make no mention of this, ever. Finally she straightened up, saying in her usual abrupt manner, "I'd raised her from a calf, you know."

John gathered up a bit of clean snow, wrapping it in his handkerchief, and she held it against her eyes, until she was well composed and her eyes less red. Then he took up her bitten hand, and looked at it critically. "I'd see to that, if I were you, Mrs. Patterson . . . this kind of small injury can go septic very easily."

"Of course, Dr. Townsend," she said, and she even managed to sound light. "My thanks."

"Yes, ma'am," And he touched the brim of his hat, and ducked back out of the thicket.

* * *

From Dr. Townsend's diary: *"Twenty-fourth of November, 1844. There is now two feet or more of snow on the ground. This day with little difficulty, our party moved five wagons from our last camp, around the margin of the lake to begin our ascent of the pass. Double-teaming with all our surviving animals has proved of some worth. Moses, Joseph, and Allen have accompanied us, leaving their winter camp half-built. They will assist us as far as the top of the pass tomorrow. It looms above us, a steep grey-granite tumble."*

From E.S. Patterson Interview, University of California Local History Archival Project 1932: *"Oh, it looked terrible high, all bare knobs of grey rock, with some pine trees and low bushes growing in the spaces between. We went as far up as we could, and then commenced to unloading the first wagon, Young Martin Murphy's I think was first. They had double-teamed it up the slope, to about halfway, then emptied it out, and commenced looking for a way up."*

* * *

The footing on the lower slopes, John decided almost immediately, was too uncertain for riding; either bare rock, bare rock with snow on it, or collections of gravel tenuously wedged into the spaces between. He roped a bag of flour on one side of Ugly Greys' saddle, balanced by the box with Elizabeth's tea set on the other, and led him after Joseph Foster, who led a single ox with the sole burden a newly felled tree. A straggle of women and children preceded them up the mountain, all but the smallest carrying some kind of burden on the back or in arms.

Isabella and her boys and Mary Miller waited for them, halfway up, sitting on the burdens they had carried so far, for there was a barrier there; a ledge too steep, too precipitous for any but the strongest and most adept to climb. John Greenwood, finding small crannies and toe-holds, had swarmed up it as spry as a lizard and let down a rope, anchored to a tree. Bernard Murphy and John Sullivan had used the rope to join him.

"Best we can do is to build a ladder, for the women and children," John had reported to Stephens, down with the wagons.

"That way, at least they can keep moving stores and goods to the top of the pass, while we figure out how to get the wagons up past the ledge."

"The wagons is no problem" Stephens squinted at the slope looming above them. "It's getting the teams above to pull them."

"I seen a lot in my time," Old Hitchcock agreed, "but I ain't seen any ox that would climb a ladder."

"Put a frill on it's neck and call it a circus," suggested Joseph Foster irreverently. "Now, I can build us a hoist and we can take them up, one by one."

"No time for that," Stephens shook his head gravely. "That's fifty, sixty beasts. Takes time, and time is something we may not have much more of. Rough out a ladder, Joe, but there's no need to make it fancy . . . the rest of us will cast about for a way around that ledge."

So Joseph and Patrick Martin had quickly felled a tree and cut a couple of poles and some anchoring stakes, and now they dragged it all up the ledge that blocked their way. The boys hauled from the top on their rope, pulling the top end into a small break in the ledge, while Joseph and Patrick labored to anchor the bottom end with stakes and rope, well pounded into a seam of earth between rocks below which offered a good purchase. Patrick took his hatchet and carved out a set of notches, a couple of quick vertical blows, and another set horizontal. He climbed up, and carved out another set, and then another, until the log had foot-holds in it, all the way to the top,

"Needs a bit of a banister, like," he remarked with satisfaction, sweating from exertion even in the cold. "Joseph, my lad, have we another place to anchor a rope, close to the bottom end, y'see? There's a fine sturdy little tree up here, for the top end. Now, ladies, I would advise a bit o' care in using this fine staircase we have built for you — you best consider passing your burdens one to another, rather than each of you carry it up and down. Who's going to be first, venturing up this excellent bit of speedy craftsmanship, worthy of the finest noble house in England, so 'tis! Ah, Mrs. Patterson, right ye are then. One step, then another. Don't ye be looking down, now, look ahead. Faith, Joseph, we should rig a small hoist, anyway. I'll fetch some more rope, and one of Captain Stephens's fine pulleys."

John carried up the flour and Elizabeth's tea set, and left them in a growing pile at the top of the ledge. He and Isabella assisted Mary-Bee Murphy up the precarious ladder, Isabella reaching from the top, and he from the bottom, and left her to rest.

"We're looking for a way to bring up the oxen." He took her hand as a way to surreptitiously check on her pulse, for she looked very grey and exhausted by the struggle so far. "And we'll see about having you ride the rest of the way, will that suit you? Until then, just rest here for a bit."

There was already a convergence on the bottom of the ladder — Old Hitchcock's two surefooted mules, and the few saddle horses and pack ponies left to them, laden with burdens from the wagons. He went down the ladder and picked up Ugly Grey's reins.

Isabella joined him; she was as nonchalant as one of the children going up and down, but now she said, "Are you good at mathematics, Doctor? If you have worked out how many trips up and down it will take to bring up all of the supplies and bedding please don't tell me. I do not want to be discouraged."

They met Stephens and old Greenwood, climbing up the slope, as they descended.

"We're going to scout along the ledge for a place to bring the wagons up," Stephens said. "Doc, if you can keep everyone moving . . . we can camp cold in the open for one night, but I'd mislike doing it more than once."

Patrick Martin passed them with a coil of rope over his shoulder, and the light of inspiration in his eyes; Mary Miller with a bundle of bedding on her back and the baby in her arms, and little Willie and his two sisters. The girls carried some small cook-pots, and Willie his father's toolbox.

"We can pack some of it on horses and mules," John allowed cheerfully. "At least, as far as the ledge; why don't you take the horse down for the next load, and the boys and I will begin packing it from the ledge to the top?"

At the bottom, Old Martin and James directed the empting out of the Murphy wagons; everything into two piles; that which could be easily carried, and that which would have to be packed onto one of the beasts. The Patterson wagon stood nearly empty, and the Sullivan's had but little in it to start with. Little by little, what was left went up the granite rampart; half a sack of dried beans and a lantern, carried by Young Martin's little son Jimmy; a pair of casks of flour, strapped to the pack-saddle of Old Hitchcock's mules, a carpetbag of clothing and three or four bedrolls piled onto the other. Nancy Patterson had two baskets of pemmican and Isabella's box of salts and medicinal herbs.

Patrick and his sons rigged a highly efficient hoist, and much of what had been transported to below the ledge moved briskly to the top of it. John gave Ugly Grey's reins over to Isabella and scrambled up the ladder, where a scattering of men and boys began packing things up to the top of the pass.

"Don't look like much this way." Joseph joined him there, and they looked at the west for a moment, a tangle of pine trees and a gentle down-slope. "But it's down hill, and that's all that matters."

John turned from it, and looked the other way, looking back at the little alpine valley which they had traversed with so much difficulty, cradling its jewel-blue lake like a precious stone, and the steep granite slope below. The winds had scoured much of the snow away from the stone, or perhaps it had melted because of exposure to the sun. If he looked hard enough, he thought he could see back along the defile where they had come and find the canyon where Elizabeth and the others had ridden south. He could easier see the field where they had culled the oxen, and where Isabella grieved for her milk cow. The place where they had camped last, and where Moses, Allen, and Joseph had begun their winter camp, was clearer yet for the piles of felled and trimmed logs. A burst of shouting came from down below, Stephens' voice chief among them, calls for an ax, for a shovel, and for someone to bring up one of the oxen.

"I think someone has found a path about the ledge." John clapped Joseph on the shoulder. "Which is fortunate, as I was not looking to walk like this all the rest of the way."

Stephens met him, at the top of the ledge with an ax over his shoulder, Dog capering after him and a look of triumph on his gargoyle face. "It ain't like what we was hoping for Doc, but it'll do good enough . . . just wide enough for one at a time, from the top to the bottom. Had to clear out some brush wood blocking the bottom."

"How did you find it?" John asked, "The boys looked all along for a break or a gully, and didn't see a thing."

"Hard to find . . . providential, I'd say. I was wondering about this big pile of scree at this end, started wondering where it had washed down from, wondered why there was enough soil to sprout some pretty good-sized pines, right at the bottom of the ledge . . . sure enough, there's a break in the ledge, runs almost sideways. I cleared out some brush, and Hitchcock and I stamped it all down good and tight . . ."

John whistled in amazement, although it was easy enough to see from the top, a narrow defile cutting down from the ledge-top, opening at the bottom. "Well, Captain, it's a good thing the best of our beasts are so skinny now, if they were in good flesh they'd stick tight here like a cork in a bottle."

"You'd think?" Stephens flashed a rare smile.

"We can always grease 'em down and hope for the best," John replied. "So, the plan would be double-team a wagon up to the bottom of the ledge . . ."

"Five, six yoke," Stephens nodded. "Unharness them, lead them up single-file through here, bring them around to that level place, harness them up again, and let down chains to the wagon below . . . and haul it straight up. Best have everything tied down fast."

"Ropes," John mused. "Something to brace the wagons with, while we lead the teams through the cleft . . ."

"It's a lot of work, Doc." Stephens said.

"It beats the alternatives," John replied. "Whose wagon first?"

"Sullivan's. It's the smallest."

* * *

From E.S. Patterson Interview, University of California Local History Archival Project 1932: *"Such a sight to see! They double-teamed that empty wagon up that pass, as far as that tall ledge, and a lot of work it was too, for even though the wagon was emptied out, it was a powerful steep grade, and those pore oxen was plum wore out."*

* * *

"Brace the back! And chock the wheels nice and tight, boys," Patrick Martin sang out. "If this beggar gets to rolling back and we lose hold, she'll be back in the desert before we even pick ourselves up and dust ourselves off."

They worried about the unhitched wagons rolling backwards, once the last yoke of oxen were unhitched. But a couple of poles braced from ground to the back axle seemed to be holding, as well as a couple of thick wooden wedges pounded in behind each wheel. Still and all, it was tedious work — unhitching the animals, one by one, for the boys to coax them up through the defile, to hoist up the ox yokes and re-hitch them, pair by pair, and to let down the chains. Young Martin took charge on top with the double-teamed animals, Patrick down with the wagon, he and Stephens together, fastening the chains, making sure that everything was equal and the wagon would be evenly pulled straight up the ledge face. Patrick and Joseph had cut a number of stout but slender poles, and laid them by, and he and Stephens held a quick parlay with the men and drovers.

"Look, you," Patrick said. "We have chosen the strongest and best conditioned of the oxen, for we shall be using them to draw up all the other wagons until they tire which Joseph Mary and Jesus hope they won't, at least not too soon. As each wagon comes up to the ledge, unhitch them and bring them up to the passage and lead them through. Take them straight up to where we will draw the wagon up, and re-yoke them. Then drive the wagon up to the top of the pass, where I think we shall be spending the night, though I like it not. We had hoped to be farther along. Now, when the team on top draws the front wheels close to the ledge, we'll be needing to lift up the front just so – and as it goes up and up and up, then we must push at the pack, even lift the back axle, using these poles when it has been pulled out of reach of our hands, so that the back wheels can rest on the ledge, just so. And all the while the team is pulling away most heartily from the top. Well, there we go, boys.

Once we get over this pass, the angels themselves will waft us down the other side, for it will be down the hill, all the way."

"One thing," Stephens added, quietly to John. "Doc – you stand aside lessen something goes wrong. If the wagon should fall, or the ledge crumbles, it'll go badly for those below. We'd need a doctor then, not another strong back now just to shove a wagon up a cliff."

"Mrs. Patterson is a most excellent . . ." John began, a little stung. He had always taken full part in the most onerous labors attendant upon moving the wagons.

"She's a midwife, and good with herbs and such, but you're the trained doctor. We'll need you for that." Stephens spoke softly. "You gave us a good scare in the desert, Doc. We were affeered there'd be no doctor for the rest of the trip."

"Besides," added old Martin just as quietly, on John's other side, "Who'd stitch up Patrick himself, the next time he gets into a fight with an Englishman, hey? If the boys are ready for the Sullivan's rig, let's the Doctor and me go and ready the next."

But John and Old Martin paused for a moment, a little way down, to watch at a safe distance.

"Pull away!" Stephens shouted from the top of the ledge, where he could see both Young Martin and the team above, and the wagon and the men below. "Steady now, steady now . . ."

Now the front of Sullivan's wagon lifted up, wheels clearing the ground. John and Old Martin watching below could hear Young Martin shouting, his whip cracking over the backs of the team, a shower of grit and rocks crumbling from the ledge as the chains bit deep, falling onto the arms and faces below. Higher, higher, Sullivan's wagon rose, until it hung entirely vertical against the ledge face.

"Mother Mary, Jesus, and Joseph," Old Martin breathed softly, murmuring almost to himself. "Steady now, steady now, haul away home."

The wagon inched slowly, higher and higher against the cliff face.

"Now lift away, lads, lift away!" shouted Patrick, and the men below converged on the rear of it, bracing against the back gate, reaching for poles as it was steadily drawn out of reach of hands.

"Steady pull now, Martin, steady as she goes!" Stephens shouted. "Front wheels over the ledge! Hold her steady!"

For an agonizing instant, Sullivan's wagon teetered on the edge, the front axle well up on solid ground, but the rear hanging in mid air, the wagon box balanced for a moment on the cliff edge."

"Pull away lads, pull away!" Patrick roared, and in one mighty heave from the oxen hitched above, and the men laboring below, Sullivan's wagon lurched up safely onto the ledge, all four wheels on solid grounding. Old Martin grinned like a maniac, and waved his hat, shouting, "Huzza, boys, huzza!" before turning to John and saying, "Oh, well done . . . now all we need do, is that again . . . four more times!"

* * *

From Dr. Townsend's diary: *"Twenty-fifth of November, 1844. Encamped at the top of the mountain pass, having with great labor lifted five wagons to the top of this precipitous incline. Moses, with Joseph Foster and Allen Montgomery took their farewells before dark, and returned to their campsite by the lake below. We fear that a winter storm may be on the way, and hope now to be able to move more swiftly, now that we are over the highest pass . . ."*

Chapter 13 – *Snowfall*

From E.S. Patterson Interview, University of California Local History Archival Project 1932: *"We looked back down from the top of the pass, and we couldn't hardly believe we had brung wagons all the way up it, but we had! The snow was all trampled to slush, there was marks of chains all over, trees chopped down, empty casks and scraps of wood all left at the bottom. And tired! We children were tired enough, but the men, they were exhausted . . . and three of them, that was going to winter over, guarding the other wagons; they said goodbye to us at the top, just at sundown.*

"We watched them climb down by the way we had come up, and they went walking off into the valley. I think now that some of us feared they might never be seen alive again, but I was just a little boy then, and I was dead envious of them, camping all winter in the snow, and hunting when they wanted, no school or chores or such.

"Doctor Townsend's foster-son, Moses, he was one of them. To me then he looked near to a man, the same as my brother Oliver. Looking back now, I know they were both just boys and I had no idea of how bad things would get, just when we were thinking we were pert near safe."

* * *

John stood with a little knot of people, just at the top of the pass, the setting sun behind them turning all the snow opposite to pink, or lavender where the shadows fell, filling up the valley below like a cup, and turning the ice-water lake to a pool of quicksilver. He and Sarah, with Stephens, Isabella with Eddie, and Old Martin huddled into coats and shawls against the bitter wind, stood in a small knot to bid their farewells.

"When you can," he overheard Isabella advising earnestly, "eat of the innards, especially of the liver – and if you can find it, strip off willow bark and brew a tea of the inner layer. It's a sovereign remedy against pain, and fevers too. Purslane . . . you know what it looks like? Fat green leaves, growing low to the ground in damp places. If you can dig down through the snow and find last summer's growing, eating it will stave off scurvy . . ."

"Lime juice is better for preventing scurvy," Old Martin said heartily. "Wish we'd remembered that, buying necessities, way back in St. Joe. Aye well. If wishes were horses, beggars would ride."

He, Stephens, and Isabella were making much of Joseph Foster, because he had no close kin amongst them and it was unseemly to part with someone who had done and would still do great service without taking some kind of notice, and of Moses for his very youth.

Sarah and Allen seemed to have little to say. "It was not so bad as all that," Allen said easily. "We'll sort things out when we get to California. You'll be taken care of, at least."

"To be taken care of!" Sarah sounded indignant, and Allen shouldered his rifle and answered indifferently. "Whatever you wish, then." They said nothing more to each other after that. Sarah pulled her shawl tightly around her elbows, and went to embrace Moses instead, while Allen seemed impatient to leave.

"I mean to thank you, for volunteering to guard our wagons," John said to him, as Allen stood a little aside from the knot of people. "We have left so much of value in them . . . and for the love of God take care of Mose, for Elizabeth's and my sake."

"Like a brother." Allen's face lightened from the dark cloud on it. "We have long been friends, you and Mose and I. Have nothing to fear for him, Joe and I will be as careful as nursemaids with the boy."

"He'll give you no credit for that, I am sure. But we will see that Sarah is safe, until we are reunited again."

Allen's face again appeared grim and dark at the mention of his wife, and he replied mordantly. "Aye, reunited. That's a cheery thought to keep a man warm of a winter."

"It does so, for me," John answered, and Allen laughed a little, saying, "You and Mrs. Elizabeth are happier in your marriage than Sarah and I have ever been. There are people who are meant for marriage, but more and more I doubt that we are such. You need not look as sour as a preacher, John. I'll see that she is always provided for."

John thought that he might have said more, but that Moses had been embraced by Isabella, and Old Martin, and Joseph Foster had shouldered his own rifle. It was time to face that wrenching farewell.

"Moses, lad," John said, in a voice that nearly gave way. "You're sure you want to partake of this enterprise? Your sister will be distraught to think of you left behind in this manner . . . it is not too late to change your mind about it. Allen and Joseph are men grown; they would not expect you to play the part of one, as well."

It almost seemed that Moses wavered; if he were still the boy he had been when they departed the Bluffs he might yet have changed his mind. But he was not; he had guarded cattle, and hunted buffalo, borne the responsibilities of a man for all those long months since, even though to John he still appeared absurdly young.

"No, Doctor John." Moses' shoulders squared under John's hands. "Liz will not be too worried; after all, she had her task. I am not a child any longer, and I have mine. I'll not be talked out of it."

"Boys, it's getting dark, we'd best mosey along," Allen said then, impatiently stepping away from the little group, starting the descent of the path tramped out by so many feet on this day.

"I thought as much." John sighed and embraced him. Joseph was already following after Allen. "Stay warm, Moses . . . keep busy as you can. I most especially recommend reading Lord Chesterfields' Letters. Dear lad . . . We'll be back in the spring, as soon as the snow melts and the passes open. That's a promise."

"Give my love to Liz when you meet her again." Moses shouldered his own rifle. "Good-bye, Doctor John, see you in the spring." He started down the trail after the other two.

Stephens called after them, "We left you two oxen, picketed out at the bottom of the pass . . . they're not in such good condition, but they'll make a couple of meals until the cabin is finished and the hunting picks up."

Allen waved his rifle, and the next moment they were out of sight, and Isabella saying distractedly, "I wish we had fed them one good supper . . . but they could not stay, with darkness falling, and who knows when the next storm will come!"

Sarah had walked on ahead, as if she cared little for a last sight of her husband.

"Your father knows." John took Isabella's arm. "He says that his rheumatic knee gives him fair warning of all changes in the weather."

Old Martin chuckled. "Me self, I feel a change of weather in my shoulder."

"Fiddlesticks! Absolute fiddlesticks!" Isabella snorted. "The stories that man tells! Eddie, my duckling, run along. Tell Nancy I will be at the fire presently."

Eddie scampered ahead; at least he still had enough energy to do so. After drawing up each of the wagons they had moved a little way down the pass to set up camp and shelter from the wind in a little dell rimmed with dark pines. Someone had started a cook fire, although no one but the children seemed in the least hungry.

"Some of his stories are true," John insisted. "And those which aren't have the benefit of being at least amusing. I'm deeply fond of the one where he spent a winter night in a cave with a hibernating colony of bears. There is a lot to be said for a man who can be good and amusing company in a tight place. Speaking of hibernation for a winter night . . . I presume that I am to share a tent with Oliver and the boys?"

"It's all such a jumble, all higgledy-piggledy now," Isabella lamented in housewifely fashion. "Sarah and the girls and I in the wagon, Eddie and the boys in the tent below. Do you know, Doctor, I nearly traded away the canvas at Fort Laramie; the boys often didn't wish to bother with it. They liked sleeping in the open or underneath the wagon if it looked like rain."

"Sheltering all of us now, with half as many wagons," Stephens ventured. "Doc, is there enough canvas for all? I was not thinking of anything beyond all the labor of moving the wagons."

"We should not use canvas after too many more nights," Old Martin answered jovially. "With luck we should soon be down below the snow. Mind you, I could sleep comfortable in a snow-bank tonight, for I am that tired with the work we did today."

"So could we all," Stephens agreed.

"Is there anyone needing medicinal aid, after today's hard business?" John yawned. "I am myself so weary I fear I would be applying my skills to the other limb or the wrong end entirely."

Isabella shook her head. "No, the only one who soon will require your aid may be Mrs. Murphy, and not for another few days, in my opinion." She gave a great sigh of relief. "Do you think it can be true, and that we are close to the end of our journeying? No, do not answer that . . . I know neither of you know, but I would so like to think that we are, just for tonight!"

And John kept silent and so did Stephens, for both of them had looked out towards the west, from the top of the pass and seen only dark forested mountains, for miles and miles beyond, and nothing of that fabled green and golden paradise that California was supposed to be. Somewhere below and beyond, Elizabeth and Helen and the others rode swift and sure for Sutter's Fort, while he plodded along with the wagons and longed for a sight of her.

* * *

From Dr. Townsend's diary: *"Twenty-seven November, 1844: Alas for hope, our labors are unceasing as the country is very rough; in one place we were forced to lower the wagons down a steep hillside by means of ropes snubbed around trees, lest the wagon overtake the team. We are descending but gradually, and fear that another great winter storm is about to break over the mountains. We are worn very thin and our remaining team animals weakened and near broken. We are wearied to the bone with the necessity of clearing trees out of our path, and Mrs. Murphy (wife of Young Martin) is close to her time . . ."*

* * *

The first John knew of it was the screaming. He was halfway down a muddy slope, leading Ugly Grey by the reins in one hand and gripping an ax in the other. He had been with Stephens, Greenwood, and Patrick Martin all morning in advance of the wagons, scouting and felling small trees this way and that, thinking, *"I used to be a professional man, with a fine library and a medical practice, and now I am a pioneer, felling trees in front of the wagons. Really, that is a waste of an education, however you look at it."*

He doubled back; it was mostly women screaming, but a man cursing too in a hoarse voice, and the meaty sound of blows, and an ox bellowing in the agonized way of a beast in pain.

"Holy Mother of God," Patrick panted, running at his side. "What is this, the Indians attacking us at long last?"

John caught his rifle from the holster on Ugly Grey's saddle, and fired a shot into the air; a signal to Stephens and Greenwood farther ahead blazing a path along a ridge above a fast-running little river.

They came up on the wagons, a grim tableau among the green pines and the white snow. Young Martin's wagon was in the lead that day, keeping to that long-established trail practice, although there were only the five of them left, and John took it all in at a look and stood stock still, frozen with horror at the scene before him. One of the lead beasts was down, fallen to its knees and dragging its yokemate with it.

Young Martin, with the face of a madman, beat it savagely with his whip handle, shouting in a frenzy of rage and despair, "Get up damn ye, get up!" as the crimson blood splashed onto the snow. Mary-Bee, half-collapsed and supported in the arms of Annie and Mary Miller, screamed from beside the wagon, begging for him to cease.

"Oh, stop, Martin, stop it! The children! Oh, stop, for the love of God!" The little boys and their cousin Mary watched in horror, some of them crying, and burying their heads in their mothers' skirts. Like John, all seemed paralyzed alike at seeing Martin, always so even-tempered and gentle, solicitous of his team, administering this frenzied and senseless beating. Only Isabella and Old Martin seemed able to move, sensibly.

Isabella ran up and snatched the bloody whip out of his hand, crying, "Oh, enough, enough!" while Old Martin took his son in his arms, pulling him away from the shuddering animal. "That's enough, child . . . come back to us now, let it go!" Young Martin collapsed to his knees, sobbing in horrible, wrenching gasps in his father's arms, while Old Martin held him fast. Just so had Isabella cried, that day of the cull in the mountains, and John met her eyes and knew she remembered it also. And Stephens appeared then, out of the woods at John's elbow, as silently as a ghost himself, and Old Martin met their eyes. "It's enough now," he said quietly. "We're done in, Captain."

Stephens nodded, acknowledging. They were exhausted, had been for weeks, and the mighty effort of getting those five wagons over the pass had sapped the last reserves of strength and endurance left to all — men, women, and the team animals. Above them, the storm clouds pressed close against the trees, blurring the sky and the mountains behind in a cloud of falling snow. A couple of fat white feathers of it drifted down on them, melting into the blood that splattered the snow already fallen.

"Mrs. Murphy's time has also come," Isabella said softly. "I do not think we dare travel any farther. And the storm is coming."

"We'll make camp then," Stephens answered. "There is a suitable place yonder, above a bend in the river." To John and Old Martin, he added quietly, "After we've set up, I'll want a meeting . . . everyone, as before, to talk over what to do."

They straggled along that little way, like survivors of a battle lost, and made camp as the snow fell thick and hard. The ox which Young Martin had beaten so savagely managed to rise and stumble that little way. John and Isabella put Mary-Bee into the Miller wagon, and Isabella tended her there.

"Tomorrow, I think," she consulted with John when they loosed the teams. "It does seem strange to be setting camp so early in the day. What do you think Captain Stephens has in mind?"

"I don't honestly know," John answered. "There doesn't seem to be much else we can do now but try and pack out with what we can carry."

"Not with Mary-Bee . . . not with the babies, and the other children, not in snow that near comes up to their chins." Isabella sighed. "What of Young Martin?"

"He's as tired as the rest of us, only worse for him, with Mary-Bee. I gave him a little tot of medicinal whiskey."

"At least they are here together," Isabella sighed again. "And the children are enjoying themselves . . . look."

Stephens had picked a campsite on a low knoll overlooking the river. They had parked the wagons in a sheltered grove by an open meadow frosted with snow, being covered deeper now by snow still falling. In it the children were romping, throwing snow-balls at each other, while their fathers cut poles and branches in the grove for firewood and to build hasty bowers and shelters for themselves.

"It is good for them not to share our cares," John said simply. "They can play for a little longer."

With poles and canvas, and using trees and the wagons themselves, they had a shelter of sorts rigged, something to keep the fast falling snow off the fire and themselves, gathering for the meeting which Stephens had called. John looked around; the contrast between them now and how they had appeared six months ago preparing to set out and cross the river into the wilderness was almost unbearable. Only Greenwood and his son appeared relatively unchanged; everyone else looked shockingly thinner, worn and sun-burnt, tired, and as ragged as some of Old Martin's tinker gypsies. Isabella and Old Martin, even Patrick Martin, surely they had not so much grey in their hair, six months ago?

By ones and twos they gathered, families and the single men, even Mary-Bee, wincing occasionally as a pain seized her, and Stephens looked into the fire and at his rough, strong blacksmith's hands as they gathered.

What do I say, now, Doc? he had asked, all those months ago when John had engineered his election to captaincy, and he had taken John's advice and made the shortest political acceptance speech that John had ever heard. But he had promised to get them to California, or wherever they were going . . . and now they were so close, so close that at every hillside prospect it seemed they could almost see that fair green and golden land, but the snow and the mountains had closed around them again, and now they were spent, out of strength and nearly out of food, but Stephens, that big, ugly, and inarticulate man had never yet failed, had always managed to keep going, to keep them all going. John dreaded that Stephens would ask his advice again, and this time he would have none to give.

"When you 'lected me, you all gambled." Stephens finally looked up from the fire and met their expectant eyes. "You gambled on me. You gambled on yourselves being able to make the trip, too. An' I made a promise then; I'd get you all to California. We're as close as anything to taking our winnings off the table. We're over the mountains, now. We found a pass. We

190

crossed the mountains in a way that no one but the Indians ever seed before. We're nearly there, folks. We're following the river downhill every day. Old Man Hitchcock, here," Stephens jerked his bearded chin toward the old mountain man, "he'll tell you that rivers lead down out of mountains, sure as the sun rises in the east and sets in the west. Caleb and Isaac and I, we b'lieve we have no more than a couple of days travel, but with the snow and the conditions of the teams and all, it's clear we can't carry on as we are. We need to make one more gamble. Most of you tell yourselves you ain't gambling folk. But you are and we need to make that last throw. We did it before, on the Green, and again when we left the Fort Hall road, and when we crossed the desert on the say-so of a naked wild Indian we couldn't say two words to . . . Hell, we gambled the day we crossed the river from Kanesville."

Stephens's water-pale eyes gleamed in his dark face; he was touched with a fire of eloquence that was not normally his. John held his breath; for once his friend was saying all the right things. Stephens took a breath and looked up at them, each of them, the wagon-owners and Isabella, the old mountain men, at John himself, and continued, "But every time we gambled, we looked around at the situation, and considered everything we might know. And then we acted on the best advice we had. You all trusted me – better then that, you all trusted each other. Every one of you had a say in each of those gambles, and every one of you all had your own kind of skill, and all of them gambles paid off. Now, we got this one last gamble and it's for stakes a man don't like to put on the table, mostly. This time it's for the lives of your women and children." Stephens paused, looking into the fire again. "We're almost to Captain Sutter's fort, so I b'lieve. We got some time; we got what's left of our teams. Greenwood here, he's been saying for weeks that our only hope is to leave the wagons and pack out fast . . . Mr. Murphy, and Miz Patterson here, they don't like that thought, since it ain't possible to pack enough supplies and all the children with what we have. Me, I think the only way out of this pickle is a compromise. We can't all go, and we can't all stay." Stephens took up a stick and poked the fire with it. The snow falling in it made little sizzling sounds, and Dog started up from sleep at his feet. She lay down again, woofing softly, sleeping with her great fawn-and-black head resting on his boot.

"I propose we leave the wagons here and build a winter camp for the women and children; slaughter the rest of the oxen, and leave a couple of men here as guards and the rest of us take the horses and mules and pack out. We take just enough for a couple of days, and leave everything else here. There should be enough to last for a while, long enough for us to come back with a rescue party. I plumb don't see any other way to play the cards, folks, and that's the plain truth of it. If anyone else can think of something, I'd 'mire to hear it, and put it up for a vote."

"I cannot, either," said Old Martin Murphy, after a silent moment, while the fire cracked and sizzled away from the snow falling into it. "I cannot bear the thought of leaving the children, but as we cannot carry them with us, we must leave them well provided for."

"How long does winter last in these parts?" James Miller asked thoughtfully. "How long could we expect until the snow melts enough in spring to admit a rescue party?"

Hitchcock and Greenwood looked at each other, and Greenwood at last spoke heavily. "I dasn't say for sure, James; at a guess, end of February at the earliest, March or April at the latest. Make that three months, four months."

"Any notion as to how good hunting might be in these mountains?" John Sullivan asked.

"There's always something about," Hitchcock answered, "if you gets hungry enough. Gen'rally, the deer and other big game go down the mountains . . . how far? Depends on how deep the snow is. They'll stay where they can paw snow off last years' grass. They won't be where it's any deeper."

No one had to look very far to see how the snow outside their wagon circle had already piled in soft billows halfway to the axles. Four months, on the scant supplies left, and the lean flesh left on forty or so oxen.

"We might yet be able to return sooner," Patrick Martin said hopefully.

"Remember, every man who goes will leave a greater share for those remaining." John added. He looked around the campfire; no, it seemed as if there were no more to say, no more questions, and certainly no alternatives.

"So it is proposed that we build a winter camp here to shelter the women and children. Shall we now go ahead and vote on it?"

"One thing," Isabella spoke up firmly. "I believe we should all vote on it, women as well as men. In remaining behind or going forth, it is asked of us all to endure a very great trial and considerable risks. When so much is then being asked of all of us, should we not all have a voice in it, not just those who have a franchise in the party? Oughtn't we at least be able to look back and say we chose our particular trial freely and fairly, and that it was not another's choice made for us?"

Old Martin nodded somberly. "'Tis a fair thing to ask, Captain. We are asking much of my daughters and Mary Sullivan, as well as Mrs. Patterson and Mrs. Montgomery."

"I think my choice is made for me already," Mary-Bee said, halfway between a laugh and a gasp. "And not by any of you!"

"A show of hands, then," John said, and the hands went up, immediately, and some reluctantly.

"I'll stay," Sarah Montgomery was one of the reluctant ones, "but I'd sooner go with the men."

"You bold thing, you!" said Mary Sullivan, half in jest, and half what sounded like malice.

"Sarah, dear, there is no other woman to be a chaperone," Isabella said, and Sarah answered sullenly, "Then I don't have a choice, only what is dictated by propriety."

"If there's no objection," Patrick Martin said heavily, "I'll stay here, for a guard, meself."

"I'll stay also," James Miller spoke up. "We'll hunt as best as we can."

"I'll not go until we have a proper cabin built for everyone," Young Martin said flatly. "And have done all that we can do for supplies and to keep them safe until our return."

"That we will," Stephens promised, and Old Martin added, "And so we must, for the safety of our own souls . . .as ye said, Captain, a man hardly likes to wager the lives of his own."

* * *

From E.S. Patterson interview, University of California Local History Archive Project 1932: *"So all decided then for the women and children to stay put, and the men would build a shelter for us, and kill the last of the oxen for food. We couldn't go any farther in the wagons then, you see the snow was halfway up the walls of the cabin that they began to build, even before the storm was over. They were out in the grove felling trees, working as fast as they could. They did not have the strength left in them, or the time to fell logs for a large cabin, so they built two small ones adjoining under one roof . . . what Mr. Greenwood said they called a "dog-trot" cabin in the place he was raised up.*

"Each little room had only a door, no windows and a little fireplace opposite. We moved in and lived like animals in a burrow; it was warmer in there than in the wagons. Ma and us children with Mrs. Montgomery and Mary Sullivan and her brothers lived in one, and Mrs. Miller and the two Mrs. Murphys all living in the other. The men covered the roof with ox-hides and canvas and piled cut branches on top of it all. They didn't go until they

were finished and the oxen slaughtered, all but two or three they took for meat for themselves."

From Dr. Townsend's diary: *"Encamped at a winter camp on a river, four days journey west of the highest pass, Mrs. Martin Murphy in labor with her child."*

* * *

"Well, at least this is easier than chopping down trees," John remarked philosophically, rolling up his sleeves. The cold bit through his shirt, for he had already set aside his coat. They had brought two kettles full of coals into the wagon in an attempt to keep it somewhat warmer; in the back of his mind John feared he would put his foot onto one of them, tip it over and set the wagon on fire.

"Speak for yourself," Mary-Bee Murphy gasped, leaning against Isabella and Annie's shoulders. She was yet able to smile at him.

"Another strong push there," crooned Isabella. "Breathe in and bear down now, Mary-Bee."

"This would be the second of Old Martin's grandchildren that I have delivered in six months," John mused thoughtfully. "There might be a very bright future for my practice in California . . . very good, now there's a bit of the head. Your father-in-law has four children, three of whom are of age and unmarried, aside from the four who are . . . the chances are excellent that I would be kept very busy as the family physician."

"That, and stitching up my Pa when he gets in fights," Annie Murphy put in, as she and Isabella lifted Mary-Bee's shoulders up.

"Breathe in and bear down, Mary-Bee, that's our brave girl," Isabella urged her and John said encouragingly. "There's the head now . . . another great push again!" Mary-Bee made a great moan that rose to a scream, and the rest of the baby slipped out of her body and into John's hands.

"It's a little girl," John said as he bound and cut the cord, and Mary-Bee fell back, laughing thinly between great gasping breaths, "Oh, the lord be praised! How she will tease and pester those imps of her brothers . . ."

John hastily swaddled the baby in a towel, and then another; she was a dusky pink, not pale like her cousin, and immediately began to wail piercingly.

"She sounds angry," Mary-Bee gasped again. "Is there something the matter with her?"

"She knows she has just been born on a mountain in the snow, in the middle of the wilderness," Isabella answered, "and will no doubt make all pay dearly for this lack of forethought."

John handed the baby to Mary-Bee, who touched her little nose with one finger and cooed, "Oh, my little sugar-dumpling . . . how you are going to plague your brothers. I can hardly wait."

"Have you thought on a name for her?" John asked.

Mary-Bee groaned a little as the afterbirth came away; all there, it looked like.

"We thought Elizabeth would be a pretty name for a girl," she answered, and John was absurdly pleased.

"Well, it would be a silly one for a boy . . . he'd be teased at school everlastingly. But if she turns out to be as pretty as my Elizabeth, she'll lead all her suitors a fine dance and need a lot of big, watchful brothers to keep them in line."

* * *

From Dr. Townsend's diary: *"Yesterday, Mrs. Martin Murphy delivered of a fine, healthy infant girl, christened by her Grandfather Murphy. We intend to leave on the morrow, the cabin being finished and all necessary preparations made; all remaining men and boys old enough to be counted as men, numbering seventeen in all, save James Miller and Patrick Martin the elder to remain behind to watch over the winter camp."*

Chapter 14 – *Winter March*

From E.S. Patterson interview, University of California Local History Archive Project 1932: *"My next oldest brother Samuel came to my mother with Paw-Paw and my oldest brother Oliver who was to go with the men . . ."*

* * *

"No!" said Isabella passionately, "I won't have it! Samuel is a boy, he is not old enough!"

"Izzy, Izzy, Izzy," Old Hitchcock chided his daughter. "Don't shame the lad in front of the others, he's sixteen and well grown, two years older than Michael Sullivan."

"Michael is going with his brother, and so would I be," Samuel pleaded.

"John Sullivan is a man grown, and Oliver is barely more than a boy himself," Isabella stormed. She dropped the armload of bedding she was carrying from the wagon just inside the doorway of the tiny cabin, and folded her arms, "And you are not too big for me to turn you over my knee!"

"Yes ma-am . . . no, ma-am, I am too big for you to do that," Samuel stammered bravely. "I've been taller than you since mid-summer. Haven't you noticed? And you've been saying at every meal seems like I eat as much as a man anyway. So why can't I go with the men, seeing as that would leave you all the more?"

"Got you there, Izzy." Old Hitchcock seemed hugely amused.

She spun on her heel, and stormed up to the campfire, where John was trying to warm the inkbottle sufficiently to thaw the ink inside, so as to be able to write a new entry. Being that there was not a shred of privacy in the camp, he already knew what the disputation was about, and had been hoping that he would not be drawn into it.

"Doctor Townsend!" Isabella demanded, "tell him! Tell Samuel he may not go with the men!"

"Why not?" John asked, reasonably. "It can't be that he is too young, for Michael is even younger and he is going. Moreover, he would be going with Oliver . . . and his grandfather . . . and Captain Stephens and myself as well. Surely you can assume that we would all be most responsible guardians?"

"Men!" cried Isabella in frustration. "You all stick together!"

John sighed and re-corked his inkbottle, putting it in his pocket. Not a good time for a full account of the building of the winter camp and the decision to split the party once again. He stood and offered her his arm. "Mrs. Patterson, may we speak privately on this matter? Please?"

She took his elbow, and he walked her a little way to the edge of the winter camp where they had been felling and trimming trees. Inadvertently they had cleared a vista looking out on the folds of snowy forest falling away to the west. He stopped at the place where they could see it all, the trackless lands along the unnamed river.

"Look at it, Mrs. Patterson," he said quietly. "It's where we're going tomorrow."

"So you are, but I don't want Samuel going with you!" She kept her voice low but her eyes were full of passionate tears.

"But is it not where Mr. Patterson is . . . Samuel and Oliver's father? You set out on this journey so that you and the children could rejoin him. He was going ahead of you all, so he could settle on a good prosperous farm, and then you would join him as soon as it was all done, and so you shall. Why not send both of them ahead, Isabella? It's only a short journey, compared to the road that we have already traveled. Captain Stephens and I can send word from Sutter's establishment, and they will be safe in the care of their father."

"But I want to keep him safe!" Isabella lost her attempt to keep her voice low, and John took her hands in his. "Samuel is a child, what more can this journey now demand of me? We have spent so much . . . Goldenrod and all the oxen, now our wagon and everything that we brought with us, perhaps the lives of my boys? I cannot endure that. I cannot!"

"Not that," John sighed. "Not that last sacrifice, not after all that. You cannot keep him safe, Isabella, not when he is of an age to think for himself. Let him go with us."

"No." Her tears brimmed over. John continued relentlessly. "Listen to me, Isabella. He cannot be rolled up in cotton-wool and protected, as you protect Sadie . . . and as you try to protect Eddie, that little imp. Listen to me. Our children at a certain age, they crave to be respected, to have responsibility, to be treated by the rest of us as if they are adults, worthy of our regard and company. We must let them have this. We must let them have this, because if they do not have this in a good way, they will become distracted and look for it in a bad way. They will become careless and idle, and seek for low company and low pleasures . . . just because they want so much to be worthy and responsible. Samuel yearns for that. Let him have it, Isabella. Let him go, and let him see that he can be a man, a brave and responsible man. It is a couple of years before he can be that in truth, but it will do him good, I think."

"Is that what you told yourself when you let Moses stay at the lake with your wagon?" Isabella demanded.

"Perhaps it was," John answered, honestly. "Perhaps it was. He has already chosen his task. Let him go, Isabella. Let him go and do it, show us all that he can rise to what is expected. We will see that he comes to no harm. Let him go with us, Isabella."

He knew he had won, when her shoulders dropped, and she looked down at their hands, and replied wearily. "As you ask, then, Doctor. I will let Samuel go with Oliver . . . but you will promise me on everything that you think holy that you and Captain Stephens will keep him safe until their father comes for them."

"We'll keep Samuel and all the boys as safe as it is possible to keep them."

John raised her hands and bowed over them. "Thank you . . . I know that Samuel will thank you, and so will Mr. Patterson when the boys rejoin him."

Isabella smiled then, a little. "Tell him . . ." Her voice quavered a little. "When you see Mr. Patterson, tell him that I am longing to see him again, and that he must come for us as soon as possible."

"If I am sure of anything," John answered, "It is that nothing will keep him from riding to your rescue . . . on a white charger, no less, and with one of your handkerchiefs as a favor. Would you like to give me one of yours, so I can take it to him as a token of your affections?"

As he had hoped, Isabella laughed outright, and answered, "That would not be necessary. He is a very dear man to me, but not, I fear, the knight-errant sort."

"Then let us go tell Samuel to make up a pack. I imagine that he has been on pins and needles, watching us talk."

* * *

From E.S. Patterson interview, University of California Local History Archive Project 1932: *"Ma was persuaded to let Samuel go with Oliver and the men. They each put on two sets of clothes and their heavy coats, and Ma packed a little food for them. They both carried a roll of blankets, and Ma made them take some extra socks, and asked Paw-Paw and Doctor Townsend to promise to send word to Pa's holdings."*

From Dr. Townsends' diary: *"Fifth of December, 1844."* *We shall depart on the morrow, having done everything possible to prepare. Snow fell heavily last night, burying the stock of meat fairly deep, as well as a great stack of fire wood which Murphy and his boys thought fit to provide, among other comforts. James Miller and Young Martin have built some rough furnishings (beds and chairs, etc.) for the cabin, so that all within may sleep in some comfort, and James Murphy has diverted himself in his usual manner by whittling toys from odd bits of wood. I perceived that he had a small box full of them, and when I asked his purpose, he replied that it would be Christmas in three weeks, and he intended to leave the collection with his brother-in-law, so that each child would have a gift on Christmas morning.*

"We take nothing but what we can carry, a bedroll and rifle and ammunition each, since we have only my horse, Mr. Hitchcock's two mules, and three of Greenwood's ponies left to us. I must leave my writing desk, although my journal, pen and ink will fit easily into my coat pockets. I must leave most of my medical implements and supplies behind also, in Mrs. Patterson's care. We leave, trusting our Savior for a safe journey and swift return."

Angeline Morrison Letter #4
3rd December,1844
Writ from Sutter's Fort, New Helvetia, California

Dearest Angeline:
My last letter was writ to you from Fort Hall, as we were about to leave the established trail and venture into the desert, following a small river into the desert sink, from where we hoped to find passage over the mountains. We were successful in this venture, although it cost us much toil.

My Dearest Husband was taken ill from sunstroke whilst crossing the desert, which distress'd me very much, but he recovered fully. Our party followed a fortuitous river up into the mountains which divide the desert from California like a great wall. With much difficulty and labor, our party brought our wagons along this river, well up into the mountains, but we were caught by winter.

Fearing that we might become stranded, Capt. Stephens call'd for a meeting, at a place where two tributaries met. Knowing not which way might prove a more straight path, it was decided to send out a small party on horseback to follow the south-ward bending fork in hopes of an easy crossing. We drew lots, among the fit and strong and without young children to care for.

You will be amazed, my dear Angeline, to know that my health is so much recovered that I was among six chosen for this desperate venture. Six of us set out on 15th November; besides myself, Helen, John, and Daniel Murphy, and two hired men, Francis Deland, whom my Dearest hired in St. Joseph all these months ago to drive our wagon, and Oliver Magnent, who was in the employ of Joseph Foster.

We each took our blankets and some little food, hoping to be able to hunt. Miss Helen and I were allowed a change of clothes each and a piece of canvas to sleep under, the men each bore a rifle and ammunition. We also had two extra horses, to bear packs, as it was hoped we could move rapidly and if necessary, bring back help and supplies upon reaching safety.

We departed from our loved ones with much anguish, Mr. Murphy and my own Dearest Husband being most particularly affected. I leave any farther description of our tender farewells to your imagination, my dear Angeline, as it causes my own tears to flow again when I reflect on them.

We ascended the southwards turning canyon with no impediment caused by snow; indeed I was pleasantly surprised at the swiftness of our passage, since we did not have to clear a way for wagons. At the end of two days, we came out on the shores of a magnificent lake, verily an ocean, as blue as a sapphire in a setting of mountains. We could not see to the end of it, but the water itself was as clear as glass. We crossed along the northern shore of it, feeling such a medley of emotions as my pen is feeble to describe; such awe and wonder at this marvel, well mix'd with apprehension of being caught in another storm and mir'd deep in snow.

After some little distance, we found an easy pass over the rim of mountains and followed it westwards, leaving behind the marvelous lake. Finding another watercourse flowing west, we descended from the mountains, fleeing the approach of a storm which covered them with impenetrable cloud for many days.

The watercourse became a broad river, as we traveled; within some days we had left the snow behind, and were traversing a country of gentle hills, very lightly wooded, and rich with game. To the inexpressible delight of the men, they were able to hunt . . . and to mine own and Miss Helen's delight, we were able to set aside certain of our heavy garments, and revel in what seemed like the balmy zephyrs of spring.

We were forced to cross the river at one point, and John Murphys' horse was o'erthrown by the swift current. His rifle was nearly lost, and himself carried some distance by the current, until he was able to catch hold of an overhanging branch. He was drenched thoroughly and nearly drown'd, although we were all wetted to some degree. We made camp immediately on the shore and built a large bonfire to dry our clothing, before proceeding farther.

Wondrously, after some two weeks or twenty days of travel following the river, we came to some houses; the dwellings of a Mr. St Clair. While astonished at our appearance – think on it, six very tired and travel-worn strangers appearing out of the mountains as if by magic – we were received with much kindness, altho' Mr. St Clair and his family and friends expressed great concern upon hearing that we were emissaries of a larger party still maroon'd in the mountains.

They conducted us down to Captain's Sutter's establishment on the confluence of two great rivers in this valley, where we were very kindly received. He is the great magnate in these parts: Miss Helen and myself were given rooms in his own house, and her brothers and the other men quartered suitably near by.

You would be astonished, my dearest Angeline, at Captain Sutter's vast establishment, for he keeps a very great estate, in a vast square fortress built out of unbaked clay bricks on top of a low hill overlooking the rivers and the territory around. There are a dozen brass cannon on the walls and in the bastions, and a troop of Indian soldiers, turned out in blue drill pantaloons and white shirts, of which Capt. Sutter is very proud.

Being informed by a messenger from Mr. St. Clair of our circumstances, we were conducted into Captain Sutter's office immediately upon our arrival. He is a gentleman of many parts, and considerable charm, and received us very warmly, with every protestation of concern at hearing of the plight of our party.

But although we all and severally begged for his assistance in organizing a relief party, Miss Helen even burst into showers of tears, to no avail. Capt. Sutter firmly demurred, although he seemed much moved, saying that winter storms make the mountains impassible, and any such attempt would only be to condemn the rescuers to an ugly fate.

We had hoped so much from our flying journey across the mountains to rescue our family and friends, and were so gratified by a successful completion; you will know that our distress was very great. Capt. Sutter seem'd most downcast, and sympathetic to our spirits, and encouraged us to hope that the party may have also been able to transport themselves closer to safety by their own efforts. He counseled patience, and offered us indefinite hospitality, saying that our lov'd ones may yet appear as we have done, and that winter has only now descended with full force upon the high mountains.

So we must wait, at least for a little while. It still seems very strange to me, having become accustomed to the trail for the last eight months, to live inside a house and sleep in a proper bedstead, and eat meals at a proper table. Civilization fits uneasily, still, like a garment I have not worn for some considerable time.

Every day, Miss Helen and I, and sometimes her brothers Johnny or Daniel, take our ponies and ride a little way along the river, by Capt. Sutter's wheat fields and pasturelands; we look at the distant mountains, and watch for a while, hoping to see our dear ones. Each day we ride back, very low in spirits, and then we say to each other, "Perhaps tomorrow we'll see them."

The post departs very infrequently from here, when there is word of a ship in port at Yerba Buena or Monterey. Capt. Sutter promises that we well be informed at such a time. I will leave this letter unsealed until then, hoping to add a post-script that my Dearest Husband and Moses and the others are safely arrived.

Until then, with deepest fondness, Thy friend
Elizabeth

* * *

"Doc, I'm goddamn glad there's no one there for me to say goodbye to," Stephens murmured to John, as they waited by the deserted wagons on the morning they had decided to leave. John nodded; he had already said his farewells long since and days back, and this desperate trek with the men and boys could be the means of reuniting with Elizabeth, anyway. He had told Isabella to make free of whatever she might be able to use from those of his medical supplies being left behind, and she had nodded distractedly.

Hitchcock stood with them, with his two pack-mules stamping impatiently, Old Greenwood and his sons, and the four hired men, who might once have sent yearning looks at Mary Sullivan, or Helen Murphy, once upon an evening when there was music around the campfire, but had no chance against the vigilance of assorted brothers. They were impatient to go. Dog nudged Stephens hand with her nose, oh, she was impatient also.

Patrick Martin took each of his sons in a mighty bear-hug, "Be off with you both then, lads. Don't start anything you can't finish."

Isabella, her eyes filling with unshed tears, pulled Oliver's coat straight, and re-knotted the muffler around his neck. She did the same with Samuel, and said fiercely, "You . . . give my love to your Pa, and tell him to hurry. Mind you pay attention to Doctor Townsend, for if I hear you ain't been behaving, I can still bend you over my knee, you know!"

"No, you can't Ma," Samuel replied, and bending down to hug her, he tightened his arms around her, and lifted her clean off her feet as he straightened up.

"Sauce!" she gasped when he put her down again. "Go on with you, you big man, then. Go on!"

"Bye, Ma. Bye, squirt," Oliver and Samuel chorused, and Oliver tousled Eddies' head, "Take care of Ma, Johnnie, this leaves you the man of the house, then." A hug each for Nancy, and another for Sadie, bewildered enough to have begun sucking her thumb again, and the two of them joined the waiting men.

Young Martin had the baby in his arms; he knelt in the snow with his boys around. John thought he might be telling them to look after their baby sister. Young Martin's brother Jamie simply stood with his arms around Annie and his adored little Mary. John Sullivan and Michael, the youngest of all those making the trip, stood close by his sister and little brother. Mary Sullivan nodded calmly, as he spoke to her; obviously last-minute directions and instructions, in John Sullivan's own level-headed fashion.

"You should be away, now," Patrick Martin rumbled finally, in his gravelly Irish voice to his old friend Martin Murphy. "Before we're all drowned in tears, and used up half the day. Ne'er fear, James and I shall keep them all safe. Be away with you, then, while the day is young. We shall see you when we see you."

Old Martin took Bernard by one arm and John by the other and said, "Martin . . . Son James . . . we'll away, and be back before you know it. Take care of the children, my dears." He came up to John and Stephens, saying, "Let's be gone from here before I commence to wail like a banshee."

And with that, they straggled off, Dog loping in the lead, dancing and leaping like a wild dervish, although there was many a mournful glance backwards as long as any could see the little straggles of smoke from the campfires and chimneys.

They followed the river, taking turns to walk in front, wading through the snow and stamping it down for an easier path for the rest, leading the mules, Ugly Grey, and Greenwood's ponies, marveling at how fast they could yet move, unburdened by wagons.

"At this great rate, we may be able to return in weeks," Jamie Murphy commented happily, and it seemed to John that their spirits rose. The country was still very rough, and thick-wooded with trees. To bring out the wagons would still be a chore, but with fresh teams . . . and as long as the snow held off.

The animals fed on rushes that evening; although it seemed that the snow was not as deep on the ground as before, it was still too thick for them to paw it away from last year's grass. But by the next day, the snow had diminished to a few rags, in deep shade, or on a northern facing slope, and they moved even faster.

"Oh, 'tis a splendid country," Old Martin said. "Look at that grass, 'tis nearly Christmas and yet it's as green as it ever was in Ireland."

Scouting a little ahead on the following day, John Greenwood and Dennis Martin shot a brace of fat deer, and they ate their fill of venison that night, at ease around the campfire.

"Oh, now 'tis sublime, that!" Old Martin sighed, and tossed the last little bit of gristle and bone to Dog, who snapped it up eagerly. Dog had been very well fed on scraps and bones this evening.

"It's a golden country. No mistake," Stephens tossed her another bit, and Michael Sullivan produced the most resoundingly noisy belch. The Patterson boys giggled.

"Manners, lads, manners." Old Martin chided them. "Pigs have none!"

"I think that was the first time in months that I ate my fill without calculating how little that would leave for the next meal," John observed idly.

"You also?" Old Martin lifted an eyebrow. "Faith an' I thought I was the only one doing so. And now we are in the land of plenty, where the rivers are full of milk and honey, and the trees full of golden fruit, and we shall not have to consider every day how many miles we have made."

"I'm glad it's nearly over." Oliver Patterson wiped his mouth on his shirtsleeve, and John said, "So am I. I think now if I had known of some of the difficulties . . ."

"Would you have stayed in St. Joseph then, Doc?" Stephens asked.

"No, but I might have thought longer on leaving it," John answered, and Old Martin said, "Doctor, when you've lived as long as I have, trust me, you'll look back on it and forget all the hardships, and weariness, and remember only the good times, fine company and marvelous sights . . . and then you'll wish it had lasted longer."

"It's lasted quite long enough for me, already," John answered, "and we are still a little short of Sutter's at that. But you are probably right about time painting a fairer picture in retrospect."

In the next days, they descended into a gentler country, of rounded hills lightly covered in fine spreading oak trees, and then into a valley so large that they could not see an end to it. The river they followed became broad and deep, flowing through lush meadows on either side. They spotted cattle grazing, fine fat cattle, and harvested fields.

At about midday, seven days after leaving the winter camp, they rounded a bend, and in the distance saw what appeared to be a great sprawling enclosure, a thick-built wall with corner bastions, surrounding a number of taller buildings within. Smoke rose from many chimneys, and a banner flew from a tall staff, and the sound of a distant bugle hung on the air.

"That can be no other than Sutter's establishment" Greenwood said with quiet satisfaction. "It is said that he keeps a greater state than the governor himself."

"There is only one other sight that could be more welcome to me," John answered honestly.

"But it is a grand one, none the less," Old Martin marveled. "Sure, and he lives like a lord, with a village outside the gates. Should we walk up to the front door, think you, or go around to the back to the stables?"

"To the front," John answered, and it seemed that they walked faster.

There were uniformed men patrolling the walls above, and the coming and going of men, horses, and wagons had beat out a road, a road that led between fine sturdy buildings, roofed with orange-red tile. They passed people going about their own business who looked at them with a little curiosity; Indians mostly, but dressed like white folk, the men in simple trousers and shirts, and women in chemises under gaily-patterned calico skirts and shawls.

The gates of Sutter's fortress stood open, but as they approached, a man called down from the bastion overhead:

"May I ask who you are, strangers, and inquire of your business here?"

"We are part of a wagon company who set out from Missouri, under Captain Stephens, some eight months ago," John answered, raising his voice a little. "And we would need to speak to Captain Sutter . . ." but his interlocutor exclaimed, "Stay . . . sir! Oh, this is happy news! You are expected! Come in, come in! We had news of your party . . . wait a moment, let me come down!"

They entered though the gate, coming out into a wide courtyard with a well in the center, all a-bustle with activity. A great arcade of structures lined the inside wall: stables and storehouses, workshops and stores. The smell of baked bread filled the air. A large house and several smaller held pride of place in the center, where a number of saddled horses were tied to hitching posts. One of them rather resembled Beau, and John's heart rose at the sight.

A bearded young man emerged from a small doorway at the foot of the bastion, saying in much excitement, "Captain Stephens, is it? Martin Murphy and Doctor Townsend? I am John Bidwell, Captain Sutter's foreman and assistant. We had much to do to reassure Mrs. Townsend, Doctor, she was most distraught."

"They are here?" Old Martin cried with much delight. "All of them with Helen and Daniel, and Johnny? They are here, and safe?"

Martin and James and their brother Bernard slapped each other's backs and crowed, "I knew it, those little scamps . . . anything to get out of chopping trees!"

"Yes, indeed, they rode in five days ago," Bidwell answered, "and Captain Sutter . . ."

But John did not hear another word, for two women had come out of the big house and down the steps and one of them was Helen Murphy, and the other was Elizabeth. And for the longest time, it was only the two of them, alone in Sutter's busy courtyard, locked in each other's arms.

Chapter 15 – *The Devils' Own Bargain*

There was a wax-flower arrangement, under a glass dome on a table between a pair of tall windows in Captain Sutter's office, the only touch of bright color in an austere room with pale rough-plastered walls. The windows were narrow and uncurtained, but there was glass in them, and frames and shutters painted a dull indigo color. John, Stephens, and Old Murphy sat in crude chairs, leather roughly sewn over a wood frame, lined up in front of an ornate inlaid desk trimmed with brass and ebony, like a trio of bad schoolboys called before the headmaster. Ragged and filthy with trail dirt, unkempt and unshaven, John couldn't help but think they were being deliberately put at a disadvantage. He did not like to think of young Bidwell being a party to this; he seemed barely older than Moses, as if he had grown that beard of his in order to seem older and more responsible.

Liz. He had come back into this world, from their embrace, to hear Bidwell urging them towards the big house and saying, "Captain Sutter gave particular orders that he meet with you at once upon your arrival."

He still had the feel of her bones impressed upon him, and she had smelt of soap and rosewater, of starched linen, and he wanted nothing more than to go apart with her alone, and pull the pins out of her hair and hold her close again, while he looked for ways to say how much he had missed her, and to work around to a way to tell her that her little brother was left behind, high in the mountains.

But instead, she had loosened her arms and stepped back a little, laughing breathlessly as she said, "Dearest, we rode out every day along the river, hoping we should see you! Captain Sutter and Mr. Bidwell assured us frequently that you must have been able to cross with safety."

"I arrived with an emigrant company myself, three years ago," Bidwell added cheerily, "We barely scraped through ourselves . . . but I had some idea of how much can be accomplished by sheer determination. We expressed every hope that we had for your safety to Mrs. Townsend and Miss Murphy."

"Mr. Bidwell and Captain Sutter have been kindness itself," Elizabeth exclaimed. "And Captain Sutter's generosity is a legend . . ."

"It is also his greatest weakness," Bidwell added, with wry affection. "With him, it is enough that a man wants employment, not that Captain Sutter can afford or even need his particular skills; which is, I think, why his enterprises here now include a brewery, a bakery, and the weaving of blankets. But as it now happens," he added with a serious face, "he may have need of your own several skills, as it happens. And that is why he wished to meet with the officers of your party at once."

Good lord, all he wanted was a few more moments with his wife. At his back, Helen Murphy asked excitedly about Mary-Bee's baby . . . a girl was it? How sweet! How far back were they camped?

Stephens himself looked more like an unhappy gargoyle than ever, and John sighed again.

"Mr. Bidwell, we have left the women and children of our party a week's journey away, camped in the mountains and awaiting our help . . . and allow me to be the first to assure yourself and Captain Sutter that they have first call on our services."

"And rightfully so, of course," answered Bidwell frankly. "But Captain Sutter will explain the nature of the service he requires himself it's not for me to anticipate."

"Well, sonny," Old Hitchcock rumbled. "Since you're his foreman, I have an idee there are things you can do on your own hook? Like send a messenger to Samuel Patterson's rancho, telling him that his two sons are safe here, but his wife and other children are marooned in the mountains?"

"Yes, of course, I know of him. Governor Micheltorena granted him lands near San Jose." Bidwell sounded distressed, and for once, rather younger. "I'll be happy to send a message . . . and we had arranged quarters for you all. I shall take you to them as soon as I have conducted your officers to Captain Sutter's office. Do you know there is not an inn or hostelry anywhere the length and breadth of this country? Travelers stay with friends or friends of friends . . . and sometimes even strangers."

Bidwell had walked John, Old Martin, and Stephens to the stairs of the big house by now, and they followed him inside, Stephens bidding Dog to stay by the doorway.

Elizabeth murmured, "Dearest, Helen and I will wait for you and Mr. Murphy in the parlor . . ." She looked up at him with a slight frown. "Where is Moses . . . I haven't seen him?"

"He stayed to guard the wagons, Liz," John stammered. It was out, then, but Liz didn't seem fearful, only rather fondly annoyed, and he realized that she must think Moses had stayed at the winter camp with the women. She kissed him again, she and Helen slipped into a doorway they passed as they followed Bidwell down the hallway to another room, the room where they sat now and waited for Sutter, the master of all they had yet surveyed.

There was a footstep in the hall, and the door opened.

"Welcome, gentlemen, all," said Captain Sutter. "Welcome to New Helvetia, and to California, and to my home. John Augustus Sutter, at your service."

The magnate of New Helvetia proved to be a sleek and stocky man of middle years, smartly turned out in a coat of vaguely military appearance that strained a little around his belly. He was slightly balding and his features described an amiable oval, supporting an immaculately barbered mustache and goatee and an expression of gentle enthusiasm and sympathy. He had a slight accent, not quite French, but not entirely German.

"Doctor John Townsend, late of St. Joseph, Missouri, our Captain, Elisha Stephens . . ." John shook Sutter's extended hand, and performed the introductions.

"Of nowhere in particular," Stephens inserted dryly.

" . . . and Mr. Martin Murphy, Senior, formerly of Missouri . . ."

"And Canada, Ireland, and everywhere in between." Old Martin added.

Sutter shook his hand, exclaiming, "A citizen of the world you are indeed, Mr. Murphy; a citizen of the world, as am I, but lately come to make my fortune in this most blessed country on the face of the earth, as I believe. And through many hardships and toils, you have come to join us in our endeavors."

"Our hardships and toils ain't over, yet." Stephens sounded particularly ungracious, and John sighed inwardly. Really, he wondered how Stephens would get on here in California if he himself were not there to intercede, to smooth over, and to apply the necessary diplomacy on his friend's behalf. Make enemies right and left, no doubt, unless he went and lived like a hermit in a cave.

Now John said, "You must understand, Captain Sutter . . . most of the men who came with us have left their wives and children in the mountains. We set up a winter camp, and slaughtered the rest of our oxen for food to leave with them. Two of our number stayed behind to guard them through the winter, but our intention now is to mount a rescue expedition, to return as swiftly as possible. We were seven days, following the river down to your . . . establishment . . . only two days of it struggling in the snow. Our guides, Mr. Greenwood and Mr. Hitchcock, were of the opinion that if we returned with pack animals at all speed we would have an excellent chance of winning through to them. But for this, we need your help, and we need it now."

"Alas," Sutter mournfully shook his head. "I regret such a daring plan is already not possible. The snows of winter in the mountains are already too deep. This is the middle of December, my friends. You were fortunate to escape the storms of winter by departing when you did." The expression of Sutter's face was sympathetic, regretful, but John noticed that it did not reach to his eyes. They were opaque, like pebbles, calculating and watchful.

"No!" Old Martin started up from his chair. "I canna sit still and hear this! Man, these are my own children and grandchildren, the wives of my sons! You tell us, there is nothing to be done? They are stranded in those mountains until spring, and meanwhile, we are able to go outside in our shirtsleeves?"

"It is indeed as mild as summer in most other places, here at the confluence of rivers," Sutter replied, his voice warm, soothing. "But the mountains are . . . well, you have seen a little of what the snow in them is like, and I can assure you that it becomes much, much worse, and with suddenness. I have been here nearly ten years, long enough to know that what trails exist are impassable. Even the deer and the Indians abandon the high country in winter. Your own General Fremont passed through here last year, and even he admitted defeat at a winter crossing."

"So, you'll do nothing?" Old Martin asked bitterly.

Sutter lifted his hands in an apologetic gesture, "I regret most sincerely, gentlemen, there is nothing that I can do for your families until spring, except offer my prayers for their continued well-being. I take that you left them with sufficient food, enough to last until spring? And two men, to hunt for them, and guard over them? But of course, you would have taken every possible care . . ." Sutter was all warm regard, and in that instant John conceived both a violent loathing of him, and the knowledge that he must keep that antipathy well-hidden.

Old Martin answered stoutly, "We left them practically every scrap we had, and all but two of the cattle."

"We ain't improvident folk." Stephens stirred himself and spoke, and it seemed that Sutter flinched slightly.

"Assuredly, they will be safe until the snow melts in spring . . . bored, perhaps, and longing to see their husbands and papas and brothers." Sutter made an expansive gesture towards the windows. "In the spring, when the paths are open, you may then make free of my stables and stores. I put no limits on my hospitality . . ."

"So we are told," John answered neutrally, and Old Martin added, "And grateful we are, Captain Sutter, grateful we are. My daughter has told of how she and her brothers have been received."

"Miss Murphy is a charming young lady." Captain Sutter seemed much amused. "She already has been the focus of romantic attentions from some of the other American settlers here. As her father, you should be forewarned perhaps." He sat back with a sigh in his own chair, the other side of his grand desk, as Stephens watched with hooded eyes and a mien of stone. Oh, here it comes, now, John thought. The point Sutter has been moving towards; what he wants of us.

"You arrive most fortuitously in California," Sutter ventured at last, making a steeple of his fingers over the gleaming surface of the desk in front of him. Stephens and John remained silent; Old Martin said only, "Aye? So you have been saying. The snows and all."

"I meant politically," Sutter replied. "Do you know much about California and its governance by Mexico? Their governor is appointed from Mexico City. At present, he's a man named Micheltorena; he's the finest of men, and a good friend to me, as well as kindly disposed to Americans. He has given out many fine grants of land . . . and that displeases some of the local grandees. They have raised a small army and a rebellion against his authority."

"And that has . . . what to do with us?" John asked, and he thought he saw a flash of impatience in those pebble-eyes. "It is, after all, a Mexican affair."

"It has much to do with you, gentlemen, whether you know or not. Should Micheltorena be overthrown, Pico or Castro, or whoever they might put forward as governor will not be so kindly disposed towards Americans. Your bright future here would be in jeopardy . . . so I have a proposal to secure it for us all. I am raising a company for Micheltorena; he is my friend and I could do no less for him. March with us to Monterey, gentlemen, and join with me assisting the governor in putting down this ridiculous little charade of an uprising. I would be indebted to you for your help, Governor Micheltorena would be grateful . . . and it would well serve your own interests. That is my offer to you and your men, Captain Stephens."

He looked at them over the desk, and they looked back for a long moment, until Stephens answered mildly, "I'd have to talk it over with the others. Prolly vote on it, too."

Old Martin scowled adding, "How long would this business take, hey? Seems to me that fifteen men would be neither here nor there."

"It will all be over well before spring; these little farces never go on for very long, more like an organized brawl, and then everyone dusts themselves off and goes back to fandangos and bear hunts," Sutter replied airily. "And fifteen armed men, just come from the trail, who would be reliable . . . you would be a very great part of my company indeed, and Doctor Townsend would be the battalion surgeon."

"As a rule, we Americans are more inclined to side with rebels against an appointed governor," John felt obliged to point out.

"As you wish, gentlemen, as you wish," and Sutter seemed about to dismiss them, but for Stephens abruptly rising.

"We'll talk it over, Captain Sutter." John inwardly sighed again, as Stephens strode towards the door; all the tact and polish of one of his own oxen.

He and Old Martin lingered for a moment, as John said, "We will let you know of our decision on this matter, Captain Sutter."

"Don't linger too long over it," Sutter answered suavely.

"In any case, we would like to render our thanks again for the care of Miss Murphy and Mrs. Townsend . . . we are in your debt in that regard alone," John owned honestly; he disliked the man, but he had to be fair.

Sutter smiled warmly." It was our pleasure as a host. They have been most enjoyable company. I presume that you would prefer to stay in the same room as your wife? I shall see that arrangements are made."

"Again, our thanks," John answered, and he and Old Martin followed after Stephens, their feet thudding on the wooden floor. Elizabeth popped out of the parlor door, as he passed.

"We have to talk to the others," he whispered. "I'll have another one of those kisses, Dearest, to tide me over."

"He put it to you to ride with his company?" she whispered in reply, and reached up to his face. "Darling, you're all bristly. You appear quite ferocious."

"You knew about this?"

"I guessed. They talk of nothing else but the governor and Castro and Pico coming out against him."

"You'll have to tell me who all these people are!" He hurriedly tore himself away. "Soon, before I make a fool of myself!"

"Tonight!" she whispered, and he hurried down the stairs after Old Murphy and Stephens. The other men had gone off towards the stable block and the corrals, and the three of them held a hasty consultation.

"Tell you what, Doc, I don't like it at all." Stephens shook his head. "Not just giving us no help until spring but wanting us to ride off on this jaunt of his? Smells like an over-full privy on a hot summer day."

"I wish we knew truly about winter conditions in the mountains." John rubbed his face. By god, he was bristly. "For all we know, he might have been exaggerating."

"Wanting us to think there was really nothing we could do until spring?" Old Martin shook his head; shrewd and stoical as ever. "Faith an' I little like the thought of dancing to another's tune . . . but he's the laird of these parts. A good friend to be having, but a worse enemy; I like it as little as you both, but I think we may have no other choice than do as he wishes."

"There's always a choice," Stephens answered. "What do you advise, Doc?"

"Stall," John replied. "Stall, and find out as much as we can."

"You'll get nothing much from Bidwell," Old Martin added. "Nice lad he is, but the way he goes on, he seems to think the sun shines out of Sutters' arse. Any else we're likely to speak to, they work for him, or are of his party."

* * *

From Dr. Townsend's diary; *"Capt. Stephens and I made the others aware of Capt. Sutter's offer, and they liked it as little as we, feeling that we are being maneuvered into taking his part against our own best interests. And he is a fair and well-thought of man, held in high esteem by all. Being newly come to this place, we do not wish to offend anyone, but there is somewhat of a bad taste resulting from his haste to recruit us to his ranks."*

* * *

"I am afraid I do not know very much," Elizabeth said late that evening, after an interminable dinner shared with Sutter and Bidwell and a number of other guests, including Old Martin, his sons and Miss Helen. Decency and a fairly late hour had finally allowed them to retire for the night in the room that Elizabeth had been allotted. "I have only been here a week myself, and have not met any of these people, but I have heard of them. Juan Castro and Pio Pico are the two most set against Governor Micheltorena, but they can hardly stand each other. There are Americans here and there, some who have been here for years, and from what I can see, most of them do as they please and humor the Mexican administrators. Is that what you needed to know, Dearest?"

"Liz, you make an admirable spy." John kissed her again.

"You seem very pleased tonight," she murmured, and he answered, "I am clean, shaved, and sharing a bed indoors with my own wife, who'd not be pleased?" But he looked at the ceiling over their heads, and sighed. "I fear for the others. I don't think I'll sleep entirely sound until they are all brought safe down from the mountains."

She took his hand, and brought it to her cheek and said calmly, "I know about Moses, you know. He is not at the winter camp with the others. Helen's brother Bernard told me, while you were in with Captain Sutter."

"I had meant to say, Dearest. There was never the right time, until we were alone."

"I know. Bernard told us, how Moses was quite set upon remaining, when you and Mr. Stephens and Mr. Foster all decided to leave your wagons."

"I couldn't talk him out of it, Liz."

"Nor could I have, Dearest. I think," she added firmly. "Moses is probably enjoying himself very much, hunting with Allen and Mr. Foster, rather than looking after all the babies and little children. He has no patience with apron strings, as I have known since that time when he went off to hunt buffalo. You were so very wise on that, Dearest . . . that I should not fuss over him, he would be able to look after himself and be safe." She burrowed into his arms then, with a sigh of complete contentment, and John thought about his last sight of Moses, walking down the pass after Allen and Joseph, and hoped she was right; or if not, could go on believing so.

Three days later, while Stephens and John were still stalling on Sutter's offer, he and Old Martin were gloomily looking over the corralled stock and discussing the chances of an expedition of their own. Elizabeth and Helen had continued the habit of a daily ride, and had ridden away some time before.

"It's not the finances, mind," Old Martin remarked frowning. "We have some funds between us, but most of it was put into our gear, stock, and supplies for the journey. We would be hard put to realize the value of the wagons in cash."

"Besides my own wagon and goods," John sighed, "I have some two hundred in gold coins and a letter of credit from my bank in St. Joseph . . . it would take time to raise cash with that, even assuming I would know whom to take it to, outside of our kindly host."

"And it would come back to buying the animals and equipment from him . . . Holy Mother Mary!" Old Martin's gaze went beyond John, towards the fort gates. "Is that not Allen Montgomery and young Foster, that we left at the lake!?"

A pair of bearded and trail-worn men with packs and rifles slung on their shoulders had just entered the compound, and stood in evident puzzlement, looking around at the heart of Captain Sutter's busy and bustling kingdom. One of the sentries approached them and exchanged a few words. The sentry turned and pointed at Old Martin and John who were already hurrying towards the gate. John was looking beyond; surely there should be one more? Elizabeth would be so pleased to know that Moses was safe, now. But there was no one else with them, just the two, no one of Moses' gawky frame and light hair anywhere to be seen, and John's heart was already cold. Allen and Joseph looked fit and well, even though dirty, but they looked at John as if they had bad news to break.

"Where's the lad?" Old Martin asked quietly, when they were in hearing. Joseph looked at them as if he would weep, and answered, "We had to leave him. I'm sorry Doc, so sorry."

"Where?" John's voice sounded harsh in his own ears, and Allen and Joseph both flinched.

"At the lake. He said goodbye to us at the top of the pass, and we went on, and left him there alone." Now Joseph was weeping, and his voice cracked; Joseph Foster, always so cheerful, who had never had a disheartened word to say even when things had been truly dreadful.

"You'd best tell us then, boys," Old Martin spoke in gentle, but stern tones, and over their head, Elizabeth looked down from Beau's saddle, like an avenging angel with the sun shining from behind her head.

"Yes," she said quietly. "Tell me what has happened to my little brother, and why you left him all alone, Allen . . . when you were the friend he looked up to?"

Elizabeth had learned much from Isabella, John decided then . . . she had that very tone in her voice, fair warning that no man or child should dare to cross, and Allen Montgomery looked fair to wilt.

"My Dearest," John cleared his throat carefully, "they have come a long way, it would only be fair to let them sit down, let them have something to eat and drink . . . and then they can tell us what has happened."

Joseph's look was piteous in its gratitude, but Allen said pleadingly, "He was alive, then, Mrs. Townsend. We left him by the fire; he said he was going to walk down to the cabin as soon as he had rested a little more. He was alive when we last had sight of him, I swear it!" and Elizabeth only looked at him, and John realized that the animus that he held towards Sutter was a pale shadow compared to what Elizabeth now bore towards Allen.

Elizabeth was partial to Sarah, and took her part when Allen had treated her badly, but now Allen had let down Moses, who was all but Elizabeth's own child. A wise man did not do harm, by commission or omission, to a woman's cub, not if he put any particular value on his own skin, or make one of her particular friends unhappy, and now Allen had done both . . . no, Allen would not be welcome in any parlor that Elizabeth kept, and John did not blame her in the least. In spite of their long friendship, John would cheerfully knock Allen down if he now showed himself responsible for abandoning Moses in the wilderness.

Captain Sutter had given them several furnished rooms in his garrison quarters, the sleeping rooms opening into an arcade that served as a sitting room and dining room combined, furnished with tables and the same sort of comfortable rawhide chairs that he had in his office. The Martin boys, Dennis and Patrick, were taking their leisure there, and welcomed Allen and Joseph happily, taking no apparent notice of John's grim face.

"Allen, man, you lazy scamp, you were supposed to be in the mountains," Patrick said cheerily. "Set your traps down anywhere.

"And what would your old father say if he saw you boys lazing away the day?" Joseph answered, and Dennis said, "Move yourselves over, and pass me the pipe, that's what he would say . . . you've just come from the women's camp?"

Allen and Joseph set down their packs, with expressions of profound relief. "A week ago . . . we'd just missed you, and your father and James said they were doing fine, and we should take ourselves after you as soon as possible, before another storm hit."

Allen looked sideways at John. "Other than the snow being nearly up to the roof, everything seemed well for them."

Old Martin had tactfully detoured to the kitchens and bakery and reappeared now with a tray bearing a couple of bowls of the good fortifying stew of beef and beans provided for the hands and local Indian workers, and a stack of thin bread.

"Sorry, boys, and it's all they had at the moment," he said apologetically, "But here's a pitcher of the good ale they brew here. Drink up and tell us what happened now . . . how and why did you come, and what news have you to tell us."

"But first, tell us what happened at the pass," John said. "We left you there to guard the wagons; are we to assume then, they are left unguarded?"

"No," replied Joseph. He had taken a cup of the ale that Old Martin had passed to him, and a bowl of the good red stew. He was gobbling it up, accompanied by handfuls of the thin folded bread made in the bake-house for the workers around here. "At least, I think not. Moses was going back to the cabin, you see."

"Tell us what happened," John said through his teeth, and Allen replied, "After we bid farewell to you at the top of the pass we all three went down again. We finished building the cabin in a couple of days. We used those two oxen to drag logs, and we had it all finished and tight, the weather was fine, and everything we needed moved into it, and then the storm set in, about four days after. We thought nothing of it, we were warm and sheltered, and thought how fine the hunting would be, when the storm was over."

"Ah," interjected Old Martin. "We were caught, just then, ourselves. Four days after crossing the high pass, that's about right, the day when we packed it in, and couldn't go any farther."

"Three feet of snow," Joseph said. "Three feet, and it didn't melt and pack down, but kept on snowing until it was up to the level of the cabin roof. We killed the oxen – there was nothing left to feed them anyway. We tried to go out hunting . . . we could barely go far enough to get firewood. There was nothing to hunt . . . so much for my plan to hunt for my supper; it was a bad one, as it turned out but we didn't know it for sure for another week or so."

"We took hickory bows from my wagon." Allen scraped a mouthful of good red stew on a fold of thin bread. "Joe said he could trim and bend them to shape; using the cowhide, he could make show-shoes of them, something that we could use and get around on the snow, better than we could in our boots. It worked, and we made three pair of them, so we could walk around on the snow, with a bit of effort."

He nudged his pack with his booted foot; two hickory bentwood objects were strapped to the back of it, the insides of the tear-drop- shaped frames filled in with a netting of ox-hide strips knotted together.

"Faith, you walked out on those?" Dennis commented, "Holy mother, I'll bet you about killed yourselves. The frame of it don't need to be all that heavy, you know."

"We went out hunting," Joseph continued. "So we did, and we did our best, but there wasn't anything, anything at all but tracks of foxes and coyotes. The deer had gone down to lower levels, the bear were all hibernating. Even the fish in the lake were gone down, and then it froze entire . . . so what could we do? There wasn't enough meat left from those oxen for

217

all three of us to make it through to spring, and the snow was piling up higher than the cabin roof."

"We talked it over then," Allen continued. "And we agreed to try and walk out. We dried the beef, and each of us took some of it, and some blankets and a rifle each, and we set out in the morning to try and catch up to you. It was hard going for us, even with the snowshoes, but we carried on. That night, we camped at the top of the pass. We had a fire, too, but we feared that it would go out, and it was bitter cold. We stayed awake all night to feed it."

"What of the lad," Old Martin said softly, and Joseph answered, "He carried on as bravely as he could – but he kept having cramps in his legs, and he fell down in the snow many times. We'd wait for him, and he would get up and walk on a little way, but by the time we made camp for the night, he could go no more than fifty yards without resting. In the morning, he could barely move."

"We couldn't carry him if he failed." Allen looked pleadingly at Elizabeth and John. "He was well grown for a lad, even if he wasn't as heavy as a man. We couldn't return to the cabin, there was only enough food left behind for one, maybe, and we feared being caught out in the open in another storm."

John, reminded piercingly of the story that Old Hitchcock had told as he and Moses and Stephens had watched the sunset on Scott's Bluffs, remained silent. Dear God, Moses had remembered how Hiram Scott had bidden his friends to leave him, accepting his own death at the price of saving theirs.

"So that's what he said," Joseph continued. "He said he would go back to the cabin alone, and live as long as he could on what was left. Perhaps he might try to walk out later on, if he recovered his strength. He shook our hands, and we said, 'Goodbye, Mose.' We left him by the fire; he said as soon as he was a little more rested, he would walk down. It had frozen overnight, so I think he would have been able to get along without the snowshoes. We promised to organize a relief party in the spring . . . it was all we could do for Mose, Mrs. Townsend, I'm so sorry. It was all we could do. He told us himself that he knew that whatever he did, he had to think of the others in the company as well as himself."

"Ah," said John. So Moses had remembered also the lecture John and Old Martin had given him, about thinking things through, after the incident with the Indians at the Sink so many months ago. With the gallantry of the very young he had decided to live up to it, courage and sacrifice and friendship, all at once, at the ice-water lake in the heart of the mountains. "I am sure he is all right, Liz, I am sure of it. There was so much left with the wagons . . . and if the snow was frozen hard, and he could walk from the pass. It was not that far from the pass to their camp." He took Elizabeth's hand as she sat with a still face and overflowing eyes.

Dennis Martin took the other, saying, "Heart up, Mrs. Townsend. I'll promise myself to go back in the spring for young Mose, with a better pair of snowshoes yet. I'd think shame on myself if I couldn't build a better pair, or teach him so as to get along without falling down." And that coaxed a softening to her face, although she still looked bitterly towards Allen.

"We know about winter snow in the mountains, now." Stephens materialized in the arcade; John had no notion of how long he had been there. "We'd best consider our answer to Captain Sutter now."

Celia Hayes

Chapter 16 – *Starvation Camp*

From E.S. Patterson Interview, University of California Local History Archival Project 1932: *"What do I recollect most clearly of the winter camp? A good many things . . . but what has stuck with me the most was how dark it was inside. Before the men went down from the mountains, following the river, they built two little cabins with a sort of porch between, a roof with no walls. But the snow soon made walls on either side, and presently all you could see of it was an opening like a burrow going down into something that looked like a tall snow-bank with a little smoky chimney on either end. It was always dark inside since there wasn't any windows; the men had been in too much of a hurry, and it made no never-mind, because the snow would have covered them up anyway. We had some fat lamps and tallow candles, too . . . and Ma would read to us during the days it was storming outside.*

"Dimness, aye, that's what I remember. And the smell of it; a wood-fire burning, and the smell of tallow candles, and dirty clothes and the babies' dirty diapers, and the chamber pots that Ma and Mrs. Montgomery kept outside in the little porch, with a couple of blankets around them for privacy. But that smell came in, too, sometimes. Nothing to do for it, as Ma and the four of us shared one cabin with Mrs. Montgomery and Mary Sullivan and her brother Robert, who was near enough to my age. Old Mr. Martin, one of the men who was staying behind to guard and hunt for us, he had a little bunk in one corner with a blanket for privacy.

"The other cabin was full of babies and children: Mr. Miller, the other man who stayed, he was living there with his wife and son William and three daughters. The youngest was the baby born at Independence Rock. Then there was Mrs. Murphy with her little girl, Mary, and the other Mrs. Murphy with her four little boys and the baby born just when the men set up the winter camp. Mr. Martin said our cabin was all peace and quiet in comparison, even if Mrs. Montgomery and Mary Sullivan fought like cats in a sack; it was still only five of us children and no babies. There was four grownups in the Murphy's cabin, but eight children and two babies. How they got through that winter without running plumb insane, I'll never know.

"Ma, I think she sent us to play outside on the fair days, as much as possible, and so did the Murphy women with the children and all. There were the other things I remember: how beautiful it was up there when it snowed; everything so clean and white, and a little ridge of snow along every twig and branch. It was so cold the snow was dry and fluffy like feathers, and the sky

220

above as blue as turquoise stone, and your shoes squeaking on the snow as you walked for it was that cold.

"We hadn't been there a week when Mr. Foster and Mr. Montgomery came down the hill, following the trail of trees the men had cut to bring the wagons over . . . there they were, just the two of them, we thought they were wintering over at the lake, guarding the other wagons we had left there.

"They talked to Ma and Mr. Martin and Mr. Miller . . . and Mr. Montgomery talked some to his wife, but they didn't have much to say; he abandoned her later, and she married another man, name of Talbot Green, came out with Bartleson and Bidwell in '41, but turned out he was wanted for embezzlement, and damned if he didn't abandon her, too. She did have good luck with her third husband, though, but I never could blame her for not thinking much of men. It was Ma, though, that taught her to read. She couldn't, you see. She was so embarrassed about that she kept quiet until we were in the winter camp and couldn't keep it a secret no longer.

"Mr. Foster and Mr. Montgomery left the lake when they saw there wasn't any hunting like they had planned. The snow was just too deep. They'd made themselves showshoes, and could walk on top of the snow, after a fashion, but it was hard going. They'd left Moses, the Doctor's boy behind, as he fell ill and there was only food enough left for one to stay the winter. They was afraid if they stayed, they'd be caught in another big storm.

"You have to remember, most of us were from Missouri, Ohio and back east. We weren't anything like accustomed to snow that piled up and stayed on the ground without melting in between a bit. They say the snow commonly was over fifteen feet or deeper. It wasn't near that deep where we were, but Mr. Miller and Mr. Martin never did have any luck hunting from our camp either. But later on, whenever we starting saying what a hard time we had, Ma would tell us to thank our lucky stars our party had Captain Stephens, and Doctor Townsend and Old Martin Murphy with us, because what happened with us wasn't near to as bad as what happened to some of them that came along later. We did have to eat some hides off the roof, though. But that came later.

"Christmas . . . I recollect Christmas. It came just after Mr. Montgomery and Mr. Foster went, following after the rest of the men. We each had a toy on Christmas morning, can you beat that? Mr. James Murphy, before he went with the other men, he had made a little toy or trifle for each one of us. A little boat with a sail or a horse or cow for us boys, a bit of a doll for the little girls, and Mrs. Murphy had sewed a little dress and apron for the dolls. Sadie loved that little doll, for she had managed to loose the shell *necklace that Ma traded for her birthday present at Laramie. Mr. James made a little trinket box for my sister Nancy, though, as she was too old for dolls. And Ma, she had a treat for us too. From the last of Doctor Townsend's stores, two little jars of jam. She brought them out and gave each of the children a spoonful. There was just enough to go around.*

"About the food . . . well, it was monotonous, but we were used to pretty slim rations by that time anyway. Ma got right ingenious. She and my brother Johnnie went out and dug down through the snow to where the men butchered the oxen, pulled up a lot of the bones they had left aside. Roasted them, cracked them for the marrow, boiled them until they were crumbly and fell apart. We'd eaten every scrap of what was left, and that includes the brains and offal. We were starving for the fat, you see.

"Another time, she and Mrs. Montgomery went down to the river, after there was a good hard crust frozen onto the snow . . . they dug down through the snow at the river edge, prospecting for water reed tubers, and plantains and stuff. It all tasted pretty awful, if you want to know the truth. But the best part of whatever we had it went to the little children, and to Mrs. Miller and Mrs. Murphy, who were nursing babies. Ma was a midwife, next to a doctor, practically. If them two didn't have enough to eat, their milk would stop up, and the babies would die; simple as that.

"She never showed how worried she was to us, but her hair went from dark brown to near enough grey in that one year, and if she ate more than a mouthful at any meal during that whole winter, then I never saw it. She was tough, too. I never saw her cry and get downhearted, but when I was older myself, I thought about the fix we'd been in, and I wondered how she managed it . . . but afterwards she never talked about that winter except on her deathbed. She went back to it in her mind at the end.

"Sadie and Nance and I, those who were with her then, we all knew then that whole dreadful winter, it had stayed with her, all the rest of her life. She wouldn't eat, you see; she wandered in her mind back to that time; all she would say to us was, 'Give it to the children, Sarah . . . Give it to Mary for the baby . . . Give it to Mary-Bee, the baby will need it.' It broke our hearts to hear that, it did . . .

"One thing, now that you've asked and brought that time back to mind; she used to walk out every fine day to the edge of the camp, and sit on a tall stump, looking out at the west, as if she were watching for someone to come up from the river. I asked her, every day that she did this, what she was looking for and she would answer, 'Eddie, my duckling, I'm waiting for your

father and Paw-Paw and the other men to come back for us, and I want to be the first to see them.'

"And I would say, 'Why is that, Ma?' and she'd answer, 'So I can give your Pa a kiss and a hug for the joy of seeing him, and a box on the ear for making us wait for him this long.' And then she would take me on her lap, and wrap her shawl around us both, and tell me about Pa's wonderful new farm, and what it looked like and all. I think she made most of it up, though, for she'd only had one letter from Pa the whole time he had been out looking for land and it were a year old when she got it anyway. That's one of the things I remember best.

"Well, that and when the snow had begun to melt and we came down the mountains, and I found a live frog and put it in Mary Sullivan's bedroll. I got a licking over that from Ma, but it was worth it."

From Dr. Townsend's diary: *"Twenty-first of December, 1844, At Sutter's Fort on the American River, New Helvetia. We have accepted Captain Sutters' terms, acknowledging that nothing can be done until spring thaw. Mr. Patterson, the mild-mannered Petruchio to our own Kate, agreed with us most regretfully as regards the impossibility of venturing a rescue before then. This gentleman arrived in haste from his rancho near San Jose yesterday, upon receipt of a messenger from Mr. Bidwell advising him of the situation. He came to fetch the boys, as I had promised Mrs. Patterson to see them into the custody of their parent . . ."*

* * *

John had often speculated in his own mind on the sort of man to have made a successful match with the formidable Isabella, so he hurried from Sutter's house to the quarters set aside for the others, and to where Mr. Patterson had been directed by the duty sentry, with curiosity lending wings.

He found Dog, that most formidable of guardians, sniffing at a wiry man of middle years with a weather-burnt face and mild blue eyes, who was sitting in one of the leather chairs, looking amused, just as Samuel and Oliver burst in, from the other direction, clamoring in unison, "Papa! You're here!"

And of course, it must be no other, for he sprang up, saying, "Oliver, and is this Samuel! Oh, you have grown so tall, the both of you!" and the boys chorused, "Oh, Pa, you'll never guess . . . we had such adventures! Ma is up in the mountains, but Doctor Townsend talked her into letting me come with the men. You'd never believe . . . Sadie is talking, and Eddie is now such a scamp . . . he broke his arm, and his head . . . Ma had to hitch Goldenrod to the wagon . . . we crossed the desert in two days, and . . . Papa, may we ride with the men and Mr. Sutter's army for Micheltorena? May we, please?"

Samuel Patterson smiled wryly, and reached across his excited and vociferous offspring. "Samuel Patterson." He shook hands firmly, "I b'lieve you must be Doctor Townsend. You have the look of a professional man. No, you may not, Oliver; absolutely not. It's a fool's errand, and I'll need both of you on the ranch, planning a campaign to rescue your mother."

"A man with priorities well fixed." John returned the handshake. "And you are correct. It is a fool's errand, to which we are committed only until the wretched man wins or looses definitively, or the snow melts, whichever first."

"A sensible man, I see." Patterson was sizing him up. "Would you allow me some moments with the boys? It has been a long time since I parted with them, and I would speak to you about this matter."

So John lounged in the verandah, with Dog's great head on his knee. Stephens must have bid her stay in the quarters, for he himself was nowhere around.

After a while, Patterson emerged from the inner room and sank into the chair opposite. "Will you accept my thanks, Doctor, for having seen to the conducting of my family? The boys are most energetic in their praise of yourself and Captain Stephens. Might I meet him, do you think, before we depart? I should like to tender my thanks and gratitude." He sighed, deeply. "I had no idea that Isabella would decide on so strenuous a route. I myself went out to California through the regular trade to Santa Fe, and the pack-trains from thence to Los Angeles. I fear that my description of the hazards attendant on the mule-train may have affected her decision." He looked pleadingly at John, and asked in tones of deepest concern, "Was she well when last you saw her, Doctor? I want to know everything, particularly in regards to my family."

"She was well when we left the winter camp, two weeks ago," John answered fairly. "Well, but wearied from the journey, as you may expect . . . and most particularly grieved at the encampment on the lake, just below the mountain pass, when we had to dispatch many of the stock. The children were well, also. To all of us," John looked at the tiled floor beneath his feet, "She has been a most amenable and trusty traveling companion, a colleague in medicine to me, and a personal friend to my wife. We have valued her company and friendship enormously."

"You can only imagine my own feelings," Patterson answered, "Knowing her qualities as a friend and companion, but intensified for me, in that she is my very dear wife, and the mother to our children. It is very disheartening to know that she has traveled all this way to rejoin me, come so close and yet be trapped by winter, just out of our reach." He sighed deeply. "And we can mount no rescue until spring. This is very bitter knowledge, Doctor Townsend, exceeding bitter."

"Captain Stephens has talked with others who are familiar with conditions in the mountains," John answered, "and they all caution us not to attempt a relief until mid-February at the earliest. So that is what we intend. Will you join us then? Captain Sutter has promised us all aid, but of course . . ." John shrugged, not liking to say more.

Samuel Patterson answered, "His generosity has long strings attached, you mean. You need say no more. I am resolved to stand aside in this Micheltorena tangle. Castro and Pico are honorable men, with whom one may honestly differ. And the truth is that just as many American settlers are taking their part in this. Most of Micheltorena's soldiers are dregs, the worst sort of criminal swept from Mexico City's jails by their government and dumped here to afflict the population. It speaks well of Sutter to be loyal to his good friend the Governor, but badly for his judgment in not seeing this whole affair for the miscalculation that it is, in alienating the local gentry. They are proud men, Doctor Townsend, and Governor Micheltorena has bungled it very badly."

"So you intend to stay home this winter and grow cabbages . . . in a manner of speaking?" John was intrigued.

"I do so intend," Samuel answered firmly. "Because, one way or another, it will make no difference at all. Micheltorena will bloody Castro's nose, or Pico will bloody Michaeltorena's, or maybe even Castro's too, for good measure, and it will make no difference at all in the long run. From the least to the grandest, the Californios care little for being indifferently and distantly ruled from Mexico. I think most of them wouldn't care two pins if Alta California fell into American hands tomorrow, or next year as it most likely will eventually. All it would mean would be indifferent and distant rule from another quarter. Less restraint upon trade and commerce and a few more emigrant parties, most likely, of which all would be in favor. Another flag and different colored uniforms on the soldiers in the presidios, which the local maidens would find enticing, I daresay. This business with Micheltorena is a schoolyard brawl magnified, and I want no part of it."

"Well, we have every intention of disentangling ourselves from it as soon as we can." John sighed. "One would hope sense can be talked to all the parties concerned. I can see how you wish to remain apart from the fray though."

"Extracting yourselves from this unhappy situation will at least give you something to think on, rather than worry constantly about your nearest and dearest," Samuel said. "Perhaps it serves as a fortunate distraction for you. Do you have family stranded in the mountains, Doctor?"

"My wife's young brother." It pained him to talk of Moses. "We raised him as our son, more or less. He is about Oliver's age. He volunteered to stay with two other men, guarding the wagons on the other side of the pass. He became ill when they attempted to walk out, and so they left him behind."

"And the other men of the party, here . . . they have family also awaiting rescue in the mountains?" Samuel sounded genuinely appalled.

"Captain Stephens does not, nor does Greenwood, our guide, or the hired men, but Martin Murphy and his sons left their wives and children, two of them infants in arms. The Murphy men will be in a perfect frenzy by the time spring comes; neither Sutter or the Governor or anyone else will stand in between them and the mountains then."

"Trusty men then." Samuel looked relieved and John said, "Will you be at Captain Sutter's table for supper? I can introduce you to my wife . . . she can then talk of her friendship with yours. They spent much time together on the trail. I am certain that Elizabeth can regale you with many cheerful accounts of the children, also."

"It would be appreciated," Samuel answered. "And it would also allow me to avoid overmuch conversation with our host. I fear he would be importuning me to join his company . . . and I rather think I might be overly blunt in turning him down."

"He is a darling," Elizabeth whispered to John that night in their bed. "Quite older, though – and quieter than I would have thought." John had sat at the other end of the table with Bidwell and Stephens, tactfully keeping Sutter's interest from Patterson, and so he had little to do with Elizabeth's conversation with him.

Now he asked, "What did you talk about?"

"Oh, the children, mostly. He does not know Sadie at all, she had not even been born when he departed for California, and Eddie only five, so he liked to hear of their doings and conversation . . . I told him of Isabella's rational costume, and he laughed and laughed, about her winning a footrace with Oliver and Samuel. We talked about the trail, of course. He went to Santa Fe, did you know? Mr. Hitchcock had connections in the trade, who made arrangements for him to travel with the yearly caravan, and he went on from there with a mule party. It sounded much more exhausting than our own travails, and most of it spent crossing a dreadful desert, and the Indians were very much more dangerous. He talked about his own rancho, and how he has had a fine house built for them all, with a view of the mountains, and many fine trees. It sounds like quite a kingly place to live. He talked much with Mr. Murphy about it."

"Old Martin liked the talk of the mission, I noticed." John added, "It pleased him greatly, to know he has come to a Catholic country, where his native beliefs are favored. He and his sons have great plans –I think most of them hinge upon engendering enough grandchildren to sweep all before them."

"You are wicked to talk so." Elizabeth tried to sound severe. "Should not we think on our own children and grandchildren then?"

"My medical practice in California may depend on attending the various Mrs. Murphys!" John kissed her most lovingly. "Have a care, for you are distracting their family physician from his duties, my Dearest."

And at that point, they lost the thread of conversation for a long time, until Elizabeth ventured sleepily, "I wish you were not so obligated to Mr. Sutter's military company, Dearest, for we could then advance our own plans. I would love to have a home of our own, one that you may bring Moses to when the snow melts, and you and Captain Stephens bring the wagons down from the mountains. Where shall we go? San Jose, like the Murphys and Mr. Patterson? I should like to be close to our friends."

"I rather liked talk of Yerba Buena," John answered. "They tell me it is on a great natural bay, and may be one of the greatest port cities in the world, but it is cold and foggy most times, from being on the ocean."

"We'll take a look." Elizabeth stretched, and then re-curled herself against him, "And maybe Moses can help us decide. When does Captain Sutter wish you all to leave with him?"

"After Christmas," John answered, "unless it does not resolve itself by then. Perhaps we can hope for that."

"I only live for the day, my Dearest . . . day to day, and for now, and content with that."

* * *

From Dr. Townsend's diary: *"Mr. Patterson and the boys parted this morning, with many protestations of regard . . . as well as a promise to meet again here, before the end of February, so as to coordinate our efforts. At supper, Captain Stephens affirmed to the company present that he was fixed most especially upon this relief. Upon being elected, he reminded us once again he had promised to bring us all to California. Since so many of our party remain trapped in the mountains, this promise remains unfulfilled, and he is honor-bound to see every last one of us delivered safely. Captain Sutter was most moved by this declaration, and by the firm intention of those few of our party who were only contracted to accompany us. Mr. Greenwood and his sons, and one or two of our hired teamsters and drovers are to remain together with the party and act under Captain Stephens' and my direction, even though their formal obligations were concluded upon our arrival. Mr. Bray, tho', has taken employment with Sutters' enterprise, as one of his foremen.*

"We departed on this day, the First of January, with Captain Sutter. We ride with little enthusiasm, but a large sense of duty towards our fellows, and for Captain Stephens. We marvel at this country, meanwhile. It is beautiful and temperate, save for the coastal regions but thinly populated . . . in many regions there are few trees, but noble and spreading ones of a species of oak peculiar to this part of the world . . .

"There are but few towns, and scattered houses of the well-to-do rancheros. The buildings are solid and low, mostly constructed of unbaked clay bricks, which are then plastered over and roofed with curving clay tiles . . .The missions are large and prosperous, tho' not as much as formerly, many of their outlying properties being sold . . . noted this day some expansive groves of cultivated olives, and terraces of grapevines . . . a pair of lemon trees, of a good size, in pretty glazed pots; such would appeal to my Dearest, in our home.

"Enthusiasm for this venture flags, the farther we go. Mr. Patterson was prescient in referring to this as an organized schoolyard brawl. There is little feeling for Governor Micheltorena, other than that which Captain Sutter feels as a friend. Most of the rest of his 'army' if you can term it thus, feel so little for his cause that we would not risk a scratch from a pin for it, let alone our lives.

"Thirteenth of February, 1845, near Monterey, on the coast. Dennis Martin has had enough of this, and the rest of us are close enough to it."

* * *

"It's a mugs game, and I've had enough," Dennis announced at their campfire. As if of old habit from the trail, the group of Stephens party men kept their own campfire and looked warily on strangers. John often wondered if they had all been too much by themselves for too long, and if they would long go on being mistrustful of outsiders to their company. "Playing patty-cake, and poncing about the countryside, while our old Da is in the mountains," Dennis continued. "I'm off in the morning. Give my regards to Captain Sutter and tell him I'll turn his horse into his own corral, and be off towards the mountains. I've seen as much of his elephant as I wish to see, and I have better things to do. Patrick . . ." he turned towards his brother, who was moodily roasting a bit of beef threaded onto a greenwood spit. "D'you want to send any message to Da?"

"Tell him there are more Englishmen here than we thought, and he's to keep his fists in his pockets until we get them sorted out," Patrick replied. "Also, we'll be along in a bit. I think this farce has about another week to run, but I want to be around to laugh when the wheels come all the way off."

"Well, please yourself." Dennis caught up his rifle and his coat and bedroll. "Matter of fact, I think I'll start now. I've eaten and rested, and I can put a good few miles behind me by dark. See you in the mountains, boys!"

He was gone, with a wave and a thunder of hoof-beats. Stephens and John looked at each other, and John said, "We won't be able to hold them to Sutter's company much longer."

"He's just hasty-tempered," Stephens answered. "He's right about the elephant, though. I reckon we're all pretty fed."

* * *

From Dr. Townsend's diary: *"Nineteenth of February, 1845. Received news from the south, via a fast courier. Governor Micheltorena has been defeated militarily in a small clash north of the Pueblo de Los Angeles, and has agreed to depart California at once. We received this news as we were about to leave for the south to link up with Micheltorena's unfortunate army. Captain Stephens and I went at once to Captain Sutter and Mr. Bidwell . . ."*

* * *

Sutter stood to receive them, seemingly with pleasure; he had a large tent set up for himself, equipped with folding camp furniture.

"We heard of the messenger from the south," John began, and Sutter replied, "The news of the Governor's surrender has not been confirmed . . . all may not be lost, gentlemen . . ."

"Yes it has," Stephens said flatly. John and Bidwell exchanged looks of amused exasperation. All the tact of one of his own oxen; even Dog had more polish to her manners. "He's gone. We're done, as we agreed. We'll move out in the morning."

"It's nearly the end of February," John added quietly. Would Sutter dare renege on his agreement? He had that pebble-calculating look to his eyes again, although his face was all kindness and concern. "You offered us anything we would need to mount a relief party, once the governorship was settled, or winter began breaking up in the mountains. We left them with food, but not much of it. They will run out in a few weeks, if they haven't already."

"It's settled." Stephens was at his flintiest, most uncompromising. "You have ambitions here, whether the Americans take over or not. How far would you go after it were known to all that you let women and children starve in the mountains, while you kept their men galloping all about the country?"

"Captain Stephens, that's hardly fair!" Bidwell was outraged, "You would have us abandon our good friends!"

"Lot of that going around," Stephens answered laconically, and bright color rose in Bidwell's face, as though he had been slapped.

"We're going," John said. "With your aid, which you promised, and which would reflect credit upon your legendary hospitality . . . or without; which might be hard to explain down the road. Either way, we're going. Good day to you, Captain Sutter." John touched his hat brim, nodded to Bidwell, and exited the tent at speed, fairly dragging Stephens after him.

When they were out of earshot, Stephens commented dryly, "Don't care for him, do you, Doc?"

"He's kindness itself, when it serves," John replied. "It fair makes my teeth hurt. He makes me want to go out and kick a cripple after every time I speak to him, and he is all saintly sympathy and no action."

"Captain Stephens, Doctor Townsend . . . wait!" It was Bidwell, hurrying after them. He looked harassed, embarrassed, and as young as Moses. "I . . . I've spoken to Captain Sutter . . . he was only surprised, taken back, as it were, by the sudden misfortune of it all. There is so much going on, with his various enterprises and affairs . . . I think it had slipped his mind entirely, the plight of your families. But he is in agreement on this, that your bargain is fulfilled, and he releases you from the company . . ."

"Mighty good of him," Stephens remarked dryly.

"We've released ourselves," John said, and Bidwell continued, "He directed that you should take whatever supplies are necessary. I am to accompany you back to the Fort, to provide any needed authority and oversee – that you have everything you need."

"We're grateful, Bidwell, very grateful, indeed," John said with some relief, and Bidwell straightened up, and answered, "Look, I know how it was, to be coming over the trail, and be lost and starving, at the end of it. We'll do for you whatever it is in Sutter's power to do."

"Grateful," Stephens said dryly, and the glance that he exchanged with John added the unspoken coda of "Or his interests."

Chapter 17 – *Rescue*

From E.S. Patterson Interview, University of California Local History Archival Project 1932: *"The Murphys, they had some little bits of meat and flour. James Miller, he managed to shoot a fox once. It started to get warmer, seemed like and there weren't any storms. Ma and Johnnie fetched down a hide off the roof, and they scraped off the hair, cut it into strips and boiled it until it dissolved, and that's what we had to eat towards the end . . . ever eaten gruel made of boiled hides? Tastes a little of beef, mostly like glue, but Ma said we had to eat it, nasty as it was, to keep up our strength.*

"Mrs. Montgomery, she couldn't bear to eat the boiled hides. She took to her bed after she fainted clean away one morning, going out to the privy. Mr. Martin, he and Ma carried her in. Ma had a little bit of sugar, saved for an emergency. She dissolved half in a little water for her to drink. Mary Sullivan had some dried meat left, but she wouldn't share with anyone but her brother and Mr. Martin. Mr. Martin though, he felt so sorry for Ma that he gave his portion to us, and Mary Sullivan didn't like that a bit, and so it was hammer and tongs for a while. Mrs. Montgomery wasn't so sick that she couldn't give Mary a piece of her mind . . . oh, yes, there was an atmosphere in that cabin, and not all from the privy pots!

"Mr. Miller, he finally got so discouraged and desperate he told us he and Willie were going to walk down from the mountains and go for help. The snow had melted and packed down a little, and there hadn't been a storm for days. He thought he might be able to get by with hunting, and so they went down the mountain, as the other men done. Mr. Martin couldn't go with them, as he had hurt his foot, and it wouldn't heal properly. He could get around the camp, all right, but not well enough to leave out with the Millers.

"This was at the end of February. Looking back afterwards, I'd guess that Ma was at her wits' end. We had nothing left to eat but the hides. One morning, maybe two days after Mr. Miller left, my brother Johnnie and I were carrying firewood, as Old Mr. Martin was splitting it for us, and Robert Sullivan came running over to us, saying there was a man coming up from the river.

'It must be Mr. Miller,' we said, and Robert said no, it was a man by himself with a big pack, and just then we heard a gunshot, and a man shouting,

'Hello, the camp! Is anyone there?'

232

Old Mr. Martin, he gave a shout and sank his ax into the chunk of wood he was splitting,

"'Tis my boy, Dennis!' he said, and so it was. Oh, my, we were glad to see him, everyone came running out of the cabins, even Mrs. Montgomery who was so weakened she could hardly stand, asking a million questions, and crying and laughing.

"As soon as he could get a word in edgeways, he said that the others were on the way, they were coming up from Sutters' Fort. He had passed Mr. Miller and Willie on the way up and told them the relief was only a few days behind him. Captain Stephens and the men, they were organizing a relief party and supplies to bring to us and take us out of the winter camp, but he was worried about his Pa and came away ahead of them, and also he had promised Mrs. Townsend to go back over the pass to the lake and look for Moses.

"Ma just sat right down, on the ground, hearing this, and couldn't speak at all for some considerable time, she was that overcome. Old Mr. Martin then told Dennis some of what our trials had been, and how little we had left. He opened up his pack right away, and gave Ma some of his supplies, saying he was right sorry he couldn't spare much; he had to keep enough to see him over the pass and back. He couldn't stay the night, even. He said that he didn't want to risk being caught by a storm, but I always wondered if it was more of what Old Mr. Martin told him of conditions in our camp. So he went off, into the higher mountains that very day. We could scarce sleep that night for excitement . . ."

From Dr. Townsend's diary: "*Twenty-fourth of February, 1845:* Mr. Patterson and some of his men have brought twenty mules and ten riding horses from his rancho, or borrowed from some of the other landholders, who hearing of the plight of our party, desired to assist us with such aid as they could render. Mr. Bidwell has drawn similar numbers from Captain Sutter's vast herds and additional supplies from larders and storehouses to support the relief party and to bring the families out and arranged for a ferry to cross our party over the Feather River. We fear the snow may be well too deep to move the wagons, referring to Allen Montgomery and Joseph Foster's witness from December.

"Mr. Patterson plans to ride with us, bringing a handful of his own drovers with him, although not Oliver and Samuel. He tells me, with a certain amount of amusement that he has left them in charge of the rancho in his *absence. I relayed to him the general thrust of what I told Mrs. Isabella, when I convinced her to allow Samuel to accompany the rest of us . . ".*

* * *

"Dearest . . . we are ready to depart." John looked into the parlor of Sutter's grand house at about mid-morning, Old Martin Murphy at his back. Elizabeth looked up from her sewing. She and Helen had quantities of white muslin, and figured calico, scissors, and spools of thread strewn about them all over the parlor. She sprang up from where she sat, a measuring-tape in one hand and a clutch of dark calico in the other, and embraced him.

"Darling, take care – bring them back to us with all haste." Then, all practicality, she ran the tape around his wrist. "Oh, good, I have got the right of the buttons and buttonholes on the cuff." She thrust the calico bundle at him. "A new shirt, Dearest . . . you have none left fit to be seen in company. Add it to your pack, I beg you. I rushed to finish it before you and the men departed." She hugged him again, whispering, "Go now. Bring them safe out of the mountains, Isabella and Sarah and all of them. It grieves both of us deeply, to think that while we enjoy such safety and generous plenty that our dearest kin and friends are lingering in despair and want."

Within the parlor, Old Martin embraced Helen, saying with gruff amusement, "So, we are away to bring our dearest children home. Fair Helen; have you any more suits of marriage offered to you that I should know of? Any princes or lords or ambassadors among them?"

"No, Papa, only the usual sort," Helen giggled. "Do you know, there was a young gentleman who came to the Fort, having heard only that some ladies from America were there, and determined therefore to make our acquaintance and Captain Sutter clapped him in chains and put him in a dungeon!"

"Has he a dungeon?" Elizabeth asked from across the room. "Not chains, surely, Helen. There are only some strong rooms under the towers."

"And he was of the opposite party in the late unpleasantness," Helen answered. "I am sure that his imprisonment was due to that, rather than any forwardness offered to me. I never was introduced to the gentleman, so he had not the opportunity."

"Put any of them off until we return, hey?" Old Martin said cheerily, "for they must have mine and your brothers' approval before they come a-courting you."

"Oh, Papa," Helen rolled her eyes, "You are so old-fashioned – be assured that anyone whom I encourage is a man you would like and approve of anyway."

"That's my darlin' girl." Old Martin kissed her firmly on the forehead. "Are these baby clothes you are making? Aye, for Mary-Bee's little one, and little Ellen . . . an excellent idea, new clothes to welcome them into the world, and better late than not at all."

"We had not a chance to do fine sewing, on the trail," Helen replied, and it seemed to John that she spoke too swiftly, and an amused glance flew between her and Elizabeth.

"Surely these are very tiny garments, Dearest." John cast a glance at a completed dress, laid out on the table nearest the window. "Ellen Miller is now more than six months old."

"But my namesake is barely three months of age," Elizabeth interjected, and exchanged another one of those amused looks with Helen as Old Martin clapped him on the shoulder, saying, "Come away then, Doctor, we've work to do, and the lads are waiting."

John kissed Elizabeth once more and followed after Old Martin, holding in his mind how lovely she looked, as if she glowed with the return of health, or maybe just the morning sunshine streaming in through the parlor window.

Stephens and Young Martin waited for them just outside the citadel gate. Dog sat panting at the feet of Stephens' horse, but lurched to her feet when Stephens handed Ugly Grey's reins to John. The pack-trail of mules, and the loose herd, chivvied by the other men, was already fairly far down the roadway along the river.

"Now, boys, let's see how fast we can move when it's our own that we are riding for!" Old Martin whooped like a boy, and they departed in a fine spray of mud flung up by their horses' hoofs.

* * *

From E.S. Patterson Interview, University of California Local History Archival Project 1932: *"We were on needles and pins, all through the days after Dennis Martin came. We watched the clouds, dreading another storm which would delay them. Ma, she sat for hours looking down the valley, with Sadie or me on her lap, all wrapped around with her shawls, and tried to work out when they would come. Dennis Martin, he said it was seven days journey on foot, and he thought they would be leaving three or four days behind him,*

'But see,' Old Mr. Martin told us, 'they might be driving cattle before them, which would slow them down some . . . unless they were mounted, which might see them moving faster . . . ah, be damned . . .'

'Mr. Martin!' said Ma, sharpish. And old Mr. Martin, he looked embarrassed and said, 'Begging your pardon . . . there's just no way of knowing until we set eyes on them.' And so it was, but it turned out we did know they was coming.

"Mary Murphy, she was Mr. James Murphy's little girl, who made us the Christmas toys? She came running into the cabins that afternoon, all excited, saying that she had heard the sound of cattle lowing, away off in the distance. O'course, we all went running outside to the overlook, everyone shushing each other, and trying to listen as hard as we could. You know how quiet it can be, away up on a high place? It's as if the noise down below floats up to you, over a long distance. We listened and listened . . . nothing but the sound of the wind in the trees, and we told Mary she must have imagined it through hoping so hard for hearing the men and her father coming to rescue us, but she said over and over again, that she heard cattle and horses at a distance.

"All the rest of that day, we kept going back to the overlook, hushing each other, and hoping to hear what she heard. I even stole out after dark to listen for a bit . . . But the next morning, though, we could all hear the sounds of hoofs and horses neighing, and sometimes very faintly a ringing as of bells; sometimes even what we thought was men shouting, faint and clear, but such a long way off! We got excited, none the less.

"When the men had built the cabins, you know, we had moved into them, and took everything necessary out of the wagons. They'd took down the wagon bows, and laid them flat, and stowed the ox yokes on top of them and tied the wagon covers tight over all, but now they were covered deep in snow, there was no way to begin to sweep off the snow, since they were buried so very deep in it. Even if we could sweep away the snow, and set the bows upright in the brackets, and put the cover on again . . . the snow was over the tops of the wheels. But Ma rounded up a wash-pan, and made us all clean up and put on our clean set of clothes. Even Mrs. Montgomery, she called up enough strength to get out of bed. By mid morning, we could hear them plain, and we kept going back and looking for them between the trees.

"Such a welcome sight they was, you cannot believe. We had waited so long for them, and there they were, looking so splendid, driving a great herd *of mules and horses in front of them, and leading strings of mules with packs behind, riding up through the trees from the river down below, shouting and waving their hats in the air: Captain Stephens, and old Mr. Murphy and his boys, John Sullivan, and Doctor Townsend, and Paw-Paw, with a man I didn't know at first.*

"He got down off his horse, and looked at Sadie and me, and after a moment I saw that he looked like my oldest brother Oliver, so I knew it must be Pa. Sadie, she was hiding around behind me; so much noise frightened her, and she never cared much for strangers.

'Sadie-girl, it's your Pa,' Paw-Paw told her, but Pa was smiling very gently, and he said, 'Hello, Eddie, you've grown so big I'd hardly know you.' He stuck out his hand, and I shook it, and I blurted out, 'Pleased to meet you, Pa. Ma says she's going to box your ears when she sees you for having taken so long.'

'Oh, I don't think she'll do that, Eddie,' he says, and he picks up Sadie, and takes my hand, and he says, '"We came as soon as we could . . . now, take me to your Ma.'

And so I led him to where Ma was, she was looking around for us, shading her eyes with her hand. She said, '"Oh, Samuel!"' like she was about to cry, and he set down Sadie, and put his arms around her . . . oh, it was a sight, it was. We hadn't seen Pa in almost three years, by that time . . ."

* * *

Patrick Martin came hobbling from the direction of the wagons, as John swung down from Ugly Grey's saddle. "Faith, but ye'are a sight for sore eyes . . . we have been longing for a sight of you, since Dennis said you were on the way . . ."

"Dennis? Isn't he here with you? He went on ahead of us he was so concerned over you, we thought sure he'd be waiting when we got here. What's the matter with your foot, Patrick?"

"Nothing at all," Patrick answered stoutly. "Just a gash that won't heal. Dennis made a promise to your lady wife before he left Sutter's. He went up to the pass, three days ago it was. She had begged him to look for your lad and bring him out if he were still alive."

A wave of gratitude threatened to overcome John's composure, gratitude and affection for the stocky, combative Irishman and his sons, and Patrick took his arm and lowered his voice. "He said you were not to wait for him, or the lad, but to get moving and get the women and the babies out of this camp before another storm hits." John looked at him very closely. Under the excitement which animated his features, Patrick appeared terribly gaunt.

"How bad is it, Patrick?" he asked very softly and Patrick replied "Ah, nothing that a little whiskey on the outside, and the inside too, couldn't have cured . . . oh, d'you mean here? Well, it were tolerable fair for all, for a month, not so fair for another month, and perilous close to starvation for the last three weeks."

John went cold. Damn Sutter. Goddamn him to hell. Damn him and his favors with strings attached, his cold pebble eyes, and his everlasting politicking.

"Who's the worst off, then, Patrick?" With an effort, he controlled his temper. He had left some medical supplies here, and brought a small assortment with him in his saddle bags. He took them from the saddle then. "Sit down, man, take off that boot so I can have a look. Over here, sit on that the stump, where you can appreciate the fine furnishings in my surgery."

Patrick hobbled to the stump, and sank down on it with relief, pulling off his battered boot. "Mrs. Montgomery, she's barely able to rise from her bed. And Mrs. Patterson has been scanting herself for two months to feed the children, so she's not all that much better. My daughter has done the same, for Mary. And she is in the way of another ween, so she told me." Patrick's shoulders slumped, and John thought he saw tears welling up in the big man's eyes. "Mother Mary and Joseph and all, Doctor Townsend, it's been the starvation times, as when I was a boy in old Wexford and we could scarce grow enough to feed ourselves thanks to the black hearts of the landlords. It breaks your heart to see it, day and day. The children are the best off, and Mary-Bee Murphy and Mary Miller too, because of the babies. They fed them the best of whatever was left to us, or what we could find. I couldn't bear another day of it, truly I couldn't. There was nothing to hunt, not a whisker of it, for Miller and me. How do you think we could endure it, seeing all their eyes growing big in the little skulls of them, and not a thing could we do, then?"

"We'll have you out of here, as soon as we can, Patrick," John promised. Patrick had a bit of cloth wound around the gash on his foot, with some dried herbs in it, binding them against the wound.

"From Mrs. Patterson, the last of her medicinal herbery, she gave me for it." Patrick explained. John sniffed at it; no putrefying flesh, no smell of infection, just not healed.

"The foot looks bad, Patrick. I'd have stitched it, if I had been here. How long ago did you say?"

"Last month."

"It should have started to heal by now, there's no inflammation," and John started to venture that Patrick must have gone without food himself, and that was why his injury was so slow to heal itself, but Stephens strode up just then, with Dog gamboling at his heels.

"We'll move them out, Doc. Now. We need to beat the weather, get below the snow line."

"We've been getting ourselves ready, so we have, Captain." Patrick pulled himself together. Hope was a powerful infusion, seemingly. "Some of our things are already packed, and out of the cabin, so. We heard you coming, so we did, and made preparations according."

"Get the rest of them ready, Patrick," Stephens answered. "We'll finish packing. We must move as soon as we can, Greenwood says he smells a storm on the air." He pulled John away with him, as Patrick hobbled towards the mule string. "Doc, I've already got men packing the traps, but if some of them are too sick to set in a saddle we'll have to make litters and carry them. Can you see who is fit to ride? Patrick looks like hell, and some of the others don't look all that well, either."

"I'll sort out who's in bad shape," John answered. "We ought to move them out first." Stephens nodded and hurried away. Fragments of reunions swam before him; Samuel Patterson, with Isabella, in the center of his children. Samuel seemed as if he were holding her up, and it struck him again how tiny she was, shrunken to the size of a child; all bones, tiny and gaunt with hardship. Old Martin, in the middle of his beloved grandchildren, all of them insane with excitement; Young Martin's sons, Frances and Theresa Miller, all but Mary Murphy, who was in her father's arms.

Old Martin had a basket of oranges, giving them out one by one, saying, "Aye, they're oranges! In the Old Country the rich folk grow them in greenhouses, but here they grow on great trees, out in the good clean air, so many that the extra fall on the ground and rot before they are eaten . . . you take off the peel, first, and isn't that a miracle? Ah, and the blossoms of them smell like the gardens of paradise, so they do! Mr. Patterson, you know, Eddie's Pa? He has a friend in the South, who sent him a great bag of them for you when he heard that there were children who had never had an orange for this Christmas."

"Don't let them eat too many, or too fast," John said to him in passing, and Old Martin whispered, with his eyes welling up, "Faith, they're fair starved, what ought we to do, then?"

"A little at a time," John answered. "Although the children are well enough, Patrick fears their mothers are in worse case." Almost to himself, he said, "I blame Sutter, that they were forced to this extremity. We should have pressed harder to return in the fall and brought them out."

Old Martin looked at him with shrewd sympathy, and answered, "Aye – we can blame him. Easier than blaming ourselves, I suppose."

Before John could consider his words, Mary Miller frantically clutched his arm as he strode towards the cabin.

She had the baby in her arms. "Doctor, where are James and Will? I don't see them anywhere, are they not with you? They went for help days ago."

"Mary, be at ease," John answered, soothingly "They're fine, we left them at our last camp, with Allen Montgomery. We cached most of the food there, and they are keeping the fires burning and waiting for us. Now, let me look at the little one – oh, yes, Mary, she looks well."

Little Ellen was well, a fat and gurgling mite, smiling up at him in the guilelessly happy way of a child who has never known anything other than contentment and love. "Let me look at you, too, Mary . . . ah, you look well, too."

"As much as can be expected," Mary Miller answered almost bitterly, and in his heart John damned Sutter again.

"Look, Mary, we plan to pack up and move today, lest we are caught by storm. You'll be with James and William tonight, if we can. I must check on Mrs. Montgomery."

"She is within," Mary gestured towards the cabin. "She did not feel well."

Stephens and the Murphy boys had already loaded the first string of mules with bedding and clothes and such few possessions as were left to the women, in a perfect storm of curses and complaints: Sutter's animals were half-wild after a winter of idleness.

Stephens called, "Let me know who needs to be carried, Doc . . . we'll put together some litters and send them out first with you. Don't wait for the rest of us, Doc. You'll be moving slow, and we'll catch up soon enough."

Young Patrick shouldered out of the cabin with another roll of bedding, and John caught his arm. "I'll be taking the first string as soon as they're packed. Get your father onto a horse, Patrick."

"I'm not sure how I'll manage to do that." Young Patrick's eyes widened at the thought of ordering his formidable parent about.

"Tell him we brought along an Englishman for him to fight," John replied, "and he's waiting for him down at the food cache."

Patrick laughed, "Aye, that would do the trick, for sure."

The cabin was all but empty, only the rough bunks left, and dark as a cave with only the light coming in from the doorway, and a little from the dying fire on the crude hearth. John thought of how crowded it would have been, with everyone and their blankets and possessions all crammed in together, and shuddered. Sarah lay on one of the stripped bunks, fully dressed, her shawl pulled around her, like a doll abandoned by a careless child. Upon hearing John moving through the rough doorway, she stirred and lifted her head.

"Good morning, Mrs. Montgomery." John sat on the opposite bunk, and set down the saddle bags next to him. "Mr. Martin told me you were feeling poorly, so I came to see you directly."

"Morning, Doctor John," she whispered, and John took up her hand to feel the pulse in her wrist. The bones of it felt tiny, fragile, like a bird's. "I thought I was feeling stronger this morning, the children were all so excited, but every time I stand up it seems like everything is whirling around me."

"You haven't been taking care of yourself, Mrs. Montgomery," John said chidingly, and Sarah replied with a faint ghost of her old spirit, "I'd just better do that, hadn't I . . . it's not like he will, now. He didn't come with you all, did he?" No need for John to ask who "he" was. He could see the bright trickle of tears out of the corners of her eyes rolling back into her hair.

"Mr. Montgomery is down the mountain, half a day's journey. We've cached food and set up a camp. He's waiting for us there, Sarah."

"Well, I am surprised," She laughed then, faint and exhausted laughter. "I thought he would have taken himself off by now. He is going to, you know. We don't want to be married, any longer, Doctor John."

"But you have spoken vows, Sarah . . . they can't be unsaid!" John was shocked, but almost equally grieved to see the depth of her unhappiness.

"Yes they can. We're the world away from where they were said. Hardly anyone will know of us here. He intends to leave me with the wagon and all that's in it but his tools and just go. Somewhere. Anywhere. We agreed, months back."

"Sarah, I think it very rash," John started, but she interrupted, "Doctor John, please don't. There is nothing you or Elizabeth could say to fix this. I'll not go back to him, nor he to me. After this, there'll be an end to it." Her eyes closed with an air of finality. After a moment, she whispered again, "I couldn't eat the hides. I tried, but I couldn't keep them down. Isabella, she and the children. They could eat them. It's all they've had for three weeks, but for some bread that Dennis Martin gave us three days ago."

Damn him, John thought again bleakly, remembering the morning in Sutter's office, and the bargain they made. Damn him. They should have just taken whatever they needed and gone back to the mountains, back to the winter camp that very day, never mind what anyone advised. But he was reacting like their leader and a hotheaded one at that, when he should be thinking like a doctor.

"Sarah," he said, making his voice sound quiet and soothing, consciously banishing the fury that he felt towards Sutter. "I am going to give you a little something to eat . . . just a little piece of flatbread, and some of the cheese they make at Sutter's fort. I brought it along for myself in my saddlebag. Here, hold out your hand. Just take little bites, go slow and careful." He waited a minute, while she chewed and swallowed carefully. "How does it sit?"

"It tastes funny . . . but good. Not like real bread," she answered cautiously.

"Now a bit of cheese . . . just a crumb, mind you. You'll not be able to manage anything rich, or very much of it."

"That was very good . . ." she said thoughtfully. "When I think on how long since I had a drink of milk . . . when did the cows stop giving milk, Doctor? Just short of Fort Laramie, I think."

"Here's some more bread." He put a larger piece of it in her hand. "I need to look at some of the others, now, but I'll come back. We need to fix up a litter for you, since you cannot ride. Is there anything you'll want to take with you?"

She frowned, thinking upon it. It seemed to take a great effort. "I had one of those Indian baskets with the rest of my things in it. I think Johnnie took it outside with the blankets."

"I'll make sure," he promised. "Now eat your bread . . . slowly, now, and I'll be back."

Outside, the swirl of activity had intensified. Old Hitchcock and Patterson were helping Jamie Murphy lash together two rough litters out of four long poles and some canvas panels which had once been part of a tent.

"All I ask," John said, "is that you hang those contraptions between the four gentlest mules you have."

"Don't worry, Doctor, we'll make sure of that!" gasped Patterson.

Underneath their feet, the ground was churned into an unsavory mixture of slush, muck, and droppings.

"You . . . young Sullivan," he reached out and reeled in a boy, who shrilled delightedly, "Doctor John! Ain't it grand?"

"Isn't," John corrected him. "Hold still Robert . . . let me look at you. Yes, it is grand. Captain Stephens asked me to look at everyone, make sure you are all well enough for the last bit of the road. You've a sore throat, then. Not enough to keep you from it. I thought sure I had a bag of horehound candy, but never mind."

He released the boy and went on, working his way among the women and children; just a few moments each and a quick assessment more by sight than anything else. Much as Old Patrick said, the children had borne semi-starvation well, and the two babies were thriving. He weighed Elizabeth Murphy thoughtfully in his hands; no, she would be too large for the tiny clothes that Elizabeth and Helen were sewing, back at Sutter's for her. Patrick's daughter Annie — she looked ill, grey and hollow-eyed.

"Put her in a litter," John told her husband, "And the girl, too. We'll sort everything out in camp tonight; I'll go in a few minutes with the sickest, and she's one of them."

Returning to the cabin for Sarah he found that she had eaten the rest of the bread and fallen into a sort of half-doze. Slipping an arm under her shoulders and another under her knees, he lifted her easily as if she were as light as one of the children. The second litter was ready: John laid Sarah in it, and covered her well with blankets against the cold. Annie and her daughter were already in the other, well wrapped, and Old Patrick had already been mounted on one of Sutter's ponies; John wondered what Young Patrick had to say to convince him. Old Patrick did look ill, so probably not much.

John put another bit of flatbread into Sarah's hand, tucked another blanket over her all, and turned his attention towards the Pattersons. According to Sarah, they'd had nothing to eat but boiled hides for three weeks. The children looked thin, but Isabella appeared emaciated, and if it weren't for her leaning against Samuel, John suspected that she would have fallen. Stephens appeared, leading Ugly Grey, Patterson's horse, and two of Sutter's Indian ponies, a hint if there ever were one.

"Ready to hitch-up, Doc? We're burning daylight."

"Just about," John answered. "Mr. Patterson – if you would conduct Mrs. Patterson and the children each to a horse, and put them onto it, we'll ride, as soon as you are ready." Isabella straightened, as if she would protest, and John sighed. "It is my considered medical opinion that eating any more boiled ox-hides or remaining in this place will have an adverse effect on your health, dear Mrs. Isabella. Let your husband and I assist you." John looked to

Samuel and added, "Just get on the damned horse, and I'll hand her up to you." Samuel set his foot into the stirrup and looked at John with a particularly amused look.

"Doctors' orders, my dear; this is really not a good time to argue." Samuel swung up into the saddle, and John picked up Isabella and lifted her up to her husband, who set her in front of him.

"Really, Mrs. Isabella, I think Mr. Patterson does have some knight-errantly qualities, after all," John added, wondering if he jested so rather than give himself over to fury. "Johnnie, you take Sadie in front of you . . . Eddie, you get to ride this one by yourself. Any monkey-shines from you and I will take over the whipping after your father gets tired."

* * *

From E.S. Patterson Interview, University of California Local History Archival Project 1932: *"They were in such a hurry because Captain Stephens feared a winter storm. The men bent every effort into moving fast, moving us down below the snow line, lest we be caught again. They didn't dare take the time to pack carefully, just lashed the bedding and bags to pack-saddles, and told us to get up and ride before we were caught by a storm.*

"We traveled all the rest of that day, and after sunset, we came to where they had camped before, and there was a great bonfire burning, and such a supper cooked for us. To eat our fill of it, after months of want, oh that was an indescribable delight . . ."

Chapter 18 – *From the Ice-Water Lake*

From E.S. Patterson Interview, University of California Local History Archival Project 1932: *"The others followed ours, as they were ready. It was a rough ride, you have no idea, but we were so glad to be moving again, and to have Pa with us at last. I think sometimes it set Ma off a little, as she had become so used to being in authority, but Pa was so very kind and good-humored and on the second day, as we were moving down below the snow, we heard someone calling . . . "*

* * *

It contented John enormously to have all of the worry and some of the guilt off his back, to be able to move along so brisk, to see Sarah and Isabella and the other women revive from their sad condition, like wilted flowers returned to a vase of fresh water. *"It is amusing to see,"* John wrote in his diary, *"how tenderly the men urge them to eat, and compete to offer them such delicacies as we brought with us, being so distressed at the conditions we found in the winter camp . . . where we had left them with such high hopes of their safety and security. We brought eggs with us, and sugar and such other rare delicacies. I had much work to do at the outset to prevent some of the children from gorging themselves . . . "*

Eddie, of course, with his unerring tendency to run straight at any available and inviting hazard, managed to make himself quite spectacularly sick from overeating on that first night. Called out of his bedroll in the middle of the night, John had administered aid (warmed milk and a mild dose of laudanum), and counseled Eddie's somewhat distraught father. Old Hitchcock was much more sanguine, being by this time more accustomed to the hazards of Eddie.

"Well, he never yet managed to kill himself, all this long way, with all the chances he had. The young imp has a guardian spirit."

"A battalion of them, I rather think," Samuel Patterson sighed "Working overtime. No wonder that Isabella's hair is almost entirely grey."

"Fortune favors the bold," John said with a yawn. "Eddie has enough bold to sell shares. He shall sleep sound, and we'll move on in the morning. Eddie's misadventures have never adversely affected his own self for long, only the rest of us."

"Funny, how that works out," Samuel Patterson remarked, wearily. "Do you have sons, Doctor Townsend?"

"Only Moses." All around the two of them were sleeping people in their rolls of blankets, and he confessed after a moment. "We still do not know if he lives yet. I have no idea of what I shall say to my wife."

"I am sorry to hear that." Samuel sounded regretful, as sympathetic as he had been the first time they met.

"Dennis Martin went to look for him; he was at the camp three days ago, so says Patrick. But he would have had to have gone higher into the mountains, over the gap where we brought the wagons, and then walk ten or fifteen miles farther."

It was the middle of the night, and John was tired, and at such times it was hard not to think of Moses and what might have happened; difficult not to see him in the minds' eye, fallen ill in the white wilderness by the ice-water lake below the pass they had crossed with such labor. The thought of Moses dying alone and abandoned by all his family and friends, like poor Scott in the tale that Hitchcock had told back at their camp by the bluffs on the Platte, brought forth such grief and regret. Those thoughts tore at him as savagely as an animal with razor-sharp claws, but only in the middle of the night or in times of such weariness, did this vision rise to torment him. Most other times, he was able to keep that cruel imagining at bay.

"He must be a dear friend to risk so much on your behalf," Samuel was saying, and John wrenched his attention back to the present, talking with Isabella's husband, while Eddie slept the sleep of the drugged.

Possibly the only time that one might relax in young Eddie's presence, thought John with a bit of wry laughter, and he answered, "No, Dennis would be more Moses' friend than mine . . . but still, we ventured so much together in each other's company. I think we became much more than friends. We were comrades in adventure and adversity. We looked to each other, in good times and bad, and were all that we had, all alone . . . so we look after each other still. It came to be a bit of habit."

"So it is in the mule trains," Samuel said wryly. "You look to and depend on each other in hard times, regardless." He looked down at Eddie." I owe you a very great debt, Doctor, for Isabella and the children; for bringing them all safely over the trail. I'll probably never be able to repay entirely, but be assured that we shall be at your beck any time you need anything at all, here in California."

"You're considerably welcome, Patterson. Except for damn near letting them starve, a little bit short of safety," John said.

"Not your doing," Samuel answered warmly. "We all had a part in deciding to wait, not yourself alone. They managed, and we were just in time, that's what I'd rather consider. Get some sleep yourself, Doctor . . . we always feel lowest in the middle of the night. I'll stay and watch Eddie awhile."

"No, I don't think I can sleep now," John answered. "It's nearly dawn anyway." So they sat together under the wheeling stars and talked idly of California, and the rich valley where Patterson had his rancho, of such crops and orchards which could be grown, and the sturdy, thick-walled house of unbaked mud brick to which Patterson had added a second storey with a wooden verandah all the way around, of books and the education of children.

"We must think of starting a school soon," Samuel ventured. "There are more and more Americans every year . . . especially in Yerba Buena. Until just the last years, there were only men, trappers, and deserting sailors from off the ships, and merchants and the like, but now with families, it changes. And do you know something else?" Patterson was looking at him, in the manner of a man who has just thought of something new. "I do believe you will be the only qualified doctor in Alta California."

"Good heavens!" John was appalled. "Surely not! There must be others with medical training, somewhere . . ."

"Well, there are those with skills, like my wife, and there are a few who are self-taught, like Mr. Marsh, and some of the mission fathers . . . they minister as best they can. But save for when a ship with a regular surgeon comes to port . . . you'll be a busy man in the years to come, you'll have all the doctoring you can do."

They moved in haste the next morning, for behind them clouds pressed down over the mountains at their back. The jaws of late-winter's trap were closing again, but this time they looked to have a good chance of escape. John did the rounds of his patients as they moved and was gratified to find Eddie demanding food, Isabella strong enough to sit alone in a saddle, although not for long, and Sarah able to sit up in the litter without becoming dizzy. Allen was with her, and it seemed that there was no animosity between them now. Allen brought her food, and sat and walked with her, and John hoped that perhaps they had been reconciled.

He reported on his patients to Stephens, riding point with Old Greenwood. Both of them looked pleased, although Greenwood looked over his shoulder and said, "It's in the nick of time, Cap'n. We'll be well below the snow line tonight, less'n that is a worse storm than anything we've yet seen . . . hold on . . ." He wheeled his pony. Back up the hill behind them, all hoof prints and mud, marked with broken branches in the wake of their passage, someone shouted.

"Stop the train," Stephens ordered tersely. Along the line of march drovers shouted to their animals, and women called out, wanting to know what was happening. Old Patrick Martin was shouting and pointing up the hill. Two men bearing packs on their backs were running clumsily downhill through the trees where they had just come from, slipping and sliding in the thin patches of snow, and the mud between them.

"'Tis Dennis!" Old Patrick shouted. "And I b'lieve that's your lad with him, Doctor!" A crackle of excitement ran along the line like ball-lightning.

John's heart lifted in a great surge of joy. Without a second thought, he spurred Ugly Gray, and sent him lunging up the hill towards the scattering of men and women around the two; yes, it was Dennis, and the other was Moses, alive and fit, but as ragged as a scarecrow. They were at the center of a fast-gathering group. He leaped out of Grey's saddle as Moses cried, "Doctor John . . . I thought never to see you again!"

"So did I, lad, so did I!" He embraced Moses; the lad was all bone, and his hair came practically to his shoulders like a wild man, but his eyes were as lively and blue as ever, although in a face worn down to skeletal gauntness. Moses returned the embrace, for a moment seeming almost frantic, a child of Eddie's age, but then he let go and stood back a little, composing himself again as John looked searchingly at him.

"We feared to have lost you, Mose."

"Came close, once or twice, Doctor John," Moses answered jauntily. "Dennis says that he promised Liz that he would come back to look for me, and we've spent two days trying to catch up and outrun the storm."

"And it's coming on fast," Dennis hitched up his pack again, "so I suggest that we keep on moving and tell tales at the campfire tonight."

"Come along, Mose, he's right, we should keep moving." John waved to Captain Stephens, and shouted, "Move on then, we're coming down . . . it is Moses and Dennis, all right."

Stephens waved to the drovers, whose animals plodded forward again, wading through snow that barely reached their hocks. Dennis ran whooping like a wild Indian towards the mules that his brother led, where his father waited to embrace him joyfully. He was wrestling the pack off his own back, tossing it onto the top of the mule's burden, and John said, "I should take yours, boy."

"Oh there isn't much in it, Dr. John, just some blankets and some of Dennis' supplies. And I am so relieved to be back with you all I could carry it easily were it twice as heavy."

"Nonetheless, tie it behind the saddle and tell me what happened, after Allen and Joseph left you."

Moses slipped his shoulders out of the straps, doing as John asked, and he said, "You can't blame them, Doctor John. You can't, knowing the qualities of them both. There wasn't enough food for one of them to have stayed with me. They knew it and I knew it, and they both said goodbye so sadly. I never held any blame to them, there was nothing any of us could do about it."

They walked on, leading Ugly Grey between them along side the pack train from which Mary Miller and the Murphy women called their welcome to Moses, and expressed their joy and happiness to see him again, alive and reunited with the company.

Old Martin Murphy slapped his back heartily, saying, "Well done, lad, well done indeed!" and Samuel Patterson said quietly, "We must indeed rejoice for you, Doctor John. What once was lost has now been found"

Joseph Foster seemed deeply moved, unable to speak for some moments. He embraced Moses silently, and then stepped back a little to shake him by the shoulders and say, "You young scamp! We thought we had left you for dead, and here you turn up again, fit as a fiddle. I see very well that you spent the winter living off the fat of the land, with never any thought for the rest of us, and all the while we've been riding for Captain Sutter all over this country!"

His very emotions choked his words, then, and Moses put his own hands on Joseph's arms and answered, "Truly, Joe, you'd no cause for worry. I made it fine down the mountain, once you and Allen had left. I had only the loneliness to fear, not knowing anything of how you all were faring."

Allen Montgomery jubilantly thumped Moses on the shoulders and said, "Mose, Mose, if there is ever a person I was gladder to see in this world . . . perhaps your sister will speak to me now, when she knows that you are safe!"

"Liz?" Moses looked abashed. "She cannot be angry with you, Allen. It was not your fault. It was my doing, to go back when I could not carry on if it meant endangering you and Joe."

"None the less, Mrs. Elizabeth blames me with particular vehemence for abandoning you in the mountains," Allen answered wryly. "We have not said more than half a dozen words to each other since we came down the mountains, most of them being 'Good morning', or 'Good Evening'."

"Ne'er mind, Allen, I shall fix it with Liz," Moses promised, and Allen shrugged and said, "Kindly said, Mose, kindly said. But it'll be of no moment, repairing my standing in your sister's parlor. Even should Mrs. Elizabeth forgive me, it may make no difference in the long run." Allen spoke with weary resignation, and John looked at him sharply, remembering Sarah's talk of the two of them separating. Was Allen still set on that course, laying aside the bonds of friendship as well as those of matrimony?

But Moses answered with cheerful determination, "I shall talk to her, Allen. You and Doctor John have been our friends for years; she cannot go on holding you responsible, not when I am safe and well, and we are all arrived in California at last."

They caught up to Stephens and Old Greenwood, who seemed just as cheered, though rather more restrained in expressing it.

"So what did you learn from a whole winter in the mountains?" Old Greenwood asked, and Moses thought for a moment before answering, "There is no way on earth to cook a coyote and make it edible." Both Stephens and Greenwood chuckled, and Moses added, "But fox is very, very good. I should thank you for the use of the traps you left, Captain Stephens . . . there was no result in hunting, although I did shoot a crow, once. But I used the traps to good effect."

"So I'd always found," Greenwood remarked in satisfaction, and Stephens asked, "How did the crow taste?"

"I couldn't make up my mind which I liked better . . . crow or coyote." Mose looked thoughtful for a long moment. "Through my efforts, I always had enough, but I could never be sure of a continuing supply. I always feared that the supply of foxes would run out . . . and I worried endlessly about all of you. Especially after the storms began, and the cabin was buried to the roof."

"We feared the worst when Joseph and Allen said they'd had to leave you," John said. "You will have to talk very convincingly to your sister before she will look kindly on either of them."

"Well, it did seem like the worst," Moses answered. "But you know, it was very odd, as soon as they were gone, I began to be very cheerful, and thought that, well I may work out something. So I got up, and picked up my blankets and the rifle, and thought about going back to the cabin. It had frozen hard during the night, and with the crust on top of the snow, I didn't need to use the snowshoes; which was good, since I was still exhausted from the day before. But I was still so tired, when I gained the cabin that I couldn't step over the sill. I had to reach down and lift up my knees one at a time to step over it. I think I slept all the night and most of the next day. And when I went to try and hunt, all I saw were tracks. Lots of them, but never a sight of anything more than that, and I was about sick with disappointment and anxiety, when I came back to the cabin. When I went to put my rifle in the corner, that's when I saw the pile of Captain Stephens' traps, and I thought, well, if I can't hunt them, maybe I can trap them. So I set them out that evening, baited with some scraps from the two oxen left to us, and in the morning I had a coyote in one of them." Moses made a face, "Well, that's when I found out about how coyotes taste. No matter how hungry I got, it just didn't set well. Three days after that I had a fox. And it was delicious. Or I thought it was delicious, compared to coyote, and could have eaten it all at once. I made it last two days. I seemed to trap one every couple of days, and now and again another coyote. I hung the coyotes up as a reserve, from the cabin eave, lest I ever run out of foxes. I think I finally had eleven, but never ran low enough to be tempted with a dish of jugged coyote again. I had plenty of salt and never used it, no bread and didn't miss it. I did have enough coffee for one cup. I saved it for Christmas Day."

"You look to have endured such hardships very well," John remarked in approval, and Moses' bright cheeriness wavered.

"I can't really describe how miserable I was, Doctor John." Suddenly Moses looked about as woebegone as Eddie after one of his escapades, and very much the same age. "I confess I was very low in spirits. It was very wearying to be alone in that place, thinking upon you all, and worrying that you might be in a worse condition. It was also burdensome to worry about where my next meal might be coming from, or even if I would even have any sort of meal at all. I consoled myself with your books. They were of great comfort."

"So they would be," Greenwood said, with enormous compassion. "So they are. I read all through Herodotus' Histories one long winter. I never felt myself alone with a volume such as that."

"I'd pile up pine knots on the fire and read aloud to myself for half the night, just to hear the sound of a human voice and pass the time." His voice wavered a bit, although his expression was rigidly controlled. "It seemed after a time that I had been there forever, that the snow would never leave the ground. When I first saw Dennis coming down the mountain I thought it was a figment of my imagining. And then I thought he was an Indian . . . I am still half-afraid that I have dreamed all this, and I will wake up back in the mountains."

"No, Mose, it is all real . . . if it is not then all the rest of us are dreaming as well. Come and tell me when you are most convinced you are dreaming, and I will box your ears, or shake your shoulders or something like that." John looked at him very closely; he did not like the way Moses' mood swung so abruptly between ebullient and bleak. But he was young, and resilient, and would recover.

"I wish we had burned that cabin though." Moses' shoulders moved as though he shuddered. "I thought of it sometimes as a prison."

"No, someone may have need of it someday," John replied.

After a long silence, Mose said, "You were right, though, Dr. John."

"About what?"

"Well, practically everything . . . but Lord Chesterfield's Letters, most especially. They were very comforting, in an odd way. I could almost imagine you or Mr. Murphy giving me such wise advice sometimes. Although . . ." Moses thought for a moment. "He was dreadfully cynical, wasn't he? About other people, I mean."

"We must live in the world as it is," John answered, "and make of it what we can . . . and look there, Mose. There is the world we will live in, now."

They had come around a bend in the river, where they could look out now and see the hills falling away below them, gentler hills, and lightly wooded, and the green valley beyond, the hazy afternoon sunshine slipping between clouds and filling it with golden light.

Moses looked, with his face alight again, and said, "It looks like a park, as far as the eye can see."

"Aye, so," Greenwood sighed. "Too soft for my liking . . . but nice enough to visit for a while. I prefer the mountains."

"It's a golden land," Stephens said. "Why would you not stay for good?"

"Itchy feet, Captain . . . the boys and I will stay, but we'll be heading east again soon . . . hire on with another party at Fort Hall, or Fort Laramie. Knowing the trail for sure, and Old Truckee's way over the mountains now, that'll make us worth our hire."

"You'd have my highest recommendation," John said honestly. "I'd be happy to write out an affidavit for you, at the very least."

"What are we going to do, now that we are here, Doctor John?" Moses asked.

"Go to Sutter's fort, and deliver you to your sister first . . . Allen and I, and Foster . . . we'll need to come back in a few months to retrieve our wagons and goods. Yerba Buena is where what little commerce there is, although I like what Patterson tells me of San Jose. What about you, Stephens . . . where are you going to settle?"

"Hadn't rightly thought on that, Doc." Stephens looked at the vista spread out before them. "But I think I'll know it when I see it."

* * *

From Dr. Townsend's diary: *"Fifth of March, 1845. This day arrived with the remainder of our party, delivered from the mountains to Sutter's Fort. We were reunited with much joy. My Dearest lavished much fond attention upon Moses, to his very great embarrassment. But he seems to have steadied by his experience in the mountains, and sobered and responsible in temperament . . . In looking through these pages, it is brought to my mind that we departed upon this road a week short of one year ago. I am much given to marvel, for we seem to have lived many years, encompassed in the space of those tumultuous twelve months just past."*

From E.S. Patterson Interview, University of California Local History Archival Project 1932: *"Pa and Paw-Paw took us to his rancho a few weeks later, when Ma was quite recovered. Pa had thought to hire a carreta, one of those carts that they commonly used in California, to transport us all but Ma saw them being used at Captain Sutters' and put her foot down, saying she would not be able to bear the screeching of it, or one of those great clumsy wheels going over a rut in the road with a great jolt, so we went on horseback with a great train of mules afterwards, as was the custom then.*

"Pa's rancho was a little west of San Jose, close by where Mountain View is today. He had been granted a tract and bought a little more land adjacent with a house on it. He improved the house, and built on a little house for Paw-Paw to stay in when he pleased. In the summer they went back with Captain Stephens and Doctor Townsend to bring out all the wagons we left in the mountains, but all the goods we left in them, they was stolen by Indians. All but the guns and Dr. Townsend's surgical kit, which they feared touching. Pa and us, we kept a wheel from our wagon as a relic; hung it up in the hallway of the house for years.

"Pa had talked so much to the others about the Santa Clara valley and Yerba Buena that the Murphys and the Millers all set up thereabouts. They all did right well, all but Bernard. He was killed in a steamship explosion in '53. The rest of them got on. When Young Martin and Mary-Bee celebrated their

wedding anniversary in . . . oh, round about '81 it was, the entire town closed down for the party. They ran in special trains for guests. He died one of the richest men in California, never foreclosed on a loan, and never did learn to write his name proper. Young Johnny Murphy, he eloped with Miss Reed, that came over with the Donners and the Reeds, two years after our party. You've heard plenty about them, I think! Such a scandal there was, he being Catholic and her just a bit of a girl then, both families were fit to be tied! Captain Stephens, he was there for a good few years, but he went strange in old age; moved to Bakersfield, pretty near became a hermit.

"*Doctor Townsend, he took his family to Yerba Buena for a while, but he eventually settled down in San Jose too. The cholera epidemic in '50 took them both. Tending the sick, they were; first him, then her. We all grieved something terrible. They left a little boy, two years old. Young Mose raised him after that. In a way, it was good to have so many friends from the trail settle close by, people you knew the qualities of. Pa and Ma lived there until they died; they always said after that they had no more interest in moving around.*

"*Mention of the Doctor's boy Moses minds me of how he spent that winter all alone in the mountains, in that little cabin he and Joe Foster and Allen Montgomery built. Two year later, some of the Donner-Reed folk took shelter in it. Them poor folks, I get the cold shivers still, thinking on how it was, trapped in the snow and waiting for help. My, I tell you we were so glad to come down from those mountains!*

"*My brothers though, they got the gold fever in '48. Oliver and Johnny got over it pretty fast; they did get lucky, but like the Murphy boys, they figured after a bit there was more money to be made from the gold miners than there was to mining it yourself. Samuel though . . . he got the gold fever bad and never recovered. He took up mining claims all up and down the foothills, went to Virginia City later on, prospecting for silver, headed up to the Yukon when they hit pay dirt there. He was killed in a fight in a bar in Dawson in '98, so we were told afterwards. You'd have thought he'd have been old enough to know better, but he was too much like Paw-Paw, I guess. Ma and Pa were long gone by then, and it had been so long since we seen him, it didn't ever seem quite real. I've imagined for years that he's still out there somewhere, working some little claim and telling yarns like Paw-Paw used to do . . . Now, if you had only took your recording machine, and have Paw-Paw and Samuel tell of their lives into it, you would have had the whole Wild West in a nutshell.*

"You know in '04, my wife had the thought that we should go back east to the World's Fair in St. Louis. First time in 60 years I had felt any urge to go back there. I went down to Mexico a couple of times, went to China and the Islands, hunting for plants, but never felt the need to go back east again. Like Ma and Pa, I didn't feel it necessary once I'd got to where I wanted to be. But the wife talked me into it, on account of my sister Sadie's husband having just died, and we thought Sadie might welcome a distraction. So we brought her with us, and my oldest son and his wife, and his children. My son worked for the railroad, and he had the use of a parlor car . . . oh my, that was the way to travel then!

"We met the train in Sacramento, where I'd been in and out of all the time, no great changes to speak of. All of them had happened after the Gold Rush and the great fire, when I'd been barely grown. Sutter's fortress had fallen down long since, and his grand house had been a stable for years, and all along the river that had been open meadows and marshes the first time I had seen it, were built up; warehouses, and businesses, and rooming houses and all.

"We looked out the parlor car windows, for the railway followed the river, pretty much . . . and that was the same road we had come down, all those years before, when it was wild and empty land, with nothing but a couple of small ranches and Captain Sutter's fort. There were a fair sprinkling of little towns now, some of which had been pretty roaring places during the Rush . . . but in between them, the mountains looked just as they had done, when it took us weeks to cross over instead of just a day.

"Pretty soon, we were going through the snow sheds approaching the top of the pass, but there were places where they'd left windows so we could look out. The train went pretty slow, too. It's a steep grade, as any of the Murphys or Captain Stephens would have testified. My son had told the engineers of how Sadie and I had come over the pass in the Earlies, so they very kindly stopped at the top of the pass, for us to get out and look down to the east and the west. So help me, I could recognize the valley and the lake where we had left some of the wagons from above. All the mountains around, I recalled them exactly as they were. But of the place where we watched those who were to stay, walking down to their little cabin, and of the little gap where we had led up the cattle one by one, and the ledge where the men dragged the wagons over . . . not a thing.

"It grieved me, for if I was sure of anything, it would be of recognizing that. My son said likely that when they had built the rail-bed, it all had been blasted away, or buried deep. I asked Sadie if she saw aught

familiar and she shook her head and said, sadly, 'No, Eddie, I barely remember anything. I was little more than a baby. I remember feelings, and being cold sometimes, and sitting in someone's lap and watching the snow fall . . . but little of events and places. There's only one thing I really remember clear.'

'What is that, Sadie-girl?' I said, and she looked out at the valley with the little quick-silver colored lake in the middle of it, and she said, 'Standing on a hillside, with nothing but green grass all around, and the wind rippling through it. The grass comes up to my waist, and it's full of flowers. There are butterflies and grasshoppers flying up out of the grass ahead of us. Someone on either side of me has my hands, and we are running through the grass and laughing; the wagons are coming over the top of the hill opposite, and the white tops of them are shaking like sails in the wind.'

"'That's the clearest thing you can remember, Sadie-girl?' I said, and she nodded, and I said to her, 'And a grand memory it is to have, if out of all of it that is the only one you have!'

"Ah, well. She enjoyed the fair. We all did. But it bothered me, to look out of the train and see a creek bed out of the window that we went over in a minute or two, and see wagon-ruts a little farther down, and know it might have taken us half the day to dig out the bank and double-team the wagons over. Just felt that it was all too easy. But they tell me now that you can fly from St. Louis to Los Angeles . . . hah! You might be able to get there in a day . . . but it'll never be the experience it was, back in the Earlies . . . is that enough for your project then? Well, thank you very much . . . Miss Birdie, was it? My pleasure.

Historical Notes

A list of the Stephens-Townsend Party members is included at the beginning of this work as a means of assisting the reader in keeping track of those members included in this narrative. With the exception of the handful listed in italics, they were all real people. I have taken some small liberties in departing from it, most notably with regard to the situation of Isabella Patterson. She was a widow, traveling with her father and a number of children, in a wagon which he owned . . . not quite the circumstances outlined here. And to judge from the existing portrait of Elizabeth Schallenberger Townsend, she had rather darker hair than I have described. Her husband was supposed to have kept a personal diary, and a log of their journey, in his capacity as the party secretary, but those documents have never been found. It is my hope that they may still exist, forgotten in an old trunk of books, or a dusty box in someone's attic. The reconstruction of his diary, based on emigrant diaries typical of the era was suggested to me as a hook upon which I could hang the rest of the story.

The other events and incidents attendant on their journey happened more or less as described, most of them taken from Moses Schallenberger's own account, dictated to his daughter many decades after the events. However, of their personalities and foibles, conversation, and small incidents which fill up these pages – although based on the scanty historical record – the overwhelming proportion have been imagined by the writer, including Dr. Townsend's engineering of Stephens' election as captain of the party.

Another notable episode drawn completely from my imagination is the scene of drawing straws for the fast-horseback party; I have no idea if anything like this was done. I deduce that some sort of fair and rational process to choose the participants for it must have been put into play, based on my own impression of a group who consulted together and reached a consensus before moving ahead in tackling an obstacle.

I also do not know if the quid pro quo put to the men of the party by Captain Sutter was as bald as I have described, or with what degree of reluctance they cooperated. It is a matter of record that they did join with Sutter's party of volunteers in the Micheltorena War. The historical record is ambiguous as to whether they were coerced or genuinely felt that there was no chance of rescuing their families for some months so they might as well join his venture.

Finally, Dr. John and Elizabeth Townsend did perish in the 1850 cholera epidemic; reportedly within hours of each other. They are buried in

San Jose's Oak Hill Cemetery, or at least memorialized there on the Pioneer Monument. Elisha Stephens died in 1884, an eccentric recluse and pauper near Bakersfield, California . . . and all but unknown.

CPSIA information can be obtained at www.ICGtesting.com
Printed in the USA
LVOW06s2124160915

454529LV00001B/62/P